I0716508

DEATH TAX

THE DEBT COLLECTION
BOOK 4

ANDREW GIVLER

DEATH TAX
Book Four of The Debt Collection
Copyright © 2024 by Sad Seagull Publishing. All rights reserved.

Editor: Laura Jorstad
Cover Illustration: Chris McGrath
Cover Design and Interior Layout: STK·Kreations

Hardcover ISBN: 978-1-958204-12-2
Trade paperback ISBN: 978-1-958204-11-5
eBook ISBN: 978-1-958204-10-8
Worldwide Rights

To the readers who have followed me this far.
Thanks for taking this journey with me.
I wouldn't have it any other way.

DEATH TAX

CHAPTER
ONE

I'**VE BEEN TOLD,** by a very powerful demon, that there is an appointed hour for my death. If I had to guess, it's exactly 12:01 a.m. in eight years, two months, and nine days, which just so happens to be my thirty-fourth birthday. Not that I'm counting.

But if I'm not careful, the appointed time could be a lot sooner than that.

Something is lurking in the Between.

A little over a year and a half ago, I got my hands on a key that lets me turn any doorway into a portal to a hallway that exists outside the mortal realm and other places—and make no mistake, there *are* other places.

So far it seems like the Key of Portunus, who is some lost and forgotten god, is the only way to access the Between. In the fifty-plus times I have traveled through it, I've never encountered a soul that I didn't bring with me. It is kind of my own personal clubhouse.

The Between looks like an abandoned office building hallway that stretches on for eternity. The walls are covered in a horrendous mustard-yellow wallpaper that is peeling. Fluorescent bulbs provide light and a persistent hum from where they hang among dingy white ceiling tiles. It's not the building that is remarkable, though; it's the white doors on either side of the hall. They lead to different worlds. For some reason they are never in the same order. I'm no physicist, but if I had to guess I'd say the rules aren't as strong out here on the border of reality.

Spooky, I know.

All that is to say: As far as I'm aware, my copy of old Porty's key is the only one in existence.

Which made the *thing* currently blocking my path off toward the horizon worrisome. The hall was endless and distance hard to estimate, but I first noticed it when I was almost a football field away.

For a long time, I stood still, watching the dark blob lying across the carpeted path. Eventually, I decided that it had to be either dead or asleep, because it hadn't so much as twitched. I considered turning around and walking in the other direction until I found the door I was looking for. But that would be admitting I wasn't the big dog in this junkyard, and I wasn't ready to do that.

Slowly, I began working my way down the hall, trying to get close enough to identify it without waking it up—if it still could be woken. Step by painstaking step, the distance between us shrank as my careful gait brought me toward it. As I began to make out a body with arms and legs, a shiver of fear ran through me.

It wasn't human.

It was a dragon—or, as I like to call them, dragoon. The creature looked almost like a human in its form; bipedal, I suppose a scientist would call it. It had two arms and two legs like us. But instead of skin, its body was covered in muddy-green scales that I could only describe as camouflage in color. It had a snout that was cousinly with an alligator's and wore a fancy suit that had been ripped to shreds.

It was also very dead.

Whatever had torn its suit apart had been only too happy to do the same to its body. The mustard carpet was full of dark stains where it had leaked all over the floor. Hesitantly, I sniffed; there was a mild foul scent but no hint of rot or decay. That meant this was a fresh kill. Whatever had done this might still be in here with me. I glanced over my shoulder, but the endless hall was still empty.

How had the lizard gotten into the Between? It shouldn't have been possible. I come in here to hide from the Dragon Dons and their ilk. If they'd managed to find a way in here, I would be in big, big trouble.

But there was no sign of any others, which meant this one had somehow gotten here by itself. I frowned as the faintest brush of something tickled the back of my mind—then the world flickered as a memory locked in the back broom closet of my brain managed to break free of its chains.

In my head are the memories of two other Matts. They are

identical to me in every way except for one choice—one that should have gotten me-us-we-them killed. But we-I did not die. In both of those instances, the Constellation Horologium, the alleged son of Time, rewound his father's kingdom to give me a second chance. I survived, but the experiences of the other mes lurk in my head like fraying threads. I don't like looking at those memories. Even the slightest nudge is enough to wake them up. They always try to take over—the alternates want to be in the driver's seat. It feels like there's three of me inside my own brain, like an overstuffed calzone ready to burst.

In one of my memories that no longer happened, I recalled tricking an identical camouflage-scaled dragoon through Portunus's door and slamming it shut. Shortly after that move, I would have died to another reptile's flaming breath. But I didn't, so this dragoon shouldn't be here.

I stared down at the lizard at my feet and gave it a little kick with my shoe. It was definitely here. As I pondered, I recalled a discrepancy between my memory and my other me's memory. When Alex and I were first confronted by the reptile gang outside the convention, there had been *three* of them. But after Horologium had rewound the cassette tape enough to let us escape, there had only been *two* left to chase us down the different hallway.

The camouflage one had been missing.

Just as I was about to turn away from the corpse, the blob of lizard twitched. Hissing in surprise, I called on Willow's flame. The fire spirit was all topped up; I had just visited the Dandelion Court in the Faerie Lands, so I had plenty of juice to work with. It would be only too easy for me to turn this narrow hallway into an inferno.

I stared at the thing for a long moment, waiting for it to move again. Now that I looked more closely, there seemed to be a light of intelligence burning in its eyes. Was it still alive?

I've never read Stephen Hawking. I'm just glad I don't get him confused with Stephen King anymore. I don't know how relativity works, or how most things do for that matter. But this place… I think it's fair to say this place is weird. Once the other-timeline version of myself locked the dragoon in here, was it somehow possible that it couldn't get out and the world just moved on?

I don't know if Time actually works in the Between. It never really seemed to take more than a moment for me to find the right door, no matter how long I wandered. That might explain why this dragoon wasn't dying. Maybe it was just…stranded. If Time didn't move here, maybe Death didn't either. Something had torn this monster to shreds, but since it was outside the normal flow of the universe, it was stuck.

A shiver ran down my spine as I studied it further. For a moment, I considered trying to put it out of its misery. Dragoons tended to be pretty resistant to fire, but surely this one, ruined as it was, could burn.

No, I decided after a moment of thought. I needed to save my firepower for whatever had done this. Even if I managed to turn the beast to ash, if it couldn't die would that even improve its situation? At least it could, like, look around currently. Maybe in time, it would heal. Although I couldn't be sure healing worked here either, now that I thought about it. The classic phrase *Time heals all wounds* implies that the tick-tock part is a key ingredient.

Turning from the lizard blob, I continued my hunt for wherever the door to Mother Earth was in this current configuration.

I was mildly confident that it was in the direction I had been traveling. I didn't have a good reason for knowing that; call it a hunch. It's kind of how the Between works. If I was right, that meant I had to keep going.

So I did.

I worked my way down the eternal hallway, ears straining for the faintest whisper of a sound. But aside from the incessant hum of the fluorescent bulbs above me, all was silent. After a few moments—if moments did indeed pass in that place—I began to relax a little. Whatever had done this seemed to have vanished. Maybe it climbed up into the ceiling, though? That was a horrifying thought.

But the real answer, I discovered, was way worse. I was so focused watching ahead of me that I didn't even notice the disturbance until I stepped on something small and hard. Dumbfounded, I glanced down to see a handful of broken chain links strewn across the ground like leaves in the wind.

The black chains were another fixture of the Between. They were put in place by some power long before I got the key to the place, to lock shut doors of places that had fallen into ruin. Dread grew in me as I turned to stare at the door to my right. The chain that had bound it in place was broken in two, and it was open.

My access to the Between came with no user manual or instructions. As far as I knew, I was just a passenger taking advantage of the secret passageway of the gods. Nothing had prepared me for this moment. What was I supposed to do? Was there a maintenance number I could call?

As I stared at the slightly open door, the sensation of being watched ran down my spine like a horde of spiders. It wasn't just the fact that a door was ajar that was giving me the heebie-jeebies.

It was which door was open.

I knew for a fact that I had never opened this particular door, or any of the others that were sealed like it. There were way too many red flags even for a rule breaker like me. Number one, a thick metal chain had held the door closed in a rather serious way. The second red flag was the sign that used to be on the door: It said the world behind the locked door had been DEVOURED.

I have always assumed this meant that the Nothing, the empty abyss that exists outside reality, had gotten it. But as I stared at the open door now, I began to wonder if maybe something else had the ability to eat a world and also fit through a doorway. For a long moment I stood frozen, straining my ears, listening for anything lurking on the other side of the door. I heard nothing.

Cautiously, I took a step forward and leaned around the open door to peer into the world waiting on the other side. I couldn't remember which devoured realm this was, and of course the warning sign was conspicuously absent. My hand hovered over the doorknob. Should I close the door? Would that even do anything, or had the chain been what kept it sealed? I had the key; maybe I could lock it.

Delicately, afraid it might shock me, I grabbed the door and began to push it shut. The hinges let out a squeal of protest loud enough to wake the dead. Panicking, I pushed the door all the way, only to find that the latch would not click. The second I let go, the door began to swing slowly open again. Somehow, it had lost the ability to hold itself shut.

I guess that's what the chains were for.

Then the door froze mid-swing, as if it had run into a brick wall. A horrific cry sounded from inside the forgotten world, making the hairs on my arm stand on end. A few seconds later the sound came again, closer this time. With a grunt, I slammed my whole body against the door, trying to push against whatever was holding it open. I might as well have been tackling a blue whale for all that it moved.

The screech rang out again. It sounded like it was just on the other side of the door. With a shout of frustration, I shoved the door another time, but whatever will held it in place refused to be budged. My heart was pounding; every instinct told me to run, that whatever was coming for me was THE END, and I was not ready for it.

I decided to trust my gut and pushed off the door into a sprint down the hall. Fear is a hell of a track coach, and I leaned into it, my sneakers pounding on the mustard carpet. I had already wandered through the hall a fair distance; the mortal realm couldn't be far.

Behind me, the ruined door burst open, slamming against the wall like it was caught in a hurricane. Curious what foul beast was coming to eat me, I risked a glance over my shoulder. It wasn't a monster at all; it was a woman. Surprised, my feet slowed down on their own as I turned to study the figure that had come into my hall.

She was beautiful but a little rough around the edges, as if she had been on the road for a bit. She wore a classic toga, but it was black and fraying. A chain of dark pearls that seemed to devour the light hung around her neck. Raven-black hair fell in waves to her shoulders. Shadowy tattoos ran down the length of her arms before vanishing underneath her clothing. Her eyes were not the black of demons or the gold of the Fae but a deep, rich purple. Was she some survivor of her fallen world?

For a moment we stared at each other, separated by about a hundred feet. I wondered what she made of me. I'm about six feet tall, with brown hair and blue eyes; I've been working out, if I do say so myself. Her eyes were focused on the fire surrounding my hands, and who could blame her? It's not exactly a normal human feature.

Suddenly embarrassed, I lowered my hands and banished Willow with a thought. Her gaze tracked up my body to my face, trying to take my measure. Still nervous, I cleared my throat. "Ah, hello," I said, feeling a little stupid. I didn't even know if she spoke English.

The woman cocked her head as I addressed her, like a bird studying a worm. Apparently she understood me just fine, because after a moment she addressed me. "You there, mortal, do you have one of the keys to this place?" It was my turn to be surprised. Whoever this woman was, she knew how the Between worked.

"What do you mean, one of the keys?" I asked.

"My cousins Portunus and Janus made this place together, and each of them had a key." Her answer squeezed my heart like a cold vise: There was another way into the Between besides mine. But that wasn't the big thing that caught my attention.

"Your cousins?" I repeated, my throat going dry. Portunus was a god, and I was pretty sure Janus was too. If this woman was one of their cousins, then logic would dictate that she was…

A god.

I was dealing with a god, and I wasn't entirely sure what that meant. I have faced fallen angels and dragons, but this was something different.

"Yes, my cousins," she snapped. "Are you one of their aco-lytes? Can you bring me forth from this place and to them?"

I no longer felt safe and comfortable. I regretted turning Willow off. My Faerie fire gives me an edge when facing down immortals or their bigger brothers: Immortals. But this god was something else entirely on the power scale. I don't know what kind of damage the Faerie spirit might be able to do to an *IMMORTAL*, but my guess was a lot less than I would like.

"No," I lied to a deity. "I'm but a custodian, here to empty the trash cans and check for any burned-out lightbulbs."

"Liar," she hissed. "I can smell his stench on you, like a rotting corpse."

"Are you sure that's not the lizard behind you?"

The goddess didn't turn to look where I gestured. Instead, she took a step toward me, and I take absolutely no shame in admitting that at her first twitch, I turned and booked it with a panicked cry. I mean, come on; what chance did I stand against something so *foundational?* An ant had better odds of stopping a charging elephant.

I lowered my head, leaning into the absolute fastest sprint I could muster. I had a decent head start; all I had to do was get lucky and get to the door to the mortal realm before she caught me—

The air around me changed suddenly from a gas to solid. One moment I was doing my best to compete with the hun-dred-meter-dash world record, and the next I was trapped in the vise-like grip of nothing. I heard the rustle of clothing and could tell that she was right behind me. She closed the distance between us in the blink of an eye. In hindsight, outrunning a goddess might have been a dream out of my reach, no matter how thorough my training.

The back of my neck itched, and I tried to turn my head to look at the deity behind me, but the air was made from granite. I could not move. My eyes widened as I spied the sign I had been looking for. The healthy door to Terra, taller and more robust than any of its neighbors, was only three down on the left.

I was so close…but still trapped in the will of some forgotten Olympian. There might as well have been two thousand doors between us for all the chance I had of reaching it. The air around me abruptly reverted to its normal gaseous state, releasing me from its grip. I turned to face the goddess, who stood three feet away. An imperial scowl rested on her face as she looked down on me. There was an ancient and terrible light in her eyes, and it scourged my mind like a whip.

Wordlessly, she held out her hand, the demand obvious. I wondered why she didn't just take it from my corpse, but I wasn't complaining. Tentatively, I reached into my pocket, grasping for the Key of Portunus. But while I moved my hand as slowly as I could, my brain raced to figure out how I was going to get out of this.

Clearly, she could stop me with her mind, but how good were her reflexes? Out of this world probably. I only had to make it three doors down, stick the key in the lock, jump through, and close the door before she got there. That was it, nothing fancy. But the last step was important. I didn't want her following me to the other side.

It would all come down to the age-old question: Who was faster, a man or a god? I held my hand out to her, the key resting in my palm like a treasure. The dark-haired goddess reached for it, and as she did, I made my move.

With a mental nudge, I summoned Willow's flames back to life, triggering a concussive blast from my right hand as my fingers closed around the key in a tight fist. The explosion sent me flying backward like a rocket. I leaned into it, letting it spin me to face my left.

I heard the deity hiss in anger, but I didn't hesitate as I slid into my landing like a baseball player coming home. With a vicious thrust, I shoved the key into the old bronze doorknob of Mother Earth and wrenched the door open, making sure to take Portunus's inheritance with me.

"You are marked!" the goddess cried, her voice tinged with the kind of fury that unmakes worlds. "No matter where you flee I will find you."

I didn't look back as I leapt through the door and slammed it shut behind me. Panting from a combination of fear and exertion, I slumped against the closet door, my knees suddenly too weak to hold me up. Desperately, I scrubbed at the sweat beading on my forehead.

Alex, my best friend, glanced up at me from the little table in our sparse bunkroom that he was writing at, his gaze mildly annoyed.

"Welcome back," he muttered, going back to his work.

"**A** *GOD?*" **ALEX** shouted when I finished explaining what I had encountered in the Between. "You set a god free?" My Nephilim friend began pacing in agitation. Tall and broad-shouldered, he had carefully coifed blond hair, and his ears were ever-so-slightly pointed.

"I didn't," I protested weakly, holding a hand against my chest. "I'm guessing the dragoon that was stuck in there might have broken one of the chains and let her in." I left out the part about how the lizard getting in there was definitely my fault. He wouldn't remember it anyway.

"How do you know she was a goddess?" Alex challenged.

"What was her name?"

"I didn't get her card," I snapped. "It wasn't a social call. But she told me that Portunus and Janus were her cousins."

"Cousins," murmured Alex thoughtfully, turning back to the table and leaning down to type on his laptop. "Portunus was a Roman god," he declared after a few moments of reading. "So was Janus."

"So she's Roman?" I asked, following his thought process.

"Maybe, the lines between Greeks and Romans get murky since the Roman pantheon basically just copied the Greeks' homework. I heard it was mostly a rebrand anyway. She might have meant the relationship literally or figuratively."

"She was wearing a black toga," I offered, "but that feels like it could be a uniform for either of those teams."

"Hmmm," Alex muttered, typing some more. After a couple moments, he sighed and leaned back in his chair, dejectedly running a hand through his hair.

"Did you figure it out?" I asked, not sure if I should be excited or worried.

"No. I was just thinking that it would be nice if we could ask Orion." My own spirit fell as I nodded in agreement. The Hunter, our former boss, had been sentenced to a millennium of imprisonment in Tartarus three months ago. Orion was the big, scary member of the group, and we had gotten used to hiding in his shadow. Things had gone downhill for Alex and me since he'd been taken. The Supernatural Crimes Division of the FBI wanted us in connection with a draconic terrorist attack that we'd helped *stop*, and the Dragon Dons were looking for us for stopping it.

The only allies we had left as former members of the Hunt

was the Dandelion Court, but the Fae were dealing with their own issues. Here in the mortal realm, we were relying on the mobster Lazarus for protection, but he too had his own game. The longer we spent in his custody, the more I felt like a prisoner rather than a guest.

"We don't have to figure out her name," Alex suggested slowly, his gaze tracking to the corner of the room, to the object I had very specifically *not* been looking at. It was a sword propped up against the wall, with a worn pommel and a red ruby set in its hilt. It was in a plain leather scabbard that didn't match its style at all.

It wasn't mine—but Orion had left it in my custody before he was thrown in the slammer. No ordinary sword, it burned with a powerful flame and had the ability to kill Immortals. I strongly suspected that it would do just fine to kill a god too.

There was only one problem: the sword didn't really like me. I know that sounds crazy, but magic swords apparently get more agency than their nonfiery brethren. The first time I ever held the blade, it burned an imprint of its hilt into my palm like a brand. The second time, after Orion handed it to me, it tolerated me. Since putting it in the scabbard, I hadn't been brave enough to draw it again.

"I'm not sure how well that would fly," I admitted, staring at the scabbarded weapon with a heavy amount of distrust. "I think I used up my hall pass already. Besides, I don't think trying to sneak up on a god and stab it is the smartest plan, even if you have a weapon to do it with."

"But she's trapped in the Between, right?" Alex pushed.

"Yes, as far as I know she can't get out without my key. I guess she could break into one of the other devoured worlds.

Maybe that Janus guy also has a key if he helped make the place."

"So how are you going to use it with an angry goddess trapped in the halls waiting for you?"

"That," I admitted, "is a very good question."

The Between was one of my greatest strengths in the supernatural world. When you're one of the little guys, being able to duck out an escape hatch that locks behind you is very useful. It was also my primary means of getting back to the Faerie Lands to visit the Dandelion Court and recharge my flame spirit's supernatural batteries. A deific interdiction would be beyond inconvenient, effectively cutting off my supply lines and stranding me without access to most of my allies.

We both looked at the sword again for a long moment before I turned away, shaking my head. That could be Plan Z, the nuclear option. But I wanted to explore any other alternatives before I tried to kill a god with a sword that did not belong to me.

"Speaking of things lurking in hallways," Alex interjected, accepting my hesitancy to use the blade, "one of Lazarus's spooks came looking for you."

The spartan bunkroom that we were currently hiding in was significantly less luxurious than the townhome we had been living in. Technically I still paid rent, but it wasn't safe for us to stay there. According to Lazarus, it was being watched by the FBI, the Dragon Dons, and the Constellation Congregation. No thank you.

I'd never had the chance to experience it myself in high school, but it turns out being popular sucks. All I wanted was my own room and bed. I loved Alex; he was my closest and most loyal friend. But never being alone was starting to wear on me like a high-pitched hum that never quite goes away.

"Oh boy." I sighed, getting out of my chair and eyeing the closet door that I had used to enter and exit the Between. "I guess I better go see what our landlord wants."

The Lazarus Corporation is a massive organization that I'm sure I've only ever gotten to see the tip of. If I've learned one thing living in one of his facilities, it's that the tweedy old man is full of surprises. His pockets are deeper than I can understand, and unlike dear Agent Richter of the FBI, he knows what is going on around him.

Lazarus had hidden Alex and me away in the basement of the same facility that my sister Meg was in. There were underground levels full of the barrack-like rooms that we were staying in, which people moved into and out of at an alarming rate.

I made my way through the sterile white hallway of the underground dorms and presented myself to the guard station that controlled the access to the elevator bank. There was no entering or exiting the lower level without passing through the checkpoint.

"Heard Lazarus was looking for me?" I asked, presenting the cool-eyed guard sitting behind the desk with my laminated badge. His eyes flicked over my name before he typed a query into his computer.

"Level Five," he confirmed with a bored nod. He pressed another button and the elevator opened with a ding. I gave him a wave and stepped into the kind of stainless-steel freight elevator you might expect to see in a hospital. The doors closed behind me, and I was off.

I wondered what he wanted from me today. Lazarus hadn't given me any good options when he recruited me to help him with this project. It was either come live in his basement or get arrested for terrorism. But since I'd begun my stay at the world's most sterile hotel, he hadn't been very forthcoming about what exactly he needed my help with. We kept doing tests and experiments, but I was no closer to understanding the bigger picture than when we started.

I felt the upward momentum fade as the elevator slid to a stop, and the doors opened with another ding. Two more black-clad security guards were waiting for me, assault rifles strapped to their chests. I'd been here long enough that I didn't find that intimidating anymore, just another day in the office.

"Morning, gentlemen," I greeted them brightly, stepping out of the elevator and setting off down the hallway. As soon as I'd heard "Level Five," I'd known where I was going. There was only one thing worth seeing on this floor. It was time for a day in the lab.

The guards didn't respond but fell in step behind me, flanking me like a color guard. Lazarus wasn't a big fan of his guests wandering around his facilities unsupervised. I'd have taken that more personally if I hadn't burned one of his other ones down.

Two turns later, I stopped at a metal door, locked with a keycard reader. I grasped my ID from where it was clipped to my shirt and slid it through the electronic eye. There was a beep, and the door opened with a hiss. I led the two guards into the air lock inside and scanned my ID again.

The outer door sealed as the room pressurized. I moved my jaw, popping my ears as the pressure built. A second tone sounded, and the inner door opened. With the guards on my heels, I strode into the lab of a scientist who had to be at least a little mad.

The white room looked like a movie set that wasn't sure if it was an arcane lair or a server hub. A massive computer bank rested against one wall, the lights on the array blinking in slow time. In the corner, several scientists in white coats peered at a mixture in a beaker. A different wall held a library's worth of ancient tomes behind a series of glass panes. In the middle of the room, a ritual circle was built into the floor. Unlike the cheap ones I had used in the past, this one was made of metal screwed into the ground and set with precious stones.

The whole room practically hummed with anxious energy like a dance floor on prom night. In the center of all the nerdy tension was the man himself, Lazarus. I knew you weren't supposed to judge a book by its cover, but Lazarus pushed that rule to the limit. An older man, he walked with the aid of a wooden cane topped with a gold creature of some sort. I'd never seen him without his tweed suit or horn-rimmed glasses. He looked like he should be lecturing students about the books on the wall behind him, not running a secret company that dabbled in the arcane.

"Ah, Matthew," he said, turning to me as the doors opened. "I had hoped you would return to this plane quickly."

"Just needed a recharge," I explained, holding up my hands. He knew all about the fire that Willow could conjure, and so did his insurance company.

"Well then, I hope you topped the tank up," he replied amicably, gesturing toward the center of the room where the circle sat. "Because we are almost ready to begin the project."

"Would now be a convenient time to tell me what the project actually is?" I asked, giving him a hefty side-eye. On the inside, I could feel my heart rate begin to increase. I had a feeling that part of the reason he had kept this a secret was because it wouldn't be fun for me.

"I suppose it might be necessary," Lazarus mused, leaning harder on his cane. His warm blue eyes scanned the room, watching his people scurry about their tasks. "It is no secret that my aim is to defeat death," he began after a few moments.

"Yes, which is why you were willing to care for Megan."

"Indeed. She is a truly unique specimen."

"So if you think about it, maybe you owe us for helping your research?"

"Nice try," he murmured in an amused tone. "You are not in the Faerie Lands anymore, Matt."

"They do rub off on you," I agreed with a shrug. I wasn't surprised that he wasn't willing to see it that way, but I figured it was worth a shot.

"But your sister is not the only one with a special condition," Lazarus continued, turning to face me. "You also exist outside of the normal rules."

"Is this about the soul thing?" I asked, getting a bad feeling.

"Yes, because of that agreement, you're governed by different rules."

"Different how?" I really did not like where this was going.

"Your soul is guaranteed to Hell when you die, but they cannot claim it for another eight years and several months," Lazarus explained as if this were the most normal thing in the world. "Which means that if you were to die now, they could not touch you."

"Where would I go if I died now?" I asked, my mouth suddenly dry. This was somehow sounding worse than I was expecting.

"Where indeed?" Something dark and twisted glinted in Lazarus's eyes behind his glasses. "That's exactly what we want to find out."

"YOU WANT TO KILL ME?" I shrieked, taking a step back. Unbidden, my hands burst into flame as Willow leapt to my aid. I heard the guards behind me click off the safeties on their rifles. Scientists around the room turned to look at us, irritated. *So sorry that my imminent death is making all this noise.*

"Only for a while," Lazarus replied, far too calm. "The idea is that we send you beyond the Veil while your soul cannot be claimed and then bring you back so you can report on what you've found. Think of it like a deep-sea dive, except to the Underworld."

"You can bring people back?" I stared at the man. Maybe he was a mad scientist.

"We could bring you back." He gestured to one of his nerds to join us. "Because you won't be completely dead."

"Lovely," I muttered to no one in particular.

A mousy woman I'd never met before approached, giving my hands a nervous glance before tucking a strand of her light-brown hair behind her ears and smiling at me earnestly. "There's really nothing to worry about," she promised. "We've done extensive research and are confident that—"

"Beatrice, maybe start from the beginning," Lazarus interrupted gently, his eyes fixed on me. He could probably see the vein pulsing in my forehead and knew I was about to burst.

"Ah yes, sorry," she responded, putting her hands in the pockets of her white lab coat. "We are going to stop your heart—"

"That's not filling me with a ton of confidence," I snapped, feeling that specific organ pounding against my chest like a monkey raging to get out of its cage.

"Then, using a combination of refrigeration technology, cryomancy, and temporal control spells, we will preserve your body at the precise moment that your soul is released and keep it until it is time to restore you to your living state."

I stared at the woman for a few moments, my mouth hanging open. "I'm sorry, but who exactly are you?"

"I'm Beatrice, lead technomancer of this project." She drew herself up, lifting her chin to peer down her nose at me. I didn't like the sound of any word that ended in *-mancer*. It was too cozy with wizards. The only magic I was interested in being a part of was someone guessing which card I drew out of a deck.

"What does a technomancer do?" I asked.

"We combine arcane knowledge with modern expertise to solve the mysteries of the universe," she told me, practically bursting with pride. Someone had read the brochure.

"Please tell me she's joking," I begged, looking past her to Lazarus. "Magic?" I knew it was real. I once saw Orion make a tracking spell out of a plastic baggie and some herbs. It worked for about thirty minutes. That did not make me feel entirely comfortable about trusting my temporarily dead body to it.

"Come. See." The old man gestured at the rest of the lab.

Beatrice led us at an excited trot to the circle built into the lab's floor. She gestured to the center. "This is where we will keep your body for the duration of your visit to the Underworld."

"Looks comfy," I muttered.

"We use Nordic runes to invoke subzero temperatures." She pointed at the far side of the ring where a bunch of Viking-esque letters were carved into the floor. "They're the best for dealing with the cold. This will minimize any decay while your soul is absent from your body."

"Awesome," I said as unenthusiastically as I could. I don't think she noticed.

"On the southern curve you will notice that we used Sumerian to blind the Reapers to your bypassing of Fate. Since it is a dead language, we expect that it will speak to them more clearly."

"Makes sense," I grumbled, feeling more uneasy by the moment. The script she indicated was written in a black polymer that was inherently creepy.

"The east and west curves are written in both Latin and Greek to catch and slow both hands of the clock, one for the hour and one for the minutes. It wouldn't do to only stop one!" She laughed at her own joke. I felt sick to my stomach.

"No second hand on this clock?" I couldn't help but ask.

"Let's not get greedy," she chided me. "Time can be slowed, but stopping it in its entirety is another matter."

"Obviously," I agreed, as if anything coming out of her mouth wasn't pure insanity.

"We will also fit you with an adapter to our quantum-powered life support technology, which will simulate brain functions and involuntary actions like heartbeats."

"Wouldn't that mean I'm alive?" This was all starting to get a little confusing. I had a fake literature degree, but this felt like it was beyond pseudoscience.

"Your heart will beat once every few minutes to prevent atrophy, but this will only begin once we detect that your soul has been collected. It's sort of like putting your body in maintenance mode."

"Classic," I agreed. "I love being in maintenance mode."

"Isn't it wonderful?" She clapped her hands together and turned to me beaming.

"Are you insane?" I demanded, looking between her and the madman who was bankrolling this whole thing. "Why would I ever do this?"

Lazarus's lips curled into a sharp smile, like a gambler holding a royal flush. He knew he had me. "Because while your soul travels across the Veil to the land of Death, you will have a chance to reclaim the other segment of your sister's soul."

I blinked in surprise. I hadn't thought about this as a rescue mission, but that was…appealing. Not enough to make me throw myself off the high dive without investigating the pool below a little further. But there was something to this line of argument.

"There is also the matter of what I am owed," he continued, fixing me with a heavy stare. Something cold slithered in my guts like a serpent. There was no kindly literature professor educator lurking behind his eyes now. More a scientist studying a beetle under a microscope.

"I have cared for your sister for almost twenty months at considerable expense to my facility in terms of time and resources. This has had a noticeable impact on our ability to conduct the research that we exist to complete. If you are not willing to do this to settle the scales, then I will be forced to take what I am owed from your sister's flesh."

Anger flared in me once more, but I clenched my fists, keeping it locked down. Lazarus gazed at me calmly with the smug patience of someone who knows he's already won. He was right. I would do anything to protect her.

Bastard.

My hands burst into flame as Willow answered my call, and I took an aggressive step toward the billionaire. "Do you want to rethink that?" I snarled, letting the fire's fury rage in my voice.

Several of Lazarus's guards raised their weapons, but the old man waved them off with an amused expression. Crossing his arms on the top of his cane, he leaned forward and fixed me with a knowing gaze.

"I have been alive for a very long time, Matthew. I am no immortal, but I'm something else—half mortal, I suppose. Do you really think that if your fire was a threat to me, you would be free to walk in this place?"

For a moment I considered calling his bluff. Willow's fire had ruined a lot of immortals' days. But something in that glittery-eyed gaze reminded me that Lazarus was not the type of man to make bets he could lose. He had too many resources to bother with risks. I could burn this building down around us, and it would only put Megan's life in even more danger. He'd probably make a profit off the supernatural insurance payout.

Glaring at the man in tweed, I dismissed the flames and drew myself up to my full height. I would play his game for now. Between the FBI hunting us and Megan needing his help, I didn't have a lot of choices. But once my sister was safe, he would pay.

"Someone's gotta ask Dawn," I told him.

ABSOLUTELY NOT," DAWN snapped at me from across the table. "Are you insane?"

"Apparently," I groaned, leaning back in my chair. I was back in the Faerie Lands, although this time I had taken the Dandelion Highway. My normal commute wasn't a safe option right now. But I had to come. I couldn't sign up to die without royal permission. "Lazarus assures me that they have tested this extensively."

"On *rats*," Ash hissed from her sister's side, her red hair reflecting her anger. The two Fae royals sat across the table, grilling me. "You, betrothed, are at least slightly more complex than a rat."

"Thanks, dear."

My plan was going over about as well as I thought it would. I knew Ash wasn't going to be a fan of the idea; betrotheds are usually supposed to be alive. It's part of the deal. But beyond that, I was one of the last three Lords of Fire. If I kicked the bucket, the Fae firepower would drop significantly. That was a no-fly zone for both sisters.

"Robin agrees that the way the contract is written prevents Hell from claiming my soul until the end of the term, even if I do expire early." I gestured at my lawyer, who sat in between us at the conference table, an uncomfortable neutral party. "Although now that I think about it, does that mean I'm supposed to be invincible or something until the contract period is up?" I glanced at Robin. "Can Lazarus and his mad scientists even kill me?"

"Oh yes," he snorted. "The ten years are a maximum, a guarantee that Hell can't *collect* you. But there's nothing stopping you from being an idiot and getting yourself killed ahead of schedule."

"What happens then?"

"Who knows?" Robin sniffed loftily, as if such questions of the universe were beneath his notice. "Maybe they put you on a shelf until collection day."

"That doesn't sound great."

"It would make it hard for you to get out of the deal if you're sitting in time-out for the rest of its duration," Robin pointed out. I nodded in understanding. Even if I couldn't go to Hell early, dying for real would probably kill any chance I had to ever get my soul back.

"I forbid it," Dawn announced, leaning back in her chair with a dismissive look on her face. She wore no crown in her blond hair, but her voice carried every ounce of her queenly authority. "Enough of this nonsense. Lazarus will have to find another guinea pig to send on his mission. The offices of Death are not a place for tourists."

Dawn's reaction was exactly what I'd expected. To her credit, I don't think she was being unreasonable. This was a stupid idea. No, it wasn't. It was so much worse; calling it a stupid idea was actually some sort of weird compliment.

"Well, actually—" I replied slowly, glancing at Robin for confirmation. He gave me a reluctant nod. He was just as opposed to this as Dawn was, but he was my lawyer. He had to tell me stuff. "—you can't stop me."

"Of course I can," Dawn replied, incredulous. "I'm your queen. It comes with the crown, darling."

"You may not forbid a Faerie citizen from making a deal in aid of a member of their bloodline," Robin told her with a reluctant smile.

"What are you talking about?" Dawn demanded, her eyes flickering from blue to gold for a heartbeat as her irritation rose. Ash's gaze snapped to me. It felt like her green orbs were trying to stare right though my skull. I didn't make eye contact with my *beloved*, just kept looking at the queen.

"It is an Elder Law, from when people would leave traps for our kind and then ransom them back for favorable deals."

"Shakespeare." The queen growled his name in disgust. My eyebrow quirked in surprise, but I didn't ask. Now was not the time. "Let's hear it." She gestured at me with a weary reluctance.

"My sister's soul is split. Part of it is here, but part of it is on the other side of the Veil. They keep calling her a shade."

"I'm familiar with the term," Dawn grumbled.

"Lazarus's team believes that while I'm in the Underworld, they can use me as an anchor to extract the other portion of her soul and restore her to some sort of normalcy."

Dawn and Ash both stared at me in furious silence for a long moment. Robin looked down at the table, displaying a rare level of discomfort. I didn't blame him. I felt a little like a chicken kebab myself, roasting on a spit between the flames of my betrothed's and my queen's ire.

Finally, Dawn turned to Robin with something like a frustrated acceptance on her face. "I assume that law is ironclad?"

"Quite," he assured her.

"You know that your sister is likely insane, right?" Dawn fixed me with a heavy stare. "Her soul has been split for over a year, with part of it in Hell. The damage that can do to one's psyche…"

"I know," I told her quietly. It might be too late to make her truly whole, but I owed it to Megan to try.

"Are you certain you want to do this?" the queen asked. The look on her face was different… The anger had been replaced by something else that I couldn't identify. "You wish to claim your right as a Faerie citizen?" Her eyes changed to solid gold as she spoke. A tightness entered Ash's face, but she didn't say anything.

I glanced among the three of them for a moment, a bad feeling in the pit of my stomach. Robin hadn't warned me that there was more to this. But it was obvious that I was agreeing to something new, instead of claiming a right that belonged to me.

"Am I not already a citizen?" I asked into the eerily silent room.

"That's complicated," Dawn admitted, rolling her shoulders as she leaned back in her chair once more. There was a hungry aura exuding from her that I definitely did not like. I'd thought I held all the cards coming into this conversation. I shot my lawyer a glare. Clearly, he had left something out.

Robin shrugged apologetically. He had rules to follow too. "You are a member of the Dandelion Court, legally speaking," he supplied after a glance at the smirking queen. "But citizens are technically Fae."

"I'm like half Fae," I protested.

"Well, mathematically, a little less." One of Dawn's cruel smiles played with the corner of her lips. I had upset her by trying to override her orders, and she was enjoying seeing me punished for it. "Damien would have to be one hundred percent *pure* Faerie in order for you to get fifty percent from him. Trust me, if you were half Fae you'd know it."

"So, what, I'm not pure enough to be a citizen?"

"On the contrary, you're mortal enough to get to choose. In the old days we called you a changeling." Goose bumps pimpled my flesh at her words. All I had been trying to do was briefly die to rescue my sister's soul from the Underworld. Somehow, this had gotten serious.

"What's the choice?" I asked her warily.

"Just declare your desire to no longer be a mortal and become a Faerie three times, and it will be so." Golden eyes flashed at me again as she watched me closely, like a master chess player waiting for my next move.

"What, uh, what are the repercussions of that?" I managed through a dry mouth.

"You become immortal, no more pesky soul." Dawn's shark-grin grew again.

"*Your mortality can be fixed,*" Gloriana's ghost whispered in my ear. I shook my shoulders to get rid of the shiver that was playing on my spine like a xylophone.

"I should note that your contract would still require the delivery of *a* soul, since you would not be in possession of one to give to Hell," Robin cut in, shooting Dawn a troubled look.

"I thought the contract said something about the force major—"

"Majeure," he corrected me absentmindedly.

"Gesundheit. I thought the force thingy included something about me Ascending as a way to cancel out the contract." For some reason I'd thought it would be harder for me to become an immortal. I guess nepotism works in all areas of life.

"Becoming an immortal is far from *Ascending*." Her emphasis was obvious. "I don't think you have any plans to become an avatar or god anytime soon, do you?"

"I dunno, sounds fun."

Ash let out a scoff. Okay, god might be a bit of stretch, but I thought I could have a chance of becoming at least a myth. My hands catch on fire. That's gotta get you to at least fanciful rumor.

"Becoming a Faerie citizen would not suffice to break the contract," Robin confirmed. "You would be required to deliver a satisfactory replacement soul, and you could become bound to all the restrictions of being a Fae."

"No more lying?" I gasped in horror.

"No more lies," Ash replied, a dark hint in her voice.

"No more art," Robin offered in an oddly sad tone. I didn't have the heart to tell him that nothing I had ever done with my life could be considered "art," unless it was very impressionistic.

"Uh," I said, trying to focus my brain and failing spectacularly. There was something oddly alluring about becoming a

Faerie. The cons didn't seem that bad, really. An immortal life of luxury and a get-out-of-jail-free card. It felt like an out that my lawyer should have brought up before. I wasn't the most comfortable with the idea of using someone else's soul as a replacement, but maybe we could get someone from death row or something. Someone who *deserved* to head downstairs anyway. Because I didn't, right?

Right?

"How come you never mentioned this as a way out?" I asked Robin, arching an eyebrow.

"Because an acceptable soul doesn't mean any old soul," he replied with a sour twist of his mouth. "In fact, given the personal nature of your conflict with Hell's CEO, I am confident that he would refuse almost any soul you offered."

"What would happen if we couldn't agree on a replacement?"

"You would be in breach of the contract, and the Devil would be within his rights to claim you, mind and body."

"I assume that's worse?" I asked, already knowing the answer.

"Much worse," he agreed. I wasn't really sure how it could be, but I realized that I didn't want to know the specifics. I had enough nightmares already.

I hesitated, trying to figure out the best path through this mess of decisions that lay before me. I felt like Theseus, but I had already defeated my Minotaur. It seemed unfair that I was thrown in the maze after. But at the end of the day, it wasn't really a decision, was it? Megan needed my help. I would do anything to save her.

I opened my mouth to agree, but Dawn cut me off. "You needn't make a full decision right this moment," she offered. "I would be willing to grant you the privilege of ignoring my command after hearing you say the phrase once, as a gesture of intent."

My eyes narrowed as I looked at her. She was going to let me thwart her—and Dawn hates being thwarted. But she looked far too smug, which meant there was more going on. I trusted her, but in the same way I would trust a tame lion.

"I assume there's no expiration date on the phrases?" I inquired. All three of the Fae across from me shook their heads. Ash was looking at me like I was the biggest idiot she knew, which might be true, she still doesn't know that many people. But even if it was a bad idea, it was only one statement. That left two more to go. How hard could it be not to say that specific phrase?

"I wish I were a Faerie," I said in as even a tone as I could manage, despite my heart racing. I held Dawn's golden gaze as the tension in the room gradually faded. The queen's lip curled into a tiny sneer as she saw my challenging stare.

With an abrupt motion she shot to her feet and stared down at me. "Do try not to die for real. Our deal doesn't extend to the grave. If you get yourself stuck in the Underworld, we will not lift a finger to break your contract before Hell comes to collect you when your time is up." I did my best not to wince at her promise.

"Fair enough," I sighed as she began to walk out. "Hey Dawn," I called after her as she got to the door. "What do you get out of this, out of me becoming a full Faerie? I already work for you."

The Queen of All Fae regarded me for a second, and the cold exterior that she wore like armor receded a little. "That," she said with a small smirk, "would be telling."

CHAPTER
FOUR

ROBIN EXCUSED HIMSELF swiftly in Dawn's wake, leaving me alone with the brewing volcano that was legally my betrothed. Ash glowered across the table at me. Her green eyes flashed with anger, but she was silent.

Nervous, I shifted in my seat. I had gotten on the Autumn Lady's nerves many a time, but I had never seen her direct this much ire my way. I'll be honest, it wasn't a great experience. Ash excelled at anger; it probably had something to do with her fiery nature and DNA. The longer she glared, the more I began to feel like a pot simmering over an open flame. Eventually my nervousness boiled over.

"Why are you so upset?" I blurted.

Ash studied me for another long moment before answering. "What is your plan?" she asked me, burning much colder than her expression had led me to believe. "What do you think happens to me if you die?"

I blinked in surprise. "Nothing?" I replied with an arched eyebrow. "You don't have to marry me, which is kind of a plus."

"Do you understand what it means to be betrothed?" she hissed, leaning forward on the table. "Our fates are tied together. Your enemies are my enemies. Your promises are my promises. You are one of the last Lord of Fires of my house. If you die—" Her voice cut off in a painful snap.

Suddenly I felt a little selfish. Ever since Orion had been locked up, I had been running a little fast and loose, like a teenager left home alone for the first time. And that wasn't entirely fair. My decisions didn't affect just me; Ash was tied to me whether she liked it or not.

"I hadn't thought about it that way," I murmured embarrassedly. "I'm sorry."

Ash kept staring until she finally let out a huff of annoyance, and her shoulders relaxed. "I understand that you have an opportunity to help your sister," she said gently. "I know that you would do anything to save her, but it's not fair to make those decisions without talking to me."

It was my turn to be silent. She was right, of course she was. She had been nothing but a staunch ally during our betrothal, and I owed her the same in return. Meg was my sister, and it was my fault that she was currently a shade, stuck between life and death. I had to make that right. Plus…the other part.

"I'm sorry I didn't communicate. But it's a little worse than

I told Dawn," I murmured, not meeting her eyes. My betrothed was silent, her arched brow asking all the questions. "If I don't do what Lazarus wants, then he's going to take what he's owed out of Megan's flesh." Ash's eyes flashed in anger, but she didn't comment. As a Faerie she was more than familiar with intense bargains.

"*You didn't talk to me either.*" Willow's voice broke into our conversation as my hands burst into a subdued, low-burning flame. From the way Ash twitched, I could tell she heard them speak too. "*I don't want to go out.*"

I felt myself go numb with shock as I realized that I had not thought about my bond with the fire spirit and how it could be affected by me dying, even temporarily. As I understood it, Willow was a collective consciousness, but each of the people they were bonded with was a unique fire. If I died, my Willow would fade into nothing.

"Willow, I'm not really dying," I protested, feeling twice as bad for my poor communication skills. I couldn't even have a conversation with the being in my head before I made decisions. I was a terrible partner. "Would Lazarus's experiment affect our bond?"

"*I don't know,*" the spirit replied slowly. "*No one has ever come back before.*"

"So there's a chance?" I pressed, hating myself a little. I knew I was asking Willow to take a personal risk, but this was for my sister. Given the choice between a being that would persist and rescuing Megan from the depths of Hell, I would make the same choice every time.

"*Maybe.*" Willow didn't sound very confident.

"Willow, if I don't, he's going to hurt my sister. More than she's already being tortured by being in the Devil's clutches." The spirit was silent, the flames on my hands were almost still, as if Willow was deep in thought.

"*The flame cannot go out*," they whispered in my head before vanishing. I felt sick to my stomach. After all the spirit had done for me, it was cavalier and cruel to risk part of their being. But I had no choice.

I hated this. Hated Lazarus for what he was making me do. Hated myself for agreeing to do it. A small coal of rage began to build in my stomach, the first ember of an inferno that was yet to come.

"You know that if my father finds out you are on the other side of the Veil, he will come for you."

"He can't," I protested. "The contract expressly forbids an early collection. I had Robin check—twice."

"We're talking about Lucifer," Ash hissed back. "Do you think that he is going to let some words on a piece of paper stop him from getting you? You will be on the other side, already halfway into Hell."

"I think I'm already halfway there, the way things stand," I said softly. Ash flinched as if hit. Sometimes I think she had enough issues with her father that she forgot why he—el Diablo—and I had beef. I'd killed his girlfriend, but that was because she wouldn't give me my stolen soul back.

The silence between us was heavy.

"Come," Ash ordered, rising to her feet. "I know that you're going to do this regardless of what I think, but I can at least walk part of the way there with you."

We made our way out of the conference room and through the meandering marble halls of Goldhall. For a moment we walked in silence, like two countries with closed borders. But after a few moments, a warm hand slipped through my arm, and we walked closer.

I guess there was no point in letting me go into the Underworld angry. This might be the last time we ever saw each other. A chill settled around my heart as I considered that. I liked Ash, and I was fairly confident that she felt the same about me. Dating someone when you're already engaged is a strange affair. It removes some of the mystery and magic. We'd sort of skipped a few steps. It was a bit like opening a Lego box to find the model was already two-thirds of the way put together.

Did we love each other? I don't think so, but we also hadn't been given the space or opportunity to find that out. She was someone I cared about, and the thought that I might never see her again felt like a heavy weight on my shoulder.

"What's the deal with Dawn wanting me to become a Faerie?" I asked her to distract both of us from the growing sense of doom. "I'm a little lost."

"She'd have more power over you," Ash replied, her hand still resting on my arm. "Right now, if the deal between you and the Dandelion Throne were to be broken, you would no longer be a part of the family."

"She'd lose one-third of her Lords of Fire instantly," I said, understanding the implication.

"But if you become a full Faerie citizen, you answer to her forever."

I nodded; that was classic Dawn, always trying to tighten the screws a little bit more whenever she could. "She doesn't like to let things go, does she?" I mused.

"It would also probably start a war."

"Not another war," I groaned. I was getting really tired of playing the role of the Archduke Ferdinand. If I wasn't careful, I'd wind up dead. "With whom, Hell?"

"It would make her look weak if one of her people was bodily dragged off to Hell. Very few immortals have ever been claimed by any of the great organizations. But *he* would never let you go so easily."

"Do we even have the firepower to throw down with the Devil and his cronies?" I was more than a little confused. "Why would she want to drag herself into a situation where she had to fight a war she couldn't win?"

"I don't know," Ash murmured softly. "And I find that terrifying."

"But it seemed like she wanted me to speak the wish three times, right?"

"I think so," Ash agreed slowly. "She certainly made sure you said it once and knew the rules." I blinked in realization. After everything I had just learned, there was no way I would ever wish to be a Faerie even one more time. That seemed like playing with a fire I couldn't hope to control. Had Dawn been worried that someone else would trick me into that path and made sure that I knew better than to go any farther down it? It didn't feel like that much of a stretch for the Queen of All Fae.

Ash and I walked in silence to the Faerie Security Administration checkpoint and into the long marble terminal that housed the gates for the Dandelion Highway. We entered the first room, and she walked over to the ancient rotary phone and began to dial. I knew from experience that the system used our mortal area codes. 310 would send me right back to LA.

She finished dialing, and the golden dandelion set into the

wall burst into motion, spinning faster and faster until it was a blur. A golden hole grew out of its center and consumed it, spreading across the entire wall like a behemoth's mouth opening to swallow its meal.

I gazed into the yellow depths for a few seconds, trying to figure out how to properly say goodbye to a betrothed. In a movie, the hero would sweep his arms around the woman he was promised to, stare into her eyes, and utter something profound.

But this isn't a movie, and I'm not a hero.

Ash surprised me by wrapping me up in a tight hug. Her red hair brushed my face as she dug her head into my chest. Stunned, I froze for a moment before returning her embrace. For a while we remained there, twin flames coiled around each other.

We had never been a particularly touchy couple. Walking arm in arm was about as exciting as it got. I could count on one hand the number of hugs that Ash had given me. But this one felt different. I couldn't exactly say why. Maybe it was because it was the first time we knew it might be the last. Maybe it was something more.

Finally, and yet too soon, we released each other. The Lady of Autumn gazed into my eyes with her own watery green ones, an uncertain expression on her face. "Do not die," she commanded.

"Well, I think technically I have to, to cross to the other side," I replied as lightly as I could. Ash gave me an unamused stare, and I relented with a small smile.

"Do not get trapped over there."

"I know. And if I do, no one will come to save me," I assured her. "I heard Dawn."

"No, if you do, *I* will come to find you," she promised. Chills ran down my spine as I looked into her intense expression. I would have known she was telling the truth even if she weren't a Faerie. I also knew that the easiest way for her to get into the Underworld was to take her father up on his invitation for a meeting. I wasn't sure I was worth such a sacrifice.

"I appreciate it," I told her through my dry mouth. I didn't know how to express my gratitude. "Let's hope it doesn't come to that."

"That would be ideal," she agreed sagely, a ghost of her smile flitting across her face. "Now scoot before I get yelled at. You're letting all the magic air out."

I swallowed and turned toward the spinning golden portal. Squaring my shoulders, I stepped into its embrace, glancing back at her one last time. The last thing I saw was Ash raising her hand in farewell, before the Dandelion Highway grabbed me like an angler setting its hook.

Something clicked into my chest and yanked, pulling me into the darkness. I don't really know how any of this works, but I like to make uneducated guesses. It's how I passed a lot of my classes in high school.

I think the blackness I was traveling through is the same stuff that the Between is in. Which means it's technically the Nothing, the void that exists between worlds. If I looked around long enough, maybe I would spot the eternal hallway running perpendicular to me off in the distance. But honestly, I tend to keep my eyes closed on the ride. I don't get carsick, but I do get interdimensional-travel-sick apparently.

The journey is quite short. There's not even time for an in-flight snack. A few disorienting moments later, I felt the pressure of the mortal world settling around me. The Fae magic seems to be able to slide me into this reality by turning the solid objects into something like Jell-O.

The drywall of Lazarus's office rippled like a lake after a heavy stone is dropped into it. I imagined I heard the wall spit "*ptooey*" as it vomited me out onto the carpet. This wasn't my first rodeo, so I managed to land on my feet.

The elderly scientist looked up at me from where he was reading at his desk, the planter of dandelions before him missing the one I had used to travel back to the Faerie Lands. "Well?" he inquired softly. "Do you have royal approval?"

I stared at him for a long moment, my heart hammering in my chest. I knew that I was going to do this, the same way that Ash had known I would. There really wasn't a choice, but I still needed a moment to collect myself before I leapt from the edge of the cliff.

"We're cleared," I said slowly. "I'll be your Underworld diver."

"Excellent." Lazarus closed the small tome he had been reading with a sharp snap. "Come, we have much to discuss in private."

LAZARUS TOOK ME to another world. It's too bad that you don't get your passport stamped every time you visit a new realm; mine would be very impressive at this point. I was beginning to learn that getting to another place doesn't seem to be that hard; there are lots of single paths running between worlds. It's finding something that leads to many worlds, like Portunus's Key, that's truly rare.

Lazarus led a group of us to a dusty old storage level deep below the earth. Off to the side, as if discarded in a sea of worthless antiques and rusting vehicles, was a blue tarp. At a nod from the man in tweed, his two guards began pulling the plastic back, revealing a pair of marble columns underneath.

One of them was missing the top half; it looked like something had sliced cleanly through it at an angle. I didn't know it was possible to cut through marble like it was butter, but something clearly had. Orion's sword probably could, come to think of it.

At the base of each pillar were carved faded words in a language I couldn't read. I thought it might be Greek given the letters. Lazarus strode forward to the pillars and placed one hand on each, bowing his head. After a moment, a square blue hole opened between them, like a door in reality.

"Come," he commanded and stepped through into somewhere else. The guards posted up on either side of the pillars, so whatever was waiting on the other side was likely safe. I ducked my head and followed him through. A pair of his scientists followed in my wake.

It turned out the blue shining through was the picturesque sky waiting for us on the other side. There wasn't a single cloud as far as I could see. We stood in some sort of wheatfield, surrounded by golden stalks dancing tall and beautiful in a warm, light breeze. LA has killer weather, but even I was impressed. This was something special.

In the distance I could make out the blue of a bright ocean, little tufts of white as waves rolled into the perfect sands of the shore. A hundred yards away lay some old buildings, long since fallen into ruin. The four of us appeared to be completely alone in a never-ending sea of wheat.

"What is this place?" I breathed in awe. "It's beautiful."

"Once, I believe, it was called Elysium," Lazarus said softly. "I paid a terrible price to recover its gates, only to find it an empty ruin."

"This was supposed to be the Good Place for someone, right?" I asked, ignoring the bad feeling the professor's words gave me. "What happened?"

"We do not know," he replied grimly, turning to face me. "When we entered, it was empty. Whatever secrets to immortality were held here vanished with its citizens. Now it is only a safe place for us to discuss our true designs for your journey to the Underworld."

"What do you mean, 'safe'?" I felt my eyes narrow. "And 'true designs'? I thought we'd already covered everything."

"We covered almost everything," Lazarus amended, his horn-rimmed glasses glinting in the brilliant sunlight. "But there is one more step to the plan."

"It seems a little late to spring this on me," I grumbled.

"We did not dare speak of it up there, for fear he was listening."

"Who?"

"Death."

I stared at Lazarus for a long moment, waiting for him to chuckle at his cute little joke. He did not. A cold, clammy hand that might have belonged to the Grim Reaper ran its fingers down my spine. "I think you better start explaining," I told him quietly, glancing at the two scientists flanking him. The guards were waiting outside, but that didn't mean I couldn't make a break for it. Even in the ruins there had to be a door I could use somewhere. Lazarus might not be killable, but I was willing to bet he ran slower than a god.

"Nothing has died here for centuries." Lazarus gestured to the ruins beyond us. "This place is barren, empty of life. Wherever there is life, there is also death. But if there is no life"—he shrugged—"there is nothing to die."

"Is the wheat not alive?" I asked suspiciously, taking a step back from the grains all around us.

"I'm talking about life with a soul."

I wondered if whatever had happened to the devoured worlds in the Between had happened here as well. The fact that the sun was shining and the crops were growing told me probably not. This wasn't the empty void of the Nothing. This was something else.

"Well?" I matched the old man's steady gaze. "Let's get this over with."

"Everything we told you is true," Lazarus reassured me. "But there is one more objective that is your true goal. You are to steal the Crown of Immortality."

"I'm to what the what?" I asked stupidly.

"We believe that Death has in his possession the Crown of Immortality. Your true mission is to steal it and bring it back to this side of the Veil." Lazarus's tone was cool and collected, as if he were ordering a cup of coffee.

"I'm not even going there for real, how am I supposed to bring anything back?" I demanded. I was very confused on the physics of all this. As far as I knew, I was going to be some kind of temporary ghost. My physical body was supposed to remain behind, hooked up to Lazarus's magical machines. It's hard to carry things when you aren't made of matter.

"May I?" Beatrice asked, glancing at her boss, who nodded. The scientist stepped toward me, crouching to pick up a rock from the ground. Staying low, she drew a line in the dirt and pointed at it. "This is the Veil. It is the border between the realms of the living and of the dead."

"Good so far," I told her when she glanced up to make sure I was paying attention.

"We are on this side. We're alive, we exist. Generally, we refer to this side of the Veil as the Living World, and the other side as the Underworld. The other side is different from ours. It is less physical and beyond time. There are only three things that we know can cross the border: souls, supernatural beings, and items of tremendous power."

I gulped. I knew which one of those I had.

"The plan is to free your soul from your body so it can cross the Veil. While a soul without a body does not have form or function on this side, we know that is not the case in the Underworld—you should be free to act over there. All you need to do is have the Crown of Immortality on your person when we summon you back, and you should act as a bridge, bringing it with you."

"What about my sister's soul?" I asked, interrupting her. If they were going to ask even more of me, I wanted to make sure I was getting my half of the bargain out of it. "Will I be able to hold on to her too?"

"Yes," she replied after checking for Lazarus's permission again. "We expect this works the same way. As you return to your body, you will briefly tear a hole in the Veil, allowing the things with you to come through."

"You '*expect*'?" I hissed. "What does that mean?"

"Based off all the research we've done, interviews with beings who have crossed the Veil, we are fairly confident—"

"But you don't know? You're just going to send me through and see what happens?"

"You are the first mortal we've encountered with your unique protection. The infernal contract you're under forbids Hell from collecting your soul until the time has expired. Anyone else with a soul who descends into the Underworld would be collected instantly."

If I hadn't had Robin check the contract for me, I would have been skeptical, but he agreed that this was standard practice. There was no collecting early, and no wiggle room on that. I'd never really thought of my curse as protection before, but in this one scenario it just might be.

Something about her explanation was bothering me. For starters, I was sure everything was more complicated than she was making it sound. People are always dumbing things down to explain them to me for some reason.

Still, I looked around the empty paradise sprawling as far as I could see in every direction and followed the hint of a thought that was nagging at me. It had to do with this empty place. It fit into the puzzle somehow, but I couldn't quite see it.

"Tell me more about hiding from Death," I pushed, still watching the golden wheat heads dance in the light breeze.

"The Crown of Immortality is mostly forgotten." Lazarus picked up the thread from his scientist, walking to stand beside me on the edge of the grainy sea. "This is by design; of all the ancient relics, it is one of the few that has the authority to forbid Death from claiming the bearer. Because of this, it is fiercely protected. If a passing Reaper overheard us even mention it…"

I shivered at the hunger in his tone and the terror in his words.

"What do you want with it?" I asked. While I knew Lazarus's aim was to cure death, I didn't really know what that meant. Immortality for all? Seemed unlikely.

"Why, to study it of course." The mobster turned to me in genuine surprise. "Tear it apart and find out how it works, then make more."

"Then sell its clones at a high price, I'm sure," I added dryly.

"Is that what unsettles you about this, boy?" Lazarus asked me softly. "You see the chance to propel our species into our rightful place among the undying, and you sneer because it might be used to make someone rich?"

The old man moved even closer to me, leaning forward to stare into my eyes with his hard blue ones. Age may have been unkind to his body, but the fire that still burned in his spirit was as bright as mine.

"Do you think that money will matter in a world where we don't die?" he half whispered at me. "Do you think that anything will be the same five years after our souls stop being fed to the bottomless grave?"

In that moment I realized that Lazarus wasn't some savvy businessman on the hunt for riches; he was a fanatic. Although I'm sure getting rich in pursuit of his insane dream didn't hurt. We all want to have our cake and to eat it too. But this wasn't just a move for him. He believed it. He believed in it more than I believed in gravity.

"Got it," I stammered, taking a step back from the lunatic. "World changing, yeah. Everyone wins, nobody dies."

"I'll make you an offer," he said calmly, adjusting his spectacles. "If you undertake this quest, you will have the chance to free your sister's soul and make her whole. If you return with the crown, I will convince Agent Richter and the FBI that you work for me and were in no way involved in the recent 'terrorist attack' downtown."

"You can do that?" I stared in amazement. "I thought you said that was impossible."

"I've decided that it is a fair trade," he grunted. "Mortals are easy. They still believe in money."

"But if I don't, then Megan gets taken apart by your team of psychopaths?"

"You think I am a monster," Lazarus replied softly. "Perhaps I am. For I would burn the world to save us all. The Immortals use us for pawns and power, and we are content to be cows, led to the slaughter. Yes, Matthew, if I cannot find a more humane way to cure us, then I will be forced to take the harsher one."

A bright light blazed in his eyes. God spare us from zealots who believe they are in the right. I glared at him but decided to move on. There was no point in arguing anymore.

"Aren't we across the Veil now? Why do I need to die if we can just walk in?" The thing that had been bothering me suddenly clicked. Elysium was supposed to be one of the places heroes went when they died, another Valhalla or whatever. Based on Beatrice's fancy line-in-the-sand diagram, that should put it firmly on the "dead" side.

"Not anymore." Lazarus sighed sadly, taking in the beautiful sights around us with a wry smile. "Once it would have been our way in around the security. But whatever doom befell this place broke it so badly that it slipped back over the line. Time passes once more, and the dead do not come to this place. It's worthless now."

I turned to give the place another scan. I felt a note of panic as I realized the black line on the horizon wasn't a storm front at all. It was too dark, too absolute. "I think I know what happened to your Underworld," I told him, pointing at the shadow.

"Hmm?" Lazarus gazed in that direction.

"That is the Nothing eating Elysium like a cancer. One day it will be consumed." This must be one of the worlds that the Between marked as devoured after all. Or very close to achieving that status.

"The Nothing," he murmured as if seeing a wonder for the first time. Together we stood and stared into the distant abyss for a time.

Slowly, he turned and began walking toward the square portal that led back to our world. "Now you know everything," he called as he left. "It is time for you to make your decision."

I watched him go for a few seconds, trying to pretend like I was going to be smart and consider this from every angle. I could practically hear Orion's growl of frustration because I *knew* he'd think this a bad idea. It wasn't like negotiating with the Fae; at least I knew they couldn't lie. Lazarus could be selling me a load of poppycock, and I'd never know.

But it was all for show. I was gonna do it. I knew it, and I suspect he did too. Megan needed me. What choice did I really have?

CHAPTER
SIX

I **STOOD IN THE** calm before the storm. Today was my death day, like a reverse birthday. I spent a mostly sleepless night in the barracks with Alex. But as the hour drew nigh, I visited my sister in her hospital room. Megan was still in a medically induced coma. It was the only way to keep her from screaming.

She lay in the same room she'd occupied since Lazarus took her into his care. Beatrice and her technomancers had made quite a few modifications since then. A thin circle had been etched into the floor, a simple metal ring that couldn't be scuffed or damaged. All the machines she was hooked up to were on the inside to prevent them from breaking the barrier.

I stood on the outside, not wanting to risk disturbing the thing that was giving her some shred of peace. Circles are sort of the magical equivalent of their own worlds. Supernatural things can't cross their borders without permission. Which meant that as long as this one was powered, the portion of Megan that was alive was at least partially sheltered from the torments that her other half was experiencing.

None of Lazarus's people were sure if the piece of Megan's soul that was in the Devil's hands could be used as a conduit to bypass the protection of the circle or not. That was "unprecedented," they said, but she still screamed every time they tried to wake her up within the circle, so my guess was yes.

"Hey, sis," I murmured softly, trying not to disturb her. "You hang in there for me, okay?" Her brown hair fanned around her head in waves. She looked peaceful. I could only hope it was true. Dawn's warning about Meg's sanity echoed in the back of my mind. It was cruel, but I knew she hadn't meant it to be. Was it true? It didn't matter. My sister was a prisoner because of me. It was my responsibility to get her out. I could only pray I was not too late.

"Give him a minute," I heard Alex snap from outside the door. My faithful friend was keeping watch, distracting the guards who'd been sent to collect me. It must be the Dying Hour. I closed my eyes and tried to drink in the peace around my slumbering sister, but there's something about hospital rooms that is too sterile to be comforting. The voices behind me rose as Alex refused to budge. I let out a long exhale and opened my eyes to look at Megan one last time.

"I'll see you soon," I promised and turned to go.

"—and I'm telling you that you can wait—" Alex was practically shouting as I opened the door into the linoleum hallway. Two armed guards wearing berets and scowls glared at me over his shoulder.

"Gentlemen," I greeted them, giving my friend a pat on the shoulder. "I understand you're looking for me?"

"You're needed in the lab," the first grunt confirmed, irritation plain on his face.

"Then let's go to the lab," I suggested, giving him a broad smile that I didn't feel. We set off, marching to my death.

"This has got to be the stupidest thing you've ever agreed to, even counting your demon deal," Alex told me as we walked.

I ignored him. Partially because I was tired of having this argument and partially because I had no good answer for him. He was right, and I didn't like that. But there's being right, and then there's doing the right thing. I was pretty sure this was the second one, which meant I was gonna do it or die trying.

Heh.

Part of me wondered if this was the specific hour that Samael had told me about. I guess we would find out. As we stepped into the elevator to shoot to the laboratory level, I marveled at how calm I felt. The two guards were clearly here to keep me from running, but I had no desire to do so.

I was about to die. Sure, it was supposed to be temporary, but I'd expected to be a nervous wreck. Instead, I was numb. It felt as if the cold hand of the grave already had me in its grasp.

The risk was massive, but that only felt fair, since my sister was still half dead. What was I going to do, leave her there? She was being pulled on by two worlds because of me, and it was my responsibility to make it right.

"How do you cross the River Styx?" Alex demanded out of

nowhere. Over the last week he had been drilling every myth of the Underworld into my head. We had no idea what I would find on the other side of the Veil, so he had tried to teach me about *everything*.

"Pay Charon one gold coin. Assuming I can even find a gold coin or carry it because I'm a ghost," I snapped. Okay, maybe I wasn't as calm as I thought.

The industrial elevator whooshed open, and we followed our escort down the hall. The room where the ritual had been prepared buzzed with a nervous energy that resonated in my chest. Lazarus and his people had been hard at work. The circle contained even more script in different-colored enamels. A second, larger circle made of gold had been laid around the original metal version.

"Magister, the subject is here," one of the scientists called as we walked in. I curled my lip a little at being called a "subject." I had a name.

Beatrice turned from where she stood in the center of the rings, white coat flaring like a cloak. She held a giant leather-bound book that looked like it might crumble into dust the next time someone tried to turn the page. I did a small double take as I realized that the words were glowing with a golden energy. I still had a healthy distrust for magic.

"Wizards," Alex grumbled, his tone full of disgust.

"They're real, right?" I asked him nervously. "Now would be a great time for you to mention that they're fake before I blindly follow one's orders and die."

"They're real and not to be trusted."

So much for that. I let one of Beatrice's assistants lead me to the massive computer bank running along the far wall. The scrawny young man gave me a small smile and gestured to a skintight black suit hanging from a clothing rack. "You'll need to put this on."

"I have to die in spandex?" I eyed the tight mesh with distaste.

"It's technically not spandex, it's actually a polymer made from various microfibers, golden flee—"

"What you need to know is that it will be hooked up to our life support system, keeping your body from atrophying while your soul is absent," Beatrice told me firmly, stepping into our conversation. The ancient grimoire she had been reading was closed and tucked under her arm like a nerdy football. "We're doing our absolute damndest to make sure that when you return, your body is in the same condition you left it in."

I gulped and gave the skinny little suit a closer inspection. It certainly didn't look special. It reminded me of the full-body wet suit I used to wear when I would go surfing with my sisters. But I had already agreed to go this far, so there was no point in complaining about the little stuff. In for a penny, in for a pound, as Damien used to say.

"Where do I change?" I asked, lifting the suit off the rack. It was lighter than I expected. Beatrice gave me a shrug and a gesture that said, *Right here will do.* I stared at the woman for a long moment, but she didn't blink.

It wasn't enough to kill me; they had to take my dignity too. With a sigh, I started pulling off my shirt. From somewhere behind me Alex whistled a catcall. I ignored him, kicking off my sneakers and unbuckling my belt. I hesitated for a second but withered under the cool gaze of the two wizard slash scientists waiting for me. I gritted my teeth and shucked my jeans before reaching for the bodysuit.

"Uh-uh," Beatrice stopped me, wagging a finger. "Your undergarments too."

I opened my mouth to protest, but she cut me off. "The suit needs to be in contact with your skin to keep atrophy at bay. You're welcome to keep your skivvies on if you're comfortable with that region losing blood flow and beginning to decay?"

I stared her dead in the eyes and dropped my boxers to the floor. This time, no one tried to stop me when I began to step into the suit. Whatever polymer this was made of sure was *grabby*. I had to jump around like a kangaroo to force my body into its tight embrace.

Across the room, Alex was choking so hard holding back his laughter I thought he might actually be the first one of us to die. My face red with embarrassment, I let the attendant zip up the back, sealing me from toe to crown in the mesh. There's just no dignified way to put one of those on, okay? It's not my fault.

I glanced down at my wrist, surprised to see some sort of display built into it. It showed anatomical stats against a heat map tracking the temperature and blood flow throughout what was soon to be my corpse.

Lazarus appeared next to me, his appraising eye running over the tech that I had been jammed into. I guess he thought it fit me because he nodded once before glancing at Beatrice. "Proceed, Magister," he commanded coolly.

Beatrice's assistant stepped forward to slide an open helmet over my head, wiggling it to make sure it was settled tightly. I felt like I was preparing to go to outer space, as the world's most underqualified astronaut.

"It is time for your friend to depart," the mobster said, turning his attention back to me. "I fear he may be a distraction."

"Absolutely not. He's my insurance," I told him.

"Insurance for what?"

"That you do your best to bring me back. If you don't, he starts stabbing people." Lazarus glanced over his shoulder to the corner where Alex was waiting, head buried in his phone. He turned back to me and rolled his eyes but didn't push the matter.

"This way, Matthew," Beatrice instructed, leading me toward the center of the circle. I didn't need to look at the digital readout on my wrist to know that my heart rate spiked as I stepped through the first ring. The technomancer stopped before entering the inner ring and gestured for me to pass her.

I hesitated; once I crossed the boundary there was a decent chance that I was never coming back. I looked up at Alex, who had put his phone away. My blond friend gave me a solemn salute, no hint of his earlier levity on his face. I gave him a nod, took a deep breath, and crossed into the center.

Nothing happened—which made sense; the circles had not been powered yet. No one had started lighting candles or doing chants. A whirring sound came from above me; I craned my head to see a mask that a fighter pilot might wear descending toward me. A long hose trailed behind it, connecting it to the ceiling.

Beatrice stepped up and fitted the mask into the gap of my helmet. It clicked into place with a series of snaps. I could feel air rushing through it, and I tried to relax. These might be some of my last breaths, so I might as well make them good ones.

"I need you to listen closely," Beatrice instructed, her voice managing to pierce the calm fog enveloping my mind. "This hourglass is made from some of the Sands of Time." She pointed at a giant sand-filled contraption set against the far wall.

"This pocket watch is linked to it." She held up an old silver timepiece on a chain. It read just after midnight—or noon, I guess, depending on how you looked at it. From a quick glance I could see that it was frozen. The second hand wasn't moving. She undid its clasp and reached around my neck to fasten it on me like a necklace. The wizard tucked it down the front of my wet suit. "The moment you cross the Veil, we will flip it over, which your watch will show. Because Time flows differently over there, this is how you will know when we are getting ready to pull you out. When the clock strikes midnight, it will be time to go."

"How long will I have?" I asked, feeling a sudden twist of fear. I hadn't thought about how long I might be stuck there. What if it was a nightmare of pain and suffering, and I was trapped there until my time ran out?

Beatrice shrugged uncomfortably. "We don't know," she said honestly. "On our side it will be three days. But over there it could be days or weeks."

"But not months?"

"Probably not months," the wizard amended.

"But definitely not years?"

"Probably not months," she repeated, patting me on the head and turning to go.

"Wait a second," I insisted, taking a half step toward her. What exactly had I signed up for? Well, I knew what I had signed up for, but some of the logistics had escaped me until now.

"Begin," intoned Lazarus.

I took another step, intending to leave the circle until a few more of my questions were answered. But my foot didn't touch the ground. Startled, I stomped harder, but all that did was make me tilt downward as my foot found no purchase. I realized that I was no longer looking Beatrice in her eyes but staring down at her from above.

Panicked, I glanced at the floor, only to find that I was floating. I drifted through the air of the inner ring like an astronaut. Dimly I could hear chanting. A crowd of wizard scientists had gathered around the outer ring, their voices crying out in Latin—the most disturbing of all languages.

Beatrice scampered to the outer ring to join them. She fished a tablet out of her coat pocket and began fiddling with it, her eyes flicking up to my floating form. A deep chill descended on me—not so much a winter's day as the heart of the North Pole itself.

It burned as it ate its way in from my fingers and toes, heading toward my core. I gasped for breath, but whatever I inhaled was not oxygen. It felt like a fog that invaded my body and mind. The cold dug deeper, and the fog spread further. Panic tried to flare inside of me, but the arctic smothered it. I was such an idiot. Why was I doing this?

Vaguely, I was aware that my heart wasn't beating normally. I could feel its slow, ponderous thumps against my rib cage. The edges of my vision began to fuzz and go black, leaving only Lazarus in the center, leaning on his cane. I took one final breath, and the darkness reached out to consume me. I let it, but I couldn't have stopped it anyway.

Then there was nothing.

With a jolt, the lights came back in an instant, like someone had just turned on the power. "You're not on my list, but lucky for you I was in the area," a warm, southern voice informed me. I jerked in surprise, reaching up to rip off the mask covering my face. I felt like a computer booting up. *Who am I again? What am I doing? They're going to* kill *me. I can't let them. Why am I just standing here?* I peered around the room, but everything was blurry. I blinked to clear my eyes, but nothing changed.

I turned in the direction of the voice and was surprised to see a man floating next to me. Unlike the rest of the world, he was perfectly in focus, as if everything had been pixelated except for us. He was tall, almost as tall as Orion, and wore a long black cloak, but the hood was down. He had thick brown hair and a mild smile on his face.

The giant black scythe he was leaning on with a two-handed grip belied the warm tone he'd used to greet me. My eyes widened as I took in his appearance.

"Sorry, what?" I asked after a few seconds.

"It's your lucky day!" the man announced cheerfully. His hint of a southern accent twanged at his *r*'s and *y*'s. A cloud passed over his face as he peered past me. "Well, I reckon it's not your *luckiest* day ever, but still. Could have been worse."

Slowly, almost against my will, I turned to look over my shoulder at what he had been peering at. There, floating just behind me, was my body. I'd know that blurry blob anywhere. *Oh, that's right, the world must be out of focus because I'm dying.*

"How could this possibly be lucky?" I hissed.

"Like I said, you weren't on my list. If I hadn't been passing through, you could have been waiting a long time for someone to come pick you up for delivery."

"Delivery? What am I, a package?

"Ah crap." He sighed, rubbing one of his hands across his face. "I'm sorry, I'm still pretty new to this. I haven't quite gotten the speech down, if you know what I mean."

I did not.

"Ahem." He dug into his cloak and pulled out an honest-to-God clipboard. "I hope you don't mind if I read from my script. It will be a little smoother." He didn't wait for me to answer before plowing on.

"Congratulations! You are dead," he read. "Your time on this mortal plane has come to an end, but your adventure continues. My name is Wilbur, and I am a duly licensed representative of Death Corp. I have been sent to collect your soul and escort you into the next life. I will be responsible for accompanying you to the DMV, where you will be able to redeem your afterlife package based on your subscription."

"I'm sorry," I interrupted flatly. "Did you say DMV?"

"Yes, sir." He beamed. "The Department of Mortal Valuation. Have you heard of it?"

"Just keep reading," I said with a sigh. Dying, it seemed, involved just as much red tape and bureaucracy as living. How disappointing.

"That's pretty much it," he admitted, scanning down the page and lifting the sheet to look underneath. "Yadda, yadda, not responsible for any damages you may encounter to your soul during delivery, void where prohibited, one ride per customer… yeah, I think we covered the important stuff." Wilbur tucked his clipboard back into his billowing black cloak. "Ready to go?"

"Uh, I guess." Suddenly panicked, I looked around, taking stock. It turned out dead me still had some sort of body. Like Wilbur, I was floating next to my blurry real one. I wiggled my fingers and toes; everything seemed okay. I was wearing a copy of the black jumpsuit, and the pocket watch dangled from my neck.

"Let's go!" Wilbur cheered, turning and raising his giant black scythe. With a downward slash, he carved a line right through the air itself. Distorted pieces of Reality curled away from the tear like sheets of paper.

The strange man who allegedly worked for Death gestured for me to go first. Hesitantly, I made my way to the edge of the gap in time and space. If I'd still had a heart, I'm sure it would have been pounding. I cast one last glance over my shoulder at the fuzzy world around us, hoping I'd get to see it clearly again one day.

Wilbur gave a polite cough. "Usually, I don't like to rush my customers," he told me, "but like I said, you weren't on my schedule, and I've got another appointment I can't be late for."

"I understand," I croaked, eyes staring into the inky darkness waiting for me. "I just didn't really expect..."

"I know, it was the same for me," he promised.

I don't know why, but that actually made me feel a little better. I had chosen this path to save my sister. It was too late to change my mind; the only way out was through. I squared my chin and took a step into the Dark. Wilbur followed behind me, and as he did, the tear zipped itself shut from bottom to top behind us.

I glanced down at the little watch hanging from my neck as the light from the real world faded just in time to see the second hand begin to move.

CHAPTER
SEVEN

MY JOURNEY THROUGH the Veil was disorienting. I felt like I had no body, but my mind was hurtling through space at Mach 10. One second there was a cold, all-consuming darkness, sort of what I imagine being buried six feet below would feel like. Then there wasn't. I saw colors I could not name and heard sounds I could never replicate.

Finally, with a familiar abrupt jerk, I snapped from the void into a white room that reminded me of a doctor's office. It was a small square, with a bed and a couple of chairs. Wilbur stood across from me, relief on his face.

Gradually, my physical form seemed to return, growing out

from my center like a slow-burning fire. As soon as I had lungs again, I started hyperventilating. I was dead. Why was I dead? This was a mistake. Any second now, Lucifer and his demons were going to appear and take me—

"There you are!" Wilbur greeted me, his southern accent pronounced. His cheerful voice cut through my panic like a knife. "I was beginning to worry I lost you for a moment. Most of the time it only takes a few seconds for a regular guy to pass through…"

His sentence trailed off as he noticed the pocket watch around my neck. His head tilted slightly, and he stared as if he'd never seen an ancient timepiece before.

"Say, whatcha got there?" he asked. "Usually, you can't bring anything with you."

"It was my…grandfather's," I lied, trying to think quickly. It didn't seem like a good idea to tell him it was a magical item counting down my return to the other side of the Veil. "He made me promise to never take it off. It was his good-luck charm."

"Huh," Wilbur mused, nonplussed. "Maybe that's why it took you so long to come through."

"What do you mean?" I asked. "That trip took like ten seconds."

"Time gets weird over on this side," he admitted. "You get used to it, but it takes a while. It actually took what you would call an hour. I was beginning to think you weren't going to make it."

I shivered uneasily. "Well, I'm here now," I said at last, looking around the small room. "Wherever this is."

"This is a transition space." Wilbur gave me a small smile. "Some folks need a moment to process the fact that their time has come to an end. Especially if it was abrupt or unexpected."

Ah, this was a freak-out room for people who weren't ready to be dead. I suppose that made sense, although it was oddly more humane than I'd expected.

"Now I really am in danger of being late," he continued. "You are welcome to stay here as long as you need; it takes up no Time. Once you're ready, head to the hall and go left. You'll find a waiting room where you can begin to get processed."

"Uh, sure," I said, eyes narrowing at the door on the far wall. Now that he mentioned it, taking a moment to catch my breath didn't sound like the worst idea. The hyperventilation had faded, but I still felt a little light-headed. What was I doing with my life?

"Okay, gotta go," he announced. "I hope your final destination has everything you wanted it to. If they give you a survey, don't forget my name was Wilbur." He drew his scythe through the air, creating another dark passage through the Veil. "Thanks for choosing Death Delivery," he called over his shoulder as he stepped through.

For one wild second every part of my being wanted to dive after him and try to claw my way back to the land of the living. But I managed to stop myself as the hole zipped itself up behind him. I had a mission. I was here to save my sister. Running now would only make me a coward and a failure. According to my father, I was already one of those things. I had no interest in giving him ammo for the second one.

But at the same time, I was *dead*. I *died*. What if that couldn't be undone? What if I was like a vase that has fallen and smashed into a thousand pieces. Even if Lazarus and his wizard scientists could fix me, would there always be scars where the cracks were?

If the King's Horses and the King's Men had put Humpty-Dumpty back together, would he ever have been the same, or just a shell of the egg he once was?

Despair crept up in my heart like a fog. Without even meaning to, I sat on the edge of the little medical bed and studied the room around me. It was so weirdly normal. It had four white walls and a wooden door that would have fit in anywhere in my world.

The only jarring element was a solid black poster on the wall that said, THE END. The small print below it read, SOMETIMES ENDS ARE NOT NEW BEGINNINGS. That didn't really make me feel better.

Speaking of beginnings, how much time had I lost? I grabbed the pocket watch and held it up, studying the little hands. It had been a while since I had used a watch that wasn't digital, but I was pretty sure that it now read 12:05 am. Wilbur said that it had taken me almost an hour to get here, but only a few minutes had passed for me. As I watched, the second hand ticked once.

Relief flowed through me: The technomancer had been right about the slowdown that happened on this side of the Veil. I'd hate to have died for nothing. But even in a place outside of Time, I was still running out of something that felt suspiciously like Time. However that worked, I needed to stop moping and get in gear. I slid off the edge of the bed and stood back up before realizing I was missing something.

My magical timepiece had made the trip with me, but what about Willow? Mentally, I called for my fire spirit to burst to life on my hands, but nothing happened. My mind echoed with an awful silence. It was as if the part of my skull where the spirit had taken up residence was completely empty. They had taken all their furniture and moved out.

Willow was right: They couldn't follow me through the Veil. I could only hope that our connection hadn't been permanently severed. The little spirit was weird, but I had gotten used to having them ride around in my head. I felt almost naked without them.

I stared at my reflection in the big mirror on the wall. I was still wearing my wet suit, which was embarrassing. My brown hair was flattened, and out of reflex I mussed it up into some semblance of shape. Wouldn't do to have helmet hair on my first day of dead school. My blue eyes stared back at me with a weariness that I felt in my bones. I could go for a nap, but I was on the clock.

With a stressed sigh, I headed for the door. Its simple bronze knob felt real; in fact, now that I thought about it, everything here felt real. Another thing that Lazarus and his crew had been right about. Hopefully they were right about everything else. I took a deep breath and opened the door. Here went everything.

My patient room opened out into a hallway that continued with the doctor's office theme. A series of brown doors on either side hinted to me that plenty of the recently deceased were composing themselves around me. I followed Wilbur's instructions and turned left, making my way past another poster that read HAPPY DEATH DAY in bright letters with drawings of confetti and balloons.

I wondered if those had been there in Virgil's era, or if they were a new addition to keep up with the times. For a moment, I worried that I had been abandoned in some other eternal hallway, à la the Between, because this one too stretched far into the distance. But my fears were unfounded; it had an end. After a short walk I emerged, like a butterfly breaking free of its chrysalis, into the next stage of processing.

A long rectangular room, painted in monotonous gray, extended a football field's length in either direction. Along the far wall ran a series of glass panes, with people sitting behind them. It reminded me of the border crossing lines at LAX. A sea of beige plastic chairs, some empty, some full, sat in rows. A banner above the glass panes read, NOW SERVING: 119,312,012,234.

At the entrance of the room a woman with shiny, red dreadlocks sat behind a desk emblazoned with a bronze seal that read: DMV. A short line of people waited their turn to speak with her. With a shrug, I got in the back of the line. Who would have thought that dying was just another chance to follow instructions?

"There must be some sort of mistake!" the elderly woman at the front of the line practically screamed at the redhead behind the desk. "I am supposed to be at my granddaughter's recital this Thursday—"

"Ma'am, if there was a mistake, and I'm sorry, but I'm sure there wasn't, I am not the person to speak to," Red interrupted with the professionally tired tone of a customer service representative. "If you take a number, the DMV agents can review your records."

"I don't want to review my records!" the dead woman shrieked. "I want to go home!" My heart broke a little as I heard the terrified note in her voice. I felt out of place, like I was overhearing something private.

"If you need some more time, you're welcome to return to one of the back rooms," the woman behind the desk offered in the same, bored tone. "But all I can do is give you a number."

With a defeated sigh, the woman reached up and accepted a scroll before staggering off toward the chairs, a vacant expression on her face.

"Bloody embarrassing that," the man in front of me murmured in a British accent. "No need to make a scene, old bird, we're already dead. Might as well go with some dignity."

"Huh?" I asked, surprised that he was talking to me.

"Bugger, you're a young one," the man replied, turning to look at me for the first time. He was sporting a monocle and pair of gray mustachios along with his striped pajamas. "Sorry about that, chap, I hope you at least had a good run of it?"

It took me a second, but I realized why I felt like such an outsider. Everyone else here was really dead. Capital D-E-A-D. I was only pretending—I hoped. The numb feeling in my chest wasn't the soul-crushing end, it was the hovering fear of apprehension. The people in line were having to come to terms with something much bigger than that.

"Uh, it was a time," I said after a moment of reflection. "How about you?"

"Well," he answered with a wink as the line moved forward. "At least Martha can't get after me about the damned hedges anymore, so things are looking up." It might have been my imagination, but I thought I heard a quavering note in his voice too. I don't think dying is easy for anyone, even the British.

"Next," called the woman, and my new friend stepped forward to accept his scroll without complaint. He gave me a small wave as he departed and made his way to the waiting area.

"Next," she said again, turning to look at me. Her thick dreadlocks shifted as she did, and I realized with a start that they were not hair at all, but *snakes*. The face of one of the copper-headed serpents came into view as it rose to look at me. I squeezed my eyes shut as hard as I could. Was that Medusa?

A soft chuckle came from across the desk, underscored by several hisses from her slithery hairdo. "You can relax, mortal," the woman said dryly. "I can't turn a soul to stone, even if I wanted to."

Oh right. My body wasn't really a body anymore. I guess that made sense. I opened my eyes and stared into the deep-green ones of the snake-haired lady. I gulped in fear but didn't feel myself beginning to solidify, so she was telling the truth.

"How do I even have a body?" I asked. "I thought that was supposed to get left behind."

"You don't—well, not really. Your soul has memory. You probably feel a heart beating in your chest, but it's not the same. Try not to think about it too much."

"You almost gave my fake heart an attack," I grumbled, holding a hand over my chest. She was right: I had definitely felt *something* jump when I encountered the Gorgon.

"Most people are too flustered to notice," she chuckled. "It's nice to feel seen every once in a while." She held out a white scroll set with gray wood on the ends. "Here's your number, wait until they call you."

"Are you…?" I started as I accepted the scroll.

She cut me off with a shake of her head. "Sister," she informed me. "Dusa had green hair." She gestured at her snakes.

"Huh. Well, I like the red." I gave her a little salute and left.

"Nice outfit," she called after me.

I walked into the large waiting area and chose a beige plastic chair away from everyone else. No one was really talking, but

I didn't want to seem inviting. I needed to get my bearings. I was on my back foot, overwhelmed by how different and yet the same everything was. If I wasn't careful, I was going to get swept away and fail my mission.

Once I was seated, I unfurled my scroll to check my number. The room didn't seem too crowded, so I figured that I wouldn't have to wait very long. My eyes narrowed as I tried to quantify the massive figure. I glanced up at the signs on the wall. The current person being processed was: 119,312,012,576. The first three digits of my number were 122. I closed my eyes and did some mental math. Arithmetic had never been my thing, but if memory served, commas went hundreds, thousands, millions… billions.

Assuming that this DMV worked like a mortal one, there were three *billion* people in line before me. That seemed insane. I was pretty sure there were only about eight billion total humans in the world. I'd seen something on the news about it.

If my number was tied to me and therefore the day that I was supposed to die for real, it made sense to me that it would be so high. A lot of people would die during the eight years and change that I had left before my contract ran out. But the number still seemed inflated.

Maybe, maybe it was some sort of hint that I would live longer than my contract. If I didn't die until I was in my sixties or seventies, would such a massive number make sense? If there were eight billion people right now, lots of them would be dead by the time I died.

Who would have thought dying would fill me with such hope?

And yet I had a time limit for this deep dive to the Underworld. I couldn't afford to sit here for fifty years waiting for my number to be called. I was gonna have to cause a scene.

Eyeing the far wall, I got out of my seat and started walking farther down the line, looking for a spot where I could jump in. I saw people of all ages, races, and creeds waiting their turn. One infant in a stroller being pushed by its mother who carried two scrolls made my heart break in a new way.

I kept going, resolved not to cut in front of those two. After a few more minutes, my hunt was rewarded in the most terrifying way possible.

"I'm telling you that you made a mistake, and it needs to be fixed right this moment!" a middle-aged man in a fancy business suit shouted, banging his fist on the glass separating him from one of the agents. His tie was undone, and he looked like he had been partying right up until the moment he ended up here. "I don't care what you say, I'm not leaving here until this is settled. Do you know who I am?" As if to punctuate his threat, he began pounding on the glass.

Looks like someone didn't spend enough time reflecting in the freak-out room.

Faster than a thought, a man appeared next to the shouter, whom I assumed was some Hollywood exec or finance bro. The new guy was dressed in the same black cloak as Wilbur. With his free hand the guard grabbed the spiraling man and slammed him against the wall.

They stared into each other's eyes for a long moment, until the dead suit began to sob, giant tears running down his face. "Please," he begged, but no one responded. He was still whimpering when the man in black dragged him away to a door on the far wall. I watched the scene with a chill growing in me. Not everything was all white picket fences on this side.

The agent behind the glass sighed and pressed something. The sign above her turned green and the number changed. Without missing a beat, I slid into the empty space with as friendly a smile as I could manage.

"Scroll," the woman commanded from behind the glass, gesturing at the slot in the window. She wore a uniform of all black, with a grinning-skull pin on each collar. Her ears weren't pointed, and her eyes were of the mortal variety. She seemed as human as me. There was something that looked suspiciously like a monitor in front of her.

"Well, I have sort of a weird issue," I replied, still clutching my absurdly large number. "My number is quite a way off, and I was wondering—"

"Count your blessings, kid. One hundred and nineteen billion, three hundred and twelve million, twelve thousand, five hundred and eighty-nine!" She rapped on the glass trying to get the attention of the crowd behind her.

"I mean that my number is a long way off." Embarrassment burned in my chest. "I suspect there might be some sort of mistake, and I'm hoping to get it fixed. I'm not trying to cause any trouble."

Another old woman shuffled toward us, holding her scroll in one hand and her cane in the other. Matthew Carver literally cuts in front of grandmothers. I guess that's who I am now.

"Sir, you will just have to wait until your number is called. Now please, let me help this woman whose turn it is, or I will have to call security."

"My number starts with one hundred twenty-two billion," I blurted out. I had no idea where the other guy had been taken, but I had no interest in joining him. I was on a deadline and needed to get a move on.

The agent blinked in surprise and turned to look at me with a sudden intensity. "Show me," she commanded, gesturing at the slot. Behind me the grandmother was still inching her way up. Not needing any more encouragement, I shoved my scroll through the hole.

Her lips pursed as she unfurled it and read my number, confirming that I was telling the truth. Her eyes flicked from the paper to me, and a single blond eyebrow arched. She typed something into her terminal.

"Matthew Steven Carver?" she asked a few seconds later.

"That's me."

"Let's see here, I do have a delivery scheduled for you. Looks like you are on the Infernal Package with Express Delivery..." Her voice trailed off as she hit a few more keys. I struggled not to shiver. That sounded about right. "For eight years, two months, one day, fourteen hours, and seven minutes from this present moment." She looked up from her screen to stare at me with a harsh, suspicious glare. "How are you here now?"

I raised my hands in a helpless shrug. "Your guess is as good as mine, ma'am. Not exactly how I thought my morning was going to go."

She frowned and began typing some more, brows furrowing in concentration. "It looks you also have racked up quite the outstanding Death Tax," she murmured, eyes still focused on the monitor.

"Tax?" I repeated, momentarily stunned. "I'm dead, why do I have to pay taxes? I thought that was, like, the only perk of kicking the bucket."

"It's part of the customs process," she replied absently, her attention still on my records. "It looks like none of the dues for your infernal contract have been paid, which comes out to a total of one thousand, six hundred and fifty-nine."

"One thousand, six hundred and fifty-nine *what*? Surely not dollars. Do you take credit cards?"

"Years." This time she did look at me with a heavy gaze.

"I owe a *millennium*?" I gasped. "I, uh, don't know how I'm going to pay that. As far as I know I'm sort of supposed to go straight to the old fiery pits."

"Yes, that is the destination for your soul," she confirmed without a hint of sympathy. "But there are standard fees and processing before your delivery can be complete. From the looks of your file, you received a hefty number of benefits as a result of your deal with Hell. Those changes to Reality need to be paid for before you can cross over. Hell can choose to pay them, but most Underworlds have the inbound soul handle them."

Of course they did.

"I didn't even—whatever, it doesn't matter," I muttered. "Surely Hell will be upset with any delays. El Diablo himself is sort of expecting me." Why was I arguing that I should be allowed to go to Hell early? If anything, a thousand-year buffer was great news. Even if it was because I had to pay surprise taxes. I don't know why I was shocked. That's why the ancients used to put gold coins on the eyes of the dead: to pay the toll. Everyone always wants a piece.

She shrugged, unbothered by the potential wrath of the Devil and his demons. "Hell has possession of your soul for eternity. A millennium of employment at Death Corp still leaves an infinite amount of time for them to take possession. It costs them nothing and helps keep our operation running."

I felt my mind twisting as I tried to understand time that never diminished or shrank. We tend to think of time as a limited resource. *I have to wake up in five hours, I get to leave work in fifteen minutes*, things like that. But on this side of the Veil there was no limit. I could spend a thousand years hiding from the Devil, and it wouldn't change how long he would have to torture me.

If I hadn't been suitably motivated to get out of this contract already, I sure was now.

"So what happens next? I'm here kind of early. Do I just sit around and wait for the proper delivery date?"

"That's above my pay grade," she told me with a tight smile. "You will need to go before the Death Board to have your case reviewed. They will decide the proper chain of events to resolve your issue."

"Excuse me." An old woman's voice cut through. "I'm number one hundred and nineteen billion—"The grandmother I had cut in front of had finally arrived.

"Yes ma'am, I will be with you in a moment." A pleasant smile spread across my agent's face. "I'm just finalizing this client's paperwork. I'll be with you in a flash, okay?"

"It took me so long to walk over here—"

"Yes ma'am, and I will personally take care of you in just a second." Another bright smile. I wondered if she'd worked retail before she died. Turning back to her console, she marked something, then stamped my scroll with a red seal. Next, she twisted the gray wooden caps off the sides and replaced them with a pair of black ones. That seemed ominous.

"Here," she said, sliding it back through the glass window. "Take this all the way down to the end." She gestured back the way I had come. "You'll find a door with a pair of guards. Show them this, and they will take you to wait for the Death Board."

"Thanks," I told her, extracting the scroll and holding it up. "When's the next time the board meets?"

She gave me a withering look like I was an idiot who wasn't getting something very basic. "I told you, Time doesn't work here," she scolded me. "They're always meeting and never meeting."

"Great," I told her with a big false smile. She could have just said *I don't know* or *Go check*. No need to give me a new existential crisis every five seconds. "Sorry," I said to the waiting grandmother.

I headed back the way I had come, looking for the door to the Death Board. It turned out to be quite a monotonous hike; I made my way past a desert of chairs, full of people waiting to be shipped off to everlasting something.

After a few minutes, I passed the desk where Medusa's sister was still funneling in the new people. She glanced over her shoulder, and her eyes narrowed as she saw my now black-capped scroll, but she didn't stop working. I gave her a wave and continued on my way.

I don't know how many people die in a given hour or day, but this facility seemed well under capacity. A somber part of my brain figured that the excess space was for infamous days. I wondered what this place had looked like on D-Day.

With a shake of my head, I banished my dark distractions. I needed to plan. It seemed that Robin and Lazarus had been correct to some degree. I wasn't supposed to go to Hell yet. But what did that mean? Would the Death Board throw me in some room until the right date? I couldn't let that happen.

I needed to be free to snoop around and find Meg's soul and the crown thingy.

As my DMV agent promised, two black-dressed security guards stood on either side of a metal door set into the wall at the end of the waiting room. They had human eyes and ears and watched me with distrust as I approached.

"Sir, you'll have to return to the waiting room," one began, but I held up the black-marked scroll to cut him off. He looked at it for a moment and then held out his hand. I passed it to him, and he unfurled the page, glancing at the stamp before letting it roll closed. He handed it back to me with an expressionless face.

He jerked his head at the door, and his companion pulled out a black key and unlocked it for me. "Head in there, and wait until you're called before the Death Board," he told me in a serious tone.

"You got it," I promised. "Do you know if they're meeting soon?"

"They're always meeting and never—"

"Right, got it." I sighed, stepping through the door before he could finish. Dying was turning out to be a lot more annoying than I'd thought it would be.

THE METAL DOOR led me into a much smaller waiting room, which finally had a bit of personality to it. Unfortunately, that personality was horrifying. Instead of a sterile government facility, everything in the room was black. Not a lot of it or most of it—all of it.

The tile floors reflected the light from the ceiling that they also devoured. A dozen leather chairs were scattered around the room, with a dark metal coffee table in the middle. On one black wall hung a painting that appeared to be a series of shadows.

The door on the far side matched the color scheme. An iron skull logo was wrought into it out of a grayish metal, making it stand out. This felt much more on brand for a place calling itself Death Corp.

I was the only soul in the room, so I plopped myself down in one of the overstuffed chairs and resigned myself to waiting no time at all, or forever. Curious, I reached out to one of the giant black books on the coffee table. I hefted it into my lap and began to idly flick through the pages. Each one was a different shade of darkness. Nothing else, just a rectangle of black.

With a sigh, I returned the book of shadows to the table and leaned back in my chair, already bored. I didn't think I was going to do well in infinity. I need way too much stimulation. Still, at least I had a moment to collect my thoughts.

I knew I should come up with some sort of plan, but I had no idea what to expect on the other side of that grim door. What was a "Death Board," anyway? I didn't even know what a "board" was in the mortal world. I knew none of the rules. But it was clear that there were rules.

If I had the right of it, Death Corp was somehow responsible for delivering souls. You die, you get brought here for processing, and eventually you end up wherever you're supposed to go. Sort of like the United States Postal Service, but more terrible—somehow.

So if I was a package, I had a delivery form and stamps, but I wasn't supposed to be dropped off before my due date. All I had to do was convince them not to take me early, and then let me wander around freely. Couldn't be that hard, right?

As if prompted by my optimism, the metal door opened with a grinding sound. I glanced around, looking for someone to come collect me, but no one appeared. After a few seconds, I rose to my feet and hesitantly made my way through the entrance to face the Death Board.

The room waiting for me was even darker, as if I were in the middle of an abyss instead of anything physical. If I weren't already dead, I would have said that I had entered a grave. At the far end of the space was a long mahogany table on a raised dais. Sitting in a line behind it was the Death Board.

There were eight figures lurking behind the table, but I didn't make it past my inspection of the first one on the left. Leaning back in his chair, with a bored expression on his face, was Zagan, chief financial officer of Hell. The demon's black eyes sharpened as he glanced up from his fingernails at the sound of my footsteps.

Slowly, he leaned forward, a stunned expression spreading across that model-like face. My cortisol levels, which were already high, skyrocketed as I stared at one of my enemy's greatest servants. But the fallen angel didn't seem thrilled to see me. His perfectly shaped brows furrowed as he studied me. It made sense. I wasn't supposed to be here yet.

"And who might you be?" asked a vaguely amused voice. With some effort I managed to tear my gaze away from Zagan. As I panned across the figures staring at me, I noticed an empty chair among the eight, just to the right of the man in the middle.

At the center of the nine seats was a man with dusty skin and all-too-human eyes. His dark hair was neatly trimmed, and heavy bags sat under his eyes. On his right hand he wore a golden ring set with a white stone that glinted as he held it toward me, demanding my scroll.

I started to walk toward him but caught myself. I wasn't here as a dead mortal to beg for mercy. I was in a room full of supernatural beings, and I knew the rules. If I wanted to be respected, I had to show them that I was not afraid.

"I'm Matthew Carver," I announced, squaring my shoulders as I looked up at the Death Board. "There seems to be some confusion about what to do with me. Who are you?" I shot Zagan a cheerful grin, as if I were delighted to see him. The CFO of Hell's eyes narrowed even further.

The figure to the far right shifted as if he'd suddenly caught on to something. I gave him a surreptitious glance. If I was going to convince this board to let me go about my business, I needed to figure out who I was in the room with, and fast.

The shifting man was lean, not in a skinny way but in a dangerous one. A knife is technically thinner than a sword, but only to slice more efficiently. He was all hard edges, from his chin to his pointed ears. The only reason I didn't think he was a demon was because his eyes blazed a solid, blinding white instead of black.

Supernatural beings are subtle except when they don't want to be. I was pretty sure I had just encountered my first angel of the non-fallen variety. A tiny little thread of intrigued hope began to sew a plan in my mind. Perhaps there was a way to work this whole scenario to my advantage. As far as I knew, the upstairs team had no idea about my soul fraud situation. Maybe that's why Zagan hadn't looked thrilled to see me.

The man in the middle gave me a tired smile and snapped his fingers. I felt the weight of the scroll vanish from my hand and saw it appear in his at the same time. I took it as a mild victory that I hadn't carried it over like a teacher's pet.

"Hello Matthew, I am Kane. Let us see what is to be done with you." He unfurled the scroll and scanned whatever was inside.

"I'm actually familiar with this case," Zagan cut in with a bored tone. "He's one of ours. I'm not sure what the issue is, but

I'd be happy to *handle* it." My heart skipped a beat.

"Yes, I see that," murmured the man reading my scroll. "It seems Mr. Carver is set for delivery to the Pit, but not for some eight years or so." He glanced up at me. "Which raises the question, what are you doing here?"

"As I said—" Zagan began.

"We object," interrupted the angel all the way on the right. The other members of the table erupted in groans, like parents on a road trip, tired of the children in the back fighting over everything. The man holding my scroll was silent, eyes unreadable.

"Of course you do, Azrael," snapped the woman to the left of center. I blinked in surprise as I realized that she was a skeleton, dressed as a bride with a dozen golden chains hanging around her neck. The empty orbs of her skull were staring at me, despite her annoyance with some of the other members of the board. For some reason, seeing her filled me with a dread that neither Heaven nor Hell could match. To me she bore the mantle of death in a visceral way that finally hit home.

I grew up in LA. I know Santa Muerte when I see her.

"It seems, Matthew, that you do pose a problem," the man said amicably, ignoring the rest of the table. "How did you come to be in this place?"

"Well, the agent behind the glass said I should—"

"He means the Veil, you imbecile," snapped a man on the other side of the empty chair. He was short, one of the shortest supernatural beings I had ever seen. His eyes were a deep purple that bordered on black, and he sneered at me with obvious contempt. Something about that felt familiar, but I couldn't quite place why.

"Oh, I don't really know," I replied with a shrug. "I was walking down the street, I heard a bang, and then Wilbur was there."

"Who is Wilbur?" the little guy demanded. "Are we supposed to know all your mortal acquaintances?"

"He is one of my Reapers," Kane rumbled softly.

"Well, I can't bloody well be expected to keep track of them all," huffed Shortstack, but he sounded less aggressive than he had a moment before.

"I'm merely offering to spare us all a headache," Zagan protested over the scorn of his peers. "He's a rounding error, and it's not worth the time to unravel whatever went wrong. Let me just stick him where he's going to get shipped anyway, and we can spend our time on things that matter."

I felt a tremor of fear at the demon's words. My impression of corporate stooges is that they are lazy and not predisposed to going out of their way to fix injustices. If Zagan gave them an easy way out, why wouldn't they take it? I turned to the angel, an obvious question in my eyes, but I needn't have bothered.

"No," Kane said in a firm tone. "He will be delivered when he is due, as the Death Treaty demands."

"No one else is asking for special favors, demon," called a man on the right side of the table. I glanced at the new voice speaking for me, who was clothed in a riot of red, blue, and yellow. He had at least four arms. Vicious fangs protruded from his mouth. He glared at Zagan.

"Right, there's never once been an exception to the rules," the fallen angel snarled.

"Surely you are not suggesting that this mortal boy is a case as momentous as one of those," Santa Muerte cut in. If she hadn't been a skeleton, I was sure she'd have arched an eyebrow with her suggestion.

The table froze, an ominous silence settling on them as they watched Zagan for his answer. "Of course not," he managed through gritted teeth. Everyone relaxed, and the pressure in the room returned to normal levels.

It took all my effort to keep my mouth from dropping open in surprise. The fallen angel did not look in my direction, which felt deliberate. Why wasn't he glaring at me and making threats? This was not the Zagan I was used to. There was something else going on here, and I was beginning to suspect I knew exactly what it was.

"The fact remains that the little snot is a problem," Shortstack injected again. "I say we throw him on a shelf and ship him off when it's his proper time. Death used to mean something. But nowadays it seems everyone is getting around the rules one way or another."

I stared at the little guy in horror. This was exactly what Robin had warned me about. If I died for real before my time was up and got thrown in storage, there would be no way for me to get out of my deal. I'd be locked up until the hour of my doom.

"Kane, be reasonable," Zagan wheedled to the man at the center of the table. "What's the point of letting one idiot mortal gum up the works?"

"That's rather the whole point," the angel on the right said quietly.

Zagan rolled his black eyes in a distorting swirl of void. "He's ours," hissed the CFO of Hell. "He made the deal. Give him to us, and let's be done with this."

A grin tugged at my mouth as I watched Zagan struggle. I had been waiting for my moment, letting him play out his rope. Now it was time to hit him with the hammer. "Well, to be fair the whole contract was forged. I never signed it," I announced gleefully into the void.

The seven other members of the Death Board all slowly turned to look at me with varying expressions on their faces. Most of them looked mildly interested, like I had told them I knew where to see a pretty rock. Shortstack didn't look intrigued, just irritated. But the angel was staring at me, his white eyes boring into mine like a laser beam.

"That's a new one," Santa Muerte observed, her voice neutral, incredibly so. If it was possible for a voice to be room temperature, then hers was exactly sixty-nine degrees.

"Yes, this human has an *overactive* imagination," Zagan chuckled, shaking his head like a disappointed parent. "I thought you all might get a kick out of that."

"We do not pass judgment here," Kane pronounced from the center of the table. "Only deliver souls to their final destination." My heart sank at his words. It seemed I would find no help from the Death Board. I glanced at the angel, but his face was expressionless. I wondered what he thought about it.

"I just don't see why we're wasting the time—" Zagan began, only to be interrupted once more.

"Even if today were his correct date of expiration, he still owes his Death Tax to cross the Veil," Kane said. "It appears to be quite the bill. What on earth did you give this man?"

"Not enough, apparently," the demon muttered, leaning back in his chair in defeat. On the right, I thought I saw the angel's eyes narrow in renewed suspicion.

"Here is what I propose," Kane announced after a moment of reflection. "This mortal is here early, but he will have to serve me for more than a millennium before he can pass through customs. What is eight years against a thousand and some change?

Let him enter my service now, in exchange for room and board until his infernal contract is fulfilled."

"What a waste of our time," snapped Shortstack. "Another mortal avoiding the rules because it's convenient. I'm sick of your softness, Kane."

I resisted the urge to cheer. Freedom to wander the Veil sounded exactly like what I was looking for. It would give me the time to find Megan's soul and figure out where they kept the Crown of Immortality. Maybe things were going to work out for Matthew Carver for once.

"All in favor?" the man in the middle pressed, ignoring the outburst. Scanning down the line, I quickly counted six raised hands. Everyone except for Zagan and Shortstack. "Opposed?" he continued. The two malcontents' hands leapt into the air.

"Then it is agreed, Matthew Carver will become one of my Reapers for a thousand and eight years." I blinked in surprise at his announcement. Somehow, I hadn't quite pieced together what workforce I was joining.

"Lucifer will hear of this!" Zagan shouted, leaping to his feet, his face a mask of fury.

Kane's head slowly turned to stare at the fallen angel, and a Presence unveiled itself, smothering the room in dry darkness. It dwarfed the power that Polaris had shown at the Constellation Convention a few months ago. The blackness of the room warped in response, coiling and slithering. I couldn't move; I couldn't breathe. The pressure holding me in place was so immense, I might as well have been at the bottom of the sea.

Even the other Immortals at the table were still. Either they could not move, or they did not dare to in the baleful eye of such power.

"Tell him whatever you like," Kane said softly. He did not shout; there was no anger in his tone. He didn't need it. "Power and Authority over Death has been given to me. This is my realm. These are my laws. You are here by my good grace, as a member of the treaty. Your Dark Star has no power here. If he has any issues with how I run my domain, he is *welcome* to come and speak to me about them."

The room was even more silent than the grave.

"Do not forget, demon, that Immortality is the greatest lie ever told. One day I will devour you all." Goose bumps flared down my spine as the Presence retreated and I could move again. I thought my eyes would pop out of my head as I watched Zagan quiver before Death himself. The fallen angel nodded once, and Kane turned back to face me. A small, tired smile spread across his face as he looked at me with his human eyes.

"It seems, Mr. Carver, that you're in need of employment. Want a job?"

"Do you guys have dental?" I asked, looking up at Death. "If everyone is going to be seeing my skull for the rest of eternity, I feel like I should get this cavity taken care of." Over his shoulder, Santa Muerte stared at me, her face—well, expressionless.

"I'll see what I can do," Kane promised, rising to his feet. As he stood, he slid a pair of black leather gloves on his hands. "But first you'll need a scythe." He strode down the table and beckoned for me to follow him deeper into the cavernous hall. I moved into Death's wake, fully aware of the seven pairs of Immortal eyes boring into my back as I left.

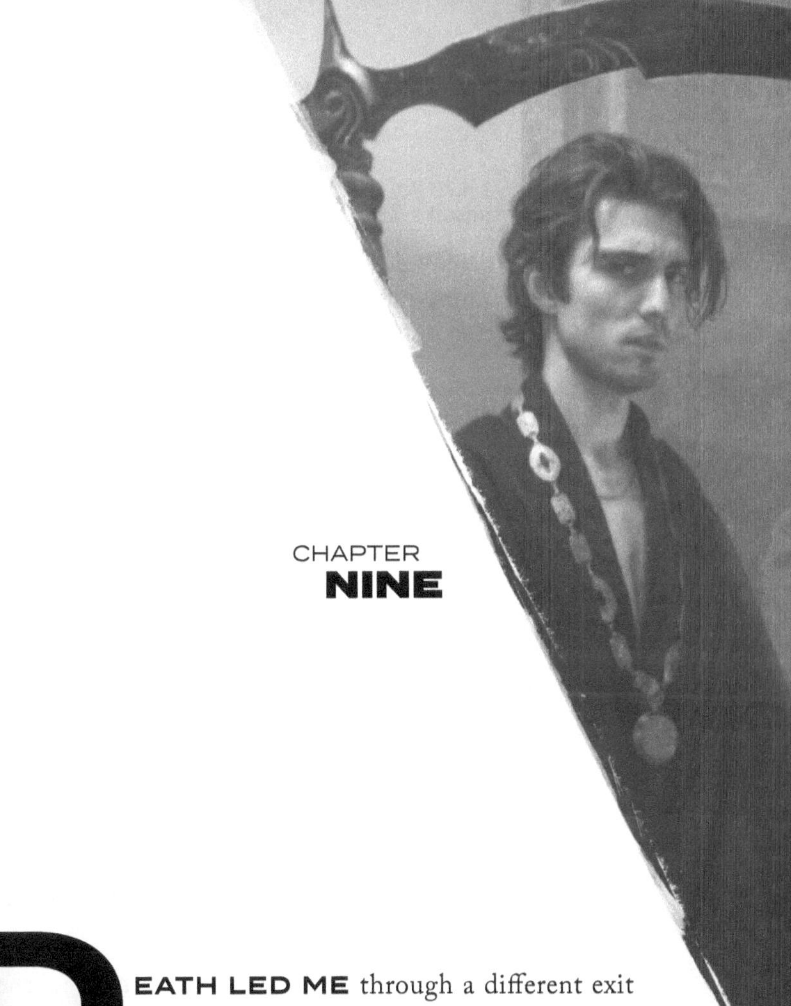

DEATH LED ME through a different exit from the room where the board was eternally meeting slash not meeting. The heavy metal door swung open as he approached and clanged shut with an ominous boom behind us. The second the Immortals were out of sight, Kane's tired smile grew into an easy one, and I swear his shoulders straightened, as if a great weight had just been lifted from them.

The hallway on the other side was back to the governmental gray; it would not have been out of place in the mortal world, down to the fluorescent bulbs and linoleum floor.

"Ah, it feels good to get out and stretch my legs," Death

said, giving himself a little shake. I eyed him askance. There was not a lot of Grim to this version of the Reaper, which didn't fit the mental picture I had of the guy.

"How long were you in there?"

Kane gave me a dour look. "Always," he replied. Right, Time here was stupid. Even stupider than back home, where it wasn't great. I still didn't understand why there had to be sixty minutes in an hour and twenty-four hours in a day. If the metric system is so good, why doesn't it work for Time too?

We barely made it a dozen paces before a gray-haired woman, dressed in the black uniform of Death Corp, appeared from a doorway, carrying a clipboard. She had a face that looked like she loved numbers. "There you are, Your Finalness," she greeted Death without hesitating. "There are a significant number of issues that require your immediate attention. Several of the minor death lords are insisting—"

"Atty," rumbled Kane, not even bothering to glance at her. "This is Matthew Carver, our newest hire."

"I'm sure there's more to him than meets the eyes," she replied, not even looking in my direction. "What department, sire?"

"Reaper," Death replied with a small, satisfied quirk of his lips. Now that I was out of my audience with the Death Board, I had time to panic at the thought of joining Death's elite troops. Had I just become a mercenary by accident? I didn't want to kill people, well, not random people. There were a few folks on my list.

"He can't be any simpler than the last one," Atty murmured, squinting at me with a jeweler's appraising eye. I smiled and gave her a small wave. She ignored it.

"I'm giving him the orientation tour. You may accompany

us if you must."

"Surely *anyone* else can do that," the assistant complained in a dry voice. "You are rather irreplaceable—the rest of your Reapers are not."

"Come now, Atty," chuckled Kane, "meeting new people is my favorite part of the job. You wouldn't take that from me, would you?" Her frosty silence told me that she was considering it. "You must have questions," he said, turning back to me. "We should try to get those out of the way before the ceremony."

"Am I going to have to murder people for you?" The gnawing worry that was bubbling at the top of my consciousness slipped out like a wisp of steam before I even thought about it.

Death stopped mid-stride and turned to stare at me, his brown eyes dark and terrible. "Did Wilbur murder you?" he asked in an absolute voice. He didn't look angry, but I still felt my mouth go dry.

"I guess not," I answered after a moment of reflection. "He showed up and said he was nearby, so he could collect me even if I wasn't on his list."

Some of the tension left Kane's shoulders, and he resumed his stroll down the hallway. "It's a common misconception that Reapers kill people."

"I'm glad that's a myth." I laughed nervously.

"Well, it's a misconception that they *always* kill," he amended after a moment of thought, tossing me a dark glance. "I am still Death."

I swallowed.

"Most of the time, Reapers are there to collect souls that have been released from their body. That's the job—gather the newly freed souls and bring them here to the Veil to be packaged and delivered. Which brings us to our first room," he added with a smile, leaning on an office door and swinging it open.

A dull roar poured from the open door, and my jaw dropped as I peered past Death's shoulder at the cold machines of industry. We stood in a small viewing room. A giant glass pane ran its length, allowing us to see the entire operation.

On the other side were rows and rows of conveyor belts, all humming along with ruthless efficiency. I watched in fascinated horror as a dark sphere, larger than a marble but smaller than a basketball, was stopped underneath a long metal arm with a glowing attachment.

The machine lowered itself and jammed its end into the sphere, passing through it as if it wasn't physical. After a few seconds, the entire arm jerked and a glow began to fill the sphere, like a lantern catching fire. After another heartbeat, the machine lifted free, leaving the glow behind. An applicator zipped out and slapped a barcode sticker on the bottom, and the conveyor moved the now glowing orb farther into the facility.

"This is where souls are given vessels," Death explained with a proud smile. "After they have been cleared through customs and paid any outstanding balances on their taxes, the deceased are put into their own orb for safekeeping and transportation."

I didn't know what to say. I stared at the sea of glowing souls with my mouth hanging open. It was horrifying seeing the most intimate part of a human reduced to a mystical night-light and processed by a row of machines.

How disappointing.

"One day, when your bill is paid, you'll go through there too," Death promised as if that were something to look forward to. I glanced at him out of the corner of my eye. He stood transfixed, the lights reflecting off his face as he watched his machines below with fanatical attention.

"Awesome," I replied after the silence had stretched long enough to be awkward even if we both were dead. "Can't wait." My voice seemed to shake him out of his reverie, and he spun away from the glass as if embarrassed.

"There's more to see," he announced brightly. "Let us continue further up and further in, as they say."

"Sire, the board?" Atty pressed, her lips settled in a flat line.

"They are Immortal. They will last another hour," Kane replied cheerfully. "Which you know as well as I."

"How does that work?" I asked him, since he was in a question-answering mood. "I thought there was no Time here."

"It's easier to think of it like that," he agreed, leading me once more down the office hallway. "But the truth is, the Veil is the dam at the end of Time." He paused, holding up a hand to form a little wall. "The waves of Time crash against us but do not pass through. It's kind of like the difference between wet and dry. We're mostly dry, but we get sprayed a little from time to time."

"Time swims," I murmured, remembering something Robin had told me what felt like a long time ago.

"Now you're getting it," Death agreed, pausing by another door. "Ready for Phase Two?"

"No," I said honestly.

"Here we go!" I had a sudden sympathy for Charlie getting his own tour of a different factory. Although now that I thought about it, maybe it wasn't that different.

"Speaking of Time, where did you get that little pocket watch around your neck? Most folks don't get to bring anything with them." Kane's voice was light and had no trace of suspicion, but I felt terror slide down my spine like a firefighter down a pole. The last thing I wanted was him taking too close a look on my dive clock.

"It was my grandfather's," I lied to Death. "He made me promise to never take it off. I guess I took him *very* seriously." I shrugged. I thought I saw a faint light glint in Kane's eyes, but he let it go.

"Sometimes those old heirlooms pick up a little hint of magic or something that lets them make their way to the Veil. That's part of what we do here—strain out all the leftover physical bits before the souls are sent to the other side."

"Huh?" I asked, not really understanding.

"You'll see." A smirk flashed across his face as he opened the next door. The noise that filled this room was deafening, even through the observation glass. Kane scooped up a pair of orange headphones and slipped them over his ears, gesturing for me to do the same. Atty didn't bother, just watched us with the same disapproving glare.

I stared out at the factory floor, in awe of the number of souls streaming in front of me. Rows and rows of glowing orbs streamed into the three-floor facility then zipped past gates where lasers scanned their barcode stickers in flickers of red lines.

One of them found a vessel it was looking for and let out a horrendous beep. The gate to the side opened, and an arm shoved the ball off its conveyor and onto a new belt. I tracked the ball as it meandered downward before being deposited in a large carton that looked like it was made to hold jumbo eggs. When the cartoon was filled, an arm closed it, stamped it with a larger barcode, and shoved it onto a belt. It vanished from sight.

The process was somehow more chilling for how efficient and clean it was. I think if I had walked through dungeons full of groaning, suffering souls, I would have been less bothered. Death being a well-oiled machine was a nightmare I hadn't mentally prepared for.

"About a hundred and fifty thousand souls come to us every day," Death shouted over the grind of the machinery. "We had to scale production to keep up with the world population over the centuries. The Industrial Revolution was a godsend."

"I can see that," I replied in horror.

"Fortunately, a lot of those inventor types owed a lot in taxes," he explained. "Rockefeller really got us running smoothly during his time. I didn't know what we were going to do after we lost Leonardo da Vinci." I opened my mouth a couple times before closing it. There was no point in asking too many questions. I wasn't going to like any of the answers anyway.

"Let's keep going," Kane told me, rubbing his hands together. "The next part is my favorite." We hung up our ear protectors and stepped back into the hall. The roar of machinery cut off abruptly as the door slammed shut behind us.

"Your End, I do think that you have been *most* thorough in your tour," Atty tried, still hoping to wrangle her boss. "But there really are severe matters that require your attention."

"All in good time," Death replied amicably. He shot me a wink with his warm brown eyes. "We're almost done anyway." I thought I heard his assistant sigh behind him, but she followed in our wake.

The third room that I was taken to was much quieter than the rest. This time, I looked through the observation glass to see pallets of soul cartons arrive, be strapped down, and then get loaded into long black vehicles that looked like a cross between an eighteen-wheeler and a spooky carriage. Grim-faced men and women in black uniforms stood watch as their trucks were loaded by other workers dressed in orange and black like jack-o'-lanterns.

"This is where the packaged souls are loaded up for delivery to their appropriate location on the other side of the Veil," he explained with a note of pride.

That final room was where it really hit me. This entire operation was a giant sorting facility. "Death really is a delivery service." I breathed. "At least you don't have to wear those ugly shorts like the USPS guys do."

"We are tasked with ushering mortal souls to their final resting place," Death agreed solemnly. "It is very serious and important work. According to the Death Treaty, no soul may cross the Veil to the Underworld without being processed and packaged by me or one of my duly appointed representatives. This is the most important function in the entire universe, and it falls to us."

"What makes it so important?"

"Do you know what a soul is, Matthew?"

"A little bit of Reality?" I guessed, remembering how the Faerie Lands had been devoured by the Nothing once they lost their ability to gain new souls.

"That's right." Kane shot me a surprised glance before continuing. "I should have known being a student of the Hunter would give you more education than most." I blinked in surprise. Death had heard of my boss. Actually, now that I thought about it, that wasn't surprising. Orion was probably one the Veil's best suppliers.

"What do you think happens if the souls stop arriving?" he pressed, interrupting my musings.

"Reality becomes unstable and falls apart?"

"Did you know that there are mortals who want to make humans immortal?" Death asked mildly. My heart skipped a beat. Why yes, yes, I did know that. "They wish to live forever, not realizing that by doing so they would destroy everything."

"There aren't enough souls on this side of the Veil to keep it running? Do they get consumed?" I eyed the trucks down below us skeptically.

"No, they don't. Things would work for a while, I suspect. But as Hubble discovered, Reality is always expanding. You need an infinite amount of souls to support an infinitely growing existence."

"So if everyone stopped dying…"

"Then eventually we'd be consumed as Reality grew too large to be maintained and collapsed in on itself." I'm not an expert, but I couldn't help but feel like Death's explanation held some water, based off what I had observed. I had been to places that hadn't been able to keep up with the rate of expansion and fallen into the dark. I wondered if Lazarus knew what future he was racing toward, or if he was just another foolish mortal fiddling around with things he didn't understand, an Icarus without the wings.

"Well, I guess I'm doing my part," I chuckled, feeling more than a little unsettled. "Seeing as how I'm dead and all."

"Well done," Death agreed warmly, like a proud parent.

"What about coming back the other way?" I asked.

"That must be approved by the Death Board, which you had the pleasure of witnessing in action." His brown eyes were locked on the pallets of soul moving below, but a wry note entered his voice.

"I can't imagine them ever really agreeing on much," I acknowledged. "When was the last time that happened?" A hunch was growing in my gut, and I didn't like it one bit.

"It's been quite a while." Death shrugged. "Sort of defeats the point if we let people wander back through at the drop of the hat." I resisted the urge to wince. It seemed that the Grim Reaper wasn't only a mailman, but a jail warden too.

"So, nothing in the last few years?" I pressed, hoping I didn't sound too desperate. I knew for a fact that someone had come back recently. That was the biggest reason I was even down here, playing dead. But if the Death Board hadn't approved Megan being sent back…how had she gotten there?

"No, it's been centuries," he clarified before turning to me, his eyes narrowing slightly. "Why, do you know someone who came back to life?"

"Not personally," I lied, my ghostly heart racing out of habit. "I thought I saw something about it on the news or something."

"No resurrections in your lifetime." Kane patted me on the shoulder. "Or anytime soon if I were to make a guess." Oh, he thought I was worried about myself. That made sense. I was worried about me. But not in the way that he was assuming. I wasn't really dead, I didn't think. So when I blew this Popsicle stand and returned to good old Time and Space, it wouldn't really be a resurrection, just a comeback.

"What would happen if someone's soul didn't get completely put in one of the orbs?" I asked, pretending to be very curious about the entire process. Which I guess I was. Who wouldn't want to know how THE END worked?

"What do you mean?" Death said, confused.

"I dunno, is it possible to, like, pour some of it out or split it into two different containers?"

"Why would you want to do that?" He looked genuinely perplexed by my question. "Hell proposed something like that eons ago, but that's because they were hoping to start claiming fractions of souls; no one else agreed to it."

"Of course they did," I muttered. "Speaking of the Death Board, what was the deal with the guy with the purple eyes? The short one? He seemed to really have it out for me."

"Ah, Pluto." Death nodded. "He's never really forgiven mortals for forgetting about him."

"Man, if he's upset about that, he'll never get over what they did to his planet," I mused.

"Something happened to his planet?" I could have been wrong, but I thought a hint of a smile was tugging at Kane's lips. Maybe I wasn't the only one whose nerves the short guy had gotten on.

"They decided it wasn't a planet anymore," I told him, resisting the urge to grin myself. I guess gossip crosses the Veil slowly. It's not every day you get to share juicy news about an annoying god. "It was too small."

Death threw back his head and let out a long and delighted laugh. The fluorescent lights in the ceiling flared brighter, and several of the black-clad Reapers on the floor below looked up at the window in alarm.

"Oh, I cannot wait to use that," Kane chuckled, muttering "too small" under his breath.

"Sire," Atty interrupted again. "If you're going to insist on leading this tour yourself, perhaps you'd at least be willing to keep it moving?"

"Very well," he replied with a sigh. "You win, Atty. No more fun."

Kane led me out of the final soul processing floor, taking our little trio deeper into the offices of Death Corp. We passed rows of cubicles, with more black-clad Reapers sitting at their desks or milling around in small groups. A janitor in a pumpkin-orange-and-black jumpsuit passed us, pushing a cart with a broom and mop. He nodded politely at Death, who returned the gesture.

It all felt so normal.

Eventually we made it to a wall of what had to be executive offices. At the end was a larger door, with tinted glass windows on either side of it. A receptionist's desk blocked access to it, and I knew from the picture-perfect organization that Atty sat there.

The sign on the white wall read: DEATH. Kane breezed in, and we followed. Everything in the room was black and gray. His giant desk was dark wood, and a gleaming skull wrought of black iron stared at me from the front. On one of his bookshelves were two very old-looking scythes and a rock stained with a dark substance. Behind him was the Nothing, the eternal, empty blackness that existed only to devour Reality lurked through the windows flanking his chair.

Death sat down and stared at me, framed by eternal hunger, all traces of good humor gone, replaced with a heavy severity. He gestured for me to sit in one of the two black-leather-and-metal chairs across from his desk.

"Do you understand the service you are agreeing to?" he asked in a calm voice.

"To be a mailman?" I replied, arching an eyebrow.

"It's more than that," Death corrected. "Being a Reaper is not a safe job. I only offer it to those who I think are dangerous enough to handle it." He glanced down at my scroll, which had appeared on his desk sometime since we sat down. "I saw that you were a disciple of the Hunter." A tight grin flashed across his face before it was gone. "I'm a big fan of his work."

I wondered if Kane would be disappointed to find out I had studied under him for less than two years. I decided not to bring it up. This was a job interview, and my résumé needed all the help it could get.

"What kind of danger are we talking about?" I pressed, managing to not get distracted for once in my life.

"You were on the right track. Being a Reaper is like being a stagecoach driver in the Wild West. Not only is it your responsibility to deliver the souls to their final resting places but also to protect them."

"Protect them from what?" I managed. I had a feeling I already knew the answer. A few months ago, the now dead Dragon Don Doyle had tried to bribe Dawn with ten thousand stolen souls. Those glowing orbs were worth their weight in Reality.

"Do you know what that is?" Death gestured at the inky, absolute darkness behind him.

"Yes," I told him.

He blinked in mild surprise, then nodded once in appreciation. "There are many places on both sides of the Veil that are forgotten shadows of what they were. Nietzsche and his friends tore down more worlds than they ever could have dreamed of. Modernity has been very bad for business for many of our Elders, and there are those who would do anything to get their hands on souls that do not belong to them."

"There are beings that would try to *rob* Death?" I demanded incredulously. "I'm new here, but that seems like a bold choice. Why don't you just go slice them up with one of those?" I gestured at the scythes decorating his bookshelf.

Kane stared at me for a long moment, his brown eyes hard and calculating. It seemed like I had finally asked a question he wasn't comfortable answering. After some thought, he grunted as if he had decided on a path and smiled.

"That is what I have people like you for. As one of my Reapers, you will bear a portion of my Authority and Power." I remembered the shadowy scythe that Wilbur had used to slash a hole in the Veil and shivered.

"This is the price you will pay for your passage to the other side of the Underworld," Death told me, holding up a finger to stall any more questions. "One thousand, six hundred and sixty-seven mortal years as one of my Reapers. Collecting souls from those who pass, bringing them here to be processed, and delivering them to their final resting place."

"Out of curiosity, what happens if I turn down the offer?" I muttered, feeling more than a little overwhelmed at the amount of Time we were talking about. Orion would be released from his prison in Tartarus before I was free to cross to the other side. I know my soul is technically locked down for eternity, but there's something about a real number that sounds more terrifying than "infinity."

"You will work in one of the sorting facilities, without a break, for twice that duration," Death shrugged. "Some prefer that to the risk."

"What risk?"

"You're already dead," Kane reminded me gently. "If you fall in my service, there are no more safety nets."

"Straight to the fiery place?" I guessed.

"Straight to Nothing," he corrected.

I bit my lip, trying to consider my best option. I didn't know how long I would be here, but working the Veil's equivalent of twenty-four hours a day, seven days a week, wouldn't leave me a lot of time to snoop around and accomplish my actual mission.

It did sound like I'd be way less likely to wind up not existing, which was a bonus.

But if I was going to find Meg's soul, I knew I was going to have go beyond the Veil. I'd have to descend into the Pit itself. That left me only one option. I was going to have to cross Death. I looked into his eyes and gave him a tight smile, hoping it didn't reflect the terror I felt on the inside.

"Guess I'm a Reaper now."

THE PROCESS OF becoming a Reaper was more straightforward than I expected. I guess that's how Death works. The End has a lot less frippery and red tape than the rest of life. He does not wait for the right moment, he simply arrives.

"I ask for no oaths. You are dead, there is nothing left to bind you," Death intoned from where he stood in front of me. He unveiled his Presence, and the Power and Authority that he held settled on me with more pressure than the crushing depths of the ocean.

Everything around us faded to black, as if the Nothing that lurked just on the border of his domain had been allowed to sweep in and crowd around us like a sea of adoring fans. Even Atty vanished. This was between me and one of the principal Powers of Reality.

"Instead, I make unto every Reaper the same promise." Kane's bemused manner had vanished with the light. His brown eyes were as unforgiving as the dirt that the dead were buried in. "Betray me, and you will never leave this place. I will unmake you and feed the scraps of your soul to the hungry dark that waits just beyond my kingdom."

Goose bumps flared up and down my arms as I nodded. A fallen angel once threatened to have me unmade, but it had a lot more weight coming from the Grim Reaper. Even Orion could learn a thing or two about threats from Kane.

"These are my three tenets, passed down for generations from Reaper to Reaper," Death continued, his voice deep and terrifying. I flinched slightly, worried I was going to find out I was already scheming to break one of them. "Guide the dead on their new journey. Protect them from the Darkness that would devour. Deliver them to their rest."

I nodded again, not trusting my dry throat to speak. Technically, I didn't think any of my plans conflicted with his list. I heard no mention of stealing powerful artifacts, or anything about bringing half of someone's soul back with me when I came back to life. That meant he couldn't get mad at me for it, right? When I had agreed to help Lazarus plunder the Veil, I hadn't really expected to develop such a personal relationship with Death before I robbed him.

"Take my hand," Death commanded. The darkness around us grew, surging forward like a furious dog on the end of its leash.

Heart racing, I reached out and clasped his wrist as he

grabbed mine in the handshake of the ancients. Kane closed his eyes for a moment, and I felt a lurch as something dark and cold twisted its way beneath my skin like a snake. I let out a gasp of surprise and tried to pull my hand free, but Death's iron grip didn't let me move an inch.

Steeling myself, I relaxed and let the chill slither into me. It didn't hurt, but it wasn't pleasant, like holding your hand underwater in a pond that is just above freezing. The creeping cold made its way up my arm and into my chest before Kane opened his eyes and released me.

"It is done," he told me gravely.

"That's it? A chilly handshake and I'm a Reaper?"

"Summon my Authority and see for yourself." Death gestured at me casually. Around us, the light returned as the dark fled. We were no longer in a pool of abyss, just a monotone office.

Hesitantly, I searched inside myself, rooting around the area of the old brain box where I would expect to find Willow. My fiery companion was still missing, and I felt their absence like a vacuum. But in the same set of cupboards there was a new void, somehow emptier and darker than the first.

I reached out to that hungry power with my will and pulled it like a sword from a stone. To my surprise it leapt at my command, eager to be set free.

A tall black scythe ripped its way into existence and settled into my right hand. The staff ran from the floor up to just shy of my head, and a long, wickedly curved blade hovered in front of my eyes like a deadly wave.

The entire thing was made of the same material, which if I had to guess was condensed shadow somehow given matter. It was lighter in weight than it should have been, but I could still feel the heft behind it. It had a gravitas that reminded me of Orion's Immortal-killing blade.

The haft was ice-cold against my palm, and as I gazed at this weapon that marked me as a servant of Death, the chill within me began to grow. Just as I thought I would freeze from the inside out, the scythe vanished with a whisper.

Warmth flooded back into me, like stepping out of an air-conditioned building into the peak of an August day in the Valley. Wordlessly, I looked back to Kane, who was watching me with an appraising eye.

"In time you will be able to channel more of my Authority," he commented, unperturbed by the weapon's vanishing. "But until your mind and soul acclimate, you will only be able to tap into a fraction of it."

"Oh," I said in a very small voice. This new power was alien. Willow was a flame, another form of life that burned with their own passion and energy. This was just a bottomless hunger that needed to devour but could never be sated. Slowly, I lifted my eyes to meet Death's brown ones. I might be crazy, but I thought I saw a hint of sympathy lurking there.

"Now to show you how to attend to your duties," Kane told me, a grim smile on his face.

"Which *any* of your Reapers can do," Atty interjected from the back of the room, her exasperation almost physical. "You are needed, sire."

"What could possible require my attention more than training the newest bearer of my scythe?" Death demanded, looking over my shoulder. A note of frustration had finally crept into his voice. Atty was silent, but I could feel her glare shoot over my shoulder.

"Matthew is one of mine now," he hissed. "He can hear whatever it is you have to say."

There was a moment of tense silence. I don't know what face Atty was making behind me, but Death did not retreat. His dark gaze was focused on his assistant as if he could pin her in place with his will alone. Granted, from what I had seen, he probably could.

"Another convoy has gone missing," the prim woman said, eventually capitulating to her boss's iron gaze. "We lost contact with them and their cargo."

I twitched in surprise. I knew firsthand that there was some sort of black market for souls. Doyle had made it clear that the dragons had suppliers who could move thousands of them. Who would dare to steal from Death himself? Only an idiot—well, an idiot who was truly desperate, since this was technically what I was in the Veil to do myself.

"How many?" he asked in a voice like the grave. The color began to leach from the room again, as if fleeing Kane's growing anger. I only wished I could follow it.

"It was a shipment to Hell, a full complement of six thousand, six hundred and sixty-six."

"What do Zagan and his ilk say?"

"That it happened outside their borders, therefore they have no knowledge of or responsibility for it. The CFO has demanded to know when they can expect a replacement shipment to meet their projected expansion quotas."

Death was terribly silent for several moments.

"It seems that I must hand over your training after all," he finally said. Darkness filled his voice. "Atty will see to it that you finish your orientation. I am needed elsewhere."

I opened my mouth to acknowledge him, but he was gone. One moment he stood before me; the next he'd vanished without a flicker or sound. I rubbed my still-chilled palm and turned to the severe-faced woman behind me. Atty stared at me with unreadable, iron eyes. Somehow I found her more intimidating than Kane.

"Well, Ms. Atty," I began, doing my best to be polite. "I guess—"

"Follow me," she interrupted in clipped tones. She turned sharply but paused before taking a step and glanced back at me. "Tell no one what you overheard here." I nodded my understanding, and she marched out of the office. Wordlessly, I followed her. It seemed that I was not in her good graces for distracting the boss for so long. That felt a little unfair. Maybe if it had been that urgent, she should have told him the real issue sooner? Just a thought.

The old woman led me at a brisk trot, her spine rigid. She made no effort to slow down to let me catch up, or to check whether I was following. I guess it made sense that Death was the most welcoming member of his organization. Everyone meets him eventually.

Death Corp employees were everywhere. Pumpkin-uniformed floor workers passed us, pushing carts loaded with boxes. I even saw a guy mopping. Everyone we encountered gave Atty a polite nod. Most ignored me, but that was fine. I wasn't here to cause a scene; I hoped to fly under the radar until it was time to go. After a few moments, we returned to the quiet office area full of black clad Reapers. She led me through the sea of cubicles down a row that dead-ended into a wall. The little boxes were doorless, about chest-high, with frosted-glass panes on top.

The Reapers took much more notice of me as Atty led me through their space. There were no smiles here, just cold, evaluating eyes. I felt like it was my first day at a school that didn't particularly want any new students.

Atty ignored the glares of the residents, gliding past them like a veteran teacher. She led me down to the end of the hallway, right up against the wall. As we drew near, I started to hear the heavy-machine hum of the factory. I guess the soundproofing wasn't as good on this side.

Atty strode into the last cubicle, and I followed her through the doorway. The area inside was larger than it looked from the outside: A double desk sat in the middle, with an office chair on either side. A familiar face looked up from a pile of scrolls as we walked in, his brown hair waving wildly.

"Well, I'll be durned," Wilbur breathed. "My unscheduled pickup, a genuine Reaper."

"Hello, Wilbur," I said, "good to see you again."

"What do you mean he was unscheduled?" Atty asked, an icy note of suspicion in her voice.

"Wasn't on my list," Wilbur said with a shrug. "But I stumbled across him and figured it would be irresponsible to leave him just dangling in the wind."

Atty turned her heavy gaze to me, evaluating me with a new level of intensity. It seemed I had just been upgraded up from "annoyance" to "curiosity" in her book, which I did not like. I gave her my most winning smile and shrugged.

"Death Board approved," I tried to reassure her. "Don't really know what's going on, but here I am."

Atty grunted but didn't appear convinced. She turned back to Wilbur and fixed him with another one of her piercing stares.

"His Finalness has been called away," she informed him. "This one needs to have the rest of his training completed. Since you went through it most recently, you should be the best candidate to make sure he's properly trained."

Wilbur's left eye twitched, but he nodded respectfully to Death's assistant. "Yes, ma'am," he confirmed in his southern drawl. "Happy to be of assistance."

"I'm sure." Atty's voice dripped with contempt, but she seemed satisfied with his acceptance. She turned, sliding past me to escape the claustrophobic cubicle. "See to it that he's properly certified by the end of the cycle, or you'll both be written up."

"Yes, ma'am," Wilbur called after her as she marched away. The skinny southern boy let out a sigh and slid down in his chair, deflating like a balloon. He gestured at the seat across from him, and I dropped into it, letting myself match his slouch.

"I don't think she likes me," I commented to the man who'd ushered my soul out of the mortal world only some hours—or days?—ago.

"Don't take it personally," Wilbur replied. "She don't like much, as far as I can tell. She reminds me of my neighbor a few farms over growing up. Mrs. Dougherty wanted things a certain way, she did, and Heaven help anyone who didn't dance to her tune."

"Never been very good at dancing," I remarked idly.

"Me neither." A genuine grin spread across Wilbur's face. For the first time it occurred to me that he was about the same age as me. It was a tragedy to see him here, bearing the Authority of Death. Something heavy settled in my chest as I realized that, unlike me, Wilbur would never wake up again. When he finished his service, he'd be bottled up and sent out of the Veil to whatever eternal deposit box had claim on his soul.

Some of my sadness must have shown on my face, because he sat up, leaning on the desk with a knowing look. "You've seen the sorting rooms, I take it?"

"Yeah," I replied quietly.

"You get used to it," he told me after a moment. "All you can do is try to make the most of it. But it is what it is, at the end of the day."

"It sure is," I agreed. I felt like I had lost my innocence. I always thought dying would be more personal. Boy, was I wrong.

"Well, I guess we oughta get started." Wilbur sighed, rising to his feet and motioning for me to join him. Together we made our way out of the cubicle and started down the long hall. "What did the boss cover before he ran out on you?"

"We did a tour of the sorting facility, and he *shook my hand.*" I emphasized that last part a little. I was sure Wilbur would know what I meant. Saying, *And then he bestowed the power of Death upon me,* felt too pretentious.

"So, none of the fieldwork, huh? Good thing I just got a new list." Wilbur sounded a little brighter. "Some company might make it go a little faster, now that I think about it."

"Hey, string-bean, who's the rookie?" A cold female voice stopped us in our tracks. I turned to find a beautiful, silver-haired Reaper leaning over her cubicle, eyeing me hungrily. I wasn't sure if she wanted to eat me or kiss me, neither of which seemed safe.

"Ah, Ms. Yuki, this here is Matt, he's new," Wilbur replied, his voice sounding even more stressed than when Atty had been bossing him around.

"Obviously he's new, that's why he's a *rookie.*" Yuki rolled her eyes, somehow never breaking eye contact with me. "But what's his deal?"

"Well, I died, and then I got a bill," I replied dryly, making sure not to look away from her. This felt like a challenge. I had been around enough supernatural beings and survived enough recesses in middle school to recognize someone who thought of themselves as an alpha.

"Janson, the new guy is talking to me," Yuki remarked coldly, her face falling flat. A middle-aged Reaper in the cubicle across from her grunted without turning to look at either of us. His attention was fixated on something on his desk.

"Sorry, Ms. Yuki, Atty just dumped him off down here without getting him fully oriented," Wilbur hurried to explain. "I'm supposed to show him the ropes."

"Well, hurry up," she snapped, finally looking away from me to glare at my new friend. "He's offending me with his breathing."

I opened my mouth to remind her that we didn't really breathe anymore, but Wilbur caught my attention and shook his head ever so slightly. With a sigh, I swallowed my commentary and played nice. I was here to lay low. I had plenty of enemies in the living world, didn't need more waiting when I bought the farm for real.

Wilbur led me away from the aggressive Reaper with an urgent nod, and reluctantly, I followed.

"Nice outfit," Yuki called after me as we walked away. "What did you die doing anyway? Looks like you fell off a surfboard and drowned, idiot." It hurt me on a fundamental level to let her have the last word, but that's how seriously I was taking this mission.

Wilbur was silent until we exited the Reaper offices and got back to the main corridors. Some of the stiffness left the tall man's shoulders, and he tossed me a grin. "Lesson number one, avoid the older Reapers."

"Yeah, what was that?"

"Near as I can tell, this job eats at you," Wilbur said softly as we walked. "There's a reason no one does it forever. The thing that Death gave you and me, it ain't for mortals like us. You can feel the hunger?"

I nodded, lightly brushing the dark void lurking in my mind. It was cold and empty and terrible, but Wilbur was right. It was also *hungry*. It was a different hunger than the one Willow had. Fire is ravenous, but this was something more…absolute.

"I think if you ain't careful, that hunger eats you from the inside out," Wilbur whispered. "The longer a Reaper's been here, the colder they get. At least that's what it seems like to me." Great, just when the stakes weren't high enough, now I had a dark power that would try to consume me from within.

"You haven't noticed it happening to you?"

The tall, skinny Reaper gave me a careless shrug. "I dunno, I've only been here a coupla centuries."

COME ON, WE gotta clock in," Wilbur told me, leading me through the back offices of Death Corp. I shook my head bemusedly as I followed my new co-worker. Capitalism seemed to have wormed its way down here too.

Our destination was a blank, empty hallway a few turns away. There was no furniture, just a large square of black tape on the linoleum floor, blocking off the end. A row of blue pouches hung from the wall, each holding a gray clipboard. The one farthest down the line had Wilbur's name on it, printed by some label maker.

"Here we go," he said, pulling the clipboard out and riffling through the pages. "Okay, a hundred names, not too bad."

"A *hundred*," I repeated, feeling a sense of dread. "We're gonna watch a hundred people die?"

It's the job," he told me in a soft tone.

"Wilbur!" a voice snapped, and we both spun to face the man behind us. He was the polar opposite of the Grim Reaper's typical depictions. Instead of a being skeleton, he was rotund. His black shirt's buttons strained against their holes. He had shrewish, dark eyes; a pencil mustache; and a bald spot that was the primary occupant of his head.

"You're way behind quota," he shouted. "You were supposed to leave forever ago. Are you trying to sabotage me? We're on pace to set a new intake record, and you're late!"

"Sorry, Ralph, Ms. Atty told me—"

"Who the devil is this?" he continued, pointing at me with a furious scowl. "This is a Reaper-only area." Ralph seemed like the kind of man who could only speak by shouting.

"I'm new," I offered, to take some heat off Wilbur. Managers are the same everywhere, I guess.

"What do you mean, 'new'?"

"I'm taking him on his orientation run," Wilbur interjected. "Matt just finished making his accord with the boss."

"Well, get him a uniform, this isn't a casual workplace," he sneered. "Can't just be lying around in whatever you *died* in. If this man is not up to dress code the next time I see him, I'll write both of you up."

"Yes, sir," Wilbur said in that neutral tone used by workers speaking to their managers since the beginning of Time. "As soon as we get back, I'll make sure he gets proper digs."

"And you," Ralph shouted, turning back to me. "Don't slow

him down. It will be a double shift if he doesn't bring his quota in before the tally closes for the day."

I nodded my understanding, feeling a little sick to my stomach. What kind of monster wanted to collect more souls? That was inhuman in a way that I couldn't even fathom. But I saw no hint of compassion behind Ralph's dead, dark eyes. Wilbur had said the hunger turns on you; maybe this was what he meant.

"Stop wasting time and get out of here." He waved toward the end of the hall. "Mush!" He waddled deeper into the facility, muttering to himself.

"So now you've met Ralph," Wilbur observed dryly as we stared at the empty space where he had just been.

"He's our manager, I assume?"

"Technically, but that doesn't mean much. Most of us just ignore him." Wilbur turned and led me back toward the black taped-off square behind us.

"First thing we gotta teach you is how to travel between the Veil and the living world," he explained. "You can do it anywhere, but we use this place so nobody wanders in when we're cutting with a knife that's too sharp, if you take my meaning."

"Even dead people have to be careful," I replied, remembering Death's warning about being unmade if I died while in his service.

"Bingo, but between you and me, there ain't much to it." My co-worker gestured at the space. "Give it a shot; your body's probably still getting used to having a bit of Death in you, but you should be able to cut just fine."

"What do I do?" I asked, licking my lips as I stepped over the tape into the box. It was sinking in that I was heading back to the mortal realm to reap souls. I was praying that Death was telling the truth when he said that we didn't do the killing. I could be a mailman. I didn't want to be a gardener, so to speak.

"Summon the scythe," he ordered.

I did, reaching inside my mind and ordering the hungry dark to come out. The same sickle blade attached to a pole grew out of nothing and settled into my hands. Its chill flooded into me as the shadows it was made of roiled darkly under the fluorescent lights.

"Now focus on the empty air in front of you," Wilbur continued, his accent fading slightly as he focused. "Tell that cold power that you want it to cut the very air."

I nodded, squaring my shoulders and trying to force my will to focus on the space in front of me. It was harder than I expected to lock onto something invisible. But eventually, I thought I felt something, a sense of a border, like a dam or closed door.

"Good!" called Wilbur after a few moments, apparently satisfied with the furrowed brow on my face. "Now cut it open."

Feeling like an idiot, I obeyed, swinging my scythe through the open air in front of me like a batter warming up before heading to the plate. To my surprise, I felt the thin edge catch on something and begin to tear, like a razor blade on a single sheet of paper.

A black wound appeared in the wake of my swing, widening as if being pulled apart by the pressure it was holding in check. Startled, I took a step back.

"Golly, first try!" Wilbur cheered, stepping up to clap me on the shoulder. "Most folks take longer. You're a natural." I wasn't sure if being a prodigy at wielding the power of Death to tear holes in Reality was something I felt good about or not. With a thought, I banished the scythe, sending the inky power back into its closet in my brain.

"Come on." Wilbur beckoned, stepping toward the crack. "We've got some souls to collect."

"Please don't let this be horrible," I murmured under my breath as I followed him through the Veil and back to the Living World.

The passage through Reality is much different when you are a part of Death Corp instead of dying yourself. Maybe direction matters too, I'm not sure. For a few moments, there was only the sound of rushing wind and the expanse of the Nothing. I kept my eyes trained on Wilbur's boots as he shot down the dark path before me.

Right when I began to wonder if we had made a wrong turn, a white tear appeared ahead of us, a mirror to the one I had made in the air of Death's lair. We burst out of the Veil and into the world I had recently left.

I landed lightly next to my fellow Reaper, trying to figure out where we were, but Wilbur interrupted my gawking. "Now use the power to close the hole," he ordered. "It's very important that we don't leave these lying open unattended."

My eyes narrowed as I looked back at the jagged wound. Mentally, I reached out to my power and felt its connection to the hole thrumming. I pushed against that connection, ordering the two sides to come together. The rent began to seal in front of my eyes and I grinned in satisfaction.

When I was done, only empty air remained. With a satisfied nod, I turned to find Wilbur's mouth hanging open.

"No one closes a rift on their first try," he stammered after a few seconds. "Who are you?"

I blinked in surprise. That had seemed self-explanatory to

me, but then again, most people didn't have a Faerie fire spirit living in their heads. I realized that I needed to be more careful. I didn't want to stand out, even if Death knew I was trained by Orion.

"I'm familiar with being loaned some power." I shrugged. "I just told it what I wanted it to do."

"Well, I'll be." Wilbur sighed in wonder. "You knew about all this supernatural mumbo jumbo before you kicked the bucket?"

"A little," I confessed. "But only for a year or so."

"That must be it," he grunted with another unbothered shrug. "I shoulda known you knew more than I did. You were way too calm when I found you. I was just a regular old human, minding my own business, and here I am now."

"It can take a minute to adjust," I commiserated. "I know I had to take some time."

"Never thought I'd see the day that I got a job," Wilbur chuckled. "Maybe dying was good for me." The two of us exchanged amused glances before we both started to laugh. Is it gallows humor if we're both dead?

Now that the rift was closed, I resumed my study of our surroundings, but everything around us was blurry. We were obviously in the middle of some street. I could make out the pavement and stripes beneath us, but everything over a few feet away was distorted. I could see moving shapes but couldn't tell what they were.

I ducked to the side and swore as a car burst through our bubble, crystalizing into perfect focus before shooting out the other side and immediately distorting. Wilbur let out a delighted laugh when the car shot right through him as if he was a…ghost.

Right. That was only mildly horrifying.

"Okay, what next?" I asked, still nervous about what exactly my new duties were.

"Let's see." Wilbur pulled out his clipboard and pointed at the first name. His eyes narrowed for a moment, then he put it back inside his jacket. "Scythes out," he ordered.

I gritted my teeth and summoned the chilly weapon, grasping it with my right hand. I figured I could hold it longer if I juggled it between my two hands to give each a chance to warm up.

"Grab my shoulder and hold on tight." He gave me a grin. "We gotta move." I followed his instructions, not sure what to expect. "Melinda Sue Brent," he announced the second I settled my grip.

My head snapped back as we leapt forward. The already horrifically blurry world distorted further as we shot away, passing through people, cars, walls, and what looked like a giant aquarium with no resistance.

Then the world crashed into focus. We were in a hospital room. Our bubble of clarity expanded to encompass the whole space. In the center of it lay an old woman, who seemed to glow from within her frail body. It reminded me of the light shining from the spheres that Death's factory filled with souls.

Around her a group of people were gathered, but none of them shone like her. It didn't take a doctor to guess who we were here to collect. I arched an eyebrow and gestured with my head toward the woman. Wilbur gave me a small smile and nodded.

It felt like it would be rude to speak, intruding on this family's last moments, even if they couldn't hear us. I resigned myself to wait, clenching my left hand to bleed out some of my rising stress.

Morbidly curious, I tried to listen in on their farewells. Who was Melinda Brent? Did her progeny love her or were they merely observing the ritual? Had she been kind or was she rich? I couldn't tell, I realized after a moment, for just as the world was blurry, so were their voices. It sounded like I had stumbled into a room full of tubas and trombones that were having a conversation.

Just when I was beginning to wonder why Wilbur had been in such a rush, the thread of her life reached its end. The glowing body in the bed seized and relaxed a moment later. The orchestra of concerned voices rose in volume, but despite Lazarus's fears, death has no ears—it cannot be pleaded with.

Suddenly we weren't alone. The woman stood before us, still old and frail but free from the physical body that had run its last race. She let out a gasp, as if she had just been dunked with cold water, and looked at us with wide eyes.

"Hello, ma'am," Wilbur said gently. "We're here to collect you."

"And who are you two supposed to be?" she asked, surprising me with a strong British accent. Dead Melinda might be, but there was iron in her gaze as she eyed the two of us.

"I'm a duly licensed representative of Death, here to escort you to whatever comes next," Wilbur replied, his voice still soft, as if he were trying not to startle a deer he had encountered on a walk.

"Death, hmm?" She snorted, glancing at me with a raised white eyebrow. "What's he supposed to be, some sort of deep-sea diver?"

"I'm new," I apologized. "I haven't gotten my uniform yet." Since she had just died, I didn't point out that a woman wearing a hospital gown was hardly in a position to criticize anyone about dress code. *Technically*, we'd both expired in stupid outfits, that's just how it goes.

"This is my associate; he's here to observe for training purposes," Wilbur confirmed smoothly. "It's probably best if you just ignore him."

"That's it then?" she murmured, her voice falling as she looked at her still body surrounded by family. "Sort of an abrupt ending, all things considered." I couldn't help but be impressed at how well she was processing her own death. I had planned on dying and still had been more out of sorts. Given her age, she might have had a little more time to come to terms with it than I did. Or maybe the Brits are just more stoic.

"If it helps, it might be better to think of it as the middle," my friend told her. "There's a lot more ground to cover."

"Is there?" The eyebrow quirked again. "Well, give it to me straight. Was I good girl or am I off to be punished?"

"Oh, I have no idea, ma'am. My job's to get you to the people who can tell you."

"Why does that smell suspiciously like bureaucracy?" she asked, her eyes narrowing.

"Only a little," Wilbur promised, gesturing at me with a wave. "If you'll come with me, my associate will open the door for us, and we can get you started."

"It's not like I've got anything else going on," she murmured, finally sounding a little bitter. She turned to look at her family once more. "I don't suppose I could say farewell one last time?" My heart broke a little at the note of despair in her voice.

"I'm sorry," Wilbur told her, his voice thick with feeling. "It's against the rules." He nodded at me to open the way back.

Feeling a little sick, I touched that dark power, summoning my scythe.

This time when I focused on the air, I pictured the waiting rooms that I had been taken to on my first trip. It took me a moment to find the thread of the Veil that I had to cut to return to Death's domain. In my defense, having one of the recently deceased watch me work made me nervous.

"Does it usually take this long?" Melinda whispered right as I prepared to slice. "If I wasn't already dead, I might have starved to death by now."

I shot her a glare out of the corner of my eye. Some of my sympathy was fading every time she criticized me. My blade hooked on that little thread, and with a wrench I cut the edge of the Veil. I stepped back as the maw began to open. Wilbur gently took her arm and led her toward it. Melinda's eyes were wide as saucers now as she eyed the rip in Reality.

"Must we?" she asked him, licking her lips.

"I'm afraid so," he confirmed.

"Well then, stiff upper lip," she said to herself and started her journey into eternity. My co-worker gestured at me to wait, then followed her through, leaving me alone in the Living World. I guess I didn't really need to be taught how to drop someone off, since I had been through that part.

I had no idea how long I'd be stuck here waiting for him to get Melinda settled. Which reminded me: How was I doing on time? I grabbed my little pocket watch necklace and held it up for inspection. Fear ran through me like a thunderbolt as I saw that the second hand was moving much faster now. Not as quickly as it would if I were alive, I decided after studying it for a few heartbeats, but the difference was a lot less than it had been when I was in the Veil.

I guessed that I was closer to Reality at the moment, which meant that things were more "normal" than on the other side of the Veil. Still, it was an issue. My new Reaper employment was going to cut into the time left in my deep dive more significantly than I had thought.

Nervous, I drummed my fingers on the shadowy shaft of my scythe, letting its aching cold push away the warmth I felt in my chest as I teetered on the edge of panicking. This whole thing was beginning to feel hopeless. Taking on the entire Underworld was too much for one Matt to handle, even one as smart and handsome as I am.

Wilbur interrupted my spiral by emerging from the tear in the Veil, a sad smile on his face. He nodded at me once he was through, and I closed the rift behind him, more confidently this time.

"Congratulations, you're a Reaper now," he told me, clapping me on the shoulder with a friendly hand.

"That was a lot," I admitted, glancing back at the bed where the shell of the dead woman still lay. "Is therapy one of the benefits?"

"Brother, that was one of the easy ones," Wilbur warned. "It gets so much worse."

He was right.

Of the ninety-nine more names on Wilbur's list, none of them went into the night as calmly and readily as Melinda. Death's tithe does not take only the old and infirm, although God help me, I wish that were so.

The worst ones were the children, so young and full of a life they would never get to lead. My heart broke as I watched

Wilbur carry a newborn through the tear to be processed. Seeing so many lights go out was tragic, and our helplessness increased the pain exponentially.

It was enough to make me feel like Lazarus might have a point.

Many people were taken by things that I could not have prevented, like disease or accidents. But others were victims. Having to stand there in a dim blurry world, guessing at what happened until their screams and terror came through the blur as Death claimed them, was a form of torture. Tears streamed down my face by the time we had carried ten souls to the next world.

Wilbur didn't cry, but the somber look he gave me as he came back through the Veil told me he carried the same weight on his shoulders; he was just used to the load.

All of the names were tragic and horrible as Death always is, but the thirteenth almost killed me again.

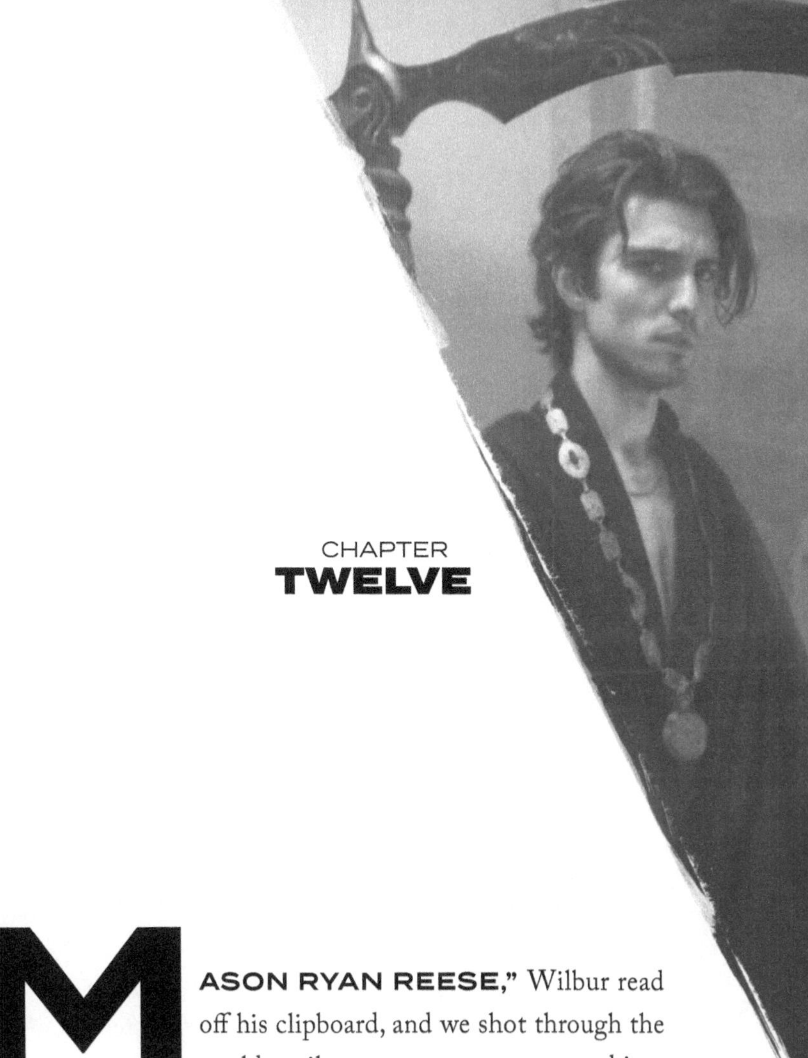

MASON RYAN REESE," Wilbur read off his clipboard, and we shot through the world until we came to rest on a road in a thick pine forest, somewhere in the Pacific Northwest or Canada if I had to guess.

The glowing form of a young man lay on the road in a pool of darkness. It was nighttime, and the only light seemed to be coming from the headlights of a car lurking where the world became blurry. Mason was in poor shape—obviously, that's why we were there.

He looked like he had gone flying through his windshield. He must have hit something—maybe a deer—and been launched out the front. He rolled slightly, a hand reaching out as if begging for help.

I tried to swallow through a lump in my throat. Wilbur shifted uncomfortably by my side, equally as affected. Both of us watched as Mason slowly bled out. Despair watched over our shoulders with as strong a gaze as his brother, Death.

I think one of the hardest parts about watching these people die was that I knew not to hope. There was none left if we were here. The story was already written, THE END loomed near, every second that remained was just a final note in their swan song. In stories, some of the people in danger survive. But no one escapes the Grim Reaper when he comes to collect.

"Helpppp." Mason's voice echoed through the blur as he raised his head weakly and seemed to stare right at us. "Pleeee-ase." Goose bumps flared up and down my arms as I realized he could see me. But he was still glowing, still alive. Instinctually, I took a step toward him, but Wilbur held up a hand, stopping me mid-stride.

"Don't," he whispered softly. "There's nothing you can do."

"Pleeeeease," Mason gasped again, his voice tearing at my heartstrings.

"Nothing?" I asked, looking at Wilbur desperately.

"We're dead, he's not—yet. You can't even touch him." With a reluctant nod, I relaxed, and he dropped his arm. As tears began streaming down my face again, I remembered the elderly woman who had been speaking to someone I couldn't see before she died the night the Dragon Dons attacked us at the restaurant. Had she seen one of my new co-workers? After tonight, I was sure of it.

Mason's strength began to fade, and his head dropped to

the pavement. It wouldn't be long now. Part of me found my-self wishing that the end would come sooner, just to spare him needless suffering. If he was already fated to die right now, why drag out the pain?

The world around us seemed to grow darker as his time ran out. The lights from his car faded, and the blur began to tighten in on us like a noose. Soon the only thing we could see clearly was his glowing form, waiting to die. Confused, I looked up at Wilbur; this hadn't happened before.

"Scythes out," he snapped sharply, his dark weapon leaping into his hand. I followed suit, summoning mine and gripping it in both hands. Wordlessly, we stood back-to-back. Something was deeply wrong.

Mocking laughter sounded from outside the circle, echo-ing as if we were at the center of a deep canyon. Wilbur and I began to circle slowly, turning to scan the blurry dark for whatever had come.

"What is it?" I whispered, adjusting my grip on my weapon.

"An interloper," he replied grimly.

"We claim this soul, Reapers," a voice called from outside the blur. It reverberated from all around us, as if it were many voices speaking together. "Depart now, and we will allow you to leave with your lives." I blinked in surprise. It seemed we weren't the only delivery service offering pickup.

"I'm afraid we can't do that," Wilbur responded, his voice hard, but I sensed an undercurrent of fear. "We're here to collect his soul, as is our right." My respect for my new friend went up immediately. I had no idea what was lurking outside our vision, but I had a feeling it wasn't going to be a pushover. Still, Wilbur hadn't even hesitated to speak for someone who couldn't stand up for themselves. That's my kind of people.

"It is ours!" the voices snapped in tones filled with rage.

"This man's soul is under the protection of Death," Wilbur shouted into the night. "The Death Treaty gives us the exclusive right to collect and deliver this mortal to—"

A thousand howls of frustration split the night. My heart leapt into my chest as the blurry wall warped inward as if something was pushing through. After a moment the wall exploded back to its original shape with a snap. In the circle on the other side of poor Mason stood a nightmare.

It was naked, with a body that was almost human, but too big and too tall. It was covered in tumors like a toad, and it stood bent over, as if bowed by the extra weight. But there was more to it than that. As I watched, its face flickered, its features vanished, and a new set appeared. This was the face of a fair woman whose skin tone did not match the rest of the body. There was another flicker, and now it was the face of an old lady.

Flicker.

Flicker.

Every time the face changed, the thing's dead eyes glowed with the same bright-orange light that Mason did as his body clung to his soul with the desperation of a dangling ice climber.

"We are Legion, and we have come to add to our host," it shouted, taking a step toward Mason. Without even looking at each other, Wilbur and I both leapt forward, blocking the monster's path to the dying man. All of a sudden, I felt a little more at home in my new job.

Legion snarled and swiped one of its long, gangly arms at Wilbur, and he jumped to the left to dodge the attack. Immediately, I cut right, forcing the interloper to split its attention to track us.

The coldness of my scythe burned in my hands as I swung it like a baseball bat, slicing through the air. Faster than I would have thought possible, the monster spun, its clawed hand coming up under the shaft of my weapon and forcing it up and over its head.

I staggered to the side, unbalanced by my wasted momentum. I was too used to swinging a sword. Wilbur pressed his attack from the other side, not allowing Legion to take advantage of me having my guard down.

Cursing myself for being an idiot, I settled into a better stance. I had never used a pole-style weapon in combat before. But I knew better than to swing wildly and lose control of my center. If the other Reaper hadn't been here, I'd already be dead. I was almost glad Orion couldn't see my pathetic attack. I'd never hear the end of it.

Hunching my shoulders, I stalked across the road, coming to Wilbur's aid. The other Reaper was on the retreat, but he clearly had more practice with his scythe than I did. As he faded back, he twirled the weapon to block Legion's attacks, then used the momentum to send lightning-quick strikes at the monster.

Despite its decrepit appearance, Legion was *fast*. The creature blurred, screaming incoherently in rage as it tried to batter its way through Wilbur's defenses. Its attention was completely focused on my friend, so I raised my weapon with the grim determination of a headsman with his ax.

The creature must have heard my footsteps. At the last moment it spun, face tortured. But not even its inhuman speed could save it from my strike. The inky-black tip of my scythe speared into its chest instead of its back.

My hands went numb as the scythe's temperature plunged from frigid to something that felt like absolute zero. Legion threw back its head and let out a horrific shriek of pain and rage. For a moment we stood like that, frozen by the power of Death coursing through my weapon into the monster.

Just when I thought my hands might turn into ice and shatter, the scythe vanished like a puff of smoke. Legion's scream choked off, and it lowered its ever-changing face to stare at me with the eyes of a teenage girl.

A black wound marred its chest where my scythe's blade had bitten into it. Legion's arm blurred in a vicious backhand that sent me crashing onto my back.

"Foolish Reaper," its echoing voice raged. "You don't have the *Authority* to kill me. I am ancient and many. You are but one little maggot."

Wilbur's black scythe sliced into its ankle, cutting through it as easily as if it were made of rotten fruit. Legion let out another horrified scream and toppled over, dark ichor spraying from its amputated stump.

Desperate to take advantage of the monster being down, I reached into my mind and tried to summon my scythe back into my icy hands. But no matter how much I called for it, the weapon did not appear.

Snarling, I charged toward the fallen creature, hoping maybe I could hold it down while Wilbur finished it off. Just because it was wounded did not mean that it wasn't dangerous. I had no doubts that Legion still had plenty of tricks up its nonexistent sleeves. Sure enough, the monster stood back up on to its single foot, hopping up and down like a demonic flamingo.

Wilbur raised his scythe for a second blow, but Legion leapt backward, out of striking range, its face shifting to a young man. For a second it looked at Mason's still-glowing form with a hint of longing. Then its dead eyes locked on me.

I glared back, my hands tightening into worthless fists. Without my scythe, there wasn't much I could do. I would have given anything for Willow's fire to answer my call, but I was still dead, and the flame was beyond my reach. Wilbur came to stand next to me, clutching his own weapon in a tight guard.

"I know you," the monster hissed in surprise. "You are marked. We remember you. Nowhere is safe from us, we are—"

"Legion, we know," I panted, interrupting its monologue.

It hissed and took a step toward me, flexing its clawed hands. I hunched and got ready to dive out of its reach. Maybe I should stop trash-talking monsters if I don't have a weapon. Wilbur hefted his scythe and moved to meet it, causing the beast to hesitate. It didn't seem eager to lose its other foot. The black wound in its chest from my scythe was leaking. Despite our failure to kill the creature, it had taken a bit of a beating.

"Marked," it snarled again, before crouching and leaping backward out of the blur bubble and into the wider world. A chill settled on my spine as I realized those were the very words that the angry goddess had said to me in the Between.

"Excuse me…" a voice said from my left shoulder. "Can you tell me what the hell is going on here?" I turned to find Mason standing next to me, staring with wide-eyed horror at his no-longer-glowing body lying in the road before us.

"Sorry," I panted, leaning on my knees, trying to catch my breath. How was I out of breath when I didn't even need to breathe? Being dead was a rip-off. "Welcome to the other side. We're here to make sure you get to where you're supposed to go."

Mason took a little convincing to get through the rift and into the Veil. I didn't blame him one bit. The only thing that might be more traumatic than dying was dying and finding two jokers fighting a monster next to your body.

My scythe was still refusing to come out and play so Wilbur took our charge to the waiting rooms, leaving me alone in the forest. Goose bumps flared on my arms as I realized that if Legion was still lurking, I would have no way to fight him off. I was marked, what was keeping him from coming back for round two?

To distract myself, I went over to study the foot it had left behind. I crouched a few feet away from the appendage, eyeing it with distaste. The stench of rot and sulfur overwhelmed me as I got closer, and I only barely managed not to gag.

It was obvious to me that Legion had been intent on stealing Mason's soul. Perhaps it absorbed souls somehow—the face thing was a pretty good clue. But that also felt too simple. I knew from my time in the Faerie Lands that souls have complex uses. I also knew that someone was making a habit out of robbing Death, which seemed like an incredibly stupid thing to do. Then there was the sulfur. If there's one thing I've learned since having my soul stolen, it's that demons always make things worse.

"So you've already encountered one of the Lost. Unsurprising, I suppose," a calm voice remarked in the stillness of my blur bubble. Gasping, I leapt to my feet. I called for the scythe to attend me, but the weapon ignored me. I was alone and unarmed. It was a moot point, I realized after I saw who had come to speak to me. If I wasn't able to kill some monster with it, I didn't think that it would be much help against an angel.

Azrael, the Heavenly Host's member of the Death Board,

stood across the clearing from me, dressed in a black peacoat and dark pants. His hands were jammed into his pockets, and his white eyes measured me with a casual curiosity. If we had been in high school, I would have said he was a theater kid who thought he was pretty cool.

Something told me this wasn't just a social call.

My heart raced as I realized this was the moment I had been looking for since the day Dan stole my soul.

"Lost?" I asked hesitantly.

He pulled one hand out of his pocket and gestured at the limb at my feet. "That one has had many names, but Legion is the most suited for it, I think. Once he was something else, but now he is Lost."

"Thanks, now I totally get it," I snorted sarcastically. "Makes complete sense."

"Instead of picking a side, some beings choose to live in the Darkness," he offered, emphasizing the word. "Outside of Reality there is only—"

"I've seen the Nothing," I interrupted, momentarily forgetting that this was an angel, and I should be polite.

"You've traveled far for a mortal." His voice was so neutral that it could have been provolone cheese.

"Unfortunate side effect of having your soul stolen." I gave him a grin that showed too much of my teeth. As far as lede burying goes, it wasn't subtle, but it wasn't every day I had the chance to tell an angel about my problems.

"Yes, you mentioned something about that when you were speaking to the board." Azrael's eyes narrowed slightly as he watched me. "How did they do it?" I swallowed as he took the bait. This felt like one of those big moments, real butterfly-effect stuff. I could finally tell my story to someone who could do *something*. I rubbed my sweaty palms on my dive suit and looked into his brilliant-white eyes.

"I was approached by a demon, a low-level salesman who made me an offer. I told him no, but he forged my signature on the contract." I shrugged as casually as I could. "Now I'm here."

"A demon offered you a deal," Azrael repeated, his tone dry.

"Correct."

"Let me guess, you were only able to reject this offer because of your devout faith?" There was a definite sarcastic tint to his words. "Get thee behind me, Satan, and all that?"

"Uh, not really," I admitted, my throat going dry. "I never quite got into all the literature. My grandmother was a big fan, though."

"If you're not a member of the flock, where did you find the strength to resist this offer for your soul?" Oh yeah, he was definitely mocking me. I don't know why I bothered telling this story anymore, even if it was the truth. No one ever believed me.

"Honestly, I've read a book before," I said, shrugging. "I don't mean…your book. Just, like, any book. Also, it wasn't really that good an offer."

The angel stared at me blankly for a moment before a slow smile spread across his face. "It wasn't that good an offer?"

"Yeah, Dan—that's the demon—he told me he was way under his quota, and honestly, I believe him. He was not good at sales." Azrael stared at me for a long moment. I could almost feel him weighing my story, deciding if he should believe me. While he pondered, my mind raced. I knew his name was familiar, but I couldn't remember why. It had been bothering me ever since I'd appeared before the Death Board, but I couldn't place it. I should have paid more attention when Grandma dragged me to Mass as a kid.

"It's a good tale," he said after a long pause. "Might be the best one I've ever heard. I almost believed you. But even Lucifer knows the price of breaking that rule." The angel turned, starting to stride off into the dark.

"Azrael," I called after him, something finally clicking in my head. "Orion believed me."

For a second, he was completely frozen, in the way that Immortals display pure shock, where they seem to step out of Time and cease to function. Then he spun and stared at me, his white eyes so narrow they looked like sunrises.

"How do you know the Hunter?" he demanded, suspicion filling his words.

I didn't answer. My nonexistent heart was so far up my throat, I was afraid it would try to escape if I opened my mouth. Instead, I raised my right fist and slowly opened it, letting the angel see where the hilt of Orion's sword had branded me when I wielded it the first time. The angel stared at my hand in cold, absolute silence. I knew he knew what my scars meant. Because I had remembered where I'd heard his name before.

Zagan said that Azrael had given Orion his sword.

This angel had personally seen to it that the Hunter bore an Immortal-killing blade. That wasn't something he would have forgotten. In the blink of an eye, he crossed the distance between us, stepping out of Time and Space and reappearing in front of me.

His black-gloved hand caught my wrist in an iron grip, and he peered closely at my palm. After a minute, he released me, a troubled expression on his sharply angled face.

"You killed Lilith." It was not a question.

"I did."

"She was involved?"

"She tried to murder me and sweep this under the rug." I shrugged. "I declined."

The angel was still for so long, I started to wonder if he had been turned into a pillar of salt. Finally, he twitched, glancing at the blank space where Wilbur had taken Mason through.

"Time to go," he murmured, which I took to mean my co-worker was on his way back.

"By the way, what brings you to this particular glade this evening?" I asked before he could leave. A nagging suspicion told me that the angel had come to talk to me. But why would he do that if he didn't already know something?

"Oh." Azrael's lips quirked up in what might have been a guilty smile. "I was in the neighborhood, and thought I'd check in on the newest Reaper." His white eyes glowed in a way that told me he knew I wasn't buying it. He turned away from me and began striding into the blurry dark.

"Hey, what's your job?" I called after him.

"My job?" He didn't turn around to face me, but I heard something amused lurking in his voice.

"Yeah. I know Zagan is the CFO of Hell. What are you the angel of?"

Azrael raised his hand and slashed through the air, opening one of the now familiar rifts into the Veil. For a moment I thought he wasn't going to answer me, but as he stepped through, he called over his shoulder, in the same tone:

"Death."

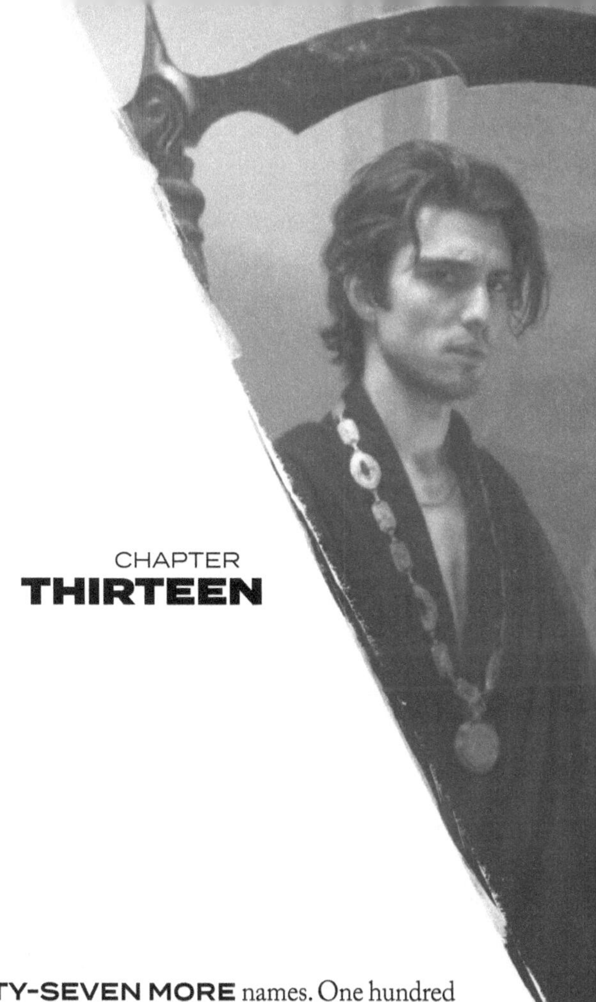

CHAPTER
THIRTEEN

EIGHTY-SEVEN MORE names. One hundred souls escorted through the Veil and brought to the Underworld. I was only carrying a clipboard, but my shoulders still sagged under the weight of it all as Wilbur and I slipped back through one of the rips to return to the empty hallway in Death's headquarters.

Wordlessly, my co-worker gestured at the pouch hanging on the wall, and I slid our completed paperwork into it. I didn't feel any lighter. Wilbur led me deeper into the facility, his mood brightening as we got farther from the entrance.

"So that's my first shift, huh?" I muttered; my throat was dry even though I didn't feel thirsty. I wasn't sure if that was because I was dead or because the work had taken away something from me.

"Yup, you're now an officially certified representative of Death Corp." Wilbur shot me a small smile to let me know he understood the layers to that congratulations.

"So, we just do that for the next thousand years?"

"More or less. The shifts usually aren't quite so eventful."

"Don't run into Lost creatures all the time then?" Somehow, I wasn't surprised. That sounded like just like my luck.

"How d'you know they're called Lost?" Wilbur asked in surprise. Mentally, I cursed myself. I had forgotten that Azrael had given me that info during his inspection. I hadn't mentioned the angel's visit to my new friend. He seemed nice enough, but I have trust issues.

"I told you, I was clued in before I died." I shrugged as if that explained everything. "I'd heard some rumors and filled in the blanks."

"Golly," Wilbur mused. "I can't imagine even trying to explain what goes on over here to anyone who's alive."

"I'm learning that it was not a thorough explanation," I admitted dryly. Lazarus and his team of mad scientist wizards had certainly left some things out.

"Now that we're off-duty, let's see about getting you a uniform," Wilbur offered. "Then we can find you a room so that you can get some rest."

"Do we still…sleep?" I asked, arching an eyebrow. "Aren't we already taking the long nap, being dead and all?"

"It's not sleeping," Wilbur told me, a serious expression on his face. "But you can still wear yourself out. The only difference is that instead of your body giving out, your soul fades."

"So naps *are* good for the soul." I'm not sure that was the appropriate takeaway, but it did feel like at least one mystery of the universe was solved.

The process to get my Reaper uniform was almost normal, just like everything else in this weird limbo between life and death. Wilbur took me to a large closet that featured rows and rows of black shirts and pants.

I made my way down one row, trying to figure out how Death's seamstresses determined sizes, but as far as I could tell every single set was the exact same. Frustrated, I turned to my friend, who was watching me with an amused expression.

"How do I find one that fits?"

"They all do." He lifted the hanger next to him off the rack and held it out to me. "One size fits all souls."

"There's no way this is my size," I replied skeptically. The shirt was clearly too small.

"Betcha twenty names," Wilbur offered with a scheming grin.

"I'm not betting you with people's lives," I growled, aghast at my friend's callous suggestion. Even if the souls we went to collect were fated to die at that time, it still felt…cold to swap them like tables at a restaurant.

"It's not like we use money here."

"This is so dumb," I grumbled, snagging the outfit from him. "Why do we even have uniforms if we're all dead?"

Wilbur didn't bother to answer my rhetorical question. Instead, he took me to an area I immediately recognized as a dormitory, or maybe *barracks* was a better word for it. The hallway was honeycombed with closely spaced doors.

The wall next to each room had a black placard that was

easily replaced, with a Reaper's name written in white. I got the last one, all the way down at the end.

Wilbur opened the door to my tiny room with a grandiose gesture, and I peeked in at the cramped space with a small sense of amusement.

At least it was bigger than my college dorm.

A single bed took up most of the space, with a metal rack for my one set of clothing. It was certainly not the nicest supernatural quarters I had ever been issued, but if it gave me some privacy I wasn't going to complain.

"Old clothes go there." Wilbur gestured at the rack. "You change back into them after your last shift before you go through processing yourself."

"I don't get to keep the uniform as a souvenir?"

"Nope, it's company property."

"All right, I get it." I sighed. "How long until our next shift?" I was desperate to get a moment to collect my thoughts and make a plan. Plus, once I ditched Wilbur, I could probably poke around better to find that crown thingy Lazarus wanted.

"When your scythe is ready," he explained, gesturing at my empty hand. "The more you grow into your power, the longer your list gets and the less rest you need to recharge. Once you're back to full strength, there will be an assignment waiting for you."

"Hard to do any reaping if you can't be a Reaper," I grunted in acknowledgment. "How long does it take to come back?"

"Depends on the Time waves." Wilbur shrugged. "Sometimes it's a while, others it's a long while." That's right, I almost forgot we were dancing on the edge of Reality here.

"It's really hard to plan without a working clock, isn't it?"

"You get used to not thinking about it. What's the rush? You're dead."

I did my best to keep a guilty expression off my face. "It will take some getting used to." I forced a smile. "Until I'm recharged, am I free to relax and process? I did die today."

"Oh yes." My co-worker blushed slightly as if he had forgotten. "I'm sorry, reckon I've gotten so used to it that I didn't consider your feelings."

"It's all right," I said, waving his concerns away. "It's been great having you as my guide through the Underworld more than once. I couldn't ask for a better one, but I think I need to do some thinking."

"I will get out of your hair so you can think as much as you need," Wilbur promised, starting to pull my door shut. "Find me when you're feeling recharged, and we'll cover the rest." The latch clicked, and I was finally alone.

I sat down on the edge of my bed, staring at the one-size-fits-all Reaper uniform in my hands. The black shirt had long sleeves and buttons; it felt coarse, like it was made of some sort of cheap polyester. I guess even old Death tried to cut costs where he could.

The loose black pants were belted at the waist, and there was a white shirt that went under the black coat. Silver scythes decorated the collars, marking me as what I was.

A Reaper.

The silence was heavier here. Suddenly the crushing weight of my solitude slammed down on me, and I bowed my head, screwing my eyes shut. I didn't know if my spiritual form was able to cry on this side of the Veil, but I certainly wanted to.

Next to the grand cosmic machine that was running everything, I felt like an inconsequential speck, a tiny dot of light smaller than a star to the naked eye. What was I doing here? What chance did someone like me have against Death himself and his army of Reapers?

Alex was right. I never should have come here.

After a long moment of self-pity, I forced my damp eyes to open and took a long, shaky breath. There was no point in wallowing. I was here, and I had a sister to save.

Absentmindedly, I slid my hands into my pockets and jumped in surprise as my right fingers brushed against a cold metal object. Hesitantly, I reached back in, pulling out a familiar weight.

I knew before I looked that it was a key.

I opened my hand to reveal the Key of Portunus lying in my palm. But as I gazed down at it, I realized that I was wrong. This wasn't old Porty's relic. This was a different key.

Instead of brass, this one was made of a dark metal. It was a matte black that reflected none of the light above it. Like my other key, this one had two performers' masks on the hilt, but the crying one was on top, above its laughing twin. It was as if someone had taken the original and inverted it.

What was it that the goddess trapped in the Between had told me? That another god named Janus had helped Portunus create that place? I'd wondered if that meant there was a second key to the eternal hallway. It seemed that there was.

But how was it here? I frowned, trying to remember every-thing the goddess had said and done. I had been confused why she hadn't just taken it out of my hand by force. Now, as I stared at its twin, I realized that it must be bound to me in some sort of magical way. How else could it follow me through the Veil?

I wonder if even Gloriana knew how powerful it was when she gave it to me.

A sudden hope burned in my chest as I stared at the relic. This changed my options dramatically. If Lazarus and his team didn't resuscitate me, or if Death took away my ability to cross the Veil, why not just let myself out the door? If I found Megan and the crown, I could simply bring them back out myself.

Eager to test my theory, I walked over to my bedroom door and held the black key out toward its knob. Just like on the other side of the Veil, a hole appeared and accepted the key readily. Hesitantly, I turned the handle. Then I froze.

The last time I saw the goddess who marked me, she was stranded in the halls of the Between, and very unhappy with me. I stared down at the twisted doorknob, torn. There was a good chance that opening this door was a mistake, but I needed to know if I had another way out.

Just a quick peek, I promised myself. I'd pop the door open, make sure that everything was hunky-dory, then slam it shut. Besides, there was every chance that she had gone back to whatever devoured world the dragoon had released her from. Last time I had made a bunch of noise and summoned her from her demesne. This time I would be as quiet as a church mouse.

Slowly, I eased the door open, my eye pressed up to the doorframe like a submarine captain peering through a periscope. As the place on the other side came into focus, my heart sank. After a moment of hesitation, I opened the door all the way, staring slack-jawed at the sterile hall waiting for me.

This was not the Between.

This was somewhere else.

Slowly, I stepped into a new hallway. Instead of a fading

office building, this one was made of marble. Janus was also a Roman god, and his style fit the imperial architecture stereotype more than his relative's.

A royal-purple carpet ran down the center of the hall, leaving the white floor exposed on either side. Tall columns were spaced evenly down the sprawling path, reaching up to the ceiling, which was filled with a roiling darkness thicker than any storm. It was at once expansive and claustrophobic, inside and outside. It reminded me of the Venetian Casino in Las Vegas with its sky-painted ceiling.

Instead of doors, this hall was dotted with iron gates that looked like they could withstand a battering ram. Slowly, my heart pounding in my chest, I made my way toward the first one. An ancient placard inscribed with Roman letters read IRKALLA, which meant nothing to me. The next one I passed was NARAKA, then JAHANNAM.

The fourth gate lay open, its hinges rusted. Nervously, I stuck my head in a few inches. The last time a door in one of these halls had been open I'd almost died horribly. All I could see was thick, overgrown jungle, and I decided to not investigate further.

I glanced at its sign and frowned. The name XIBALBA was familiar to me, but I couldn't explain why. Feeling more confident that this side of the Between wasn't inhabited by an angry god, I wandered boldly down the hall, cursing my schooling for not teaching me things that were useful. Clearly, I had not been exposed to enough of the classics.

Finally, I found a clue that my half-educated brain recognized. Like Xibalba's gate, this one was rusted and falling off its hinges. It hung open, as if whatever treasures it once held were no longer worth guarding. As I read the name chiseled into the marble wall, I knew why.

Once, this had been the gate to Elysium.

I strode through its entrance, wondering if I could find the gate that led to Lazarus's basement. The eternal fields looked exactly how I remembered, with beautiful golden wheat dancing in the breeze. I made it three steps before I ran into a solid wall that I couldn't see.

I bounced off the barrier with a yelp, rubbing at my stinging nose, noting once again that being dead was not all it was cracked up to be.

A dozen puzzle pieces clicked into place for me as I glared at the invisible wall. Lazarus had told me that when this paradise fell, it had "slipped back over the line." He meant the Veil. Elysium was no longer part of the Underworld, which was why its gate was a ruin.

This *was* the Between, but on the other side of the Veil. I was no longer between worlds, but between Underworlds. I made my way back into the marble hall and looked up and down.

There must be a door here that would lead to my own bad place. One of these gates had to open into Hell itself. I licked my lips nervously. If I wanted to rescue the other half of my sister's soul, there was a good chance that I was going to have to venture into Perdition. This other Between might be my way in.

I glanced down at my pocket watch. It was just after 1 p.m.. I had already used up an hour, but that was after a long period across the Veil. I stared at the little timepiece for a long moment, but the second hand remained frozen. I still had plenty of time. I'd save walking up to Lucifer's house and knocking on the front door until I got desperate.

Well, more desperate anyway.

Cognizant that I had been gone for a while, I started to make my way back toward the gate I had come through. If Janus's Key was going to be the ace up my sleeve, then I shouldn't get caught the first time I used it.

My entrance's sign read THE VEIL in the same carved Roman lettering. Out of curiosity, I glanced at the next one down: HADES. Intrigued by a name I actually knew, I walked toward it, key still in hand.

The gate seemed to be in good repair, closed and locked. If my memory wasn't playing tricks on me, the ruler of the Roman version of Hades was none other than…Pluto. Technically this could have been the Greek one, but I was guessing that would use a different font on its sign. My eyes narrowed as I realized that must be how Pluto got his seat on the Death Board. Every figure I had recognized was responsible for Death in their organization.

Hell seemed daunting, but compared with the Devil himself, diminutive Pluto seemed practically manageable, even if he was a god. Some whispering instinct told me that there was something worth finding in there.

In a split second, I made a rash decision. I strode over to the Hades gate and jammed the Key of Janus into the lock. The metal hinges squealed in protest as I pulled them open, in urgent need of some WD-40. I guess that made sense. It was unlikely that many souls still found their way to Pluto's halls. He was on a budget these days.

A thick mist coiled around the entrance, obscuring whatever was waiting for me on the other side. For a moment I debated closing the noisy gate and returning to the Veil. But I had to start somewhere.

Hunching my shoulders, I strode into the mist and descended into Hades.

FOURTEEN

THE FOG OF Hades swirled around me. I walked forward, missing Willow's comforting flame more than ever. The dim murk threatened to swallow me, but I put my head down and kept moving. I had come too far to turn back now.

Just when my courage was about to break, the fog abated, and the sound of rushing water filled my ears. I emerged into the glade of a forest that was fading from autumn into winter. The trees were bare, skeletal limbs raised to the sky like corpses.

The grass was green, but a sickly green, the plants on their last legs. The whole countryside hovered on the verge of death. I felt like the entire world had a layer of gray over it, draining the colors.

A wide, dark river roared past, its current strong and power-ful. I saw no ferryman, but instinct told me that I was looking upon the River Styx. It seemed I was already on the right side, which was good because I had no coin to purchase passage. As I studied the raging water, I noticed a path winding its way into the naked trees. A sign next to the entrance read KEEP OFF THE GRASS.

Mentally, I cursed myself for being a fool and set off on the path. After twenty yards it began to make its way up a slight incline. I tried to see where it led, but the dead trees were thick enough to block my sight. There was nothing to do but keep walking.

Why was I here? What did I really think I could gain from sneaking into a lord of death's domain? My task was to rob Kane himself, and my sister's splintered soul was not stored here. This place had nothing for me.

But my gut told me that precisely because it was on the border of turning into a ruin, this was the perfect place to start. A thief needed practice before he was ready to rob a bank. I was here to learn the game before I had to play for real.

After a few twists, I emerged into an open space that had been cut into the forest. It ran from the base of the hill I was climbing all the way up. On a patch of flat ground at the bottom sat a massive boulder. The earth behind it was torn by a matching rut, as if the stone had rolled up and down many times.

A skeleton lay in a pile at the foot of the rock. I paused for a moment staring at the remains of a myth even I knew. I wondered if his eternal task had been completed, or if he had finally just given up.

Unsettled in a new way, I continued my trek. The hill rose

more swiftly now, keeping pace with Sisyphus's track, carving back and forth in relentless switchbacks. My breath grew ragged, but I kept on marching. Somehow I knew that at the top, I would find answers to some of my questions.

Time had no meaning here. In fact, I suspected it didn't exist in this place. The dam of the Veil had cut off the clock's waves and left this place a desert. I walked for eons and for only a moment. Abruptly I emerged from the dead forest, feeling like I had lived a thousand lifetimes but learned nothing.

The trees stopped before the top, marking a clearly defined circle around a low, dark building made of stone. The fog swirled around the fortress like appendages of a living thing, hunting. I swallowed as fear grew in my chest. This was where I had chosen to come.

With a sigh of self-hatred, I continued up the path, making sure that I never left it. Something told me there was a reason it existed. If Pluto wanted people to stay off his dying grass, I was only too happy to oblige.

The fortress's mighty gate was cracked open, its walls un-manned. I stepped into courtyard, spinning slowly as I took in the scene before me. The building wasn't a military structure at all, I realized as I studied it. It reminded me of an abandoned outlet mall. There were three open floors' worth of small square rooms carved into the dark walls like stores, with balconies connecting them all.

Most of them had shattered glass windows. Curious, I walked to the first one and peered in. All I saw was a slowly spinning wheel, a leering skeleton still tied to it.

Tearing my eyes from the rotating corpse, I made my way farther into the mall of punishments. Another room had only an apple tree and a pool of water. Not sure what the deal was with that one. The second floor was more of the same, full of empty shops, or whatever the Hadesian equivalent was.

I turned away from a particularly gruesome one and froze. Something grated across the ground below me. I dropped into a crouch behind the railing of the balcony and peered down to the first floor.

A massive beast was dragging itself across the floor with a limp. Once its fur had been dark, but now it was white and eaten by mange. I thought I heard a swarm of flies hovering around it. A deep snuffling sounded as it investigated around where I had wandered.

Terror gripped me as I watched one of its heads rise from the ground and sniff deeply at the air, while its other two stayed glued to the ground. The dog's rotting teeth dripped with yellow mucus, and its eyes were filled with the blue fog of glaucoma. Cerberus, the hound of Hades, didn't look good, but I had a feeling he was healthy enough to tear me to shreds.

Slowly, I crouched, not daring even a peek at the dog. Yeah, that head's eyes weren't holding up so well, but he had plenty more to try to see me with. The snuffling increased as the monstrous canine followed my path across the first floor.

It was only a matter of time until he tracked me to where I hid on the second floor. I shifted, trying to keep my shoes from grating on the dark stone. The dog below me let out a low growl, which froze me in my tracks.

I rose, risking a peek over the railing. All of the beast's heads were staring forward, away from me, three sets of horrific teeth bared in identical snarls. With a roar, the dog leapt forward, faster than I thought he would be able to move in his sickly state. A series of dull barks echoed out of his mouth as he scrabbled across the floor and dashed deeper into the mall.

I let out a long sigh and collapsed to the floor, leaning against the railing for support. My heart pounded in my chest, trying to convince me of a fundamental fact: I should not be here. I should not be here. I should not be here.

But I was here.

I might as well get something out of it.

Eventually, I managed to get my wobbly legs under me and pulled myself to my feet, leaning on the balcony rail like a support. The bazaar of horrors was silent and empty, so I made my way to the open staircase that led to the third floor.

As on the floors below, there were boxy spaces carved out here for prisoners that had long since been broken open. But these were bigger, more dramatic. One in particular was massive. If this were a real mall, the store that occupied that space would have been a major chain.

Curious, I wandered across the narrow balcony that ran through the middle of the room, glancing over the railing as I went to see if Cerberus had returned. There was no sign of the ancient hellhound, which made me feel a little better. But not completely, because I was still wandering unsupervised in *Hades*. I seem to recall that not going so well for either Heracles or Odysseus.

As I drew near to the mega store display, I realized that it was completely gilded, from the floor to the furniture. The Fae, who adore gold above all things, would kill to have Goldhall be as aureate as this prison.

I drew up short at the edge of the giant space. Unlike the other storefronts, this one seemed to never have been sealed off by glass. Instead, a series of golden ropes hung from matching posts, forming a mostly ceremonial barrier. Staring at the sea of shiny objects, I tried to understand what kind of punishment this had been. Maybe it was the tomb of a fallen warrior, buried with his spoils.

Something stirred in the center of the room. My gaze snapped to a giant golden chair facing away from me. It was almost big enough to be called a throne. It was also not empty, I realized.

"It's impolite to stare," a man's voice called in bored tones.

"Sorry, I got a little lost," I admitted, my mouth so dry that it took me a few tries to get it out.

The man didn't answer for so long, I began to wonder if I had hallucinated the whole exchange. Just as I was about to turn away and explore a less weird part of the mall, he let out a long dramatic sigh and rose.

I bent my knees, preparing to flee at the first sign of another one of Pluto's monsters. All I had to do to escape was get down three flights of stairs, make it to the bottom of the winding path, and run out the gate. At least it was all downhill.

It was not a monster who rose to meet me, but a man. He had dark features, with a large golden crown nestled in his black hair. Even his robes were made of gold; they moved leadenly as he walked. His brown, human eyes gazed at me with an unknowable weariness, but they sharpened slightly as he took in my outfit.

Suddenly I knew whose punishment this was.

"You're not supposed to be here," he said flatly.

"I got *lost*," I repeated.

The man stared at me with untrusting eyes before he let

out an amused snort and dropped to sit on the armrest of his throne. The solid-gold clothing looked like it was a significant amount of weight to carry.

"What do I care?" he muttered to no one in particular. "There's hardly any trouble left for you to get into here." I glanced around the empty mall. He had a point. The front door hadn't even been shut.

"You're Midas, right?" I wondered if he would be flattered by being recognized. "The gold thing is pretty legendary."

"Once they put *King* in front of my name." He didn't seem to be offended, just tired.

"Sorry, it's been a while," I told him.

"How long?" A note of curiosity entered his voice, which was the most energized he had been since I found him.

"Uh, let me think." I'd never been good with dates, historical or otherwise. "Were you B.C. or A.D.?"

"What are you babbling about?" He was giving me the same disappointed look that most of my professors had given me after calling on me.

"Okay, right, definitely B.C. It's one of those things that you would know if you knew. I think the Greek Empire came before the Roman one anyway." Maybe this was the Greek Hades after all—but that didn't make complete sense. The Romans named their gods after the planets which would make Pluto one of theirs.

"It's not like there's a difference worth mentioning," Midas grumbled.

"Three thousand years?" I said. "Give or take a few hundred probably?"

Midas stared at me in shock. Then his face sagged and

somehow, he looked even more tired than before.

"What happened here?" I asked, changing the subject.

"The same thing that happens everywhere that touches the mortal realm," he lamented softly. "Entropy."

A shiver ran down my spine as I realized he was talking about souls. They were the fuel that allowed Underworlds like this to exist. With the fall of the Greek and Roman Empires, I had to imagine that fewer and fewer souls made their way to Hades. This place was hanging on by a thread as Hubble's expansion ripped it apart.

"What made you one of the lucky last men standing?"

"There are no others left, only me." Midas's lips compressed into a flat line. "Once I am gone, this place will fade into nothing. A piece of advice, boy: Don't antagonize the gods. No creature in all the worlds is more petty."

No wonder Pluto wasn't any fun. He was one lightbulb away from losing his entire kingdom. Do you still get to be a god of death if you no longer have an Underworld? My gut told me the answer was no. His entire career was teetering on the brink of the abyss.

"Speaking of the gods," I began after a moment of thought. "What happened to Hades? I thought that he ran this place, not Pluto."

"One and the same." Midas shrugged as if that was the most boring question I could possibly have asked him. "When the pantheon changed from Greek to Roman, some of the less agreeable members were replaced. Others changed their names. Many of the ancients have worn more than one face through the eons."

Everything is real, but not everything is true, Alex had once told me. A shiver ran down my spine as I realized how right he had been. The major difference between the Greeks and Romans was just *branding*? Was Zeus really Jupiter? What about Poseidon and Neptune? I guess the answer was duh. When one empire fell from grace, most of the pantheon picked up and switched teams. Wild.

Reeling with a new understanding of the world and the things that lived in its shadows, I shook my head to clear it. Midas let out another sigh, bored by the only visitor that he had received in a couple hundred years. My small talk was clearly not up to courtly expectations.

"What is one of Death's Reapers doing in the halls of Hades?" He arched a dark eyebrow. "You are most certainly *not* allowed in here."

"Why?" I asked, a little surprised. We brought the souls; why wouldn't we be allowed inside?

"You are glorified couriers." Midas spread his hands to take in the ruins of the mall mausoleum around us. "Do you think that Pluto would want anyone to see the ruin that has befallen his halls?"

Understanding flooded into my brain, and I realized that I knew a secret a god of death would kill to keep. We deliver the souls, but we aren't their bankers. No one knew that Hades was hanging on by a thread. Surely Kane knew that it had been a while since any new mortals had been brought to the River Styx. But how could he know the rot on the inside?

"I should go," I murmured, feeling a new sense of dread. Coming here had been a mistake. I had wandered into something much more complex and dangerous than I could ever have imagined. Surprise, surprise.

"I might recommend it," Midas smirked, seeing the fear on my face. "The damn hound will drag his way through the ruins soon, and even though he's past his prime, I wouldn't let him catch me, were I you."

"Thanks for the tip, see you around." Waving, I took a single step, then froze, my foot hovering a few inches off the floor.

Eureka. Sometimes I'm so stupid that I'm brilliant.

"Hey, Midas," I called, turning back to stare at the man in the gilded cage. "You wouldn't happen to be a Sorcerer King, would you?"

"WHAT IS A Sorcerer King?" Midas's face screwed up in confusion.

"Well, it's a king who is a sorcerer, generally."

"Thank you, that answered all my questions." He glowered at me from inside his prison.

I chuckled, trying to think of another way to explain this to someone born three millennia before me. Come to think of it, it was rather surprising that we had been able to communicate at all. "Your English is incredible, by the way," I commented. "Where did you study?"

"What is English?"

"The language we're using to talk to each other?"

"Boy, you are speaking flawless Greek."

I arched an eyebrow in surprise. Maybe dying did bring people together in some ways. "Okay," I said, deciding to cut to the chase. "Let's try this another way. I am searching for someone who can bestow an Impossible Task. Can you do that?"

Midas's reaction was immediate. He slid off the side of his throne and strode to the front of his cell, the heavy gold clothes he wore banging as he moved. "An Impossible Task?" he repeated in breathless tones.

"I need one," I confirmed, my heart racing. Carina had told me that all the Sorcerer Kings were dead. But Death was not a barrier to me anymore. Hope began to grow within me as a door I thought was closed began to open.

"An Impossible Task can only be fulfilled by the living," he objected, his eyes narrowing. "It would be worthless to you."

"Let me worry about that," I assured him, a grin tugging at my lips. He could do it. I was sure of it. My palms felt clammy, and I rubbed them against my pants as I watched him consider me.

"Yes," he affirmed after a moment of thought. "I can give you what you seek."

A giant grin battled its away across my face.

"But." He held up a finger. "In order for me to grant you one, I will require a service from you."

Nothing is ever free. I knew that all too well by now.

"What's your price?" I asked, crossing my arms. It didn't matter what it was, I'd find a way to pay it, and I suspected he knew that too.

"Release me," he demanded simply. "Send me into the beyond." I thought I saw hope on his face, and I realized that we were the same. Both of us were trapped and desperate for any chance to get out.

"Wouldn't that take this whole place with it?" I glanced around the ruins with a skeptical eye.

"Hades would be no more," Midas confirmed. "It would finally be swallowed by the dark."

"So all I have to do for you to give me what I want is destroy Hades?" I swallowed. "Are you sure you don't want to make that the Impossible Task? That's no small thing you ask."

"Pfft, you have no idea what you are seeking for, do you?" Midas said, a disgusted look on his face. "If you are worthy of being given such a challenge, you will destroy this place."

"Okay, okay." I held up my hands in surrender. "I'll do it. Any idea how to make you die for a second time?"

"You are a servant of Death," the king replied, sounding puzzled. "Use the Authority that was given to you and command it to be thus."

I tried not to gulp with fear. If my scythe had winked out after striking Legion, there was no way I had enough control of it yet to send Midas into the waiting dark that was the Nothing. But I didn't want to fail—I couldn't! Too much was riding on this.

I held out my right hand and called to the cold darkness that lurked inside me. The power responded sluggishly, like a snake disturbed in the middle of winter. A shadow began to fill in the space of my hand, but it was thinner and more transparent than it had been before. Instead of a thick, inky black, it was a translucent gray. I squeezed the haft of the scythe, and it gave a little, like Jell-O.

"Ah," I muttered, shuffling my feet. "About that. I may need a little time to get it to your level."

Midas glowered at me and my shadow of a weapon for a long moment, frustration drawing across his face like a storm cloud. "Then return here when you are worthy of the task you ask for!" he snapped. "I will still be here, rotting into nothing."

I opened my mouth to reply, then paused as I heard a low growl. Midas's eyes went wide, and I turned to glance over the railing to the floor of the mall, three stories below. Cerberus's mangy form glared up at me from where he sat on the floor, like a dog with a treed squirrel.

As I made eye contact with the beast, he threw back all three of his heads and let out an entire pack's worth of eerie howls. The hairs on the back of my neck stood at attention as the sound rebounded through the ruins of Hades. For a moment, I was frozen with fear. My scythe vanished like a blown-out candle.

"Run, mortal!" Midas cried, his voice kicking me into action.

I spun, sprinting across the top walkway, back toward the staircase I had used earlier. Below me, Cerberus let out another series of barks, and I heard his toenails clicking on the floor as he began to hunt.

I dropped low as I rushed, trying to keep the canine from guessing where I was. As I did, I scanned the mall for an avenue of escape. I needed to get out of here before anyone came to investigate the source of all the noise. I didn't see any other doors, which meant my only way out was back down by the river. That seemed like a problem.

Generally speaking, there's no escaping from a dog in a straight sprint, unless it's a Chihuahua. They're faster than us, and there's not much I can do about that. But Cerberus wasn't in peak condition. If I could lose him for a minute, perhaps I could slip out and make my escape down the hill.

That was a pretty big if.

Slowly, I made my way to the top of the stairs and risked a glance down. The monstrous dog was pacing the floor, his heads tilted upward, looking for me. He didn't seem to know where I was, but that didn't matter because to escape I'd have to run right past him.

I needed a distraction. I glanced into the ruined exhibit next to me, which had some sort of empty riverbed running through it. *That will work*, I thought, striding over to reach through the broken glass.

I grabbed a fistful of the thick pebbles and started making my way down to the second floor. Drawing back my arm, I turned and threw one of the stones toward the far side of the mall as hard as I could. The rock *click-clacked* against the ground, and I heard Cerberus snarl as he turned to investigate.

Moving swiftly, I trotted down to the second floor and raced toward the staircase to the first level. As I sprinted, I tossed the rest of my pebbles toward a corner behind me, trying to confuse the beast. I didn't dare pause to see if he took the bait. I knew that if I hesitated, I might freeze again.

I heard my stones fall like a miniature hailstorm as my foot landed on the main floor, and I took that as my cue. I put my head down and sprinted toward the gate, pouring on all my speed. Behind me, the dog's heads growled in discordant harmony as he caught sight of me.

A chorus of howls chased me as I burst out of the mausoleum and careened down the winding path through the dead forest. Fear coiled around my heart as I ran, making it hard for me to take a full breath. All I could think about was being mauled by those different heads and snapped like a wishbone.

Of all the deaths that had threatened me, this was one of the most horrible.

Cerberus's cries echoed off the corpses of the trees as I rounded the bend next to Sisyphus's remains. I could hear the monster thumping along behind me, only my ability to take sharp turns smoothly was keeping me ahead. I glanced over my shoulder in time to see him burst through some low-hanging branches, snapping them like twigs. I let out a scream of terror at the sight and somehow began to run even faster.

After what felt like an eternity, I emerged onto the shore of the River Styx. The dark waters roared loud enough to drown out the sound of the hound on my heels.

Thick fog still coiled around the edges of the glade, but I thought I could see the bright light of the Between shining through the depths. Without risking another look behind me, I raced toward that light.

"WHO DARES?" a voice thundered above the crashing of the rapids. I froze in my tracks, then slowly turned to see a tiny, angry god.

Pluto stood aboard a flat ferry crossing the river. It cut through the rapids without hesitation, even though no one seemed to be actually rowing or poling the thing. There was no sign of Charon either, I noticed. I wonder if he had been fired during the economic downturn that was affecting this place.

The fog around me parted as if it had been hit by gale-force winds, ruining my cover. The master of Hades was glaring at me, his purple eyes blazing with wildfire. So much for getting out cleanly.

"YOU!" he raged as he recognized me. The fear that spiked in my body gave me enough of an adrenaline kick to break through whatever had been holding me still. I didn't know if he just hadn't been using his whole power, or if having only one soul in the bank made him weaker.

Cerberus howled as he burst in the clearing, and I lowered my head as I charged into the remnants of the fog. It was so thick that the world grew dim and sound began to distort. Ahead of me, the bright lights of the Between beckoned, and after a few moments, the deep fog parted to reveal the gate.

"WHERE ARE YOU, REAPER?" Pluto's voice blasted from all sides. "YOU CANNOT HIDE FROM ME IN MY OWN REALM. THERE IS NO ESCAPE."

It seemed that the god of death didn't know everything about his home. I raced to the open gate and risked one last glance over my shoulder. As I did, the fog parted once more, and the Olympian leered at me with a mocking smile.

My heart skipped a beat, and I began backpedaling through the exit. I watched as the god's confidence faded.

"NO!" Pluto cried, realizing that he was too late to stop me. He raised a hand. Clearly I had more than overstayed my welcome. I turned and leapt through the glowing gate, slamming it shut behind me. Janus's version of the key clicked in the lock, and I slid to the floor, leaning against the wall.

For a long time, I lay there outside of Time and Space, letting my nonexistent heart rate calm down, catching my useless breath, and gathering my wits. I know that's a paradox. I had no physical form to tire out, but my mind wasn't ready to let go yet.

I glanced down at the pocket watch around my neck, the time still hadn't changed. I guess being this far on the other side of the Veil really did slow things down. That was good to know. I couldn't stay here forever, though. I had a chance to get my Impossible Task. But I wasn't worthy—not yet. I had to learn to use my dark powers of Death, and to do that, I had to go back to work.

I wasn't sure what I was going to do about Pluto. He knew that I had been in his domain, which according to Midas was forbidden. Not only had I broken the rules, but now I knew his dirty secret—Hades was broke. I grinned as I realized that was probably the best security I could have. Knowing what I did of Immortals, I was guessing the god would do anything to keep his reputation intact. I had some leverage. I would just have to use it carefully until I could destroy his home and revoke his status as a god of death.

A year and a half ago, I used to go to the movies to hide from my friends. Now I conspired against deities. I wasn't sure which version of my life was better, but I couldn't deny this one was more interesting.

Wearily, I climbed to my feet and made my way down the marble halls Between Underworlds. I ran my hand along the cool wall, letting its firmness ground me. It reminded me of my time in Goldhall. They weren't particularly restful or relaxing memories, but I had survived them, and that gave me an odd sort of courage.

I found the gate marked THE VEIL and slipped my key into the lock, picturing the little dorm room I had exited from. I hesitated a second before I turned it, making sure my mental image was perfect. It would suck if I popped out in a room full of Reapers. They would have a lot of questions that I couldn't really answer.

The gate opened, and I let out a sigh of relief as I peered out into my own room. My ridiculous death scuba suit was still hanging next to the bed. Feeling lighter already, I stepped back into the Veil and closed the door behind me.

Suddenly light-headed, I collapsed onto the edge of the bed like a sack of heavy Matt potatoes. The adrenaline began to fade, and my brain finally had enough spare processing power to actually feel the terror that I had just experienced. Running from a god of death and his insane dog might have been the scariest thing I had ever done. Even the unchained Doyle had *only* been a dragon.

I flopped onto my back and stared at the ceiling. If Pluto hadn't been my enemy before, he definitely would be now. I could only hope that my time in the Veil would run out before he sought his revenge.

CHAPTER
SIXTEEN

I **'M NOT SURE** how long I lay on my bed, staring at the ceiling, but I do know that I didn't fall asleep. Wilbur was right, that's another thing that you lose when you die. I felt like I was in some sort of weird meditative trance, but that might just be a trauma response from everything I had just been through. This wasn't my first time being chased by gods and monsters, but it still hadn't gotten any easier on the old psyche.

Eventually my brain turned back on, and it occurred to me that since my trip to the Underworlds had taken no time I was still on break. This was a great opportunity for me to poke around the Veil without anyone watching over my shoulders. I fished out my pocket watch and confirmed that the second hand was moving again. It was just after 2 p.m., which meant I still had a lot of my death journey left, but I couldn't get comfortable.

On top of my looming deadline, I had no idea how Pluto was going to react to finding me lurking in his domain. If he went to the boss and complained, I could find myself in a cell or sitting on a shelf long before my time was up. All the more reason to get on with it.

I tucked the watch back under my Reaper blacks and set off to explore. As I wandered through the corporate side of the Veil, I was struck by how much it felt like every office building I had ever been in. Some people sat at desks doing paperwork, while others marched around on tasks. The whole place was hustling and bustling, which I guess makes sense if you're handling the entire volume of the mortal realm's incoming souls every day.

"Reaper Carver," a woman's voice demanded from behind me as I made my way through a sea of administrative cubicles, looking for anything interesting. Surprised and feeling a little guilty, I turned to find Atty standing behind me. I put on my warmest smile and tried to look like I wasn't doing anything wrong.

Death's gaunt assistant gave me a sour look. "The master wishes to see you. Come with me."

Without waiting, she set off at a brisk pace. Now truly panicked that I was in trouble, I raced after her. With every step I felt like a man being walked to the gallows. Pluto must have gone straight to the big cheese himself after all. How much trouble was I in? Obviously, I had broken a rule, but in my defense, no one had told me it was a rule. I hadn't meant to trespass; I had just been lost.

"Did he say what he wanted to see me about?" I asked Atty after a few moments of extremely loud silence. Death's assistant hadn't been impressed with me during my orientation and seemed even less so now. She reminded me of a great-aunt who was eternally disappointed with everyone around her.

"Yes."

"Oh good," I replied after her long pause made it clear that she wasn't going to share that with me. "As long as someone knows why."

Atty and I continued in pristine quiet. Her heels clicked on the linoleum floor in a tempo that I matched my march to. Visions of being walked to the principal's office in school flashed through my mind, but worse.

Before I had a chance to settle my nerves, we were there. Death's assistant led me to his office and opened the door for me, gesturing for me to enter, her gray eyes flat and unreadable. I gave her a small nod and stepped in, ready to die.

Kane was sitting behind his desk framed by the giant windows that stared out into the empty night beyond. He gestured for me to sit in one of the chairs in front of his dark desk. As I did so, he put down the scroll he was reading and glowered at me through the steeples of his fingers.

Maybe I just needed to get out ahead of him chastising me for my invasion of Hades. The longer I sat in anxious silence, the worse it would likely be. If I played dumb, no one could blame me too much. I was new here and wandered through a door I shouldn't have. I'm very good at playing dumb—I could sell it.

I opened my mouth, only to be interrupted. "Atty tells me that you encountered Legion while reaping?" he asked in a serious tone.

Oh yeah, I had almost forgotten about that particular horror. There had been so many other ones already. Maybe this experience wouldn't be so bad; Wilbur and I had fought it off and protected Mason's soul. That's what we were supposed to do.

"Yes, sir," I managed, my voice cracking slightly with nerves.

"Only one?" Death pressed, still eyeing me with what I would almost call a distrustful gaze.

"It seemed to be alone," I agreed. "I stabbed it in the chest, but that didn't do a whole lot. Then Wilbur cut off one of its feet. It didn't like that very much."

"That was it?" Kane blinked incredulously. "You cut off its foot, and it ran away?"

"Wilbur did," I repeated. "Then it made some threats and scampered off."

"It didn't touch the mortal's soul?"

"Mason," I offered quietly.

Death's face softened slightly at my tone. "It didn't touch Mason's soul?" he repeated.

"We kept him safe and brought him to the Veil," I confirmed, feeling a little sick. While I understood that if you did this job long enough, there was no way that people wouldn't become numbers, I was going to do everything in my power to prevent that from happening to me.

Death leaned back in his chair and drummed his gloved fingers on his desk as a small frown grew on his face. It was an oddly human gesture. For some reason, I couldn't picture Orion or any of the other Constellations doing such a thing.

"Did anything else unusual happen?" he asked after a moment of contemplation. "Something that might have spooked it. It is not like Legion to flee once it has a mortal's soul in its sight."

With a start, I realized he was talking about Azrael. The Angel of Death had appeared after Legion had fled, while Wilbur was escorting Mason through the Veil. Maybe the Lost creature had sensed his Presence and decided it wasn't worth the risk. But that seemed like something I should play closer to my chest.

"Can you define unusual? That entire experience was pretty weird, if we're being honest."

"Of course," he replied, inclining his head to me. "I told you that there are creatures who seek to steal the souls in our care, but I confess that I did not delve into the subject. I expected it to be a long time before you saw your first Lost."

"Why is that?"

"Because they rarely venture onto the mortal side of the Veil," Death answered. "They are weaker there."

"That was Legion *weak*?" I said in horror. "It was a nightmare."

"The Lost tend to prefer high-risk, high-reward targets," Kane continued grimly. "Why battle a Reaper for a single soul when they can fight a handful for a thousand on a battleground better suited for them?"

"The shipments," I breathed, dots finally connecting. "That was what Atty interrupted my training for."

"Yes, the Lost swarmed and captured a delivery that was being escorted to one of our clients. Three Reapers were sent into the final dark."

"Wait, he was here, right before we ran into him?"

"The thing that calls itself Legion is more than one body," he told me. "The size of its host is incalculable." I blinked. I had assumed the changing faces and bodies were the extent of its collection. I hadn't realized there were more of those too.

"Which Reapers died?" I had only met a few, but they were my co-workers. It seemed rude not to ask.

"Ivar, Kareem, and Leila." Death spoke their names in a reverent whisper. I hadn't met any of them, but I still found myself struck by how human their names were. I wondered if Kane remembered everyone he had lost—all the souls that never made it to their final resting places. Looking at the twisted expression on his face, I suspected the answer was yes.

"Weaker or not, I am…grateful to you," he continued after a moment of thought. "Neither of you should have had to face a threat like that yet. And not only did you survive, you protected the soul that had been trusted to my charge."

Had Death just thanked me? That was unexpected. Maybe Pluto wasn't as much of a tattletale as I'd thought. I put on my supernatural thinking cap and tried to look at this situation from his perspective. In a way, Kane was like Orion with the Hunt. The souls of mortals were his domain, his responsibility. If one was stolen, it would weaken him to some degree. Maybe not on a physical level, but it would demonstrate that he couldn't protect his domain.

Immortals and their ilk are all apex predators. A king who cannot protect his kingdom isn't likely to remain king for very long—just ask Pluto. If it were my old mentor sitting across the table, he would be thanking Alex and me for defending something under the Hunt's protection. From that point of view, Wilbur and I were up for Employee of the Month.

"Of course, sir," I managed in an embarrassed tone. "It didn't sit right with either of us, letting that thing drag Mason into the dark." I nodded as Death fiddled with his hands once more. Something in his hesitation told me there was more to this meeting than a debrief.

"It seems that you are a more competent warrior than most

of my servants," he admitted, still watching me closely. "I suppose given the teacher you had, that is no surprise."

Even Death respects the Hunter. I promised myself that if I ever saw Orion again, I wouldn't tell him that little fact—there'd be no living with him. It would be as if Bacchus appeared out of the forest and told some winemaker that he loved their wine.

Three Reapers had just died to the Lost, while we had survived an attack. If there's one thing I've learned from being employed, it's that doing a good job has a bad habit of getting you more responsibilities without a raise.

"Uh-oh," was all I said. I thought I knew where this was going.

"There is an oversized shipment due for delivery to one of the Underworlds, and I am light on guards. There have been too many disruptions lately and we cannot afford another one. I'm going to send you with the convoy."

"I could barely tickle a weak member of Legion," I protested. "What am I supposed to do against a stronger version on the far side of the Veil?"

Death's heavy gaze settled on me, and if there had been an actual beating heart in my chest, it would have stilled under the weight of that stare. I got the sense that he was judging me, trying to decide if he could trust me. I felt a tiny twinge of guilt somewhere in my chest.

Despite his unfortunate duty, Kane didn't seem like a villain. He was an elemental force, a fact of life. But he took the protection of his souls and the execution of his duty seriously. Sure, he was *Death*, but he didn't take some horrific delight in what he was. He didn't seem to be involved in the actual timing of someone's end, only collecting them when their Time was up. He was more janitor than murderer.

He must have seen whatever he was looking for, because after a moment, he let out a frustrated grunt and rose to his feet. Wordlessly, I copied him, as if he were a king. He gestured to the open area of his office where he had given me his power, and we met in front of his bookshelves.

Slowly, he pulled off his gloves, revealing a pair of leathery, weathered hands that looked like they were used to hard work. His left hand had the golden ring with the white stone that I had seen before. But on his right, he wore a ring that I didn't recognize. It coiled like a black serpent and was carved to look like a leering human skull, with a pair of leg bones beneath it forming an X.

The Jolly Roger is a lot less fun when the guy whom it's made to reflect is holding it instead of some pirate ship ride at a theme park. With another long look at me, he removed the ring, then slipped his leather gloves back on.

"This ring is a mark of my trust," Kane told me, staring at the light-eating jewelry in his palm. "When a Reaper is given access to my power, they must learn to use it over time. As they do my will and prove their trustworthiness, they gain access to more of it. This is why the senior Reapers are used for deliveries: They are stronger than you. This will grant you an extra measure of my Authority."

"You keep using that word."

"Authority?" Kane's brow wrinkled in confusion.

"Never really got along with it." Death rolled his eyes. "But seriously, what is it? What have you given me?"

"Authority can only be held by someone who has Power over a thing." As often happens in supernatural conversations, the capitalization in his voice was obvious.

"Is that different from willpower?"

"Will is different," Kane replied, giving me a surprised look. "What have you seen?" Memories of Polaris, of the mysterious Presence that had shown itself during the battle with Doyle, and of Kane all flashed through my mind.

"Enough," I told him.

"Willpower is the fuel you need to exert Authority," he offered after a moment of thought. "But having fuel does someone no good if they don't have tires. The most stubborn man in the world cannot hold Death at bay. It is like a car sitting on cinder blocks."

"But a man with complete Authority over Death couldn't live forever if he didn't have the Will to fuel it?" I asked, continuing his metaphor.

"Just so."

"So this will give me better tires or something?"

"It will give you direct access to me. No tires needed."

I swallowed.

"But there is a price."

He didn't have to say that. I knew it. There is no other way to get power. Carbon may be the building block of the universe, but it is not as foundational as one basic fact: Nothing is free, and anyone who says otherwise is selling something.

But I didn't care what it might cost. I needed this power. I had a dead king to kill. It took all of my will not to lick my lips as I stared at the death ring in his hand. I could practically taste my Impossible Task. It tasted like apple pie and freedom.

"I'm listening," I managed after I realized he was waiting for me to respond.

"The other Reapers and death gods will seek to kill you and take it for themselves." Kane shrugged as if this weren't a big deal. "Because anyone who is wearing this ring cannot be compelled to leave the Veil when their service has ended, unless they give it up."

My head came up at his words. That sounded like quite a blessing. I could see why. Hypothetically—let's say—anyone who knew that their soul was heading to a fiery, unfun place once their service to Death was over would do anything to get their hands on one of these rings.

"Not even you?" I arched an eyebrow at the original Grim Reaper.

"This ring signifies that the bearer is a member of my lineage," he replied far too calmly.

"You're adopting me?" I couldn't help the incredulous tone that seeped into my words.

"In a way." I wondered if having Kane as a dad would be more fun than Damien. There was a decent chance it would be. "It might be more accurate to say that I am choosing you as my successor." My jaw crashed into the floor as I processed what he had said. That was not a small price.

"I don't mean to be disrespectful, but why don't you protect the convoys yourself? Surely the Lost wouldn't dare strike at a shipment you delivered personally."

A tired smile flashed across Death's face. "Because only a mortal who has died can pass beyond the Veil, and I've never gotten around to it."

"You never died?" I asked incredulously. "How does that work?"

"I suspect that I'm supposed to be the last one out," Death

commented darkly. "Turn off the lights and lock the door behind me." I shivered, realizing that he was talking about the moment after every single being with a soul was dead, when some jerk wrote THE END on the story of the universe.

"Then how would I be your successor?" I asked, thoroughly confused. Nothing in this conversation was going how I thought it would. "Don't you have to die for someone to succeed you?"

"Things go wrong sometimes, Matthew," Kane replied cryptically. Didn't I know it.

"Why me?" I pressed, still confused. "There are other Reapers who could use this power better than I could, even if they're not warriors. I don't think you recruit just anyone to be one of your servants."

Kane was still for a moment, his brown eyes boring into mine as he once again tried to take my measure. There was something he wasn't telling me. After spending so much time with my Faerie lawyer, I had started to develop a pretty good sense for when the game is afoot.

Why would he not want to use another Reaper? What possible reason could he have for using me, the newest member of his crew? Yes, Wilbur and I had fought off Legion, and I was a disciple of the Hunter, but that seemed like smoke—an excuse. There was only one reason I could think of why he would choose me over them.

"You don't trust them," I breathed. Death's eyes furrowed as he narrowed them. He didn't deny it. I took that as an invitation to keep talking. "You think some of your Reapers are dirty, giving souls to the Lost, and I'm the only one that you know for certain *wasn't* involved."

"What makes you think I don't trust my servants? They

received the same promises as you."

"Before I died, I witnessed a Dragon Don try to bribe the Queen of All Fae with ten thousand stolen souls," I replied.

"What?" Death's voice was colder than the grave that he ruled. I flinched against the icy fury in his words. He might not be a monster, but he was *terrifying* when he wanted to be.

"She didn't accept them, but I'm guessing that the Lost somehow provided—"

"The Lost are mindless devourers! They don't steal, they don't plot, they don't barter," Kane interrupted with a snap. He spun away from me and began to pace along the glass panes of his office like a caged tiger. "You can't negotiate with something that is only made of hunger. It doesn't need anything else."

I stood in silence as he paced out his fury. "You're sure that this Don had these souls?" He paused mid-stride to fix me with a stare. "He wasn't bluffing?"

"The Queen turned him down. I never personally saw any souls, but I think he had them. He made a comment about things 'falling off trucks' and getting lost."

"Then it is worse than I feared," Death murmured to himself, his eyes unfocused. "They must have found a way to control the creatures."

"Who? The Dragon Dons?"

Once more, he raised his gloved hand and held it forward, the black ring gleaming darkly. "You are right, Matthew. I do not know if I can trust my own Reapers, and I recently lost my most trusted ally. I need more Reapers to protect the shipments if we are going to keep the order of the universe flowing."

"But since it's been going on longer than I've been here, I'm the safest choice?" I prompted, finishing his thought for him. I stared at that cold ring in his hand, wrestling with my dread. I needed the power if I was going to be able to kill Midas before my time ran out, but I also didn't want to become Death's understudy.

Not even a little bit.

"That is part of it," Kane agreed.

"And the other part?"

"I've always considered the Hunter to be an excellent judge of character." Death shrugged as if slightly embarrassed. He really was a fan. "I don't think that any student of Orion would stand by while innocent souls were stolen and abused."

I closed my eyes for a moment as guilt settled around my ankles to weigh me down like a pair of cement shoes. He had a point. If Orion were being offered this ring, he would already have been wearing it. I let out a long sigh. "No, they wouldn't," I agreed.

I wanted to tell him to shove it. That I was here to do a job and do my time. But I felt the example of my master pulling at me like the damn Pied Piper's siren song.

I scooped up the ring and slid it onto my right ring finger. A deeper cold than I had ever felt, like the center of Winter's heart, settled around my finger. It was a twin flame to the dark power that Death had already given me, but denser.

"Reach out to my Authority through the ring," Kane commanded.

I did as he instructed, looking inward to where the darkness he had already given me lurked. But this time I found something new. A beacon of shadow shone on my finger like an inverted lighthouse. Instead of grasping for the scythe directly, I poured my will through the ring and threaded it to where the darkness waited.

The power roared as it surged into me through the ring, as if I were wearing a magnifying glass. Absolute coldness settled across my body. Whatever amount of Kane's nature I had used before was but a sliver of the vast and insatiable power of Death.

My knees buckled as my body responded to the torrent pouring through it. I would have fallen, but the Grim Reaper caught me with his gloved hand, his brown eyes looking almost sympathetic.

"It's a lot," he said.

"What, the entirety of your power? Nah, barely noticed," I panted as I got my feet back under me. "Is it cold in here, or is it just me?"

"You'll need to use it sparingly," he warned, eyeing me with the same bemused disapproval with which most Immortals greeted my sarcasm. "Your soul will adapt to the power over time. But in a pinch, this will let you draw on more of my Authority than you could otherwise."

"So I still have to grow my personal connection, and this is just a brief burst of power?" I asked, thinking deeply. If nothing else, the ring would let me train my own access to the scythe faster, which would in turn help me finish off poor Midas.

"The more you use it, the more you will be able to handle," Death confirmed. "It takes time for a soul, the *thing* of life, to get used to carrying me with it." It made sense, sort of a matter-and-antimatter kind of thing. Romeo and Juliet, I dunno. I'm not a scientist, and the only ones I know killed me, so I'm not sure I trust them.

"Does this mean I'm your heir now?"

"Technically." The Grim Reaper chuckled as if that weren't terrifying. "But you don't need to worry about it anytime soon.

My work is far from done."

"You been to a doctor recently? Had a colonoscopy? I don't know how to tell you this, but I'm something of a bad-luck charm for Immortals. They tend to drop dead around me." I was beginning to think I should have said no. I mean, the man had said that I could give it up if I wanted to, but what if he died while I wasn't looking?

"Matthew, I have been alive almost since the beginning. I am very tired, but still just as here as ever." Kane gave me a thin smile. "My final hour still feels eons away."

"Well, from now on you're getting all your essential vitamins and minerals," I told Death to his face. "I'm willing to help you figure out how souls are being stolen, but I have no interest in taking over your spot."

"The convoy is waiting for you," he told me. "The sooner you start, the sooner you can give me that ring back."

"Where are we delivering these souls anyway?" I suddenly thought to ask.

"Right to the Gates of Hell."

It seemed that I had an appointment at my final destination a few years early.

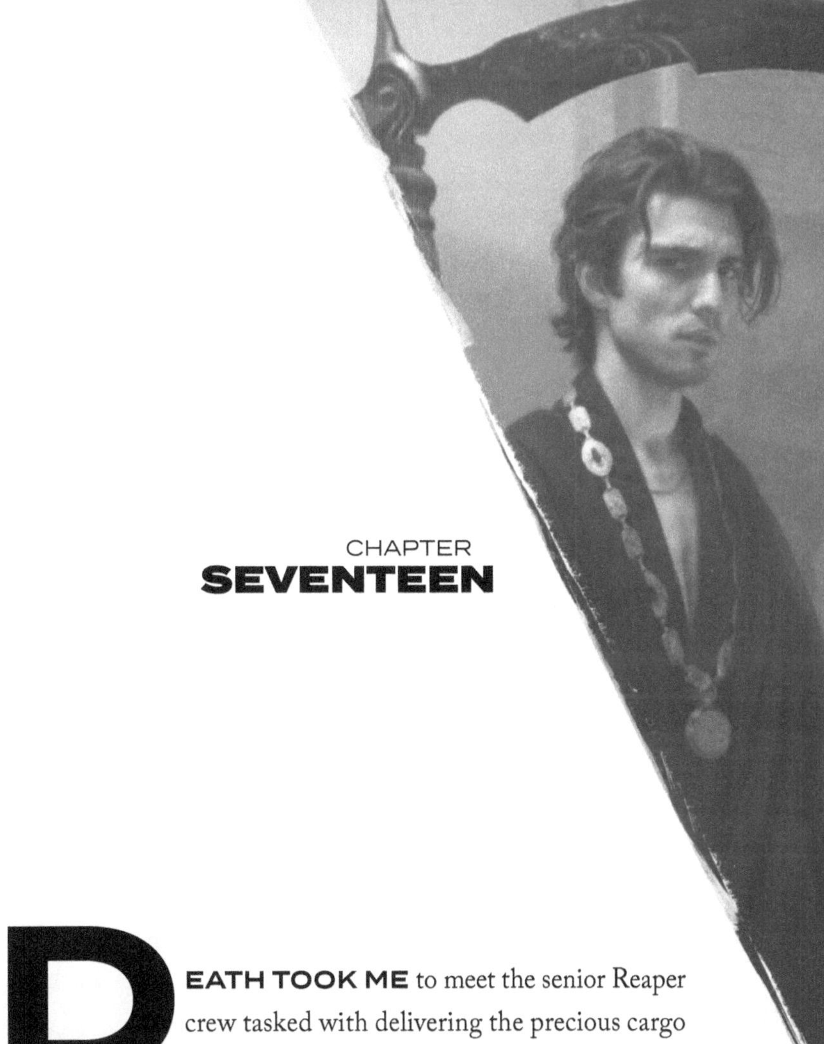

CHAPTER
SEVENTEEN

DEATH TOOK ME to meet the senior Reaper crew tasked with delivering the precious cargo to Hell. I might not have been as eager to sign up if I knew people's souls were being prevented from going to the fiery Pit. In my head, I had thought about folks missing out on their chance at Paradise or something.

I'm sure getting eaten by the Lost in the murky edges of the Nothing isn't pleasant, but could it be worse than *Hell?* That seemed sort of impossible. The whole point of Satan's domain was to be the land of eternal suffering, right? I also didn't have any sympathy that the guy might miss out on getting some of his pieces of the mortal pie. He was currently set to gain my soul illegitimately; I didn't really feel like helping him collect some of the ones he was owed.

"Are all of the souls that are missing from Hell?" I asked Kane as we walked.

"No," the Grim Reaper replied, giving me a knowing look. "Shipments to many of the Underworlds have been hit."

"But not all of them?" I pressed, noticing a tone in his words.

"Not all of them," he confirmed. "Most of the places that have been affected are not in a position to do much about it."

"Do you mean from a power standpoint?"

"The places of Damnation tend to be less likely to make a fuss. They're all stealing from one another anyway." That made sense in the same way the mob wouldn't call the cops if another gang stole from them.

"So, whoever is involved in this is trying to be annoying, but not so annoying that they get squashed by the superpowers?"

"Exactly."

I let that information digest for a bit as we made our way deeper into the soul sorting facility. "That means they're smart."

"They might be clever," Death hissed, "but no one escapes me forever."

"Technically haven't a few people…" My question trailed off under the pressure of Kane's dark gaze. So, no answers to the mysteries of the universe today. They do say the grave is the best secret keeper.

Four other Reapers waited for us in what I can only describe as a locker room. Each wore the same black, long-sleeved uniform as me. My heart skipped a beat as I recognized one of them from the office: Yuki stared at me with a dark gaze, her expressions revealing nothing.

"Sire," A big Reaper intoned as we entered. He was a tall black, bald man who rippled with muscle and looked like he had been a soldier or gladiator in his past life. I wondered if I was supposed to be calling Kane by a more formal title. He hadn't mentioned it, but now that I thought about it, it might behoove me to show old Death a little more respect.

"I've brought your fifth member, Rex," our leader rumbled.

"Five? Do we really need to move so heavily armed? The bridge will be unhappy with so many free souls on it," the leader protested.

"We cannot afford any more losses, especially not to this client. This is an overloaded shipment; I don't want to take any risks," Kane replied, dismissing the protest. "Matthew was trained by one whom I respect. He will suffice."

"There's no way the rookie packs enough of a punch to be useful yet," Yuki remarked, her eyes narrowed. "He'll only slow us down."

"He'll be fine," Death rumbled in a *final* tone. "He fought off Legion in the living world on his first Harvest. He's a natural."

No one dared to argue with him after that, so I joined the team. The other two members were both women, fair-haired Foxa and dour Karen, who resembled her namesake in every way.

Rex opened one of the lockers and pulled out a collection of small glass spheres, each attached to a thick golden chain. One by one he slipped them over our heads. Curious, I lifted the ball and peered inside. A nebulous light glowed faintly from within; it reminded me of the light in the soul containers that this factory produced.

"It's a Reality Anchor, rookie," Yuki sneered over her shoulder when she saw me investigating it. Her silver hair was tied back in pigtails, and she was slipping a familiar pair of black leather gloves over her hands.

"What's it do?" I asked, humoring her. At least she wasn't being as rude as before. No one seemed to have noticed my new ring, but I was glad to have a way to hide it for the time being. Nothing good could come from letting the cat out of the bag early.

"It creates a little bubble of reality around you so the Nothing doesn't devour you," Rex answered for her. He didn't look at me, but I got the sense that it was because he was focused, rather than rudeness.

"Don't let that come off your neck, or it's bye-bye, new guy," Yuki sang.

"Got it," I replied, my fist tightening around the chain. Surely there was a better way to secure this if it was so important? "It's soul-powered, I take it?"

"A little borrowed strength from the people who want the mail to keep on being delivered," Rex interjected again, finishing pulling his gloves on. "You don't need to know how it works. Just stay behind me and keep your eyes open." I felt like I had just joined a SWAT team but also kind of like I was dressing up for a Halloween party.

Rex led us out of the locker room and onto the floor of the final sorting facility that Kane had shown me on my tour. Death drifted along behind us, like a parent watching their kid pack for college. It must be infuriating to have all that power and be stuck here inside the Veil.

The roar of the sorting machinery hammered us as we walked to the end of the line, where a row of black trucks waited, loaded with souls. Tension flooded through me. Was I really going to do this?

"If it makes you feel any better," Yuki shouted at me over the hum of the conveyor belts, "this is a black band shipment."

"What does that mean?" I called back.

"Murderers, monsters, and worse," she replied cheerfully. "We do deliveries by strata to make intake faster, so we don't have to stay out in the dark too long."

"How does that help?"

"All the bigger places have some sort of organization system, circles, terraces, whatever. We take them deliveries that all go to the same zone so that we don't have to spend a long time sorting."

"How efficient," I murmured, a little horrified. Although I must admit, it did make me feel a little better about my current role.

As we neared the trucks, I realized that they weren't typical eighteen-wheelers, but more like a modern wagon train. There was a driver's cab on the front one, and two rectangular cargo trailers were hitched end-to-end behind it. Each had its back door open, ready for inspection.

"Okay, people, run your final checks," Rex called. "Verify each soul container is packed up tight, then we roll."

"Come on, rookie," Yuki told me, jumping into the back of one of the trucks. "Let's make sure we don't die." I followed the woman through the shelves of the structure, eyeing the boxes holding souls.

"Do you know why we make sure that everything is sealed before we go out?" she asked me as we did our walk-through.

"So nothing gets damaged in shipping?"

"There are things out there in the dark that can smell a single soul like a shark can smell blood. The crates act as dampeners on the scent to make it harder for them to track us down." I felt a trickle of fear at her warning, and I looked back over my shoulder, triple-checking our work.

"Never go out into the Nothing with an unsealed soul if you want to come back."

"Got it," I promised. Together we exited our truck, and Yuki closed and locked the doors. It was time.

"Karen, you drive. Foxa, ride shotgun." The two women nodded and headed to the cabin, following Rex's orders. "Yuki, you walk on the right." The man turned his serious, dark eyes on me with a frown. "New guy, you take the rear."

"You got it, boss." I tossed him a salute, but he didn't react. I couldn't tell if he disliked me or simply had the personality of an ice cube.

An overwhelming grinding sound emerged, drowning out the hum of the conveyors. I turned toward the far wall in time to see it split into a pair of massive bay doors, slowly opening like the maw of a leviathan. A translucent orange barrier filled the gap between them. The empty dark of the Nothing peered in from the other side, pressing against the glowing shield like a wave.

I swallowed as I stared at that cold, hungry abyss. It hadn't occurred to me that delivering the souls to Hell would require us to walk *through* the Nothing. My trip to the back entrance of Hades had been pleasantly lit and air-conditioned.

But it seemed the front doors of these kingdoms were much less inviting. Nervously, I grasped the glowing Reality Anchor that hung around my neck and stared at it, trying to make sure the batteries weren't running low. It felt like I was on a space station about to take my first walk in zero gravity but had somehow missed out on astronaut school. As I stared into the exposed Nothing, I felt it pull at me, like it had the first time Gloriana showed it to me.

"Breathe, rookie," Yuki commanded from next to me, snapping me out of the lulling trance of the abyss. "You gotta learn not to look at it directly."

"How? It's everywhere!" I gestured at the expanse in front of us.

"Technically, it's nowhere." The cocky Reaper sauntered away, tossing me a wink over her shoulder. I couldn't get a read on her. When Wilbur introduced us, she had been nothing but rude. Now here she was being almost playful.

Whatever her deal was, it was super weird.

"Okay, people, let's move out," Rex called as Death made an impatient gesture. The giant hangar doors finished sliding open and settled into place with a boom that echoed through the room. I shot a glance at Kane, who was still lurking in the corner. He was trying to be stoic, but I could feel the tension radiating from him. He saw me looking and gave me a slow nod, which I returned. Once I was outside of the Veil, he couldn't protect me anymore. It would be just me and the other Reapers against the empty dark.

The truck came to life with a muted hum that was surprisingly quiet. I guess even Death Corp had switched to electric vehicles. On a hunch, I glanced at the orange glow from their undersides and realized the fuel was probably not electricity, but souls. That made more sense. Where would they even get fossils to turn into gas?

I had just enough time to wonder how we were going to

drive the truck through the emptiness when Kane walked to the front of the bay and stood in front of the door. He closed his eyes and raised his hands, his scythe coalescing in his right palm, like a wizard's staff. He raised the weapon and a translucent bridge dancing with all the colors of the rainbow began to extend from the floor, shooting out into the Nothing.

When I was fourteen, our family dog, Shadow, passed away. That first night as I lay in my bed crying, my mother had reassured me that he was in a better place. "He's gone over the Rainbow Bridge to play forever," she told me. Of all the myths that I had discovered to be based in truth, this one was most surprising.

Slowly, like an overburdened ox pulling a wagon, the truck began to roll, heading for the dancing orange barrier and the pathway of many colors. Ahead of me, I saw Rex and Yuki begin to walk along their respective sides of the caravan, easily keeping pace with its slow plod.

As I took my first steps following them, my nonexistent heart began to race. I could sense the unquenchable hunger of the Nothing trying to reach into the Veil and devour us all. Was I really going to walk out into that dark abyss and make my way to the front door of Hell? This had to be the stupidest thing I had ever done in my life.

And that's saying something.

The front of the truck reached the shimmering border and rolled through it as if it weren't there. The second trailer followed, with Yuki and Rex flanking it. Then the third exited the safety of the Veil, leaving me trailing behind the final link, trying not to have a panic attack.

I could feel Death's eyes on the back of my head as I approached the orange force field. I made my feet keep moving, even as every instinct in my brain screamed for me to turn around and flee. Only one thought burned in my mind with each step.

Hell was where Meg's splintered soul was being kept. If I was going to help her, then I was going to have to go there eventually. I might as well walk up and knock on the door on official business, when Zagan and his boss couldn't touch me.

I only had a limited amount of time to save her. If I had to walk through the dark to get to her, then that was what I was going to do. I hadn't come this far only to let fear stop me. The toes of my boot brushed the barrier—I kept walking.

I passed through the edge of the Veil without feeling a thing. I expected the Nothing to be bitterly cold, like how I imagine the void of space is. But it was dreadfully room temperature. I didn't feel it at all. A thin orange cocoon sprang up around me, swirling on invisible currents. It was translucent but added a bit of warmth to the air, like a campfire.

I guess that meant my Reality Anchor was working as intended.

The shimmering walkway rumbled under my feet, like a suspension bridge tormented by high winds. A trickle of fear ran down my spine as I remembered Rex complaining that free souls cause issues for structural integrity. I glanced over my shoulder at where Death waited. Was the Rainbow Bridge strong enough to hold five of us? I'm sure he knew what he was doing, but it would have been nice to hear an engineer's opinion before we walked out into the dark.

Too late now, I guess.

The Veil filled the space behind us, an infinite wall made of solid steel. It stretched as far as I could see to the left, right, up, *and* down. The bridge we were walking on was connected to the only opening, a lonely beacon of light against the immeasurable titan that was the border of Reality.

The convoy kept moving, and so did I, covering the rear as I had been ordered. As I walked, I let my eyes wander. Eventually, the dark swallowed up even the iron wall behind us. We were alone, traveling on the Rainbow Bridge through the Nothing.

I had never felt so small and insignificant in my entire life.

The yawning emptiness pressed in on me. I could feel it eating at my mind like a poison, trying to find a crack in my sanity that it could infiltrate. It was massive and incomprehensible. This thing didn't exist yet could swallow the entire mortal realm like a whale swallows a single plankton.

Nothing mattered. I did not matter. When I was dead and devoured, no one would remember me. I would fade into the night and be forgotten, as all things were. Why was I even trying to get my soul back? No matter how I got shuffled, the darkness would find me eventually. I felt clammy, even inside the bubble of my Reality Anchor. The abyss was staring into me, and not even Atlas could have held up against its weight.

"Get a grip, rookie," Yuki called, pulling me out of my downward spiral. Startled, I glanced up to see that the feisty Reaper had dropped back closer to me on the right side of the trucks. Her dark eyes were fixed on me, and she gave me an arrogant smile.

"Turn off your brain, it hurts less." She turned away and resumed her walk. Her voice sounded dampened, as if it were coming from far away. I guess the void even tore at the sound coming out of our mouths.

"I don't know how to do that," I called back. "Overthinking is my passion."

"Then this place will eat you alive," Yuki replied with a chuckle.

"What am I supposed to do instead of think?" I demanded.

"Keep your eyes open for Lost," Rex snapped from the left.

"Yeah, yeah, our eyes are open," Yuki grumbled, seeming not at all contrite. "Just making sure the new kid doesn't get brain rot on his first trip." Rex grunted but did not protest.

"You can get brain rot?" I whispered to myself in horror.

We rumbled on in silence for a few minutes. I found myself wondering if this was what travelers on the Oregon Trail felt like in the old days, walking alongside a row of wagons for an eternity. It was somehow boring and terrifying at the same time.

I should have gone to the little undead boy's room before we left.

"How long does it take to get to Hell?" I asked Yuki, who was still hovering closer to me than she needed to. Maybe she didn't like being alone in the dark either.

"It doesn't take any time," she scolded me, as if I should know better. Right, there was absolutely no Time this far from the Veil. The second hand on my pocket watch would not move while I was on this mission. I knew that—but we weren't there yet, and I wanted to know how close we were.

"Fine, how many steps does it usually take?" I corrected myself in an exasperated tone. "Is there still distance here? We can use the metric or imperial system, or paces, whatever you prefer."

"It's never in the same place twice," Yuki said, tossing me another grin over her shoulder. Was this really the same woman who had refused to let me speak to her before? Maybe the fact that Death had told everyone I'd fought off Legion had given me some street cred.

"Will you please shut up and stay alert?" Rex growled.

"Oh, relax, big guy," Yuki threw back. "The Lost never hit two convoys in a row. They're probably all fat and happy from the last shipment they stole. There'd have to be something particularly enticing to draw them out of sleeping off their bender."

Rex didn't reply, but his silence was so brittle that I didn't think he agreed; he just figured it was a waste of time to keep arguing. I didn't blame him. The only thing sharper than Yuki's scythe was her tongue.

"What would draw them out?" I asked her, curious. I was new here and needed to learn.

"Something more appealing than a regular batch of souls," she said, laughing. "Who knows what makes those monsters tick?" I had just enough time to remember that Legion had told me I was marked when the howls began.

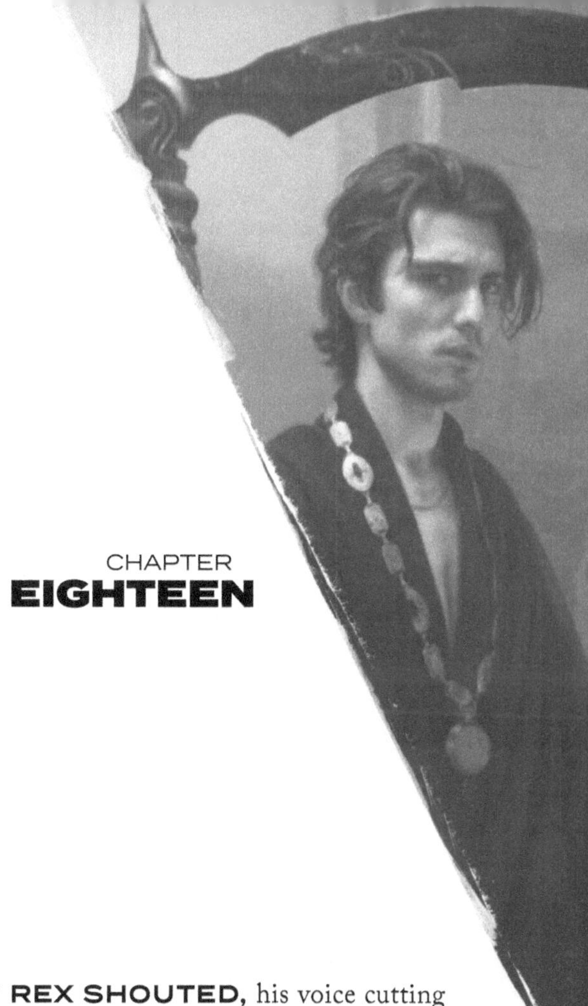

LOST!" REX SHOUTED, his voice cutting through the discordant howls echoing in the abyss. "Form up on me." I scanned the dark behind us, looking for more of Legion's kin, but all I saw was the empty Nothing. I caught Yuki's eye and shot her a questioning look. She gave me a tight frown before turning away.

"Keep up, rookie," Yuki called, coiling her legs, summoning her scythe, and leaping straight to the top of the truck in a single bound. She landed gracefully, like a trained martial artist, and beckoned to me with an impatient wave.

Holy crap. I didn't know that she could jump.

Hoping my weaker connection to Death would supplement my own leap, I summoned my scythe and launched myself upward. Right as my feet left the Rainbow Bridge, I knew I wasn't going to make it. There wasn't enough force behind my jump. But as I soared, I didn't slow down, floating upward like a hot-air balloon.

Of course, I realized with a flash. In the Nothing, gravity also didn't exist. Somehow the glowing walkway exerted its own force to hold us down, but once I got far enough away, it grew weaker. I landed lightly on the top of the caravan, as if I were walking on the moon. I shot Yuki a pleased grin, and after a second, she returned it. Two more figures landed on the front, striding toward us as we joined up with Rex. Karen and Foxa both bore their scythes and grim expressions.

The howls grew louder.

"Back-to-back," Rex ordered.

Following his orders, we formed a loose circle facing outward. I shifted my hands on the haft of my weapon, feeling its dark chill settling into my bones. I guess I was gonna find out if being Death's successor was as much of a power-up as he had promised.

"Don't let them get into the trucks," Rex ordered, his tone serious. "Work together. Karen, you and Foxa are a team. Yuki, you take the new kid."

"What about you?" I asked, feeling like a burden.

"I'll be fine."

"There." Foxa pointed out into the dark, and I craned my neck to see what she had found. I thought I saw a rippling, like the movement of a shadow against a deeper shadow. I gasped as I realized it was a long, narrow ship, like a canoe. Figures crawled all over its black surface like insects. Their screams grew as it drew closer.

"Dark Abyss, it's a full raiding party," Karen swore in hushed tones.

"Good thing the boss sent reinforcements, I guess," Yuki muttered.

"Look," Rex snapped, gesturing toward the center where a giant figure rested, the only one still in the swarm of ants. "They have a Dreadknight with them. Kill him and the rest of them will flee."

"Kill a Dreadknight? Are you insane? Do you have enough Authority to bring one of them down?" Yuki demanded. "There's no way the rest of us have even a fraction of what it would take." Kane's ring on my finger pulsed with cold fire. Something told me that wasn't true. It better not be, because I could die for real out here. In hindsight, maybe it wasn't the brightest plan to entrust my survival to Death. It wasn't really his area of expertise.

"New plan," Rex replied grimly. "Cover me while I cut the head off the raiders."

There was no more time for strategizing. The black raft slammed into the Rainbow Bridge ahead of us, like a Viking ship beaching. Immediately, a dozen figures boiled out.

They were wildly different sizes, but all of them flickered with changing features like their brother that had tried to kidnap poor Mason. They howled in discordant tones as they raced across the glowing walkway toward our convoy.

Behind them came their Dreadknight. The thing was massive; it had to be at least eight feet tall. The Lost Knight was decidedly more non-Euclidean than the Legion it brought with it. It walked toward us on three legs, dragging a sword almost as long as one of the trailers.

It had seven arms, each different in size, scale, and form. One appeared to be just a long tentacle, wrapped around another appendage like a whip. Its face was hidden inside a long, tall helmet that glowed with malevolence, more tentacles poked out of the bottom in a wriggling mass. Horror crept down my spine as I took it in. Something in my mind cracked like a dam under pressure.

This was nightmare made flesh, come out of the dark to devour mortal souls.

"Reapers!" the Knight cried, drawing closer, its pack of Legionnaires crouched in front of it like wolfhounds waiting to be released. The creature extended one of its many arms and pointed directly at me. "Come face True Death!" At his challenge, the host charged forward.

"Let's go!" Rex commanded. We raced across the top of the trucks to meet the wave of Lost sweeping toward us. I still brought up the rear, and I copied Yuki's pose, letting the scythe trail behind me like a tail.

The low gravity let us bound forward, and we picked up momentum like an avalanche as we closed with the leading edge of our enemies. My fake heart raced with fear, and my body thrummed with synthetic adrenaline. At least if I died here, Satan couldn't get his grubby hands on my soul.

Yuki leapt in front of Rex, her pigtails flowing behind her like a shadow, and slashed her scythe in an arc at the leading Legionnaire. The bulbous creature danced to the side with more grace than should have been possible for something that size.

As fluid as it was, it wasn't quick enough to dodge her attack completely. The sharp edge of Death slashed through its left arm like a razor through a sheet of paper. The monster screamed as its limb went flying in a spray of ichor. Its face stopped flickering among all its stolen souls for a second, as if it had to reboot. After a heartbeat it resumed, faster than before.

I had no more time to watch Yuki's fight, because it was time for my own debut. Deliberately, I angled at the smallest Legionnaire. It was tall and thin, like a gaunt stickman walking on two legs, but its face flickered as quickly as its brethren's.

My working theory was that the skinny one wouldn't be as resistant to the weak Authority of my scythe as the thicker ones. Less mass meant there was less for me to digest right? Even though Kane had given me his signet ring and made me his heir, I wasn't in any rush to tap into that power if I didn't have to.

I leapt to the left, twisting my hips as I had seen Yuki do, to let my trailing scythe whip forward like a scorpion's tail. Twiggy was faster. It bent to the side, leaning like a willow tree in the wind. My weapon swished harmlessly through the abyss between us. Off balance, I staggered behind it, a prisoner to my own momentum. Twiggy raised a vicious three-fingered claw and swept it at me.

"Ack," I shouted, dropping to my knees and sliding underneath the Lost creature's attack. Whatever the Rainbow Bridge was made of was significantly gentler on my body than asphalt would have been. It wasn't hard at all, more spongy, like a playground mat.

I leapt to my feet, spinning to face the gangly horror. I focused on its two long-fingered hands and did my best to ignore the revolving Lazy Susan of faces that this thing had devoured. Seeing them was heartbreaking in a way that I didn't have words to express.

I twirled my scythe in my cold hands, trying to get a feel

for it. Twiggy didn't give me a chance to reset, leaping forward and slashing wildly with both claws like a Weedwacker. Trusting my footwork, I let the Lost push me backward, retreating from the trucks step by step, looking for my moment.

Whatever the Legionnaire had been before it ventured into the outer darkness, it had not been a trained fighter. It fell into a mindless rhythm I found contemptible. If Orion had been here, this thing would already be dead.

But seeing as how he was locked away in a timeless prison, I'd have to fill in for the big guy.

Confident in my timing, I stopped retreating as its right claw came through the windmill to slash at me. I raised the pole of my scythe to block the attack. The force of Twiggy's blow shoved the bottom of the weapon toward the floor. I stepped forward, using the seesaw-like momentum to drive the point of the blade into the thing's chest.

The Legionnaire let out a bloodcurdling scream that ground the entire battle to a halt for a moment. Reapers and Lost alike stared at my scythe jutting out of the monster's bony chest. Cold flooded into my hands as the power of Death tried to exert itself over my foe. Slowly, Twiggy looked down at it, as if shocked that it was still alive. It might have been surprised that it still had a heartbeat, but I wasn't.

This was exactly what I had been afraid of.

I didn't have enough Authority to handle even the smallest Legionnaire. If I was going to play in the big leagues, I was going to have to level up. Gritting my teeth against the chill settling in my bones, I reached out with my will toward the dark ring lurking on my finger.

Before I could seize its power, the dark edge of a second

scythe burst through Twiggy's neck from the other side. The tip sliced through the Lost like the dorsal fin of a hungry shark. As it cut, the Lost's face stopped changing, freezing on the tortured expression of someone's grandfather. After a moment, even that disappeared, exposing the empty nightmare of Legion's true face, which had been hidden underneath. It was twisted and wrong, made of shapes I could not describe or re-create even though they were instantly seared into my brain. I knew I would see that visage in my nightmares for the rest of my life. I looked over its shoulder into the wide eyes of Yuki, my savior.

A shriek escaped from the creature. Her scythe pulsed and seemed to drink in the very color from the Lost. A thousand lights, like a swarm of fireflies, erupted from the wound and shot into the blade. My eyes widened as I realized that Yuki was drawing the stolen souls out of the Lost and into her. The Legionnaire's cry grew in intensity, and if I hadn't been holding my own scythe, I would have used my hands to cover my ears against the shrill siren.

Just when I thought I couldn't bear it anymore, the creature's neck exploded in a burst of gore as its head was ripped from its body. The tall Legionnaire crumpled like an empty balloon, revealing Yuki on the other side, a cocky grin on her face. "Need some help, rookie?"

A host of lights pulsed from under her flesh. I've heard of people glowing, but this was ridiculous. Before I could thank her for the save, a second scream tore through the night, this one distinctly more human.

I spun in time to see Karen writhing in the grasp of the Dreadknight. Its whiplike tentacle was wrapped around her throat, while more of its seven bulky arms grasped her head and legs. I watched in horror as Karen's scythe fell from her fingers, vanishing before it could land on the Rainbow Bridge.

Rex let out a roar of rage, trying to battle his way past a pair of Legionnaires. Foxa was nowhere to be seen. "Dark Abyss," Yuki swore as the Knight began to *pull*. Its bulgy muscles rippled while Karen screamed in pain. With a horrifying, wet pop the Reaper's head popped free of her body in a spray of blood.

Another soul lost to the hungry dark.

The Dreadknight dropped her body to the ground like an empty wrapper, raising its grisly trophy to anoint its towering helm. Blood dripped down the dark metal.

Behind him, one of the Legionnaires exploded in a burst of light as Rex's scythe cut down another of the Lost. Apparently satisfied with its horrifying ritual, the Dreadknight hurled Karen's head off the bridge into the abyss before turning to fix its attention on Yuki and me.

"Do you have enough juice to kill that?" I asked her as the monstrous Lost took a ponderous step toward us. Its massive sword still trailed behind it in one of its many hands.

"No." For once the Reaper's voice wasn't brimming with brash confidence. Startled, I glanced at her, but her attention was focused on the Dreadknight. A small frown creased her face.

"Maybe if we tag-team it?" I offered.

"No offense, rookie, but I'm not sure you can even *cut* it." There was no condescension in her voice, just a tired practicality. "No one's seen a Dreadknight for eons. I wonder where this one came from."

"What makes it different?"

"It's an aspect of Legion that's feasted on enough stolen souls to warp into something worse." The creature took another step toward us. It didn't seem to be in a particular hurry. Then again, it wasn't exactly in danger.

"So we run cover for Rex so he can handle the big guy?" I suggested. At this point we just needed a plan. The senior Reaper was still battling three Legionnaires in a fury, his weapon slowly carving them up bit by bit.

"Can't." She shook her head, still staring at the Dreadknight. "If we rabbit, it will just start eating." She gestured to the trucks behind us brimming with fresh souls for it to devour.

Silly me, I hadn't realized that we were the only thing between it and its feast. That's why it wasn't in a hurry: It was hoping we would run. It didn't care about us, it just wanted to eat.

"Would that really be so bad?" I grumbled, remembering where this delivery was destined. "We're not exactly protecting the crown jewels of society here."

"I don't know about you, but I have no desire to see how much stronger it can get." Yuki scolded, but there was no heat in her voice. After a moment, I nodded. Things can always get worse.

"So we slow it down until Dad can come and save us? Got it."

"Don't let it grab you," she warned.

"Yeah, picked up on that." Its tentacle was wrapped around one of the other arms again, coiled until it was needed. The cold steel of Death's signet ring burned on my finger like a beacon.

"Follow me, keep moving." Yuki dashed forward, letting her scythe trail behind her once more. I copied her, angling myself toward the other side of the Dreadknight so it would have to pick one of us to strike at.

Well, in theory.

I hadn't fought anything with seven arms and a completely

distorted sense of reality before. For all I knew, it had some sort of spidery compound-eye situation going on underneath its towering helmet that would let it track both of us. But in the absence of knowledge, I had to do my best with what I had.

Yuki shot past the lumbering titan's left side, her scythe striking out like a streak of lightning. Her weapon's edge sliced the Dreadknight's armored leg, and the creature squealed in protest. Then she was behind it, sprinting to get out of range of its arms. If she had managed only a little scratch, I had a feeling that my Authority wouldn't even dent the plate. Steeling myself, I reached for the burning cold of Death.

But the Dreadknight had other plans.

Its tentacle arm shot out at blinding speed, suckers pulsing. With a squeak, I gave up on trying to summon my power and twisted to the side, dancing out of reach of the horrifying appendage. Cognizant of Yuki's warning, I started running as soon as my feet landed.

The Dreadknight spun, swinging one of its giant arms at me in a vicious hook. The monster had taken its time wandering toward us, but it was startlingly fast under all that armor. I dropped to my knees again, letting the strike pass over my head. This time I could feel my hair dance in the wake of its attack.

Unfortunately for me, that dodge cost me all my momentum. I looked up at a whistling sound just in time to see the Dreadknight's massive sword rise over its shoulder like a tsunami of steel. I had only a second to dive to the side in a roll as the weapon crashed down on the Rainbow Bridge with enough force to rattle the teeth in my head.

For a moment, I could only stare at the pillar-sized blade lying on the ground a few inches from my face. I've had some near-death experiences, but this one was close enough to shave with. I had almost been sent to the dark forever.

"Rookie! Keep moving!" Yuki's command snapped me out of my stunned pause.

I scrambled out of the way as one of the Dreadknight's three feet came stomping down right where I had just been. I sprinted out of range of the monster. How were we supposed to kill something like this? It didn't have any weaknesses, just more strengths.

That was a dumb question. I knew how I was supposed to kill it. Death himself had told me how to do it. And he had also commanded me to keep my new power secret. So what was I supposed to do when none of my allies had enough Authority to challenge a Dreadknight?

A shrill scream echoed behind me as Rex reaped another one of the Legionnaires he was battling. I glanced over my shoulder to see that his dark skin was almost translucent from the lights of all the souls burning within him—as if a million fireflies were crammed inside his body, jockeying for a place. A twisted expression crossed his face, like a man who's just finished one too many slices of pizza. I didn't think he could hold much more.

I was going to have to disobey Death.

Yuki flashed by the Dreadknight again, her scythe aiming for the same ankle. But the monster had seen that move before and was smart enough to not fall for it twice.

With its unnerving speed, the creature charged the small Reaper like a linebacker trying to tackle a gymnast. Quick on her feet, Yuki leapt to the side, aborting her attack.

The Dreadknight stormed through the empty air past her

like a rhinoceros, and I let out a small sigh of relief as my partner managed to avoid being crushed. But my joy turned to horror as the monster's tentacle arm snapped out behind it like a lasso, wrapping around Yuki's neck. The Reaper had just enough time to look at me in terror before she was jerked off her feet. Her scythe vanished as her hands flashed to her neck.

"Yuki!" I shouted, chasing after them.

The Dreadknight ignored me, maintaining its charge down the Rainbow Bridge toward the convoy of souls. And why shouldn't it? Rex was still occupied by its soldiers, Yuki was under control, and I wasn't a threat.

Well, maybe that last part wasn't as true as the Lost thought.

"Hey!" I shouted at the monster's back. It ignored me, dragging my comrade and its massive sword across the bridge behind it. Slowly, I let my sprint peter out until I was still. Yuki stared at me with wide eyes, still struggling with the tentacle around her neck.

There was no point in me chasing the creature like this. I had to show it something that it couldn't ignore. I had to use the ring. I hoped Kane would agree with my decision. With a gesture, I banished the scythe in my hands. Warmth began to flow back into me, but I ignored it. No use in getting comfortable—I was about to plunge into even colder depths.

I gritted my teeth and set my stance, mentally *and* physically, for the onslaught that I knew the ring would bring. Last time it had caught me off guard, but now I knew what to expect. With a long breath, I reached out with the Authority that Kane had given me and channeled it through the ring that marked me as his heir.

Glacial fury poured down on me with the force of a fire

hydrant. I staggered as the frigid power filled me and consumed me—staggered but did not fall. Hunger bloomed in me like a fire. Slowly, I raised my head and unbent my back as I struggled for control of the source inside me.

A Presence bloomed in the emptiness that did not belong. Death might be barred from passing through the Veil, but for a moment his power was here in its entirety. It was like a single malicious eye glaring down on us.

I was numb, I couldn't feel my toes—forget about them, I couldn't feel my legs.

The two Legionnaires fighting with Rex froze like deer in the headlights as the power washed over them. I felt a vicious satisfaction as my Reaper cut them down with my own power, reclaiming a part of me that had been lost.

"LOST ONE," I called, channeling a power that was not my own.

This time the Dreadknight heeded my call. The monster paused mid-stride. Slowly, it turned to face me. Its massive helm tilted as it studied me, like an insect trying to solve a logic puzzle.

Guided by an instinct that I didn't understand, I took my gloves off, tucking them in one of my pockets. Kane's dark ring pulsed in time with the hunger inside me. Without another thought, I began walking toward the creature.

The Dreadknight let out a vicious battle cry and charged, releasing Yuki from its tentacled grasp. Its footsteps shook the Rainbow Bridge; six of its arms spread out, ready to strike.

Fool.

The Lost Dreadknight thundered toward me, and I walked forward to meet it, empty-handed. Why didn't I have my weapon? Because I didn't need it anymore.

I was the weapon.

As the monster lumbered into range, the last of its massive arms bulged, bringing its long sword up and around in a vicious arc designed to slice me in half. I bent my knees and leapt, using the lower gravity of the Nothing to my advantage. I shot forward, getting inside the strike's arc before it passed harmlessly behind me.

Practically floating, I brought my feet under me and landed smoothly, resuming my walk. The Dreadknight was almost close enough. It let out a keening wail of rage as its attack failed to land, and the cold part of my brain smiled as I saw it backpedal, trying to halt its charge. I didn't pick up the pace. There was no need to hurry. Death comes when it comes.

Too late it realized that it was no longer the apex predator on the bridge. The Lost raised its sword again to bring it down in another smashing blow, but it was a futile effort. I shot forward like a spear, my hands extended.

The massive beast had too much bulk to start reversing before I could grapple with it. I slammed into the Dreadknight, both of my hands grasping one of its many arms. It let out another keening wail—this one full of fear instead of rage.

With a thought, I released my hold on the cold hunger that filled me to the brim. It raced out like a starved tiger after a fresh steak. The Knight screamed as Death's dark power poured into him, struggling in my grip. Even though it was physically stronger than me, it had no hope of breaking my grasp. I was no longer just Matthew Carver.

I was the Starving Dark.

The Eternal Hunger.

The Unfillable Void.

That Which Devours All Things.

I was Death.

I pulled with the hunger, urging it to devour him. In some ways it was like an inversion of Willow's power, it had the same desire to consume, but was frigid to its core. The Lost let out one final scream as its defenses were overwhelmed by that frozen fire, and I gasped as lights burst from the creature and raced into me with the sound of rushing wind.

It was like staring into the high beams of a hundred oncoming cars. Slowly, the chill began to retreat, pushed back by all the *life* I was carrying inside me like a proud seahorse father.

Heat began to build in me like a raging fire, and I didn't know if I could bear it. Each soul that Death's power ripped from the Dreadknight felt like one too many. But the hunger didn't care. It was not full, so it kept eating. Death had been robbed and neither it, nor I as its heir, would be satisfied until every single one of the lost souls was back in our possession.

I closed my eyes as I braced against the building pressure, but it didn't help. The light behind my eyelids was just as blinding. At some point my mouth opened, and I started screaming in harmony with the tortured sounds coming out of the Lost in my grasp.

As the flood of souls built to a crescendo, I cursed Kane for sending me to die in the Nothing. Whatever fire hydrant of power he had given me clearly should have come with an instruction manual or warning label.

With a pop, the last glowing orb shot out of the Dreadknight and into my chest. Surprised, I staggered back a half step as Death's Presence winked out, finally sated. The Lost slumped as I released it, then began to collapse in on itself, as if all its bones had turned to jelly. Horrified, I watched it implode, its stained armor clattering to the ground as the being that had filled it turned into liquid before my eyes.

My attention was diverted from the melting monster at the sight of my hands. They glowed like the sun was shining from the other side of my flesh. As I inspected my wrist closer, I saw that there were many small lights dancing and twisting through my body like blood cells. I half expected to be able to see the shadow of my bones as they moved.

My head came up at the sound of a footstep behind me. The two living Reapers had approached while I was distracted. Each of them still carried their scythe, and both had apprehensive looks on their faces. Yuki's flesh had a light glow from the souls she carried, and Rex's dark skin shone even brighter, but neither of them could hold a candle to the incandescence that was clinging to me.

"Guys, I can explain," I promised, raising both my hands as they stared at me, eyes full of distrust.

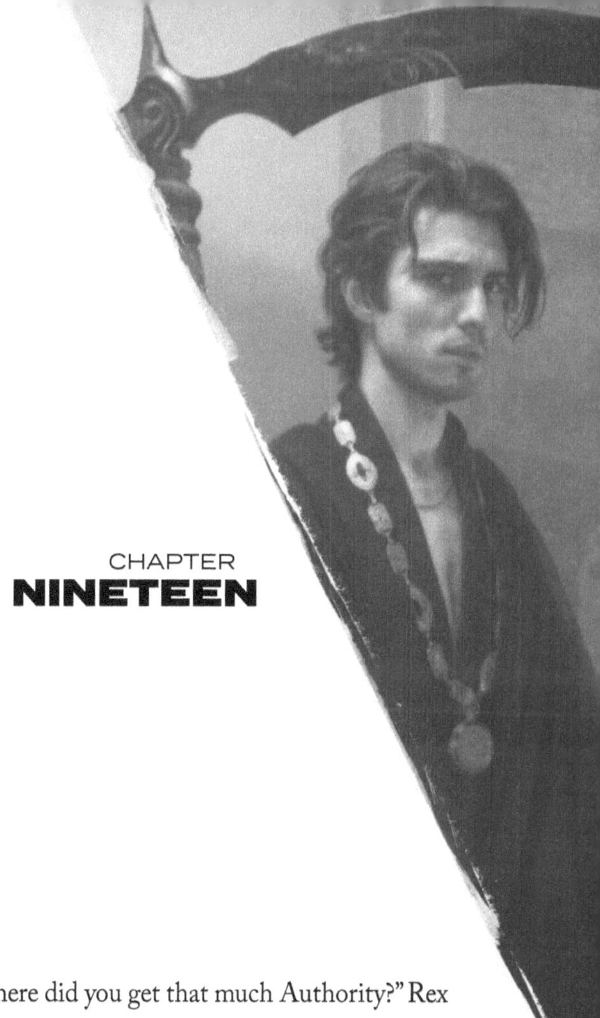

Where did you get that much Authority?" Rex demanded, waving his scythe in my general direction with enough force to make me feel a little uncomfortable. I probably would have felt more threatened if the three of us weren't twinkling like we had just survived some sort of glitter fight. There's just something about everyone's skin glistening that drains the tension out of a scene.

"It was like *he* was here himself," Yuki breathed in agreement. "I don't care how much of a prodigy Old Grim said you were, there's no way you pulled that out of nowhere, Rookie."

"You're right," I admitted, nodding at the black ring on my finger. "I had help." Yes, Kane had told me to keep this to myself, but I'd sucked all the souls out of a Dreadknight with my bare hands; there wasn't much room left to fudge the truth with.

"Dark Abyss," Rex swore. "Is that what I think it is?"

"Probably?" I replied with a shrug. "He told me it would let me channel enough of his power to be helpful out here."

"An heir?" Yuki gaped like a fish. "He finally names an heir, and it's *you*?"

"Rude."

"Why would he trust you with this power?" Rex agreed suspiciously. "You're new. Why not one of us who has been here longer?" Something dark flickered through the glowing Reaper's gaze. A chill ran down my spine as I guessed that he knew one reason why Kane had not trusted any of his existing staff. Fortunately, that particular question was easier for me to blow off.

"When I was alive, I was trained by a Nephilim called the Hunter," I explained with a small shrug. "Orion? You might have heard of him. I guess our boss is a fan. He said that meant I was ready for the big leagues sooner." Yuki and Rex both stared at me for a moment, blank expressions on their faces.

Even if they weren't traitors, I understood their skepticism. Whenever the new guy gets promoted over the people who have been at a job for a while, it upsets the apple cart. Who was I really? None of us knew that much about the others. We had lived separate lives. The only thing we had in common was that we had all died. Well, or come close enough to count, I guess.

Which reminded me, what had happened to Foxa? I had been given a horrifying front-row seat to Karen's gruesome end, but I'd lost track of our other companion.

"Over the side," Yuki told me when I asked. I shuddered in sympathy. Something told me that was not a swift or pleasant ending. I wondered how long the Reality Anchor around her neck would keep the Nothing at bay before she was finally consumed.

"What do we do now?" I gestured toward the convoy of souls resting behind me, somehow untouched in the violence. "I think we still have a delivery to make."

Rex's gaze flickered from me to the trucks, distrust threatening to boil over. For a moment, I thought that he was going to throw himself at me. The danger in his hard eyes made me start to reach for Death's icy power.

"He's right." Yuki interrupted our staring contest with a helpless shrug. "We survived. The souls gotta get to where they're going."

"Fine," Rex growled, finally turning away from me. "You and the *heir* are on guard duty. I'll drive." Without another word, the senior Reaper stormed toward the cab, his scythe blinking out of existence.

"Come on, rookie," Yuki said softly, gathering herself for another low-gravity leap. "Let's take a walk."

The convoy restarted itself with a quiet rumble as we landed on top of the trucks. I barely felt a bump as Rex drove over the corpses of the Lost who had waylaid us. Yuki was silent for a while as we rolled down the Rainbow Bridge. I stood next to her, staring out into the endless dark.

"Thanks for saving us," she said after a long silence, still not looking at me.

"Oh," I replied, surprised. "You saved me too."

"You didn't need help. You tore a Dreadknight apart with your bare hands."

"But I didn't know I could do that yet," I protested. "It

took me a few minutes to figure out what all the levers on this thing do."

"He didn't train you?" She looked at me now, one dark eyebrow arched.

"He showed me how to turn it on and wished me good luck," I grumbled, still more than a little irked about it. He had told me that I was his heir, but like all supernatural beings, he was extremely stingy when it came to filling in the blanks.

"Well, you certainly managed to figure it out," she murmured, a hint of amusement lurking in her voice. "What happens next, Your Highness?"

There it was. I resisted the urge to roll my eyes at the sarcasm in her tone. But we both knew there was a little bit of truth lurking in that comment, like a dagger under an assassin's clothes. If I was truly the sole heir of Death, that would make me something like a prince—maybe executive vice president, depending on how the Postmortem Constitution structured the government around here.

"No idea," I told her. "Phase one is to get back to the Veil without dying."

"I wouldn't worry about that," she replied airily. "No convoy has ever been attacked more than once." *You've been marked*, Legion's voice hissed in my mind like a curse.

"That's good to know," I said, wishing it made me feel better.

"If I were you, I'd be more worried about surviving once we get back."

The stick then. Fine by me, I've never cared for carrots. "Is that something you can help with?" I asked dryly, not bothering to keep my sarcasm to myself.

The Reaper shot me another look, this one evaluating.

"Maybe." She crossed her arms. "Do you think you need help?"

Before I could answer, we were there. From the distant blackness, dark walls burst into view, emerging from the Nothing like it was a fog. Vicious spikes ran along their edges like some Gothic nightmare. As we got closer, I could see that the whole construction was decorated with the tortured, screaming faces of gargoyles. The Rainbow Bridge stopped just short of it, where a massive drawbridge was lowering. The opening beyond glowed like a red-hot coal. It reminded me too much of being downrange of Doyle's mouth right before he unleashed an inferno from his guts.

"We'll find out," I muttered.

We had arrived at the Gates of Hell.

The doors continued to open like a monster's maw. Massive chains groaned with the strain of millions of pounds of rock and metal. Slowly, the drawbridge descended until it attached to the end of the Rainbow Bridge.

My body began to shake with fear as the front of the convoy left Death's bridge and made its way onto hellish ground. I was about to walk in the front door of Hell. This was a special sort of madness, exclusive only to Matthew Carver. There was no other place in the known worlds that was more dangerous for me.

I should be anywhere but here. With my final eight years and change, I should be sitting on a beach in the tropics, spending my five million demon dollars on margaritas and better times, not knocking on the Devil's front door. Robin better be right about how ironclad our contract was on the collection terms, or I would never make it out of this place.

Yuki let out a long sigh and summoned her scythe, leaning on it like a staff. With a start, I realized that she was also shaking.

"You too?" she asked softly, her eyes full of despair.

Oh.

I hadn't considered that my experience might not be that unique. We were all dead, and one day our souls were going to be delivered to their final resting place. I guess she knew hers too. Wordlessly, I nodded, not trusting my voice to work.

"The cold helps." She nodded at the black weapon next to her. "But it never gets easier."

Reluctantly, I followed her advice, calling on Death's Authority, letting my own Reaper weapon fill my hands. True to her word, the frigid pulse pouring into me brought clarity like an ice-cold shower before a date.

I was on the clock, I reminded myself, pressing a hand to the frozen pocket watch hanging around my neck. This was my chance to take a look under Hell's hood and find a way to break Megan out. The chance to save my sister was worth any amount of risk.

Yet despite my good intentions, it was hard to feel optimistic about my chances as we passed through the walls of a fortress that towered above me, taller than the Empire State Building. I didn't remember Dante mentioning them. Maybe the Devil and his cronies had upped their security in the last few centuries.

I found myself doubly glad for my scythe's cold embrace. The heat that poured off everything here was *oppressive*. The effect was magnified by the sudden return of gravity's full weight settling on my shoulders like a yoke. I didn't see any lakes of fire, but I certainly felt like I was near one.

The way ahead of us was blocked by another closed gate, so Rex hung left as we entered the compound. Blackened cobblestones clattered under our wheels as I craned my neck, trying to catch a glimpse of my future home.

Everything glowed an evil orange, as if a forest fire's smoke had swept across the sky, hiding the sun. My guess about increased security felt more accurate as the convoy rumbled toward an honest-to-goodness truck loading dock. There were three raised spaces for our trucks, with metal garage doors waiting to devour the souls we had brought.

A pair of red demons wearing yellow safety vests and hard hats stood out front watching us. One of them produced a pair of green, glowing lights like an air traffic controller and gestured at Rex, guiding our approach. Slowly, we backed up, and under the fiends' directions, he dropped off one cargo truck at each of the bays. I couldn't help but be impressed. I never even got the hang of parallel parking; this was a whole other level.

Following Yuki's lead, I leapt down to the cobblestones as the last truck settled into place. Rex emerged from the cab, and the three of us went to confer with the demonic dockmasters. Part of me was worried that they'd recognize me at first glance. Other supernatural beings had been able to *smell* the sulfuric influence of my demonic deal, but if these two fiends clocked me, they made no sign.

"You're late," the first one complained as we approached. This close, I was struck by how similar they both looked to my least favorite demon of them all. While the boss demons tended to look mortal, like Zagan, these guys were bad stereotypes. They had tomato-red skin, thick black fur instead of pants, and cloven hoofs. Horns poked out of each head, and a pointed tail curled out of each butt.

"Ran into a Lost raiding party," Rex grunted, crossing his arms.

"Damn, they're getting bolder," the dockdemon remarked,

flipping through the pages on his clipboard with his long black talons. "How much of the product was lost?" This close, I realized how short these inferior demons were. The tips of their horns barely reached my shoulders.

"None."

Both of their faces snapped up at Rex in surprise. "None? Most impressive. Hell appreciates Death taking the enforcing along these routes seriously." He let out a theatrical sigh as he scanned his sheets some more. "Let's see, this is a delivery for the Seventh Circle, correct?"

"Murderers," Rex agreed.

The scarlet assistant let out a little groan, and the dockdemon seemed like he agreed from the small frown that crossed his face.

"Well, those are class seven, so we'll have to call a supervisor…" he began.

"How convenient, then, that one is present," a smooth baritone voice cut in, making my heart sink. I knew it all too well. I glanced to my right and found myself staring into the black eyes of Zagan, Hell's CFO. He recognized me, that was for sure. The fallen angel's attention was fixed firmly on me as his staff reacted to his appearance.

"Executive Zagan!" the dockdemon squeaked in surprise, dropping his clipboard as he dove into a deep bow that his assistant hurriedly copied. "We were just beginning the intake process for this delivery—"

"I heard; murderers bound for the Seventh Circle, is it?"

"Yes, Your Avariciousness, we were just about to find the on-duty manager to approve—"

"Who is supposed to be on the clock?" Zagan asked coolly.

"Sloth, sir."

"Figures," the executive muttered to no one in particular. "Well, I am here, I'll take care of it." He held out a perfectly manicured hand for the clipboard that lay on the asphalt. The dock-demon turned to his assistant and gestured. Slowly, the smaller demon crouched and picked up the fallen manifest, passing it to Zagan like a terrified deer, ready to bolt at the slightest sound.

I drew on a little more of Death's power, burying myself in its frigid depths to keep myself calm. Zagan was one of the most terrifying beings that I had ever encountered. And that was on *earth* where there were more favorable rules for mortals. I didn't want to know what he was capable of down here in the dark.

The CFO watched the little red fiends scurry around him with a flat expression on his face, like a parent who is fed up with his toddler's antics. "Let's see," he said after a moment, flipping through the documents he had been handed. "Three trucks full of murderers, a supplemental shipment totaling thirty thousand souls." He let the pages drop and fixed us with a skeptical look.

"I can't help but notice that all of you are *glowing*," he muttered dryly. "That wouldn't happen to be some of my product, would it? What's the final number—twenty-seven thousand? Less?"

Rex glanced over his shoulder, tracking Zagan's obsessive stare to me, and stepped to the side. I glared at him, but he just shrugged. I guess if I was wearing the ring of the heir, I had to converse with foreign dignitaries.

"They're not yours," I reassured him, leaning on my scythe metaphorically and physically for support. "These are lost souls that we reclaimed from some Legionnaires who mistook us for prey on the road."

"Matthew, you are practically bright enough to be one of the stars in Orion's former constellation," he chided me condescendingly. "You would have to consume a hundred Legions to shine like that." He gestured contemptuously at the parked trucks behind us. "Perhaps you thought you could deny Hell a little of its due? You wouldn't be the first Reaper to skim off the top of a shipment."

"Or maybe he devoured a Dreadknight," Yuki offered laconically from the side. She hung off her scythe, both hands wrapped up around the top like it was a jungle gym.

"A Dreadknight?" Zagan scoffed, glancing at her for a moment before looking back at me. "There hasn't been a confirmed sighting of a Dreadknight in eons. Besides, none of you would have the Authority to..." His voice trailed off as his black eyes narrowed in the direction of my right hand, where Death's ring gleamed in the orange light. Mentally, I cursed myself as an idiot. After Yuki and Rex figured it out, I had let my guard down. I should have put my gloves back on.

After a moment of studying, the CFO let out a disgusted snort and shook his head. "Regardless, we are owed souls that have been lost by your shipments. I see no reason that you should not make good on some of that debt with these."

My stress exploded as the other two Reapers looked at me with studiously blank gazes. Of course he wanted the extra souls too. I'm no accountant, but I'm pretty sure that they were kind of like laundered money. They must have been reported lost by Death and his staff after they had been taken by the Lost. No one was looking for them anymore. If they somehow made their way into Hell's coffers, who would notice?

I would.

It's one thing to deliver the souls of murderers to an eternity of torment. It still doesn't feel great, if I'm being honest—I'd much rather be the guy who delivers puppies to sick children. But being a courier for the universe's delivery service wouldn't eat at me for the rest of my existence if people were getting just deserts.

Giving the Devil and his kin a bunch of souls that didn't belong to them just because it was easy was something I would never be able to scrub myself clean of.

The tension in the docking bay grew exponentially as I remained silent.

I wasn't going to give him the souls. I knew it, and from the evil glint in his eyes, he knew it too. But what could I do about it? I wondered if the ring marking me as Death's heir would be enough to strike Zagan down. What was it Kane had said when the Death Board adjourned? "One day I will devour you." I didn't think that day had come yet. That would just be too convenient, and I never get to do things the easy way.

So how exactly was I supposed to stop him, standing in his house without a fancy burning sword or any other way to kill an Immortal? I couldn't see a way around it. Which left me only one choice—straight ahead.

"No," I replied calmly, without a plan. "These souls will be returned to the Veil to be repackaged and delivered to their *appropriate* destination."

Zagan's smile widened, as if I had just given him an excuse. "Careful, little Reaper," he admonished. "You wouldn't want to be caught taking a soul that belongs to my master off his property." In a flash I figured out his angle. If he could implicate me in some sort of crime against Hell, he'd have a legal reason to keep me from leaving.

Gulp. Even Death's icy power wasn't strong enough to keep that fiery fear in check.

"Inspection!" a new voice barked from behind us, interrupting our confrontation. A sneer of disgust rippled across the CFO's face as he lifted his gaze over my shoulder. Dreading whatever fresh nightmare the demons had coughed up to torment me, I glanced behind me—only to see the last thing I expected.

A man and woman strode into the docking area, dressed in matching white robes. Both wore burnished golden breastplates over their clothes and sword belts cinched around their waists. Their armor was stamped with a crest bearing three arrows grasped by a hand. But it was not what they were wearing, but who they were that was the most shocking. Two angels of the unfallen variety stalked into Hell, their white eyes blazing.

CHAPTER
TWENTY

LOVELY TO SEE you," Zagan told them with the overly polite greeting that is reserved for a host who hates his guests but can't do anything about it.

I barely heard his remark. My eyes were locked on the weapon that rode on the hip of the woman in front. It was a short sword, with a minimal cross guard and a pommel for one or two hands as needed. The end of the hilt was set with a large ruby that glinted with its own light. A glance at the woman's companion revealed another weapon made in the same style. If that wasn't enough of a clue, the branded scar on my right palm began to itch. That was one theory confirmed.

"Cease any unloading of the delivery immediately," the man

demanded, his white eyes sweeping over me without stopping.

"Of course," Zagan agreed, fake smile still plastered on his face. "We had just begun going over the manifest. You are right on time."

The female angel held out an imperious hand and snapped her fingers for the demon to give her the clipboard. Something ugly flashed through Zagan's expression, and for a moment, angel and demon stared at each other in open distaste.

"The Death Treaty states that any duly appointed representative of a signatory member has the right to audit any shipment of souls from Death or his surrogates—"

"I am familiar with the rules, Kelilah," Zagan hissed, shoving the manifest into her waiting hands. I blinked in surprise at his reaction. I had seen the CFO upset before, even gotten under his skin myself, but it seemed the angels were a sore spot for him.

I guess that made sense, in the grand scheme of things.

"Murderers today, is it?" she mused, flipping through the list. "Excellent." Her finger traced down the sheet before pausing on a random line. She tapped the name twice, looking at me for the first time.

"Let's see item number nine thousand, three hundred eighty-one," she ordered. The two senior Reapers looked at me, making it clear that neither of them was interested in being in charge anymore. I had an inkling of what she wanted, but I figured it was better not to look like an idiot in front of this audience. I gave Rex a nod, and he walked to the first truck, inserting a black key into its ancient lock.

The mechanism turned with a heavy click and a series of dull thuds as some *heavy* bolts retracted. The dark-skinned Reaper swung the door open and leapt up into the cargo space.

Slowly, Rex worked down the aisles, looking for the SKU number that designated someone's soul. It was more than a little horrifying even if they were murderers.

After a moment, he found the orb that he had been looking for and pulled it out of its crate. Cradling it in his hands, he returned, holding soul number 9,381 out for inspection. Kelilah accepted it, holding it up into the air and peering into it, like a jeweler trying to look at a diamond in better light.

My heart began to race as I realized that she was trying to see if the name on the list matched the number. As far as I knew, it should, but I hadn't loaded these trucks myself. Kane was worried about corruption inside his own ranks; what if this delivery wasn't up to par?

"Let's see," she mused, glancing back down at the page. "Frederick Black…there you are." A note of satisfaction entered her voice, like a chef taste-tasing a perfect sauce. "Accepted," she declared after another look, handing the orb back to Rex. "Now let's take a look at truck two." The angel flipped a few pages deeper in the manifest.

"How about fifteen thousand, six hundred nineteen this time?" she inquired.

We went through this same process three times, once for each of the trucks. It was a spot check of sorts. If the randomly chosen soul didn't match the name on the list, the angels would know something was up and could demand to inspect the shipment in more detail.

But as long as the names they checked were correct, the heavenly representatives assumed that every other glowing soul was headed to the right place. It seemed like a pretty casual security system if I'm being honest.

"Very well," Kelilah said after checking the last one. She tossed the clipboard to Zagan with a casual disinterest. "Everything seems to be in order for this shipment."

"As always," Zagan chimed in cheerfully. He seemed a lot less stressed now that the inspection was over. I wondered if he knew more than I did about the corruption in the Veil. Probably.

"Tell me, Reapers, how many souls are you now carrying within you?" It took me a moment to realize that she was asking me the same question that Zagan had. The angel's eyes were narrowed in suspicion as they flicked over my two co-workers to land on me. "You're practically glowing like the sun," she noted.

I felt two gazes on me as my fellow Death employees once again demurred to me. I resisted the urge to sneer at them. I was so going to bring this up at the next all-hands meeting. Gritting my teeth, I gave the angelic inspectors a tight smile.

"None of these are from today's shipment," I assured her. "On our way here, we encountered a detachment of the Lost and devoured them, reclaiming some souls that had previously been lost."

"You expect me to believe that a few Legionnaires had gobbled down enough souls to make you shine like that, Reaper? Be reasonable."

"No," I admitted, annoyed that she also seemed to know what she was talking about. If this was the first time such a heavy hitter had been seen recently, I didn't really want to tell the whole Underworld until I had a chance to inform Kane, but I thought it was probably a worse idea to get caught lying to an angel.

"The Legionnaires were led by a creature known as a Dreadknight. Do you know of it?"

"A Dreadknight?" she scoffed. "They haven't been seen—"

"In eons, I know," I cut in smoothly. "Yet it seems that the Legions of the Lost had managed to raise one. With any luck, it will be eons before we see another."

"You devoured a Dreadknight?" the male angel asked skeptically.

"Where else would I have found all these little lights?" I held my hands out for their inspection, letting them watch the galaxy dancing under my skin.

"What do you intend to do with them?" Kelilah pressed.

"We could sort them here—" Zagan began.

"I'm sure you'd love that," the male angel snapped at his fallen cousin.

"We will be taking them with us to the Veil," I interjected, preventing the Immortals from bickering any further. "They will be inspected and re-sorted under the watch of Death before being delivered to their *appropriate* resting place." I let a little heat enter my voice as I glared at the three of them.

Kelilah and Zagan stared at me with uncannily similar surprised expressions. For a moment they practically looked related. I returned their gazes with as toothy a smile as I could manage. "As is our purview," I reminded both of them flatly.

I had no idea if that was really true. Kane hadn't bothered to tell me what to do if I found any extra souls lying around. But as far as I could tell, Death Corp had been designated a sort of neutral third party whose sole responsibility was to deliver folks to where they were going.

The various Underworlds all had their own marketing campaigns convincing folks to sign up for their particular resort, but all the travel and logistics fell on Death and his merry band of

Reapers. That was what the Death Treaty was all about.

My guess proved right enough. Kelilah snorted after a few seconds and turned away. "Very well," she agreed. "But rest assured that Raguel will hear of this, and our representative will be ensuring that these souls are properly returned to the Veil."

I had no idea who this Ragu guy was, but I gave her a thumbs-up.

It occurred to me that this might be a great time to get some more eyes on my whole soul fraud thing. These two angels seemed to work in a department that would find my situation very relevant.

"What happens if a soul is ever in the wrong place?" I asked, adopting an honest expression.

Kelilah turned to look at me again, shrewishly. "It is returned to its rightful place, and the perpetrator of such a mistake is pursued most vigorously," she replied, her tone full of a hidden threat.

I felt a small smile tug at the corner of my mouth. This random encounter might prove to be the best thing that had happened to me in a long time. "Excellent," I replied brightly. "Because my soul is flagged to go to the wrong place. It seems a demon forged my signature on a contract—"

With a smooth glide, Zagan slid between me and the angels, clasping his hands in front of himself. "I wondered if this might come up," he said, chuckling at the small frown building on the two angels' faces. "Have no fear, this particular young man has had the opportunity to plead his case in front of the Death Board, and Azrael himself was unconvinced."

"Well, that's that then, isn't it?" The male angel replied dryly, turning away from me, leaving the small hope I had in my chest to plummet in free fall.

"See to the unloading, Reapers," Zagan ordered, not even bothering to look back at us. "Kelilah, Mishpat, a moment if you don't mind." The CFO led his two counterparts a few feet away, leaning in to murmur to them in a subdued conversation. Suddenly I realized that Zagan might not have cared whether the souls in the shipment were legitimate, only what I might have said to the angels.

Cursing myself for missing another opportunity, I turned back toward the trucks, following my two co-workers.

"What was that?" Yuki hissed, dropping back to walk next to me.

"Nothing." I waved her question away with a dejected sigh. "Let's get this over with so we can get out of here."

Rex was already unlocking the first truck. As he finished, he turned and tossed the black key to Yuki, who went to the second one and opened it again. The gray metal doors of Hell's delivery bay began to rattle as they rolled open, revealing a small horde of red demons waiting to accept the souls.

Grasping the pattern, I held up my hand. Yuki threw the key to me, and I turned to the final vehicle, feeling an odd sense of foreboding as I undid the lock. This was it—I was about to literally deliver thousands to Hell.

Maybe they had sent themselves with their actions, but I still wasn't exactly comfortable as the doors swung open, and I leapt into the back of the truck. Death's cold ring burned on my finger, and I clenched my hand in irritation. It was a little late to back out now.

I sighed, turning and nodding toward the waiting junior demons. Like the dockmaster and his assistant, they all wore fluorescent-yellow vests. Their orange hard hats clashed horribly with their cherry skin.

At my gesture, four of them ran forward with a metal ramp and set it down, bridging the gap between truck and delivery bay. Another demon pushed a cart forward, and the sound of its rattling wheels somehow filled me with dread.

The worker demon stopped his cart at the edge of the truck and made his way into the back with familiarity. Something told me this was not his first rodeo. A heavy sadness settled in my heart as I watched him begin lifting crates of souls off their shelves.

So much tragedy was contained in these vehicles, and it was only a fraction of the suffering of the human experience. Something existential pressed on me as I took it in. What even was the point if this was the end that waited for so many of us? I hadn't seen any literal flames, but I had no doubt that whatever lurked on the other side of this loading bay was not pleasant.

"Excuse me, Reaper." A snively voice interrupted my dark thoughts. "Need to get at that set of pallets behind you."

My eyes were dragged down by a force stronger than gravity and crashed on the diminutive demon trying to get past me. He wore the same yellow safety vest as the rest of the workers, and this close I could tell that he was wearing a black back brace too.

What kind of demon needs to wear support gear?

A pathetic one.

An inferno of rage erupted in my chest, like a volcano that's been lying dormant ready to remind the world of its awesome power. My heart knew that voice before my brain connected the dots and pulled up the right file.

No wonder Zagan was nervous.

In a heartbeat, Death's power was pouring through me as I drew on the ring for an Authority deeper than my own. The cold strength filled me, and with a single hand I grabbed the short, red creature by the neck and slammed him against one of the now empty frames of the truck.

The demon let out a startled squawk, his eyes coming up to meet mine for the first time. I saw those black orbs widen in horror as he recognized me as quickly as I had recognized him.

"Hello, Dan," I snarled, my voice full of the void.

TWENTY-ONE

DAN THE DEMON, the architect of my suffering, my greatest enemy, clawed desperately at the iron grip I had around his throat. But no matter how fiercely he dug, I felt nothing. The power afforded to me as Death's heir mingled with the rage that was boiling over in my heart to make a perfect numbing cocktail.

"Gack! Hi, Matt," Dan managed after a moment, still trying to pry himself free of my hands. "Fancy seeing you here. Has it been a decade already?"

I held out my left hand and let my scythe fill it with its inky sharpness, which only made the demon's black eyes go wider. "No," I growled. "It hasn't."

"Wait, you're a *Reaper*?" He gasped in disbelief. "How did that happen? I'm pretty sure I didn't put that—"

"You didn't."

Dan went completely still, sagging in my grip like a deflated balloon. His hands flopped down to his sides, and he gave me a mournful look. "Will you please let me go?" he asked in a flat tone. "I don't even need to breathe, man."

I remembered hitting Dan in the face with a baseball bat in my alley a year and a half ago. I might as well have been trying to smash a mountain for all the good it did. My eyes flicked to the scythe, emanating cold power in my hands. How much Authority did I really have? Part of me was tempted to find out. My hand, glowing with the souls hiding inside me, tightened around his neck a little.

But then a more cunning thought wormed its way through my mind. I blame all the time I've spent with Robin. He's a bad influence. "I have a better idea." I grinned at the demon. "Why don't we go have a chat with the two angels out front?"

Dan's face turned pink, which I guess was the same thing as someone going pale if their complexion was that of a fire truck to begin with. "Are you insane?" he demanded. "Do you know what that might do—?"

"Get me my soul back?"

"It would go on my permanent record!"

"You realize I don't have a ton of sympathy for any fallout that you might get for stealing my soul, right?"

"You don't understand," he protested pathetically. "I could get *unmade*." I felt a shiver run through his body that wasn't faked. I didn't really know what goes into the unmaking process, but I assumed it probably wasn't fun. I wasn't planning on dragging him out there anyway. His reaction told me exactly what I had been looking for—he was afraid of them. I could use that.

"And I'm going to *Hell*," I hissed back at him.

"Dude, it's not so bad. We have a buffet."

"There's no way it's any good," I replied, begrudgingly allowing him to distract me from my point.

"Depends. Do you like garbage Parmesan?"

I winced, imaging glorious chicken Parm where the poultry had been replaced by rubbish. "No."

"Okay, it might not be your kinda buffet then," Dan admitted, giving a tiny shrug.

"It doesn't matter," I snarled, shaking my head to rid it of the demon's asinine distractions. "Because we're going to go talk to those lovely white-eyed people from the other corporation, and you're going to tell them what you did."

"Come on, man," he whined, clawing at my hand around his neck once more. "They probably won't even believe you, and then we'll both be in trouble."

I struggled to keep a frown from growing on my face. From the apathetic response I had gotten just a few moments ago, I had a feeling he was right. If I relied on those two glorified border guards to do their job, I was gonna end up in the fiery pits right next to Dan. That didn't bode well for future attempts to recruit them as allies. But it didn't mean I had no use for the little fiend. He was my pathway to Megan.

"Fine, you don't want to 'fess up?" I snarled, inching the black scythe a little closer toward him. "Then let's make a new deal."

A strange expression passed over his features. I'm no expert on demonic emotions, but I would have said that he looked sad. "I can't make deals anymore," he told me dejectedly. "I got demoted."

I resisted the urge to roll my eyes. Gee, I wonder why he might have gotten sent to the Shipping and Handling Department. What possible reason could his bosses have to criticize his performance?

"That's fine," I snapped. "I'm going to make the terms this time."

Dan's eyes narrowed as he looked at me.

"Here's my offer. I won't drag you out in front of the angels and tell them you're the demon that did me dirty. In exchange, you have to help me retrieve something."

"I'm not really allowed to leave the premises anymore," Dan muttered. "My visa got revoked when I got disciplined."

"Perfect. The thing I need is here."

The demon's head snapped up, and he fixed me with a terrified glare. "Are you crazy? You want to steal something from here? What is it?"

"My sister's soul has been split. Half of her has been kept here, trapping her in suffering. I want it back."

Dan's jaw hung open, and his mouth worked soundlessly for a few moments. "You want to lift a soul from Hell?" he gasped at last.

"Half of one, technically," I replied.

"Are you insane?"

"An interesting question," I admitted, blinking in surprise and glancing around my surroundings. "I don't think so, but then again I do think that I'm a Reaper in service to Death delivering souls to Hell right now, so there's a chance I'm just wildly hallucinating." I arched an inquisitive eyebrow at him.

"'Fraid not," Dan told me.

"Well then, that's the offer."

"You don't realize what you're asking. Even if I could get past the security for it, there's no way I'd be able to get it to you. I can't leave, remember?"

"What kind of security?" I asked.

"Her soul is probably being kept in one of *his* private vaults, which are impossible to break into. Plus, even if you managed to get ahold of her soul, it's not like I have a key to let you out the front."

"Let me worry about that," I grunted, trying to stop a wicked smile from growing on my face. "Can you get me to the door?"

"Weren't you listening?" he demanded. "You can't just waltz into *Hell*. There isn't a guest pass or visiting hours."

"I have that covered. It won't be a part of your duties." I insisted. If I could sneak into Hades, why not Hell? Sure, a lot more people worked here, making the risk of discovery much higher. But in theory it was the same thing, right?

"Is there an out-of-the-way room or broom closet I can meet you?" I pressed.

"Hmm, hard to say. The boss really likes to keep it open concept."

I resisted the urge to roll my eyes. Of course he did. "Think harder," I snarled, giving Dan a little shake, my body fueled by Death's strength.

The creature let out a little whine as he rattled. "I am—I am! When did you get so freakishly strong? I'm pretty sure that wasn't in the contract. Oh! You could hide in the Trust and Safety Department's offices. The boss fired the whole team recently."

"Trust and Safety," I repeated dryly, not feeling the need to make a joke. It sort of wrote itself. "Got it. Here's the deal. You meet me there, guide me to where Megan's soul is being kept, and don't tell anyone or sabotage my mission, and in exchange I don't drag your red ass out in front the angels. Deal?"

My heart was hammering so hard in my chest that I was worried he would feel my nervousness through the hand I had clamped around his throat. This was my chance. I was never going to get a better opportunity to rescue my sister.

"How will I know when to meet you there?" he asked nervously.

"How long's your shift on the docks?"

"Thirty-eight more chronons."

I stared at him blankly. "That's some sort of unit of time for places where Time doesn't exist, isn't it?" I asked with a heavy sigh. Dan nodded. "And it's not useful to anyone who isn't in the exact same place of Time not existing, is it?" Another nod.

"Fine," I growled. "Then you wait there every chance you get from now until I show up. From now until THE END. And you're not allowed to report this to anyone. Ever."

Dan sighed but nodded. "This is acceptable," he told me. "Put me down so we can shake on it?"

My eyes narrowed as I watched him for a second. I had never willingly made a deal with a demon before, but it seemed that being dead was making me break all my rules. Mentally I ran through the agreement, trying to find a loophole. I knew it wasn't perfect, but I wasn't smart enough to see any obvious flaws.

Plus, Dan and I had been here for a while now. At some point, one of his bosses was going to notice that the souls weren't being unloaded from my truck and come to investigate. Sometimes you gotta get out with what you can.

With a snort, I released my grip on his neck and let him drop to the ground.

A sense of dread was growing in my gut like a kindling flame, but nevertheless I held my glowing hand out toward him. I had come too far to go back now, and this was a thing worth dying—again—for.

Dan reached out with one of his claws and we shook. His flesh was warm and gross, like he was running a deep fever in his bones. "We have a deal," he said somberly. I hoped that he was as bound to his word as a Faerie.

With a grimace of disgust, I let go and resisted the urge to wipe my palm on my Reaper uniform. I felt like I had demon sweat on me and needed a shower for my insides and outsides.

"What's the holdup in here?" a new voice demanded. I turned to see one of the dock supervisors entering, a frown on his cherry-red face. His black eyes snapped from Dan backed against the wall to the scythe looming in my left hand.

"This idiot was being clumsy," I snarled before Dan could stammer some awful excuse. For a demon he was a terrible liar. I'm not sure what it says about me that I think I'm better at fibbing than a fiend of Hell itself, but here we are. "I told him if he knocked over even one of the orbs, I was going to take it out of his hide." I let the cold hunger of Death fill my tone, lowering the hellish temperature around us a few degrees.

"Well, we're on a schedule," the boss snapped, waving his clipboard at me in irritation. "Stop holding him up. And you, loser, be more careful." With an irritated grunt, he stormed off to check on one of the other trucks.

"You heard the fiend," I muttered, giving Dan a long glance. "Get back to work." He gave me a slow nod and started pulling orbs off the shelves. Not wanting to cause anymore suspicion,

I followed the boss's lead, banishing my scythe and storming out of the truck.

The moment I emerged into the docking bay, I felt the heavy pressure of Zagan's gaze on my back. Slowly, I turned to meet the fallen angel's stare. He was still off to the side speaking with his counterparts, but it seemed casual. Clearly the scions of Heaven were satisfied with what they had inspected. Although how anyone can feel confident when dealing with the Devil and his ilk is beyond me. Familiarity tends to breed contempt, I guess.

I gave the CFO a smile and a wave from my glowing hand as I headed back toward where the other two Reapers waited. He didn't react, but his gaze continued to track me with a suspicious air. His eyes flicked back to the truck behind me, and somehow I was sure he had seen Dan enter it. The CFO knew I was up to something. He just didn't know what. I tried not to let that worry me. Zagan was the second trickiest demon I had ever met, and while Samael was in a league of her own, he was no slouch. I didn't want him thinking too hard about what Dan and I might have been talking about.

"You good?" Yuki asked as I joined them. "Something hold you up?"

"This is my first time," I replied with a shrug. "I don't know what I'm doing."

"Whatever you say, *heir*," Rex grumbled, shooting me a dark look.

"Just because I got a promotion doesn't mean that I'm qualified," I told him honestly. "Feel free to keep running this thing, big guy."

"No, I'm good," he sniffed, crossing his arms.

We lurked in awkward silence for a while, watching the little red demons scurry to empty our trucks of souls like worker ants bringing food back to their colony. The same sadness washed over me as I watched thousands of mortals take their final journey to eternal torment. I knew that most of them "deserved" to be here, but I didn't feel great about the fact that I had to take that at face value. At the same time, somehow my sister had ended up here as well. I tried not to think about the "whys" of it all very often. For all I knew, this was where I was always going to end up too. I didn't know who made these decisions, but from my point of view, Megan was always a better person than I am. And yet...

Through history, lots of people have had lots of rules about how everything works. From here under the hood, though, I saw no answers. It seemed that these Underworlds were only too happy to cast a wide net to keep their profit margins high. It didn't feel right or fair. But what in the Living World is either of those things? Why should it be any different here?

I don't know how many chronons passed, but thirty thousand souls were unloaded in an impressively short amount of time, swallowed by the large metal doors that rumbled closed after Hell had eaten its fill. Zagan and the angels turned toward us expectantly.

"Why are they looking at me?" I muttered out of the side of my mouth to Yuki, since she was the only one who seemed willing to help me.

"Delivery isn't finished until everyone signs," she whispered back.

Of course. How very reasonable and normal. I glanced around our trio and spotted a black clipboard in Rex's hand. I made eye contact with him and held out my hand. Wordlessly, he passed me the board and then began walking toward the trucks.

"Good luck," Yuki called softly as she moved to follow him.

Heart hammering in my chest, I glanced down at the form as I made my way to the cluster of Immortals. It had far too many words that were far too formal for me to process while I walked. I didn't even know what "The signatures hereafter referenced accept delivery of appropriate and proportionate amounts of mortal souls from their entrusted allotment with Death Corp" means, but it sounded important.

Fortunately, at the bottom were three lines that you didn't need a legal degree to figure out:

DELIVERED BY ___________

INSPECTED BY ___________

RECEIVED BY ___________

"Okay," I announced as I approached them. "I just need a couple of signatures and then we can pack up and get out of your hair." I froze as I realized that I didn't seem to have a pen. Rex really was out to get me.

I patted my pockets, half hoping that a writing implement would appear. But apparently the power of Death could summon only scythes out of a hat. My pants remained empty.

"I seem to not have a…" I trailed off as Zagan produced a long black feathered quill from somewhere within his suit, a wry smile on his face. "Thanks," I told him as cheerfully as I could, taking the gaudy thing and signing MATTHEW CARVER next to the appropriate line.

"If I could just get your John Hancock," I said, extending the clipboard and pen toward Kelilah. She accepted it with a strange look, which made me realize that the expression probably hadn't made it to this side of the Veil. Although as far as I knew he was around here somewhere. Well, maybe not *here* but in the neighborhood.

Confused or not, she signed the page with a tight scrawl and passed the kit to Zagan, who paused, making a show of reading the document. I resisted the urge to roll my eyes. Kane didn't strike me as the type to try to sneak something through on a technicality in a delivery receipt. Since I was standing there as his representative, I certainly hoped not, anyway. But I guessed you didn't become the CFO of Hell—or anywhere—by signing things without reading.

"Looks to be in order," he sniffed after a few long moments of silence. Finally, the quill twitched again as he signed with a large flourish.

"Thank you very much." I gave them all a big grin as I took the work order back. Briefly I glanced down at the page and immediately I wished I hadn't. Below my name were symbols that I could not begin to define or explain. The second I laid eyes on them, I felt them bore into my mind like worms, wriggling like living, twisting things. With a grunt, I forced myself to look away, blinking rapidly to clear my vision.

I guess it made sense that angels' real names weren't in English or any other man-made language. But it would have been nice if they warned a guy. The three Immortals chuckled as if amused by seeing a toddler bonk its head on the coffee table. I speared them all with a pointed stare but didn't comment.

"We appreciate your business," I told them through a false smile and gave a cheery little wave before heading toward the trucks. I could feel their eyes all burning holes in my back.

"I'll be sure to say hello to your sister for you," Zagan called after me as I walked.

I gritted my teeth and clenched my fist but didn't turn around.

As I approached the lead vehicle of the caravan, I let out a whistle to get Rex's attention. What? If he was going to be a jerk about my promotion, then I was going to let him know about it. The older Reaper glanced up, eyes narrowing as he realized that he had just admitted that he would come when I called.

I tossed him the clipboard to stow away in the cabin. I don't think bosses do paperwork. That sounds like something you entrust to your staff. Plus, I had no idea what to do with it. Although that was in keeping with the boss theme.

"Let's get out of here," I called. "You drive. We got some souls to finish recovering."

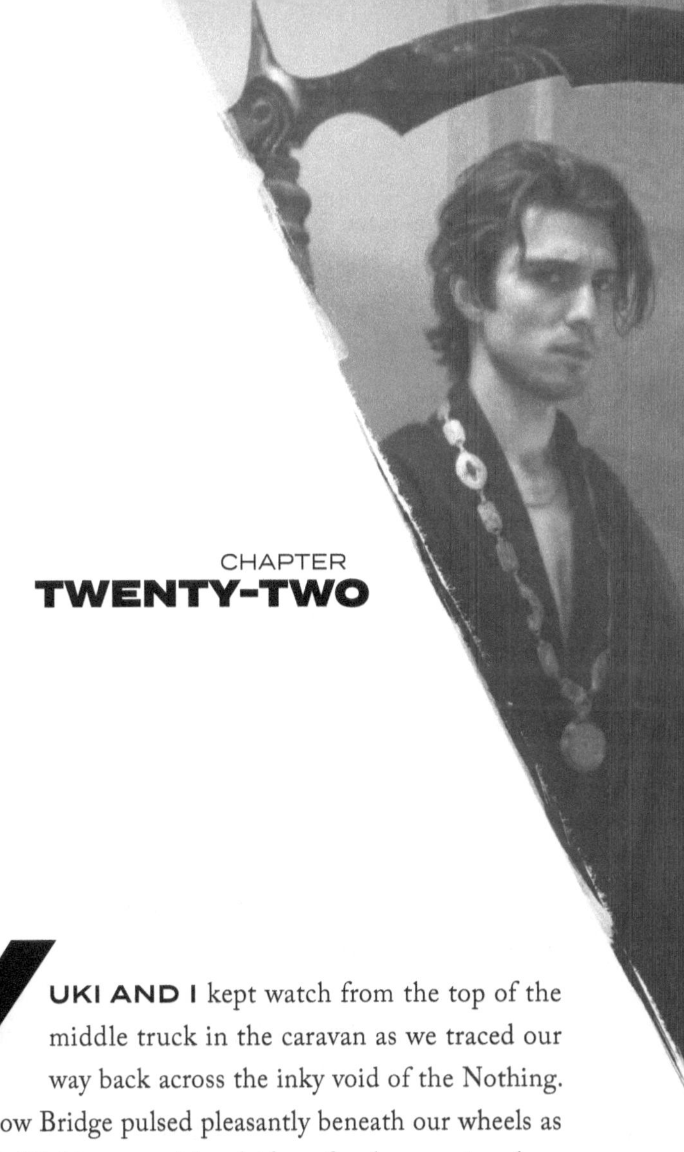

TWENTY-TWO

YUKI AND I kept watch from the top of the middle truck in the caravan as we traced our way back across the inky void of the Nothing. The Rainbow Bridge pulsed pleasantly beneath our wheels as we cruised. All things considered, if not for the yawning abyss surrounding us, I might have thought it was kind of beautiful. Maybe it was, but in the way that the deep ocean is beautiful—and full of terrors. I guess monsters with squid arms come out of the darkness of both of them.

The moody Reaper didn't speak much as we traveled, and I was content to let her have her silence. I needed some time to think myself. Seeing Hell with my own two eyes had made it more of a real place. Now my mission felt like it had a weight to it that it hadn't before. Somehow I was even more afraid of it.

But what else was I supposed to do? This is what I had died for. Sure, Lazarus had threatened me, but that had been less important.

For a chance to save Megan, I'd risk it all.

I knew beyond a shadow of a doubt that she'd do the same. If our positions were reversed, she'd be here wearing the black ring of Death, ready to carve me out of Hell itself. Or, I mused as the stark white Veil began to appear in the distance like a mountain range, she'd have been smart enough never to end up in this situation.

"Much smoother ride back, huh?" I asked Yuki, breaking the silence.

"It always is," she replied softly. "Nothing for them to eat."

"You sure about that?" I held up my hand to show the lights glowing beneath my skin like the Milky Way. "Seems like there's plenty still on the table."

"Fair point." She glanced behind us as if suddenly nervous.

"Doesn't matter now." I gestured at the safety in the distance. "We're almost home."

Somewhere in the darkness a deep horn began to sound, like the awakening of some long-forgotten god. I fell to my knees as my chest began to vibrate under the pressure of its low bass note. Dimly, I was aware of Yuki crashing down next to me. The souls swirling around in my frame squirmed so aggressively at the eldritch call that my whole body shook.

Just when I thought I could bear it no longer, the horn stopped, cutting out like a dream.

The caravan jerked as Rex floored it. Groaning, I staggered

to my feet and held a hand to Yuki, who was still collecting herself. She gave it an odd look before rising on her own.

"What the hell was that?" I demanded, starting to turn to look behind us.

"Don't." Yuki's sharp tone matched the fierce grip that she wrapped around my arm. Surprised, I paused, looking from her intense stare down to the hand holding me fast. "Don't," she repeated more softly. "Some things can't be unseen."

"What do you mean?"

"That is the cry of one of the Elders. To gaze upon their face is to stare into madness."

"Oh, great now I gotta deal with—" I started, but the anguished cry came again, and once more we were both driven to our knees. As I knelt, pressed down by the pain of something I could not comprehend, I stared at the growing presence of the Veil.

We were so close.

This time when the cry ended, I didn't even think about turning around. I had no idea what was following us, but given how weird its kin had been, I was good without that knowledge. I leapt forward to the first truck and stomped on the roof in encouragement to Rex.

"We're good! Go, go, go," I shouted. He must have been able to understand me because the caravan picked up even more speed, hurtling over the Rainbow Bridge like an arrow toward the target that was the Veil.

The white superstructure loomed in front of us now, close enough to see the glowing orange air lock that we had exited through when this nightmare of a trip had started. My naked eye could trace the path of the road leading right into the bay.

When the third cry came, we were almost there. This time I was ready for it, and I dropped down, wrapping my hands around the front of the truck. I didn't want to risk falling off. The other Reapers would leave me behind in a heartbeat.

I must not look back.

I gritted my teeth and hung on for dear life, eyes closed as that call began to bewitch me and make the souls hitching a ride in my body dance. It was a siren call, I realized, daring me to look back and welcome its dark embrace. This wasn't my first rodeo with one of them.

No thanks.

The hum dropped in volume, and I cracked an eye open to realize that we had burst through the open orange bay doors like a bat into Hell. The protective nature of the Veil muted whatever power was calling out in the dark.

Slowly, I sat up and looked around the room. Reapers and soul sorters stood stock-still, staring out into the void behind us with tight expressions. Even Kane himself was lurking apart from the rest, his gaze set on the thing that had been following us.

Well, if they were all looking, I guess that meant it was safe now. I turned and looked back out into the Nothing. The Elder being that moved through it was massive. It's hard to get a sense of scale in the void, but it seemed like this thing could dunk on a hoop at the top of a skyscraper without getting on its tippy-toes.

I could only make out the shape of it as a shadow against the darkness, and even that was strange. Things wriggled and bent, but I could not categorize or explain them. Whatever this being was, I could never even begin to understand it. I just knew how wrong it was.

You are marked, Legion had told me. A chill ran down my spine as I wondered if the Elder was after the souls we stole from its Dreadknight, or if it wanted something else. I really hoped it was just the souls.

After a few moments, Kane turned from the eldritch horror and stared at us. I saw his brown eyes take in the three living Reapers and the glowing souls carried in our bodies.

"Come with me," he ordered, turning on his heel and marching toward the exit of the loading bay.

I guess there wasn't a welcome-back-from-the-abyss party waiting for us. Or cake—I didn't see cake anywhere. With a sigh, I dropped off the roof, groaning in surprise as my knees had to catch my entire body's weight. We were back in Reality now, no more low-grav.

"What about that?" I asked Yuki, jerking my head over my shoulder at the being raging in the dark. "Shouldn't we be, like, battening the hatches or something?"

"It can't cross the Veil," she reassured me as we fell into Death's footsteps. "It'll probably moan and whine for a bit then go back into the dark."

"How fun," I mused, pausing for just a moment to watch the dark shape pace back and forth like a caged tiger. Even through the orange shielding I could feel its dark call tugging at my soul, urging me to come into the dark. Maybe it wouldn't be so bad.

"Matthew," Death snapped. His voice was cold and heavy with Authority, more Grim Reaper than Kane. Startled, I spun to see Yuki and Rex standing next to him looking at me with confused expressions. Huh? I had only looked at the Elder thing for a few seconds…or had it been a century?

"Whoops!" I called, jogging to catch up with them.

"It is dangerous to gaze at one of the Elder Lost for too long, even on this side of the Veil," Kane cautioned me grimly as I approached, his voice warmer.

"Noted," I said brightly. "I must have missed that page in the training pamphlet. My bad." The three of them ignored my comment as we swept out of the loading bay and into the main offices.

"Karen and Foxa?" the boss asked Rex as we made our way deeper into the factory.

"You should ask him." The dark Reaper gestured at me with a flippant jerk of his thumb. "Your *heir* was in charge, not me."

Kane stared at him for a long moment before turning to face me, his brown eyes judgmental. I held up my own glowing hand and shook it, as if to say, *What else was I supposed to do?* The boss turned away from me without commenting, which made me suspect I would get a special lecture later.

I love special lectures. They always make me feel great.

"Very well," he said stiffly. Oh yeah, I was going to get an earful. "First we extract your precious cargo." He turned down an unfamiliar hallway that slowly shifted from the dull white of the Veil to a matte black as we went.

"What is this?" I murmured. A chill began to fill the air. The path deadened into a large round door that was emblazoned with a golden skull, its face locked in a rictus grin. Without a word from Kane it began to swing open to greet us. A thrill ran through me as I realized that this was his vault. Death's power permeated everything here. It felt like an ancient cave tomb with the stone rolling away. Who would dare to rob Death in his own home?

Kane led us through the entrance, and the shadows on the

wall grew larger. My attention was ripped away from the gathering darkness when I saw what was waiting for us on the other side. Rows of shelves were stocked with trinkets that glittered against the dark like stars in the night sky. Everything was made of gold or silver and sparkled with jewels. Each piece sat on a pillow next to a white placard written in a sharp, precise hand.

I'm not the most possession-oriented guy, but this opulence took my breath away. Around the room I saw swords, paintings, and everything in between. They were cool, but my nonexistent heart skipped a beat as I found the crown section. There were rows of them, but one immediately called to me. It was black like the Nothing. Each of the seven gemstones had been carved into a diamond shape, and together they glittered in a row like stars. Even before I read the placard, I knew this was the CROWN OF IMMORTALITY.

I had found it. Now all I had to do was figure out how to get it.

I schooled my face into a still mask as Yuki turned back to glance at me. "The Veil acts like a giant strainer," she explained, nodding at the priceless treasures all around us.

"What?"

"Sometimes people's souls bring interesting things with them," Death answered without turning. "This is my collection."

"Wow, this is the real lost and found, huh?" I tried to look as uninterested as possible, but on the inside, I was memorizing everything I could.

Kane led us down the center aisle to the back of the vault where a larger golden skull was set into the black wall, leering. A door sat in the center of its mouth. We paused just before it.

"Rex, go first," Death commanded, and the Reaper nodded,

slipping through the door without any apprehension, closing it behind him with a heavy click. The eyes of the skull began to glow red, which was either ominous or a sign that the room was occupied.

The three of us stood in uncomfortable silence in the vault. It felt a little like waiting in line for an airplane bathroom, everyone awkwardly standing in the aisle, trying not to make eye contact.

"How long do you think Rex will be in the deathroom?" I asked after the silence became insufferable. "I'm about to explode." Kane ignored me. Yuki let out a reluctant giggle but didn't comment.

A few moments later, the other Reaper emerged from behind the door, his skin no longer glowing with the light of rescued souls. I guess it was kind of like a bathroom then.

"Yuki," our boss prompted, and the woman slipped down the hall and into the room, once again turning the eyes on the skull red. Rex tossed Kane a nod as he passed but didn't pause, beating a quick retreat out of the dark vault, leaving me alone with Death.

Oh boy, lecture time.

"Listen, I know you told me not to let people know—" I started, trying to cut him off at the pass, but he had other plans.

"How did you reclaim so many souls?" he asked softly, his brown eyes boring into mine.

"We were attacked."

"Obviously."

I glared at him but continued. "There were a bunch of Legionnaires, but they had this big guy with them. Yuki told me it was called a Dreadknight." Kane sucked in his breath in surprise. "It was tearing us up. It literally ripped Karen limb from limb with its bare hands. I don't know if Rex himself would have been able to bring it down."

"Because you did."

"Obviously." I gestured to my glowing body with a bit of a sarcastic smile.

Death was silent for a long moment, his gaze fixed on a spot on the wall above my head. "A Dreadknight," he murmured at last. The death bathroom door clicked, and Yuki emerged, also freed from her glowing companions.

"Go," he murmured, gesturing.

Obediently, I started walking toward the door as Yuki came back. When we passed, I whispered, "I hope you flushed."

"Do you even know how it works?" An amused smile flickered across her tired face.

"Nope, no one at this company believes in training."

"Just put your hand on it, you'll be fine."

Not feeling particularly reassured, I walked up to the skull door and stepped inside. The interior of the small room was even darker than the vault. Shadows gathered on the walls like living things. It was empty except for yet another skull. This one, made of crystal, was set into the far wall. Emblazoned in silver above the death's-head was the phrase MEMENTO MORI, which even I could translate. "Remember, you shall die."

A deeper chill settled around my shoulders as I took in the altar. Despite the lack of light in the room, it twinkled as if lit from within. I glanced down at my own skin, which burned with an inner light, and frowned.

Without any other guidance, I decided to follow Yuki's advice and stepped forward to the skull. Slowly, I placed my right hand on its forehead, yelping in surprise at its frigid touch.

Power surged into me like a dark serpent, twisting up my arm. I tried to leap backward, but *something* held me in place; my hand might as well have been superglued to the sculpture.

Then the energy began to pull, and I felt the souls rush out of me as if sucked up into a straw, each one like a little bead passing through me. It wasn't painful, but it felt weird. Sort of like the pins and needles of a limb waking back up.

More and more of them shot toward the skull, and I gasped as the sensation grew from a small stream to a torrent. Finally, I knew how a balloon feels during its last moments. It took a while for me to empty my soul bladder but eventually the flood faded, and then it was done. The skull withdrew its presence, and I staggered to the side in surprise.

"Holy crap," I mumbled, choking for air. "That has to be the least fun way possible to do that." At least those souls were back in the system and had a chance to go where they deserved. I felt pretty good about that. On shaky legs, I stumbled back to the door and let myself out into the slightly better lit vault. I saw no sign of Yuki or Rex.

Only the old man waited for me. I swallowed a nervous gulp and strode to meet Death alone in what was basically a dark alley. Which I guess doesn't make me particularly special. Everyone meets Death on their own in the end—I was just doing it a little earlier than usual.

"Did you finish?" he asked, eyeing my no-longer-glowing skin with a critical eye.

"Waited until it spit me out," I reassured him.

"Do you understand what you just did?" There was a softness to his eyes that I couldn't quite place.

"I put the souls back into the system so they could be sorted?"

"You rescued more than a hundred thousand people from oblivion." I blinked in surprise at the mental picture of that many humans filling a giant stadium. No wonder it had felt so crowded in there.

"Oh, is that all?" I managed weakly. "Well, some of them are likely to find their way back to another kind of torment, right?"

"Even the deepest circle of Hell pales in comparison with the horrors of being slowly devoured by one of the Lost on the edge of Reality," Kane told me grimly. "There isn't a soul among them who would rather go back to that existence than to where they are supposed to be delivered."

I resisted the urge to shudder at the gruesome information. I was still having a hard time processing the number of souls who had been lost in the dark. I suppose in the grand scheme of the universe, it wasn't that many people…but still. I didn't know whether to feel proud or to feel sick.

"So—the Reapers know," he prodded in a flat tone.

"The Reapers know," I confirmed. "I could have kept it a secret, but then we'd all be dead, and that Dreadknight would have been thirty thousand souls fatter. That seemed like the worse outcome to me."

Kane looked away in irritation but didn't say anything. I got the sense that he agreed with me but didn't like that those had been the only two options. He reminded me of Orion when the Hunter was forced to watch from the sidelines. Sometimes he criticized Alex and me for not solving a problem the way he would have. I've got a few tricks up my sleeve, but I'm not the Hunter or the Grim Reaper. At best, I'm some sort of pale shadow imitating the real thing.

"A Dreadknight…" Kane murmured as if he still couldn't

believe it. "And one of the Elders stirred in the dark."

"Yeah, about that," I said, interrupting him. "Is that what I think it is? Some sort of thing from beyond or horror from outside our universe?" Kane jerked his head for me to follow him, and he led me out of the vault. The circular door groaned shut behind us as we left. I could have sworn its golden skull winked at me as I watched. How was I going to get back in there?

"I don't think they are from beyond," he replied after the door closed. I had almost forgotten my question. "They were the first to be Lost and have lived on the edge of Reality feeding on the souls of mortals for so long, they have been twisted into something that should never have been."

I was silent for a moment processing that. The Legionnaires and Dreadknight had certainly been weird and warped. I guess it made sense that their parents were even stranger.

"Things will get worse now," Kane informed me.

"Worse how?"

"When one of the Elders stirs, it's like someone kicked over their anthill; they come out in force. We'll have to send out convoys with heavier guards and move smaller shipments. I must inform the Death Board."

"Plus," I continued for him, "you still don't know whom you can trust."

"I still don't know whom I can trust," he confirmed grimly. "Did you learn anything?"

"Not really. Everyone seemed equally motivated to not die." I shrugged. "What are the odds that Foxa or Karen was a mole?"

"No way of knowing now."

I frowned, trying to think of anything that might have been a clue. Everyone had been a consummate professional as far as

I could tell. The only hiccup had been when they had found out about my new title, but that didn't implicate Rex or Yuki. That was just office politics.

"What if it was just bad luck?" I asked.

"Bad luck that a *Dreadknight* appeared to attack an extra-heavy convoy of thirty thousand souls heading to Hell?" Kane arched an eyebrow.

"Well, when you put it like that, I guess it does seem a little too convenient," I admitted.

"You are my heir now. Help me root out this cancer before it is too late."

"Uh, when exactly would it be too late?"

"When the leaders of one of the Underworlds decide that they are no longer willing to abide by the Death Treaty and allow us to collect souls on their behalf. Instead, they will go to the mortal realm to claim souls themselves on the timetable they prefer."

"They can do that?"

"Of course." Kane gave me a skeptical look. "But part of the peace that currently exists is that they use me as a neutral third party. Otherwise, it would be total anarchy." In my head I pictured Dan the demon being sent out as a Reaper instead of as a salesman, just whacking whomever he could get his grubby little claws on to meet his quota. That didn't sound good for anyone.

"Yeah, I see how that could be a worse system."

"Then help me stop it from becoming the new one."

"What do you need me to do, boss?" I tossed him a mock salute, but my heart was plummeting. This was starting to feel like a lot. All I had to do was infiltrate Hell to steal my sister's missing half soul, sneak back into Hades to kill Midas so he could give me my Impossible Task, then break into Death's vault and steal the Crown of Immortality for Lazarus, while also catching the traitors hiding among the Reapers.

At least it wasn't boring.

"Do whatever you must to do gain their trust." Kane stared into me. "You have already seen that there are places where Death cannot go. You must follow the rot back to the source. It is not enough to find out who is the traitor; I need to know whom they have betrayed me to. Otherwise, this cycle will repeat itself forever."

"Just consider me your own private eye. Sounds fun."

"They will come for you now," he told me coldly, ignoring my enthusiasm. "You had better be ready."

I had a bad feeling I wasn't.

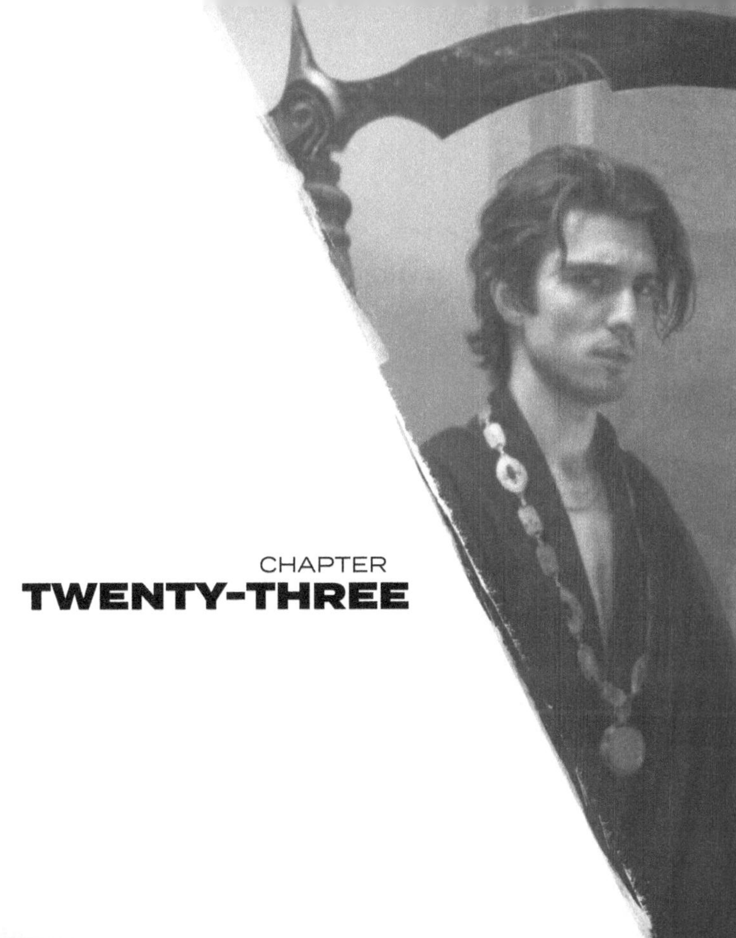

TWENTY-THREE

THE DEATH BOARD might always be meeting, but I was beginning to feel like I was always being dragged in front of it too. I had barely gotten to take my boots off before I was summoned to yet another dumb meeting.

I guess that's corporate life for you.

Three of us stood in the abyssal, cavernous hall, the only survivors of the delivery to Hell. Across from us sat the eight members of the Death Board at the nine-person table. The chair to Kane's right was still empty. Somehow the heavy darkness of the room felt thicker than it had when I was here the first time.

My favorite Olympian, Pluto, glared daggers at me from

his side of the table, while Santa Muerte's empty eye sockets made it hard for me to tell which of us she was staring at, but somehow her gaze was the heaviest of them all.

"Your report?" Kane asked lightly, but there was a hint of deadly steel lurking in his voice. His attention rested heavily on Rex, who stood in the center. The Reaper squared his jaw, staring up at the board.

"Why are you talking to me?" he demanded. "Why pretend that I was in charge? Ask him." He jerked a thumb at me.

I managed to hold back a wince as the other seven Immortals at the table shifted at his words. They turned their gazes from Rex to me, each with its own crushing weight. Thanks for that, buddy. Yuki shot me a sympathetic glance but was silent.

"And yet, I am asking *you*," Death replied, his voice no longer friendly. A chill sliced through me. Rex must have gotten an even heavier dose of the cold. The man collapsed to his knees as the power of the grave tore into him.

"We set out from the Veil as ordered, with an extra-large delivery of souls for Hell," he began. There was no more defiance in his voice.

"Only because of previous delays," Zagan cut in. "I want to make it clear that we were not getting special treatment." A couple other members of the board rolled their eyes.

Rex ignored him. "After traveling the Rainbow Bridge for quite a while, we heard one of the Lost's raiding horns and saw one of their vessels hurtling toward us through the Nothing. We prepared to defend the convoy, but they were led by a Dreadknight."

"Impossible!" Pluto interrupted, leaping out of his chair like a weed sprouting overnight. "What sort of nonsense is this,

Kane? A Dreadknight hasn't been spotted in—"

The diminutive god of Hades abruptly fell silent as Old Grim turned to stare at him. Death and the god of death stared at each other for a moment that might have stretched an eternity. I don't know how Time works, but if the Death Board is always meeting, then they might still be locked in that silent showdown in some splinter of the universe.

"It does sound a bit unbelievable," Santa Muerte ventured gently after the silence had grown unbearable. "Surely none of you three has been a Reaper long enough to know what they look like."

"Big guy, way too many arms?" I offered, taking a step forward. I don't know why I felt the need to stand up for Rex. I was pretty sure he would not do the same for me. Maybe it was because we had fought for each other out in the Nothing. Maybe I just really didn't like Pluto. Whatever the reason, I hadn't made a conscious decision. My feet and mouth volunteered me without checking in with the home office first.

I felt my butt clench as the intense weight of the room's attention descended back on me. Even Kane and Pluto broke off their stare-down. It felt like I had just dunked myself in a tub of blood and then jumped into the shark tank.

"It was full of more than a hundred thousand souls?" I continued, glaring up at them as best I could. "This ringing any bells?"

Santa Muerte was silent, but the sound of her necklaces clacking together as she shifted in her chair was plenty loud.

"So, the Dreadknights walk again," the dusky man in bright colors with four arms breathed. "How many souls did you lose to this monster?"

"None," Rex replied, still on his knees.

"None?" Pluto sputtered, his earlier cowing by Kane apparently forgotten. "How exactly did you prevent a *Dreadknight* from devouring every single soul in your convoy including your own? Even most of this board—"

"He killed it." The kneeling Reaper gestured at me with a twitch of his head, cutting off the god's rant as efficiently as a headsman.

The silence this time was deeper, the attention on me heavier.

"So." Azrael spoke for the first time, his white eyes locked on mine. "You have finally chosen an heir." For some reason, I hadn't been truly afraid in this meeting until those words came out of the angel's mouth.

Kane had warned me that things would get worse, that people would be out to get me now. But it had been hard for me to understand how that would be possible.

But now I understood there were things worse than Reapers here in the dark.

Most of the members of the Death Board were staring at me with the kind of naked hunger that made me feel like I had suddenly turned into a juicy piece of steak before their eyes. The only exceptions were Azrael, who looked bored, and Santa Muerte, whose skull made her impossible to read.

"I have," Death admitted heavily after a few moments, gazing down at me with a small frown on his face. I could only shrug back. If he didn't want an obnoxious heir, then maybe he should have had a more rigorous hiring process.

"You should have informed us," Santa Muerte scolded, her skull turning to stare at Kane.

"The board has every right—" the four-armed man began.

"An Elder has stirred in the Dark," Death told the room, killing every protest with one fell blow.

"Which one?" Azrael asked sharply, leaning forward in his chair. For the first time, the Angel of Death looked disturbed, his angled features drawn tight.

"Ubizekal, the Herald." Kane told him. I swallowed remembering the Elder's massive shadow moving through the darkness as it chased us to the Veil. I don't know how much stronger it was than a Dreadknight, but I also don't know exactly how much stronger Godzilla is than an iguana. I don't need hard numbers to get the idea.

"Were there others? Have Sharizan, Rykismash, or Ssserkai been seen in the deep?" The angel's white eyes burned with intensity as he stared at Death. I'd never heard any of those names before, but I wondered if that was the point. Some things are better being forgotten.

"Only the Herald. I would not keep such things from you, Azrael."

"It is rare but not unheard of for the Herald to wake," Zagan mused, eyeing his fingernails without a care in the world. He seemed to have the opposite reaction to this news than the angel—par for the course, I guess. "I'm sure he'll get bored and return to his slumber soon enough."

I hated the fact that I found some hope in his words, but if the Elders were anything like the stories I knew, I thought he had a point. Ancient things often tend to be a sleepy lot in myth and legends.

"I will have to inform the Host about this," Azrael warned, his eyes scanning the rest of the table. Several of the board members shifted uncomfortably at the angel's proclamation.

Zagan merely wrinkled his nose, dark eyes dancing.

"What do you intend to do about this, Kane?" Pluto demanded, evidently bolstered by the terrible news. "How will you keep our deliveries safe?"

"My esteemed Olympian colleague does have a point," Zagan offered from his side of the table. "Things are already far from satisfactory, and I can't imagine they're about to get better. The Death Treaty demands a certain level of security."

"We will change our delivery pattern immediately," Death replied without a moment's thought. "If bigger predators are out hunting, then we shall make the meals so small that they're not worth the effort."

"You'll have to increase the frequency then," Santa Muerte pointed out, a brittleness in her voice. "No one will be willing to subsist on starvation rations for long."

"I concur," the four-armed man replied vehemently, leaping to his feet. "We have been more than patient with you so far, *Death*. If you cannot protect our deliveries as is your duty, then maybe it is time we did it ourselves." An angry murmur spread through the middle of the of the table, although I noticed that both Zagan and Azrael were studiously silent. This was what Kane had been warning me about. There was more at stake than some souls being lost, which was already horrible enough. If the Underworlds stopped using Death as their delivery system, I was confident mortals would suffer even more than we already did.

"Ever since Mother Ruin's last assault, you've lost your touch," Pluto sneered, gesturing at the empty seat at Death's right hand with a dramatic flair. "Yama's death made you lose your nerve."

I guess that explained the missing board member.

Something violent flashed across Kane's face, a ripple of rage that was gone as quickly as it had appeared. But as I studied him closer, I could see the light of anger still burning brightly in his eyes.

"Weren't you just complaining that I had appointed an heir?" Death asked in a cold voice, glaring at his rowdy board. "Now you complain that I have not taken enough steps to protect the delivery of your souls?" Pluto fell silent. I barely managed to hide a smile at seeing the little god caught by his own words.

"One wonders how the Dreadknight knew how to find this specific convoy with such accuracy," Zagan mused from his side of the table in a tone that implied he didn't wonder at all. His black eyes were focused on me with a sudden intensity that I did not like. The fallen angel had a trick up his sleeve.

"What are you implying, demon?" Santa Muerte demanded, turning to look at him.

"It's just that there were five Reapers who knew where our large delivery was headed, and the three living ones are right here." Another murmur swept through the room as the Death Board's attention returned to us.

I felt a cold hand settle around my heart and squeeze as the demon began to lay his trap. Fortunately, I was prepared. Kane had given me the same thought about the other Reapers. The whole reason he had made me his heir in the first place was that this had been going on long before I had died.

"Technically, I had no idea until we left," I protested. "I'm new."

"All the same, I know that *I*, for one, would feel better if these three were taken off the field for a bit, until we can find the source of the leak," Zagan replied, pressing a hand to his chest.

Amusement glittered in his eyes as he watched my expression.

Had he guessed my plans with Dan the demon? Or was he just being difficult? If I was stuck in the Veil, how would I be able to rescue Meg's missing soul from the Devil's personal lair? I struggled to keep my expression confused as I met his gaze, then glanced at Kane for backup. My boss gave me an irritated look, like I was somehow to blame here instead of loose-lipped Rex.

"Heaven agrees," Azrael barked after a moment of silence. Shocked, I glanced at the Angel of Death, but he wasn't looking at me; his white orbs were locked on his counterpart down the table. The rest of the board looked stunned. When was the last time those two had agreed on anything?

Suitably bullied, the other five members voiced their agreement in short order, leaving Kane with a unanimous vote to stable Rex, Yuki, and me.

Death shook with a barely constrained rage, but his voice was as cold as ever. "Very well," he agreed. "I will abide by this board's wishes and place these three Reapers on administrative duties until they are cleared of involvement."

"Or caught," Zagan prodded.

"Or caught," Kane growled. My heart sank at the delighted little smirk on the CFO of Hell's face. I had a bad feeling that I was about to become a work of art and get framed. I'd have to keep my nose clean.

We were dismissed, and the meeting continued, or it didn't. Or maybe it continued, and it also did not. However the physicists would explain it, I quickly found myself alone as I entered the black marble waiting room outside Death's lair.

Yuki gave me another small smile but didn't say anything as she followed in Rex's angry wake. The bald Reaper didn't even acknowledge that I'd stepped in to help him. I watched his broad back as he stormed away and shrugged. *See if I ever help you again, bucko.*

I exited into the employee halls of the Veil. The sterile white corridor felt almost warm and refreshing after the inky darkness I had just spent too long in. Then I spotted my least favorite god of death.

Pluto stood in the center of the walkway with his arms crossed, waiting for someone. From the way his lips thinned and his purple eyes narrowed when he saw me, I had a hunch I knew who.

Joy.

"What can I do ya for?" I gave him a friendly smile.

"How did you get into my realm?" the short god demanded, glaring up at me. I knew he was some sort of Immortal with an incredible amount of power, but it was impossible for me to take him seriously. If I stiff-armed his forehead, he wouldn't be able to punch me.

I wondered if this was how Orion felt all the time.

"Oh, I'm not really sure," I lied earnestly. "I was looking for the little Reaper's room, and I think I took three lefts instead of two lefts and a right? Suddenly there was fog everywhere and a river…I'm still learning my way around."

"Don't lie to me, mortal!" Pluto took a step toward me, his hands balling into fists. The air around him sizzled with power, like the atmosphere seconds before a thunderstorm breaks. A dark crown flickered into being on his head. Despite my earlier confidence, I felt myself take an involuntary step back at his display of rage. He might be a baby, but his tantrum could fry me like a fish.

For a second, I considered summoning the full Authority of Death that the ring would give me, but that felt wrong. For one, I wasn't even sure that would be enough power to bring down a god. But also, I had better leverage to use on the master of Hades. I realized that he wasn't sure what I knew. He had only run into me as I was fleeing through the mist.

"Yeah, I was in there," I snapped at him, jutting my chin out in challenge. "I saw *everything*." Pluto froze in his tracks, and I saw uncertainty in his eyes.

"Quite the *packed* house," I continued condescendingly. *That's right, you bully. I know the secret of your failing Underworld. You're broker than a college student living off ninety-nine-cent ramen.*

Pluto lowered his fists and took a step back, his face burning bright red with embarrassment. If only Homer could have seen this. I had made a god blush.

"Stay out of my property," he warned, shaking his fist in my direction. "Or I will crush you."

"Sure thing," I lied, knowing full well that I would be returning there very soon. "It was kind of gross in there, dude. Maybe you should look into getting a cleaner." I turned, planning on leaving him after that absolute zinger, but the god moved to block my path.

"Give me the key," he demanded in low, cold tones. I felt my heart skip a beat as I matched his purple stare. He had gotten control of his temper, and for the first time, I saw that he was dangerous.

"What key?" I stammered, stopping my hand from straying to my pant pocket. "I don't think our rooms even have locks…"

"You have something that my cousins made. By rights, it belongs to me."

It made sense that Pluto was tied into that family tree the same way the goddess in the other Between had been. All the Roman and Greek gods must be related somehow.

"What key?" I replied, keeping my face as smooth as possible.

"Don't treat me like a fool, boy," Pluto snapped, taking another step toward me. "I saw you flee into the marble halls of Janus's Way Between Worlds. There is only one key that will unlock those doors."

"That sounds kind of risky. What if someone loses it? Can't you just get a locksmith?"

"Give me the key, or I will make you suffer," he hissed, sliding toward me once more.

"Pluto! Control yourself!" A woman's voice cut through the tension like a whip crack. The god and I spun to stare at Santa Muerte, who had snuck up behind us. The skull's eyeless sockets bored into both of us as she glared at us.

"You are a member of this board," she scolded in a tone so short that even he could see over it. "Act like it for once, you child."

"How dare you?" Pluto snarled, clenching his hands into fists. For a moment, I felt like an innocent bystander, trapped between two gunslingers who were about to draw iron. I don't know if Santa Muerte qualified as a god the same way that Pluto did, but I had no doubt she packed a powerful punch.

For a moment, the two Immortals stared at each other. I held my breath, not even daring to move lest I set them off. Eventually, Pluto backed down, a disgusted sneer on his face. "This isn't over," he snarled at me, spinning on his heel and storming down the hall.

"Thanks for the save," I told Santa Muerte as I let out a long breath. "I don't think he's a big fan of me."

"Be careful, little Reaper," she warned me, her empty sockets filling my vision. "The master of Hades does not forgive anything that hurts his pride. Before, he did not like you, but now he will hate you."

"Who doesn't at this point?" I muttered. "You probably hate me too."

"I don't care about you in the slightest." Her necklaces rattled as she shook with a silent laugh. "I just like seeing that little fool get angry." She strode down the hall without a second glance.

Frustrated, I dug my pocket watch necklace out from under my shirt and glared at its face: 6 p.m. Half of my time was gone. I needed to get moving if I was going to fix all this before I came back from the dead.

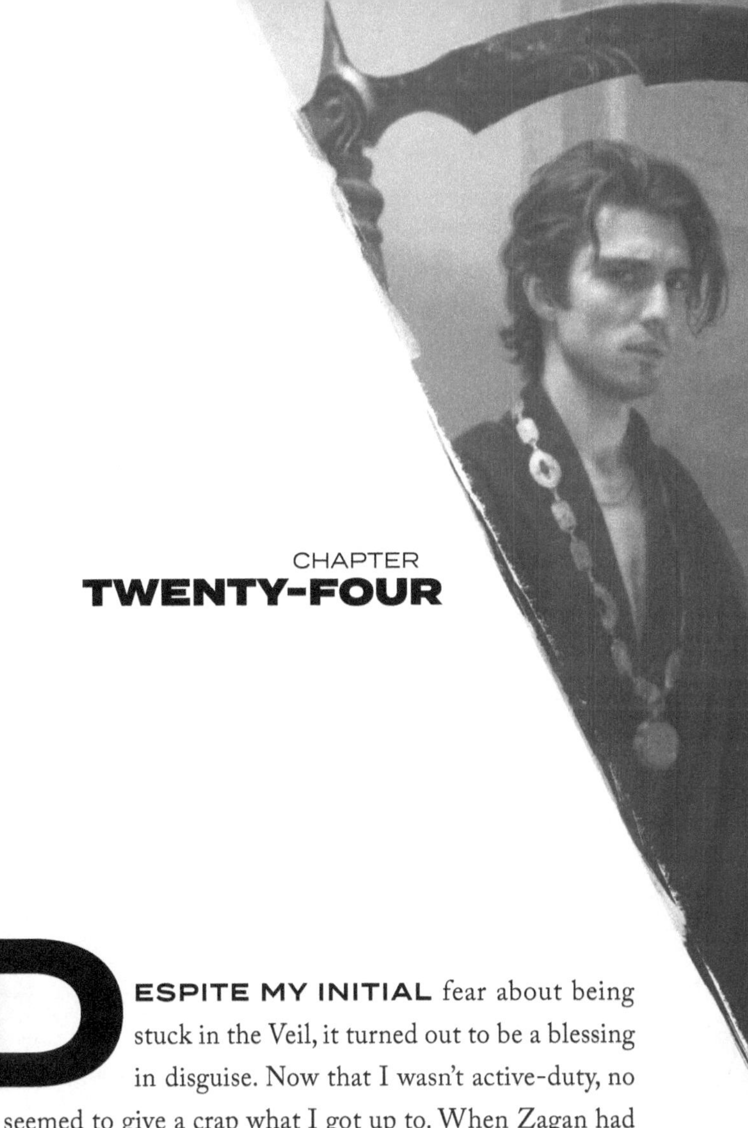

TWENTY-FOUR

DESPITE MY INITIAL fear about being stuck in the Veil, it turned out to be a blessing in disguise. Now that I wasn't active-duty, no one seemed to give a crap what I got up to. When Zagan had proposed that I be held in the Veil, I had imagined it would be a lot more invasive than this. It only took a few shifts of being chained to a desk before I realized this was the perfect time for me to go back into the Between.

As long as my butt was in my seat when I was supposed to clock in, not a soul bothered me. It was oddly isolating. For the first time since I had died, I was beginning to feel a little... dead. There had been so much human interaction, or at least action, up till now that I hadn't felt like I was no longer among the living. That was fine. I didn't come here to make friends. The only question now was: What do I do first, rescue Megan or kill Midas?

Thanks to my excellent negotiation skills, Dan was locked into waiting for me for as long as I needed. There was no rush on that end. But I had a few problems to solve before I could stage my jailbreak. For a while now, I hadn't known how I was going to get her soul out in the first place. But my run-in with the Dreadknight gave me an idea. I didn't like it, but I was pretty sure it would work. But once I had Meg's soul and brought it out from Hell, then what? I had no idea where I was going to hide it until resurrection time.

I had no delusions that carrying around a soul I had removed from an Underworld without its master's permission was anything other than crime of the highest order for a Reaper. I'd never hidden anything this serious from my parents.

So it might be smarter to save Megan's soul till last and get the Impossible Task and Crown of Immortality now. Buuuut, I had a feeling that when I took out the final soul powering Hades, Pluto wasn't going to take it well, and I didn't want to stick around the Veil to see how that investigation went down. If I took the crown first, I'd have to hide it, which had its own set of problems.

There was also the fact that Megan was in *Hell*. She was suffering, and the sooner I got her out the better. Already I feared what damage might have been done to her mind or soul. Dawn had warned me that she might never be whole, and I didn't think the Queen of All Fae was exaggerating. I don't know if any amount of therapy can help someone recover from that kind of trauma.

The problem was that all of these things were BAD IDEAS, and no amount of holding them up to the light and looking at them from different angles would change that. But as terrible as they were, they were also necessary. So I decided that it would be easier to hide a stolen soul for a while than to cover up a murder, which meant I was going to Hell first. Hopefully it wouldn't be the last thing too.

All that academic reasoning made it sound so easy, but as I stood in my tiny Reaper dorm room, holding the Key of Janus in my hand, my feet felt like they were wearing cement shoes. It took all my willpower to take the final steps to the door.

I don't think that made me a coward. It was Hell for Pete's sake. Virgil and Dante hadn't had a blast while they were there. I was allowed to be a little *apprehensive*. Even the Underworld version of my key had a giant frowny face on the top of it. But apprehension didn't pay the bills, and I had a lot of them coming due, so I jammed the key into the lock and gave it a twist.

The door swung open to the marbled halls of the Between, Underworld Edition. Licking my lips nervously, I slipped through and pulled the gate shut behind me. I don't know how it was a door on one side and a gate on the other, but that's a question I leave to the scientists.

The metal click of the latch echoed through the empty hall, and I struggled not to wince. I was trying to be sneaky. Walking softly, I made my way down the red carpet, past gates to worlds I wasn't looking to visit.

I drew up short as I passed one labeled ANNWN—DEVOURED. The name tickled the back of my mind like the ghost of a sneeze. I stared at the rusty and chained entrance, racking my brain for where I had heard that name before—

Gloriana.

Gloriana told me that had been the name of the Fae Underworld before it fell to the Nothing. A chill crept over me as I realized that this ruin represented a portion of the fall of my family tree. Oh, the atrocities Dawn would be willing to commit to restore it.

Shaking myself out of my daydreams, I resumed walking, leaving the fallen place behind me. I made my way past the gates to: HADES, MICTLAN, FERRI, and more. The farther I walked, the more my anxiety grew. Where was the one for Hell? Had the Devil and his goons somehow sealed off the back door to their realm?

YOMI, ADLIVUN, and METNAL passed by as I continued my search.

And then I was there. The sign simply said HELL, but somehow reading it in person made it feel even more real than it had when I made a delivery. No heat came through its gate, but I still imagined that I could feel a whisper of a warm breeze.

Now came the hard part.

The Key of Portunus wasn't exactly a GPS-accurate delivery system to new worlds. It seemed to spit me out in a place that it thought fit my desires. For the most part, when I visited the Faerie Lands, the stakes were pretty low. Being off by a few degrees wouldn't result in my eternal torture and damnation.

But this trip, we were playing for keeps. I bowed my head to stare at the metal key in my hands, trying to focus on the directions that Dan had given me. "The offices of Trust and Safety," I whispered to the frowning mask over and over, not sure if I was praying or casting a magic spell.

With my heart in my throat, I inserted the key into the large metal lock and turned. The click of it unlocking was so loud that I thought every Underworld would be able to hear it, not just the one I was trying to sneak into. I pulled the gate open and stared at the foggy dark waiting for me.

"Here goes nothing," I grumbled and strode into the mist.

The moment I crossed over the threshold between Janus's realm and Hell, the temperature spiked at least twenty degrees, and I felt sweat begin to bead on the back of my neck. Which was a bummer, because if my body wasn't real, why did it still think it had to sweat?

But despite the sudden heat, I couldn't make out any other changes. Blindly, I made my way forward in the dark, feeling more and more lost. When I had snuck into Hades, I'd come out through a gate right by the river, but the change had been obvious. Was Hell just empty? Had I gone to the wrong— My panic cut out as I ran smack into a wall that I couldn't see.

"Son of a—" I hissed before remembering that I was supposed to be sneaking into the most dangerous place in the universe and clamped my mouth shut.

I stuck my hands out and felt across the surface that I had run into. It was wooden and rattled a little as I pushed on it. As my palms traveled lower, they found a…doorknob. I was in a closet.

Steeling myself, I turned the knob and peered out into Hell.

My first glimpse of the Devil's realm was disappointing. It was seemed so much more normal than I'd expected. I was in some sort of office space. Thirty empty cubicles stretched across the dim room. If Death ran his empire like some corporate monstrosity, then I shouldn't have been shocked to find out that the demons did too.

I had met their CFO after all.

The place was empty, so I slipped out of their closet and let the door close behind me, sealing off the access to the Between. I had learned my lesson about letting creatures sneak in there. The last thing I needed was a demon infestation to go with my angry goddess and dead dragon.

Practically on my tiptoes, I shuffled down one of the two rows of cubicles. My feet clicked on the linoleum-like floor. I guess there are no carpets in Hell—probably a fire hazard. A poster on the wall showed a fluffy black kitten preparing to pounce on a baby bird. The caption at the bottom read:

WORK EVILER

NOT

SMARTER

I wasn't entirely sure that *eviler* was a real word, though I guess it sounded better than *Work more evil*. Still, what do I know?

As I made my way toward the front of the room, I saw another door waiting for me. The crack glowed with a wicked red light. Would it open right onto one of those pits of fire I had heard so much about?

I drew up short, eyeing the exit with distaste. It would really suck if I snuck in here, only to open the wrong door and have my face melted off by lava. The goal was to not do that. As I paused, I suddenly realized I could hear a soft, rumbling sound that my footsteps had covered. My heart skipped a beat as I strained my ears, trying to listen.

Whatever was making that sound was here in the room with me.

I dropped into a crouch, below the running wall of cubicles, feeling my heart beginning to race. I was certain that whatever beasts el Diablo kept on the premises were going to be in better shape than old Cerberus, and I had barely survived my tangle with that dog.

The rumbling continued at an even pace, undisturbed by my presence. It was the sound of someone sleeping, I realized after listening for a few more moments. It wasn't quite a full-on snore; more the heavy breathing of someone who had a deviated septum.

Staying low to the ground, I began a slow walk down the line. There were only a few cubicles left in the row before I got to the entrance, which meant that the sleeping creature had to be below one of…

I halted as I caught a flash of bright red under the desk to my right. This was it.

Slowly, ever so slowly, I inched forward, doing my best to be silent.

One step.

Another.

A third—this time the demon shifted in its sleep, rolling to the side slightly. My insides clenched as it situated itself. If it moved just a few inches, it would be able to see me. My eyes narrowed as I traced the spiked red tail that had flopped out into the aisle, and the black fur encasing its cloven-hoofed feet and legs.

"Dan?" I demanded, feeling a sense of irritation as I realized that I had just tried to tiptoe past my help. The red creature jolted awake, sitting straight up and slamming his horned head into the bottom of the desk with a dull *thunk*.

I enjoyed that.

A dry chuckle escaped my lips as I rose out of my crouch.

"Wake up, Dan, you've got a deal to complete," I sang as my nemesis let out a little groan. The short demon crawled out from his hidey-hole and rose to his feet, fixing me with a belligerent black stare.

"How did you get here?" he demanded. "There's no way you actually found the Trust and Safety offices."

I gave him a grin that was all teeth. When he'd stolen my soul almost two years ago, I had no idea what was going on. It felt good to turn the tables on the fiend.

His eyes tracked to the closet behind me and narrowed slightly. "Did you come out of the closet?"

"I told you not to worry about that," I told him in a condescending tone. "I'm here now, and it's time for you to make good on your part."

He clearly hadn't expected me to get this far without being caught, which meant that he hadn't been making the deal in good faith. But I guess that wasn't really surprising. He was a demon; faith was not their thing.

"Are you sure?" he whined, wringing his hands together like an old washcloth. "It's pretty—bad out there."

"That's kind of the point," I snapped. "If this was a vacation resort, my sister's soul being stuck here wouldn't be a problem, would it?"

The short demon muttered something under his breath but stopped protesting. He reached back under the desk and pulled out a brown paper bag that seemed full. "Put these on," he told me, shoving it into my arms. I peered through the top of the bag and eyed what looked like clothes.

"What is this?"

"You can't just wander around the place dressed like a *Reaper*," Dan told me, making it clear that I was an idiot. "I got you a uniform so you won't stick out like a dead thumb."

I lifted out a pair of black pants, revealing a matching long-sleeved shirt, and…a full helmet. I lifted it free of the bag and stared at it for a long moment. It was made of some sort of glossy black ceramic that glinted, even in the low light. It weighed much less than a steel version would have. The face was worked into the snarling visage of some monster-demon.

A chill settled on me as I stared into the creature's empty eyes. This was somehow more terrifying than seeing a bunch of cackling demons running around. I eyed Dan distrustfully as I lowered the helmet.

"What is this for?"

"It's a shock trooper uniform," he replied unhelpfully. "They're mostly about your height so I figured it would work."

"Shock trooper?"

"They're the enforcers around here, rank-and-file type. Just put it on, man, this is already going to be hard enough without you throwing a fit every five seconds."

"Fine," I snapped, dropping the bag and reaching for the pants. Dan stood there watching. I glared at his beady black eyes, and the two of us held this stare-down for almost a minute.

"*What?*" the demon demanded eventually, throwing his hands up in exasperation.

"Turn around," I told him primly. "I'd like some privacy."

Dan did as I asked, muttering something about "stupid

furless monkeys" under his breath. I ignored him and began changing, swapping out my Reaper blacks for the dark suit of a Hell enforcer. It wasn't embarrassment that led to my request; I didn't want him to see the pocket watch hanging around my neck. While Death hadn't been fazed by its presence, I felt like the fewer people were asking questions about it, the better. The last thing I needed was for someone to figure out I wasn't actually dead, just playing possum.

The shirt and pants fit like a pair of dress fatigues, although I noticed the shoulders were a little too broad and the thighs a bit thicker than mine. Clearly, regulation shock troopers were bulkier than me. Which was just great news. One of these days, I'd like to be the bigger guy in a fight. Just to see how it feels.

"You can turn around now," I told him after the watch was safely tucked away under my new uniform. I held the mask in my hands and gave him a little twirl as he looked at me. "What do you think, should I keep it?"

"You're a little small," he grunted, "but it's probably fine."

"That's not exactly reassuring."

"You decided to infiltrate Hell to steal a soul from the Devil himself, bucko. You left reassuring behind a long time ago. Now put on the helmet and shut up."

I detest when Dan has a point. It just bothers me on a fundamental level. I hate him so much that if he says the sky is blue, I want it to be red. But even I had to agree with his logic on this one. With a shrug, I settled the helmet over my head.

The cool ceramic hugged my skull tightly, and I was pleased to find I could actually see out of the mask. I'd worried a little when I realized it didn't have eyeholes. On the plus side, it would be impossible for anyone to tell that I had human eyes instead of demonic ones. Maybe Dan actually had thought of everything.

"Let's do this," I told him, panic rising in my chest as I glanced at the door behind him. So far, I hadn't really been in much danger. I could leave at any time, and no one would ever know I'd been here. But once we stepped out that door into whatever else Hell had to offer, I'd run into other demons, and my chances of escaping would plummet.

"Not so fast," the fiend told me, holding up one of his bright-red claws like a crossing guard. "You gotta learn how to walk first."

"What do you mean 'how to walk,'" I demanded.

"Shock troopers don't just schlep around like a California surfer boy. They march."

"First of all, I don't surf. Second of all, fine—how does it go?"

"Like this." Dan stiffened his spine and turned to the side. He stuck out his straight left leg and then followed with his right leg equally unbent. His arms were clapped tight to his sides, and he stared straight ahead as he crossed the room.

He looked like an idiot.

"You're kidding," I protested. "Your crack troops are goose-stepping around the Pit of Hell?"

"You gotta walk the walk before you can talk the talk," Dan replied with a shrug.

"That's not what that means."

"Just practice, will you? I have a shift eventually, and if I miss it, *things* will come looking."

I suppressed a shudder at the thought of what a demon might consider to be a *thing*. Feeling like a parody of a villain, I strode to the side of the room and repeated Dan's stiff movements.

"Faster! No, not that fast!" Dan snapped out instructions as I clomped back and forth like a soldier in boot camp. After a few passes I had the timing down enough that the short demon shrugged, chewing on one of his long black talons. "Guess that will have to do. Lunch break's about to start."

"You guys eat?"

"You guys eat?" Dan mimicked my question in a high-pitched voice, a hint of annoyance crossing his face. I guess that was a sore subject for him. Maybe too many high schoolers had made fun of the little guy.

"Stay behind me and stare straight ahead while we move through the hallways," the nervous demon told me. "Whatever you do, do *not* speak. If anyone asks you a question, let me handle it."

I nodded; my mouth was too dry to speak anyway. I didn't think keeping quiet was going to be too much of a problem just this once. Dan gave me one more appraisal, his black gaze running up and down my body before he let out a little sigh and turned to the door.

"Let's go die," he muttered more to himself than me.

He grasped the handle of the door and turned it, swinging it open. Together we stepped out into Hell.

TWENTY-FIVE

I KNOW DAN TOLD me to stare straight ahead like one of those British royal guards, but that was *impossible*. Our feet clicked on the shiny black linoleum floor as I goose-stepped behind the red fiend, doing my best to match the tempo he had shown me. It was hard to focus, because my brain was more than a little distracted by the spectacle around me.

I didn't know if Dante was a liar or if Hell had just gotten a lot of work done since his visit, but the place was decidedly more modern than it had been in the *Inferno*. We moved along a hallway that would have fit into the set of a sci-fi movie. Black walls and floors were lit by bright, sterile lights. To our left the drab color scheme was offset by white doors that led to more offices.

There was a steady hum of air-conditioning as powerful HVAC machines pumped air into the facility, keeping the heat in check. That must be why I could only catch a faint whiff of rotten eggs—the telltale scent of sulfur, the official deodorant of demons everywhere.

The entire right side of the hallway was made of glass that looked out into the Pit. There was a gap between our wall and the drab land that seemed to stretch into the horizon. The ground was a burned sort of gray, as if it had been choked with ash. A few trees clung to life, empty of more than a handful of colorless leaves. Open pools of bright-red magma were scattered throughout, belching toxic-looking black smoke into the air.

I could make out the forms of humans wandering listlessly around the dungeon. I tensed myself to witness horrors I could never forget as I looked at the first man. His gray skin was thin, as if he hadn't had enough to eat for a while. But other than looking a little skinny, he didn't appear to be in any pain. If anything, he looked kind of bored.

I glanced down the gap and could make out another floor floating below the first. More levels stretched downward before the angle cut off and I couldn't see any farther.

"I *said* look straight ahead," Dan hissed from in front of me, his voice snapping me back into position. A rhythmic clicking began to sound ahead of us, and I felt my heart race as a group of shock troops, dressed identically to me, came into view.

They marched past us, a squad of ten, with a leader in the front and three rows of three following him in perfect unison. I did my best to match their timing, feeling a cold bead of sweat begin to run down the back of my spine.

It took a will of iron for me not to crane my neck and watch them as they marched past, to see if they turned to inspect me with suspicious stares. But I continued in Dan's footsteps and forced myself to breathe. If they came for me, I had a way out. I'd make a break for the nearest door and use Janus's Key to get to the Between before anyone could grab me.

A haunting little voice in the back of my mind chose that moment to remind me that someone had blocked my access to the Between while Doyle had been on his rampage. I decided not to think about that. I'd never figured out who had done that or how. Hopefully that interdiction had been accidental rather than intentional. It was too late to worry about it now; I was already here.

The sound of the shock troopers faded behind us, and I let my shoulders sag in relief for a moment before stiffening my spine back into the correct ramrod posture. Ahead, the hall began to curve slightly to the right, and everything suddenly clicked for me.

We were walking in a circle. This hallway was part of some superstructure that surrounded the Fiery Pits of Hell like a sphere. The dingy world that we saw out of the window was only the First Circle, the one that wasn't supposed to be that bad. On first glance it didn't seem great.

That meant the other layers I had caught a glimpse of floating below this one were likely the other circles Dante had described so long ago. I racked my memory for the list, but it evaded me. In my defense, it had been a while.

If I wasn't completely wrong, there were…nine levels to this place. I was pretty sure there were ones for things like lust, gluttony, violence, and some of the other deadly sins. Stealing maybe? That didn't feel quite right. However many there were, this was probably the tamest section of Hell. Everything we would encounter from here on out would be worse. Joy.

Dan turned to the left, and I followed him as he stepped onto the last thing I expected to find on this side of the Veil: an honest-to-God escalator. I swear it really was. I stood at stiff attention behind the little demon as we began to descend deeper into the Pits. Out of the corner of my eye, I got my first glimpse of the Second Circle of Hell.

As I've admitted more than once, my Dante is *rusty*, but I didn't remember the circle where a vicious storm raged on a beach. As I watched, people in bathing suits raced around in the sand, being thrown about by winds, battered by heavy rains, and dragged to sea by crushing waves.

A placard on the wall at the bottom of the escalator read: LEVEL TWO: LUST. I wasn't entirely sure I got the metaphor. As we marched around the ring, the storm began to fade. A bright light shone as if the sun had come out, and the beach dried up. It was as if the tempest had never been. I watched in fascinated revulsion as the prisoners danced and partied once more without a care in the world.

But in the distance, dark clouds began to gather once again.

As I looked closer, I noticed the haggard expressions on some of the partiers' faces, as if they were run ragged but couldn't stop, compelled by some sort of horrible siren to continue their revelry. Maybe the metaphor made a little more sense now. Dan and I entered another escalator.

LEVEL THREE: GLUTTONY.

More shock troopers marched on this floor, and it took all my attention to match their tempo as they stomped by. Other demons made their way past us in lab coats, their skin as tomato-red as Dan's. Some eyed us with curiosity but didn't question us. The Third Circle of Hell was a weird one. People were trapped in mud while it rained, and something huge and horrifying moved in the dark, illuminated only by pools of lava that cast everything in a, well, hellish glow. Another escalator.

LEVEL FOUR: GREED.

I saw men and women buried in coins, drowning in pools of molten gold, and other horrors that I could barely process. It was certainly worse than the others, and I knew that it would get worse still.

LEVEL FIVE: WRATH.

Wrath was the most straightforward of any the circles we had passed so far. Men and women fought in an arena that constantly shrank as lava closed like a noose, forcing the combatants together. Fighters that were slain would be consumed by the magma only to reappear a few moments later, doomed to die over and over for eternity.

I couldn't help but wonder what circle I would have been assigned to if I were to wind up here the normal way. I didn't think I was driven by lust. Greed and gluttony didn't feel right either. But wrath was harder for me to ignore. I had some anger that lurked deep down on the inside. Sometimes it was righteous, but did that count?

I don't know, I don't work here.

It was on the escalator down from the Fifth Circle that we finally ran into trouble. We descended into a security checkpoint. Instead of an unobstructed view of LEVEL SIX: HERESY, we ran into a pair of double doors organized like an air lock.

"Here we go," Dan muttered to himself. My nerves, which had begun to calm after passing so many demons without issue, spiked again. The little fiend was very bad at pep talks.

Shock troopers stood on either side of the entrance at rigid attention. The teeth etched in their masks gleamed in the pristine light of the high-tech infrastructure. Dan led us between them without a second glance, and I followed, my feet drumming out Hell's marching tempo. The first door opened to admit us, then shut behind us, sealing us in the security air lock. The placard along the top read: DIS—AUTHORIZED PERSONNEL ONLY.

I wondered why the name sounded so familiar. It gave me an eerie sense of doom. It felt like it was short for one of those old scary words that we don't use often, like *discordia*, the name for great strife. It evoked in me a feeling of permanent despair, which matched the aesthetic of the place.

A bored-looking guard, wearing similar black fatigues but with an officer's hat instead of a mask, stood in the chamber before the second door. Unlike any of the other demons I had seen so far, he appeared human, except for his black eyes. "Credentials please," he insisted in a tired tone.

A sense of true terror flared in my chest as I took in the appearance of this guard. So far, the only infernals I had met that looked human had been fallen angels or Lilith, who had been her own special thing.

Was this one of those ancient Immortals? My disguise might have been good enough to fool some of their offspring like Dan and his contemporaries, but what about one of the original nightmares? My guide produced an ID badge from somewhere. He didn't have any pockets; where had it been? I eyed his furry legs with distaste. Maybe I didn't want to know.

"What brings you to the Red Sector, Zero Nine Nine Seven One Two Six?" the officer inquired, giving the ID a cursory glance as he accepted it. He stuck it into a slot in the wall before turning back to us.

"Control ordered someone from Intake to inspect the special project," Dan grumbled, sounding like a bored construction worker. "Guess who drew the bad lot?"

"Not your lucky day, eh?" The officer nodded knowingly.

"This isn't my lucky century," my guide groused. I resisted the urge to roll my eyes. They were hidden behind my mask, but it still felt like a risk. The panel above the slot turned red and a harsh buzz sounded before it spit out Dan's credentials.

A spike of fear ran down my neck as it failed. Did he not have a way to get through the checkpoint? What if this was some way to get us caught without him breaking the terms of our deal? I tried to remember the exact wording that we had agreed to. Could he have found a way to betray me without technically violating his side?

"Hmm," the officer said, taking the ID out and sticking it back in. After a few seconds, the light again buzzed red and spit it out. "Seems like you're not authorized," he told Dan, not sounding too concerned.

"Those blighted goats in Control are as worthless as they are lazy," Dan spat. "They promised I'd be cleared by the time I got down here."

"Front office is always slower than they say," the officer agreed with an unbothered shrug.

"Listen, let me level with you, infernal-to-infernal." Dan leaned in toward the officer. "This inspection was ordered by CFO Zagan himself, and he's already been down to my boss's office to chew him out for it taking so long."

"Damn, that's a tough spot," the officer agreed, a genuine

look of sympathy crossing his demonic face.

"Boss said it had to get done during the lunch break, so we don't disrupt the construction. But if it doesn't get finished, my manager is gonna put the heat on me when Zagan comes looking for a demon to blame."

"Typical."

"But if they send it to me, I don't have anywhere to put it but on the people who wouldn't let me in…"

"Well done, you bastard," the guard breathed. Although from the way he said it, he sounded more impressed than upset. I guess a demon can appreciate when someone screws someone else over. It's probably as close as the soulless creatures can get to art. Even I had to marvel at Dan's daring. When he had tried to get my soul, he had been a terrible salesman. It seemed the little guy had gotten a bit better since then.

"Gotta pass it along," Dan replied with a helpless shrug. The officer demon nodded, his lips pursed in thought. His black-eyed gaze flicked between us and the exit as he contemplated his options.

"Zagan himself, you say?" he asked, arching an eyebrow. Even this fallen angel was impressed by hearing that name.

"Right from number two."

"Well, far be it from me to get in the way of the C-suite." The officer stuck his own credentials into the wall. After a moment, the light turned green and the door across from us slid open, revealing the same glass-covered walkway that the other floors had featured.

"Best get a move on," he urged.

Dan tossed him a nod of thanks, and we resumed our walk.

"Oh hey, why do you need a shock trooper for an inspection?" the officer called as I crossed to the other side of the door. Heart thudding in my chest, I froze mid-stride, trying to maintain the rigid indifference that all the other guards had shown.

Dan shot me a nervous look as he turned to glance past me to the guard. "It's dangerous down there," he explained with a shrug. "They told me not to go alone."

"Fair enough. I'm not jealous of you having to go into there at all. Good luck!" The doors of the air lock slid shut with a hiss, and we were alone with the prisoners of the Sixth Circle.

Of all the different tortures we had seen so far, the heretics seemed to get the punishment that best fit traditional expectations of Hell. People screamed in agony as they burned in different cells.

I did my best not to look too closely.

On this side of Dis, there were far fewer staff demons wandering around. That made sense to me since it was a restricted area. The ones that passed us were mostly more scientists, who ignored us, striding with purpose.

It occurred to me that the demons of Hell probably weren't on guard for someone to break in. As far as I know, it had been a while since anyone had done it. If Dante was the most recent, then it would have been almost seven hundred years. I'm not sure if any of the other characters of myth and legend who raided an Underworld had come to this specific one. Odysseus and Heracles went to their respective Hadeses—which I guess weren't that different, just under new management. Persephone ended up in the same place too. I'm sure there's a few others, but my education is like my credit score, decent but not great.

The point is, it takes a special sort of madman to insert himself into the Devil's lair. We must only be born every few hundred years. No wonder the demonic employees weren't on edge. They were watching for people trying to get out, not waltz right in.

That made me feel better until I remembered that in a short amount of time, I'd be one of the poor suckers trying to get out too.

LEVEL SEVEN: VIOLENCE.

Apparently, there's a difference between violence and wrath, and as I gazed upon the Seventh Circle, I could tell that whatever it was, it was a big deal. The plane before us was made entirely of some viscous, boiling red liquid. If I didn't know better, I'd say it was blood—an ocean of it. As I looked, I saw figures struggling in the midst of its oozing grasp, trying to swim to the end.

One made it to the volcanic rocks at the edge and struggled to claw his way out of the nightmare seas. An arrow slammed into his chest, knocking him back into the bubbling liquid, and he sank.

So did my heart as I watched this terror. The souls I brought here as a Reaper had been bound for this circle. I didn't care if they deserved it; seeing their torture firsthand only made me feel complicit. I might as well have been one of the demons myself. Consumed by guilt, I turned away.

The circles on this side of Dis had truly become things of nightmares that lived up to the reputation of el Diablo and his fallen angels. Plus, now that I thought of it, if I had a besetting sin, it wasn't wrath.

I was a killer, a man of violence.

One day this could be my home too.

LEVEL EIGHT: FRAUD.

I felt a little better as we rode the escalator down to this level. This was a circle that I wasn't really in any danger of visiting. If anything, I was a *victim* of fraud, soul fraud that is. My eyes drilled into the back of Dan's skull as he led me through the empty halls. It might have been my imagination, but I felt like he twitched uncomfortably.

Whatever was going on in this circle didn't really make a lot of sense to me. There were rings within the rings, and people marched this way and that. Some were being whipped, others buried, and others still were being burned. I'm sure there was some sort of rhyme or reason to it, but I couldn't put it together. Maybe I'd get it if I had finished reading *Inferno*. But as I recall I had more important things to do that week, like take naps and eat cookies.

LEVEL NINE: TREACHERY.

My whole life, I've heard people use the expression *when Hell freezes over* as an indicator when something would change. I have bad news for them. It already has and nothing is different. The Ninth Circle of Hell was a frozen lake, completely still and tranquil. It reminded me of the Nothing. It was as close to a void as you could find while still existing. As far as the eye could see, people were encased in ice, unmoving.

For some reason, this level terrified me more than all the others before.

Once again, we walked halfway around the circle, and Dan led me to another escalator. I blinked in surprise; Dante had only ever spoken of nine levels. Maybe some service tunnels ran below everything.

Halfway down the escalator, Dan turned to stare at me, a curious expression on his face. I cocked my head to ask him *What?* without speaking. Just because there were fewer fiends down here didn't mean it was safe to talk.

The short demon didn't reply. Instead, he gestured with his hand at the placard waiting for me at the entrance to the new floor.

LEVEL TEN: MATTHEW CARVER—WICKED ABOVE ALL.

Oh crap.

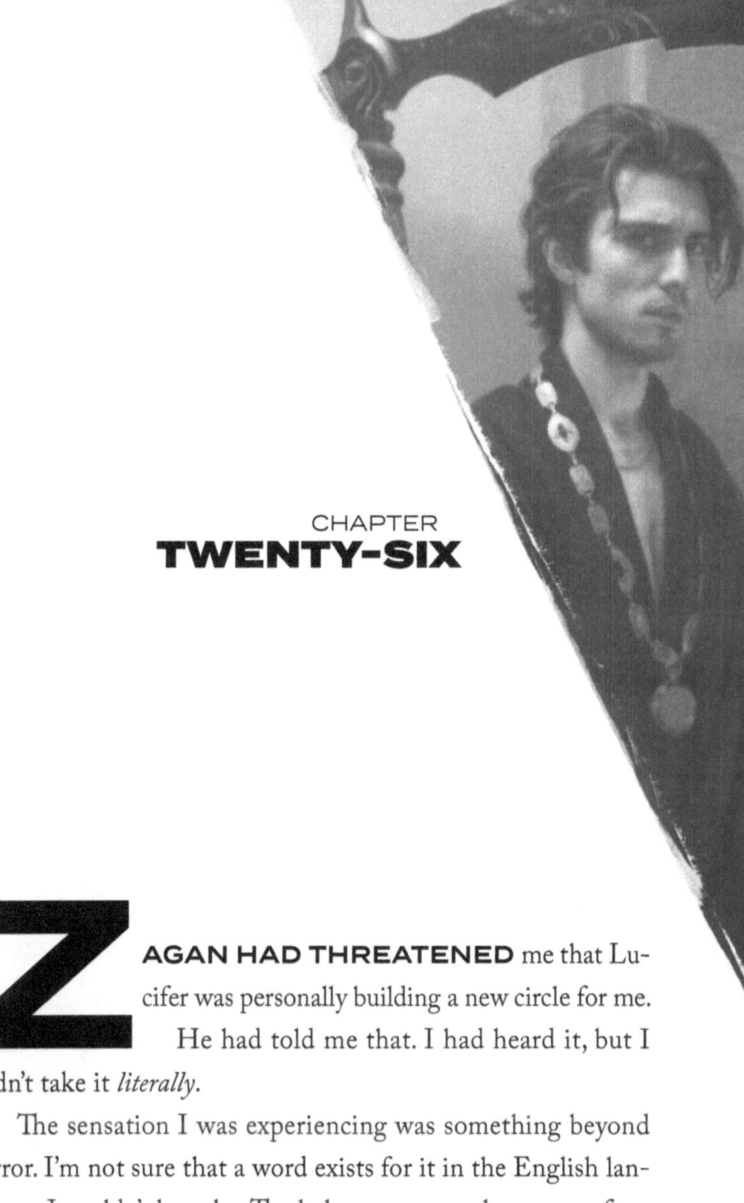

ZAGAN HAD THREATENED me that Lucifer was personally building a new circle for me. He had told me that. I had heard it, but I didn't take it *literally*.

The sensation I was experiencing was something beyond terror. I'm not sure that a word exists for it in the English language. I couldn't breathe. The helmet was too close to my face. Red swam at the edges of my vision as I followed Dan out into the circle of Hell dedicated to me. The first thing I noticed was that it was still under construction. The glass wall wasn't built yet, and planks extended out to the floating plane like bridges.

I found that oddly reassuring. Given that there was an

appointed hour for my death and all, I figured they would be in more of a hurry if they were expecting me to show up early.

Scaffolding was everywhere, draped with plastic tarps. It looked like the workers had just been here before heading off on their lunch break. I still couldn't believe that demons *ate* lunch, but it worked out for me, so who was I to look a gift horse in the mouth?

As I looked toward the center of the circle, though, the little thread of cheer I had managed to find quickly faded. In the center of the flat plane was a perfect re-creation of the cul-de-sac I had grown up on.

Every inch was exactly how I remembered it. The Richards' lawn even had the weird fountain that was crooked after my oldest sister Lily ran into it. There was the tree I fell out of, getting a scar on my knee for my troubles.

I didn't know what *He* was planning by re-creating the Weston Court cul-de-sac from Northridge, California, but after seeing all the other levels, I knew I was not going to like it.

I drifted forward on feet that I didn't remember ordering to walk. Slowly, against my own will, I made my way across my front yard and past the circle drive, where I knocked on the front door—my front door. I struggled to find a breath as I stood on my own porch. *Please be okay, Megan*, I prayed.

I wasn't surprised in the slightest when it swung open.

My sister, ghostly and translucent, stood inside the doorway. My heart leapt with joy to see her. The last time I spoke to her she had been a whimpering mess—which, I assume, I would be too if half of my soul were stranded in Hell. She seemed…better than I'd expected. I had been worried that I would burst in on a torture scene, but she looked like she had just woken up from a nap.

Megan crossed her arms and glowered at me. Relief flooded through me. I wasn't too late. They hadn't broken her spirit. "Aren't you a little short for a shock trooper?" she demanded.

"What? Oh, it's just a—" I ripped my helmet off without another thought. Megan's eyes widened in shock as she saw me, then a look of horror crossed her face.

"Surpriiiiiise!" I called, giving her a small smile. "This here is a rescue."

"What are you doing here, you idiot?" she gasped, her gaze flicking over my shoulder to the empty circle of Hell.

"What, you thought I was just gonna *leave* you here?" I demanded. "It's my fault that you're being tormented by the—"

"I told you to run." She wore the disapproving look of an older sister, one I had seen plenty of times before.

"Well, yeah, I've been doing plenty of that, don't worry. But I wasn't going to let you—"

"Oh, Matthew," Megan breathed, her expression softening to earnest disappointment. "You should have. *He* wanted you to come here, and here you are."

"What? Oh no! It's not—I'm not really—" I cut off my sentence abruptly, remembering that Dan was still here. I glanced at the fiend, who gazed at me with an almost pleasantly neutral expression on his face, his clawed hands clasped in front of him. He didn't need to know that I wasn't dead-dead. "This is an off-the-books operation. I'm just here to bust you out. That's why we came during lunch hour."

"Matt." Megan sighed disappointedly. "Did you really think that demons get breaks?" A cold fury settled over my heart as I looked down at the tiny demon who was no longer making eye contact with at me.

"Daniel," I said softly. "Did you set me up?"

"No!" he protested, waving his arms wildly at me. "I couldn't even if I wanted to! We *shook* on it."

"Are all the worker demons really on lunch break?"

"Yes."

My eyes narrowed as I tried to twist my mind like Robin, analyzing his response from every angle. "Do demons normally get a lunch break?"

"No."

"Why are they getting one today, Dan?" Part of me marveled at how cool and detached my voice was. By rights, I should be a gibbering mess. There was literally nowhere worse for me to be than in the center of the Tenth Circle of Hell, the wheelhouse of the Devil who hated me.

"Fallen angels have really good hearing," he muttered, his shoulders sagging.

Zagan.

The CFO had been listening when I negotiated with Dan to get my sister's soul back. I scrubbed my memory, trying to remember what the fiend had agreed to. He had promised not to betray me or sabotage me, but he hadn't said anything about warning me if they found out on their own.

"Dark Abyss," I swore.

In response, the lights went out.

The eerie re-creation of my neighborhood was plunged into darkness so deep that, for a second, I thought I had somehow died again and been sent into the hungry dark waiting to devour me. But after a moment, I realized I still had a body; I just couldn't see.

A beam of light, like the spotlight for a stage performer's

monologue, clicked on with an audible *clunk*. It shone down on the center of the cul-de-sac. A single figure stood there, wearing a smug expression as he inspected his fingernails.

Zagan, model-esque CFO of Hell and member of the Death Board, flicked his gaze up from his cuticles to spear me with a heavy stare. "I'm getting an insane bonus this Christmas," he drawled.

My heart stopped for a beat. My mind raced at the glee in his voice. This was so very bad. I was not supposed to be here on *so* many levels. I wasn't just Matthew Carver, the mortal whose soul had been stolen. I was also the heir of Death, and I had no jurisdiction here. The whole point of a heist is not to get caught.

Whoops. That's what I get for skipping out on the other nine members of the crew, I guess. But after the panic had its moment to flare, I realized I wasn't completely out of options. The Key of Janus still sat in my pocket. All I had to do was grab Megan and get the hell out of…Hell.

I just needed to find the right moment to make my move. So I matched the empty abyss of Zagan's stare with my own and tried to think of something clever to say, but I had nothing. I'll admit, I was rattled. How could I not be? I think even Alex would be stumped by this situation, and he's almost as good at one-liners as me.

As the silence stretched between us, Zagan arched an amused eyebrow, as if he couldn't believe I was still frozen. I couldn't either. Just when I needed my sarcasm the most, it had vanished. As the tension between us grew awkward, I decided there was only one thing to do.

"See ya!" I yelled, and spun, dashing into the home I had grown up in.

It was pitch black, but that didn't matter. I had snuck out of that place in the dead of night a thousand times. I had it *memorized*. Five steps down the hall, I took a right into the den. Twelve steps to the kitchen, but two of those were to the left to dodge the couch.

I thought I heard Zagan give an amused chuckle as I made a break for it. I probably seemed ridiculous, trying to run from an executive of Hell while at the very bottom of the Pit, like a toddler trying to run from its babysitter.

"Megan, follow me!" I shouted as I burst into the kitchen.

"Where? There is nowhere to run. Trust me, I've checked," she called after me, her voice annoyed. Despite her doubt, she trailed in my wake. That was fine. I was used to being underestimated by demons and older sisters alike.

"I have a plan!" I snapped.

"Not again," she groaned.

"Shut up and run."

I spun and dashed up the stairs, holding my hand in front of me so I would know when to turn to the left with the staircase. I never bothered to count the steps as a kid. How I wished I had now. I made it to the top and ran down the hall, letting my hand trail on the left wall. Megan's shade followed me, despite her doubts. I just needed to get away from the demon for a second.

"Knock, knock," Zagan called in a singsong voice from the front. His knuckles echoed off the door a few times. "Howdy, neighbor, new to the area?"

I ran faster.

Not the first door, but the second. As I encountered the recess in the hall, I dropped my hand to the knob and burst into Megan's room. I spun, motioning for her to follow me in.

I slammed the door shut behind us. This was it: time to find out if my plan would actually work.

"What now, genius?"

With my left hand, I scooped out the soul orb that I had snagged from the Death Corp offices. It was empty and lifeless, but hopefully not for long. With my right, I summoned the dark scythe of Death. Megan recoiled in the dim light as the weapon appeared out of thin air. Horror bloomed across her features, and I wondered what tortures she had been subjected to during her time here. Originally, I had hoped to walk her through why I needed to cut her with the scythe, but we were out of time. I could apologize later—if I didn't kill her again.

"It's not what it looks like."

"It looks like you're about to kill me!" She was panicking. Her eyes were wild with fear.

"Okay, well…kind of. But not permanently! I don't have time to explain. All you need to know is that I'm going to put your soul in this ball and get you out of here. Sound good?"

"Not really!"

"Sorry," I told my sister, steeling myself to do what needed to be done. My heart was hammering in my chest. If I was wrong, there would be no undoing this. *Please let me be right.*

"We're out of time," I whispered, my heart breaking to see the fear in her eyes. Megan had just enough time to scream before the hungry black blade passed through her shade. I felt no resistance—there was nothing physical about my sister's presence here. But the scythe drank up her shade greedily. I closed my eyes in horror as Megan's form faded.

I couldn't bear to watch. This was where I found out if my theory was correct. Either my sister's soul could be collected like the ones on the Rainbow Bridge, or I had just killed a part of her for good. My whole body sagged in relief as I opened my eyes and saw a single orange light hovering where Megan had been. With the Authority of Death, I called to it, and it came. Just like the souls I had rescued before, it sank into me, shining through my skin. I watched, transfixed, as it traveled up my right hand before vanishing under my uniform until it emerged onto my left. The orb seemed to call to her soul like the skull in Death's vault.

With a faint *pop*, the light zipped into the empty ball sitting in my right hand. A wild surge of joy shot through me as I watched the orb illuminate. Unlike any I had seen before, Megan's was filled only halfway. The top portion was gray and dull. That made sense, given her particular condition. The important part was, it was glowing. She was in there.

Good enough for now.

The stairs creaked as they always had when someone began making their way up. "Matthew, why are we doing this?" Zagan chuckled. "It's a bit late to run, isn't it?"

I barely managed not to whimper in fear as I realized how close the fallen angel was. Heart racing, I shoved Megan's soul into my pocket and fished out Janus's Key. This was it. If Zagan had turned off my access to the Between, I was so dead.

Well, I was technically already dead. This would be worse.

Megan's door opened inward, and I wasn't completely sure that would work. The Between always had me push the door into it. I had never tried to pull one open. But I knew exactly where I needed to go. My room was right across the hall.

Gripping the key in my hand, I sprinted out of Megan's room, lowering my shoulder toward my door as I jammed it forward like a knight's lance. I felt it settle into place as it always did. Thankfully, the magic that made the key always fit still worked. I twisted it to the right, unlocking the door a split second before I slammed into it with the full weight of my body.

It burst open and the sterile, white light of the space Between Underworlds shone through. My heart leapt in my chest as I crashed through the wrought-iron gate. I slid out of the smallest gap possible so I could slam it behind me swiftly.

I had just enough time to hear Zagan's furious shout before the gate clicked shut and I was alone in the Between. For a long time, I stood there doubled over. Ragged breaths came out of my mouth, and my shaking hands were still wrapped around the bars. I kept pushing against the gate, bracing to hold it shut against anything that might try to smash through after me.

Zagan wouldn't just let me go. He would follow me. He was a fallen angel; there was no stopping him. My plan wouldn't work. I wasn't smart enough. Something would go wrong—it always did.

But no attack came. Eventually, the shakes faded, and I let go of the gate, falling back on my rump as I sat on the floor. I leaned against one of the cold marble pillars, letting its chill ground me.

Slowly, I reached my hand into my pocket, terrified that the thing I had risked it all for wouldn't be there. I let out a sob of relief as my fingers closed around a familiar orb the size of a tennis ball. I pulled out Megan's soul and stared at the half-filled container, letting the sight of it fill me with a hope the rest of me didn't feel.

Short of getting captured and smuggled away into Hell early, getting seen was one of the worst possible outcomes for me. I had broken all sorts of rules that Zagan would be only too happy to bring up to Kane.

I had stolen a soul from the Devil. Sure, it was half a soul, and technically, he wasn't supposed to have it right now per the contract. But I don't think rules are a thing that bother the Devil when he decides to hold a grudge. I'd just poked the bear.

The Death Treaty itself might be damaged by my actions. Even so, as I gazed at the orb, knowing that Megan was no longer in his clutches made it all feel worth it. But the job wasn't done yet. I had gotten her out of Hell, but now I had to get her home.

TWENTY-SEVEN

ONCE TERROR FADES to a dull throb, corporate work after death is even more boring than it is in life. After slipping back into the Veil from the Between, I changed out of my shock trooper uniform and threw it back into the hallway. Getting caught with those fatigues in my closet would only lead to questions I did not want to answer. I managed to steal another pair of Reaper blacks without anyone noticing and did my best to lay low.

For the first few shifts, I kept waiting for Kane or Zagan to appear and drag me down a hall to Perdition. But after nothing happened, I began to suspect that there was something else going on. I mean, duh, when isn't there? Clearly the fallen angel's first move hadn't been to go and tattle to Daddy Death, but why?

I remembered how pleased he had been to catch me in the Tenth Circle. I wondered if he'd failed to warn His Devilness that I was coming, hoping to deliver me as a surprise gift. But instead of now having me as a prize, he had lost something of immense value. I found more than a little bit of joy in the thought of Zagan and Dan being on the hook for letting Megan's soul get stolen.

But yeah, once the fear wasn't overwhelming, desk duty was super boring. There's something crushingly depressing about the fact that it's possible for a human soul to spend its entire mortal life chained to a desk, just to end up back at one on the other side.

Ralph, the Reaper office manager, seemed to take perverse delight in assigning me the most mundane tasks he could, which seemed like a bold choice for how to treat the next in line. I didn't want to end up running this place, but if I ever do, there's a couple of people at the top of my list for downsizing.

That's how I found myself sitting on an office chair in the Reaper staging hallway, the same one that Wilbur and I had used to return to the real world and collect souls. Now instead of being sent out, I marked Reapers in and out of their shifts, then double-checked that they'd finished their lists. It was so simple, a six-year-old could do it.

There are no days in that place on the edge of Time, so I had no idea how long I had been trapped. My watch now read 8:17 p.m., and I was beginning to get stressed.

Since I was laying low, I had decided to wait a bit before making a run at Hades to complete Midas's request. I still needed to get my hands on the Crown of Immortality, but I was saving that problem for last. Stealing from Death was even scarier than robbing the Devil.

I snapped out of my brooding as a dark slash appeared in the air at the end of the hall announcing that a Reaper was returning from the Living World. Time for me to do my three minutes of work.

The rip in the Veil widened, and I relaxed a little as Wilbur stepped through. The crack began to close behind him, shrinking to nothing as he exited. I gave him a friendly smile and rose from my chair, clipboard in hand.

"Hey man, welcome back!" I said cheerfully. "Everything go okay?"

"Yeah," Wilbur replied quietly, not quite meeting my eyes. Now that the heir thing wasn't a secret anymore, the other Reapers avoided me like the plague. I don't know if it was fear or jealousy, but I was surprised at how lonely I began to feel after a while. Even my first friend treated me differently now.

"Nice. No more Lost running around lately?"

"Not since the one we saw together." I felt my smile tighten as I held back a wince. If he wouldn't talk to me, there was no way I was ever going to get along with the other animals in the zoo.

"Well, I'm glad you haven't had to face one on your own then," I offered.

"Yeah, that's nice I guess." Wilbur's eyes remained firmly fixed on the floor, as if he was too embarrassed to even look at me.

"Okay, I have you down for a hundred souls. All done?" He handed me his clipboard without reply. Each name had his initials, WJM, next to it. I nodded, marking him off-duty on my sheet.

"Nice. Dude, you're a machine," I told him as I finished the paperwork. "You were my last Reaper in the field, so I'm on break too. Wanna hang out?"

"Oh, I don't know, I'm pretty tired," Wilbur murmured, a flush creeping up his cheeks. "I was going to rest for a little bit."

"Right." I swallowed, feeling a surprising sting of disappointment. The willowy Reaper scurried down the hall like a cockroach fleeing the light.

I wished Alex were here. Well, kind of. I didn't wish he was dead or anything. But doing this on my own was harder than I'd thought. My friend had been with me every step of the way since my soul had been stolen. This was the longest I had gone without his advice and backup, and I was getting tired of it. Feeling more than a little dour, I decided to take a page out of Wilbur's advice book and get some rest myself.

A pair of Reapers I hadn't seen before walked past me as I made my way toward the dormitories. Now that I had been signing the field gatherers in and out, I had been introduced to more of Death's employees, but that still left a lot of unknowns.

If I was going to trace the stolen souls back to their source, then I had to find a way to break into Reaper social circles. So I turned, opening my mouth to call after the two of them, just in time to see a scythe hurtling toward my face at lightning speed.

Instead of a nap, I got jumped in a hallway.

Orion's training took over, and I dropped into a crouch, springing to the side as the blade carved through where my torso had just been. Instinctively, my brain called for power to help me fight back. Usually that meant a cheerful red fire would burst into being and engulf my fists. But Willow couldn't reach me on this side of the Veil. Instead, my mind found a different power lurking within me.

A black scythe of my own sprang into being, and I raised it in time to stop the second Reaper's swing. There was a muted peal like a distant bell as our two weapons struck, and I stared in horror as white cracks began to run down the haft of mine. It seemed that these Reapers had more Authority than I did.

We'll see about that. Outrage bubbled in my chest. These two idiots thought they could take me? They thought that just because I was new to being a Reaper, they were my equal? They must not know about the Hunter. I would be more than happy to show them his teachings.

The first attacker, a short, balding man who, given how red his face was, looked like he had died of either a heart attack or extreme sunburn, came at me again. In death he was light on his feet and moved more fluidly than I would have thought possible given his physique.

I sidestepped his attack, retreating down the hallway. The long, narrow space gave me a natural defense against my would-be attackers. Our scythes were long enough that they could only come at me one at a time. The second Reaper stepped in to take a crack at me. Tall and lanky, his weapon flashed toward me with confidence. He'd been at this longer than I had.

The white fissures widened on my scythe when his blows landed. String Bean definitely had more Authority at his command than Sunburn. That meant I'd use him as my example. If my fellow Reapers didn't respect me yet, maybe after today they would.

They switched places, and I retreated from the bright-faced Reaper, blocking his somewhat clumsy attacks with ease. What an idiot. It was clear that he didn't know what he was doing.

"Say, fellas, why don't we talk about this?" I asked between breaths. Although I didn't have a lot of experience fighting with a scythe, this was pretty basic stuff. My feet already knew what to do.

String Bean stepped forward, a frustrated look in his eyes. It was clear to him that his ally wasn't putting me under pressure, but he could see the damage his weapon had done to mine. I could tell that he thought he had me.

Good.

This time he stepped toward me aggressively, assuming that I would continue to fall back under his attacks. But my time retreating was over. The lean man set his stance like a baseball player and swung his scythe as if he were preparing to hit a home run. I channeled Death's power through his signet ring on my finger, using my will to coerce all that cold strength into reinforcing my weapon.

String Bean's scythe crashed into mine and shattered under the force of the blow like a piece of balsa wood smashing into a cement wall. Shards of the black weapon flew past me like shrapnel, fading as they went. My opponent collapsed to his knees, screaming in agony at the disruption of his power. Slowly, I lowered my scythe so that the blade rested horizontally on his shoulders.

That shut him up.

Sunburn froze, his eyes wide. I held his gaze and let a mocking, sinister smile grow on my face. On the inside, though, I was panicking. Kane had been right when he told me that the other Reapers would come for me. I was no longer safe here—and I wouldn't be unless something changed.

They needed to fear me.

String Bean opened his eyes and looked at me in horror, his mouth hanging open. For a moment we just stared at each other, him pleading, me panicking—not sure what I should do.

I knew what Orion would do.

I knew what Kane would do.

But I didn't know if killing him was what I wanted. Sure, he was already dead. But one of the few things they had covered during orientation was that dying again while on the job was even *worse*. I'd sent people down to meet their maker and check in for their final stay in the Underworld, but unmaking someone was a different step.

I also couldn't afford to show weakness. If one of us was going to end up in the dark beyond, I had a vote on who. But what if there was a different outcome? Maybe there was a way I could use mercy to make them fear me more.

With meticulous patience, I drew my scythe back like a headsman preparing for his final swing. String Bean's eyes closed, and he let out a pathetic whimper. I snarled and swung the blade toward his neck, rotating my wrist as I did so the blade turned away and the back of the pole hit him instead. The force lifted him up and slammed him into the wall.

I ignored him as he slid to the ground like a sack of potatoes, turning my glare onto Sunburn, who was staring at me with horrified awe. I bared my teeth and took a step toward the short man, who spun and began sprinting as fast as he could.

A savage smile grew on my face as I lowered my head and gave chase. There were two parts to this plan: I wanted lots of people to see him gibbering in fear as he ran from me. If being dead is anything like being in high school, only a handful of people needed to spot that before everyone would know about it tomorrow. But I also was curious where he would run. Who did he think would protect him from me?

I cackled madly as I chased Sunburn down the halls, passing other employees of Death Delivery Corp. By the twelfth shocked face I didn't even have to fake my grin anymore. This was kinda funny. They tried to murder me; the embarrassment was on the house.

The fleeing Reaper made deliberate turns as he raced through the corridors, strengthening my suspicion that he had somewhere to go, so I dropped into a comfortable lope and settled in to follow him as long as I needed to.

All rats scurry back into their hole eventually.

Sure enough, he led me out of the front office and back into the warehouses where the souls were sorted. I frowned as he ducked through a pair of double doors into a room marked STORAGE AB–AC. I hadn't been down here since Death had given me my introductory tour.

I followed the man into the room and let the doors swing shut behind me with a loud crash. There was no point in trying to be subtle. I was here to intimidate, after all.

Looking around the room, my eyes narrowed as I realized there was no sign of Sunburn. I stood in a giant warehouse whose center aisle ran back as far as I could see. It was dimly lit, with only the lights running down the middle turned on, creating a series of bright pools surrounded by the dark. Rows and rows of shelves were stacked with soul cartons, their orange lights glowing in the dusk.

Hanging from the ceiling of each row was a sign marking the names of the people waiting to be delivered to their final destination. The first sign on my left read ABERNATHY–ABHANG;

the next continued in the same vein. It was like a library of people, and I felt the hair on the back of my neck prickle as I took in the sheer size of it. I had helped deliver thirty thousand souls to Hell, but this was another order of magnitude.

Forcing myself to focus, I strode down the center aisle, glancing down the rows as I passed, looking for the fleeing Sunburn. If he had tucked himself away in one of these shelf structures, this was going to be the most annoying game of hide and seek of all time.

"Come out, come out, wherever you are," I called. "I just want to talk," I promised, then chuckled darkly. Let him figure out what that meant. I allowed the scythe in my hand to fade away but kept Death's power humming in my veins.

In any other room, I might have missed the slight rustle of cloth as something dashed past me to my right, but this room carried the silence of the grave. Out of the corner of my eye I caught a flicker of motion to my left, the shifting of shadow on shadow.

Ah.

I knew what this was. Sunburn and String Bean weren't acting alone. With a sigh, I slowed to a stop in one of the pools of light, trying to act bored. I placed one hand on my hip and summoned my scythe, leaning on it like a doorpost. Internally, I pulled Death's ring as hard as I could, letting the cold power fill me to the brim. I could make out more sounds of movement now. I was more surrounded than a southern belle at a line dance. For a moment, I worried that Sunburn had led me to a forgotten basement full of mummies and crypt-keepers, some of Death's forgotten minions.

But after a moment of reflection, I realized the only monsters here were men. The more the mysterious figures circled, the more I realized they were trying to rattle me.

"You might as well come out," I called into the dark. "I've got a nap to take, and all this swirling is eating into my break time." The rustling of circling Reapers fell silent, and after a moment, dark figures began to emerge from the wings and into the low light of the center aisle to surround me.

I felt my fake heart skip a beat as I counted six—no, seven—of my fellow Death Corp employees all carrying their scythes, but I pulled a page from Orion's book and kept my face as blank as a stone. I recognized Rex and Yuki right away, both of them gave me blank looks. A few of the others were Reapers I had signed in and out since my stint in administration had begun. Goosebumps flared down my arms as I realized that the corrupt Reapers I had been looking for were right under my nose the whole time.

But I hadn't expected to see Wilbur here. The skinny southern boy stared at the ground at my feet, not meeting my eyes, as I felt my guts twist with the knife of betrayal. Postmortem friendships don't seem to have much sticking power.

"Guess we ended up hanging out after all, huh?" I asked him softly, not sure if my voice was cold with the Authority of Death or with my own hurt. Wilbur winced but didn't look up, something like shame lurking around his furrowed eyebrows. I held my stare, letting him feel the weight of it for a moment.

I didn't recognize the man standing at the head of the ring. He had dark black hair that matched his Reaper blacks. He alone hadn't bothered to summon his weapon, and he stared at me with pursed lips, hands in the pockets of his uniform. It would be a lot more convincing if he hadn't felt the need to bring an entire strike force with him.

Sunburn stood next to him, even redder in the face after our little run. He held his scythe with something of a death grip, knuckles tight and white. I gave him a little wink, and impossibly his complexion moved even closer to that of a tomato.

"Seriously, how did you die?" I asked him, ignoring their leader. "It has to be skin cancer, right? If you had just used a good SPF like at least once, you would not be here right now."

"Enough," the stranger's British accent cut through my banter coolly, oddly flat. "It is time that we met."

"Fine. Let's meet. I'm Matt. We good?"

"And I am Jack, the boss of the Reapers."

"Actually," I snorted, raising my hand to show him the skull signet around my finger, "I think that's me." The rest of his gang shuffled like dogs waiting to be fed.

"Give me the ring."

I arched an eyebrow. "Want to run that by me again?" I asked softly, matching his flat tone. A lot of beings had been demanding I give them my stuff lately. Compared with gods, this guy was just an annoying puff of wind.

"Give me the ring that makes you Death's heir," he repeated. His eyes too had gone flat, like a reptile's. I shuddered slightly, reminded of the cold-blooded dragoons that had plagued me a few months ago.

Glancing at the murder of Reapers that surrounded me, I shifted my scythe forward but kept leaning on it, as if I didn't have a care in the world. Rex and Yuki were both dangerous fighters; I knew that firsthand. Wilbur didn't worry me too much. He was too new and hadn't benefited from the teachings of the Hunter. The others I didn't know much about, but if they were still retrieving souls, I was guessing they wouldn't be able to summon as much Authority as either of the two Reapers who'd gone into the Nothing with me. If things got spicy, I'd go for one of them first.

"No," I replied with a smile that did not reach my eyes.

"You're not better than us!" shrieked Sunburn, his red face dangerously close to being the same shade as a fire alarm. Drawing back his scythe, he took an angry step toward me, his courage apparently restored by the presence of six of his friends.

I eyed his approach without any fear, a dark instinct whispering in my mind. The Authority that I carried knew the outcome even before I did. It seemed that my earlier mercy had been a waste.

Sunburn stepped into range—well, he stepped into *my* range, which was different from his. In one explosive movement, I stood up straight and swung my scythe across my body, parallel to the ground.

As the weapon traveled, it grew like the long hand of Death, covering the distance between us in a heartbeat. The red-faced Reaper had just enough time to scream and raise his own scythe in a feeble attempt to block my strike.

But on his best day, he didn't have the Authority to tell me no.

The scythe in his hands turned to glass and shattered, jagged dark pieces falling to the floor like the remains of a precious vase. My weapon continued in its deadly arc and sliced through him as if he were made of paper. For a moment there were two halves of the sunburned man, but then they began to fade, becoming translucent. Before either part of him could hit the floor, he was gone. I felt the spark of his soul trying to find refuge under my skin, but I rejected it, banishing it to the dark with my will. It vanished, collapsing in on itself like a star going supernova.

The room became very, *very* still.

I dropped the butt of my weapon to the floor, and it shrank in on itself, returning to its normal proportions in the blink of an eye. I swallowed my discomfort at the thought that I had just unmade someone, sending them to the True Death that waited beyond death, and forced myself to meet Jack's cold, dead eyes.

"Sorry, you were just saying something, but I got distracted."

"Where'd you steal that soul from?" Jack replied as if nothing had happened, hands still in his pockets.

The darkness around us grew deeper as I froze. For a moment, I thought my entire body had turned solid. I couldn't think, only feel as an overwhelming terror swept over me, conquering even Death's icy clarity. Unconsciously, my left hand slipped toward my pocket where Megan's soul was squirreled away. Somehow the corrupt Reaper knew. I was so dead.

"What soul?" I demanded, but my voice was shaky. I might as well have admitted it. Jack's toothy grin slashed me as sharply as my scythe had sliced through Sunburn.

"A pity Wilbur hadn't brought you to see me first. We could have shown you how it was done." I narrowed my eyes at his blatant admission to soul stealing. Sure, I was technically guilty of a similar crime, but I wasn't bold enough to go around saying it *out loud*. Either he thought that he had enough to hold over my head to keep me silent or he wasn't planning on letting me leave this warehouse.

"I won't give her to you."

"I don't want you to give it to me, are you daft? If old Grim finds out what you're carrying, he'll tear you to bits. I don't want my prints anywhere near you and your smuggled cargo. Never bring it here, that's the trick."

"What do you want then?"

"I need my lot off desk duty,"

"What?" I blinked in surprise at the change of topic. I was expecting him to demand the ring again.

"You asked what I want. I want the rest of my crew restored to active service. Pronto." Huh, maybe Zagan hadn't demanded that the three of us be put on the bench just to screw with me. Jack's crew must have been feeling the pressure if he was trying to extort me to undo it. Interesting.

"And if I don't make this happen, Kane finds out about my passenger?" I guessed. Jack may not have wanted Megan's soul, but he was happy to use the leverage that the knowledge gave him.

"Bingo," Jack's smile turned into more of a sneer.

"What if I give him a list of names of Reapers who have been stealing souls right under his nose?"

"Go ahead, mate, you're one of us too." Jack's mocking laughter was sharp enough to cut. My eyes strayed to the scythe lurking in my right hand. Maybe there was another way to settle this.

"Uh-uh" the cold man warned, wagging a finger at me. "Don't go getting any big ideas, Matthew. If I don't return from this little parlay, one of my men will take this news straight to Death on my behalf." Of course.

"What about them? Why not get them to ask Dad to let us back out to play?" I jerked my head back at where Yuki and Rex lurked behind me.

"They've already tried. But they're not the heir."

"Why try to take the ring from me if you need me to talk him into releasing us?"

A grin passed across the other Reaper's face. "I had to know if you had the mettle to look Death in the face and lie to him."

"You want me to go barge into Death's office and demand to be put back on duty?" I asked, feeling a little incredulous.

"If that's what it takes."

Kane had promised the Death Board that we would be prevented from any meaningful work until our names could be cleared. There was no way I was going to be able to talk him into breaking his word. But what choice did I have?

"If I do this, we're square? You'll forget about this whole situation?"

"Of course," Jack shrugged as if it was no big deal. "Cross my heart and hope to die."

"Fine," I agreed, not believing him in the slightest. "I'll see what I can do." At a nod from Jack, the ring around me broke, freeing me to leave. I paused as I turned away, looking back at the somber form of Wilbur.

"You don't have to be like them. I know we're dead, but what we do still matters." He was still for several moments as if struggling to think of the right words to say. I didn't wait for him to find them. It was time to go see Death.

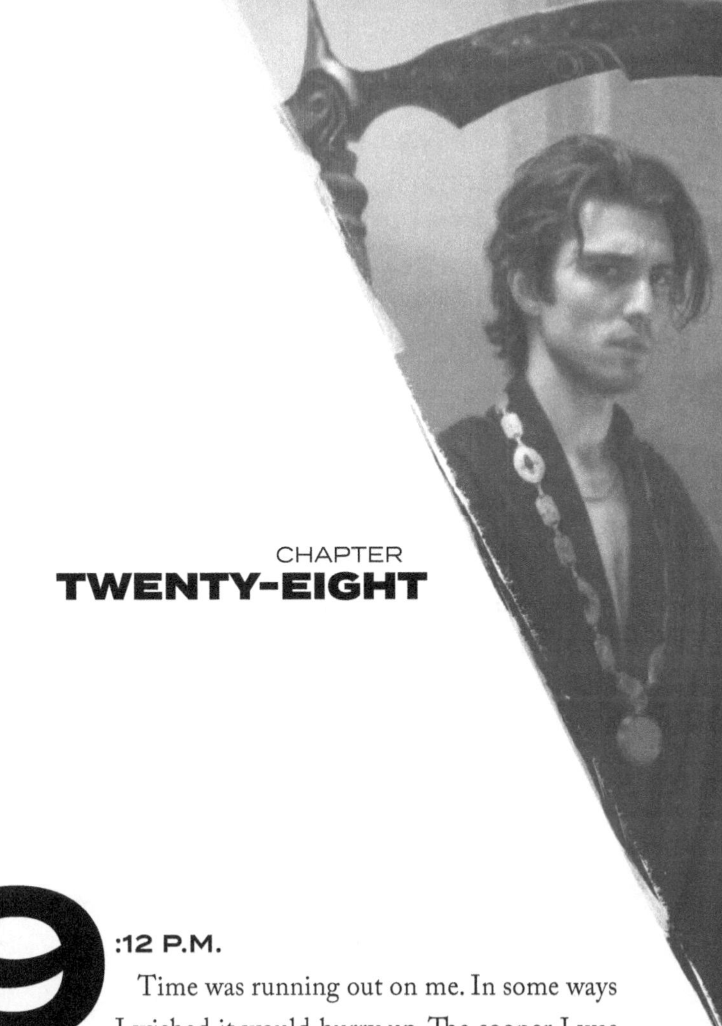

CHAPTER
TWENTY-EIGHT

9:12 P.M.

Time was running out on me. In some ways I wished it would hurry up. The sooner I was back on the Living side of the Veil, the sooner I would be out from underneath Jack's thumb. But I still needed to collect my Impossible Task from Midas before it was too late. According to Atalanta, all the Sorcerer Kings capable of granting me one were dead. This would be my one opportunity to take advantage of that loophole in my contract.

I also needed to steal the Crown of Immortality to keep Lazarus from trying to carve my sister up like a science experiment. As if it wasn't enough to be smuggling a soul out from under Kane's nose, I had to plunder his own vaults too.

But first, I had to get Jack off my back or there wasn't going to be any Matthew Carver to bring back to life. So, I did what he asked and went to see Death.

As with all good quests, in order to reach the final boss, I had to first make my way past the guards. Kane was brooding in his office, which was something of a common occurrence for Old Grim. I guess when you're trapped inside the Veil, unable to venture beyond, there isn't much more to do.

But between me and his door was a powerful fortification, a large marble desk staffed by Atty, more fearsome than any infantry division. The older woman eyed me distastefully at the sound of my approach, her dour face somehow twisting into an even more severe frown.

On her desk was one of those stenographer's keyboards, made up of far too few keys. Her fingers flashed at an inhuman speed as she typed, even with her glare fixed on me.

"What do you want?" she sniffed. An old-timey printer at the edge of her desk was processing what she typed line by line, gears whining. The paper appeared to be from one spool, and it curled in on itself as it went, like one of those eternally long pharmacy receipts.

Distracted from her glare, I glanced at the printout, eyes narrowing as I strained to read the faint print:

Dord, Phillip

Dork, Caleb

Dormand, Pier

Dorne, Bailey

Dornt, Peter

Dornt, Rachel

Dornt, Victoria
Doro, Jace
Dorpe, Tyrone
Dort, Kev—

"I said, what do you want?" Atty's crisp voice ripped my attention away from the list of names. A sinister feeling spread through my body as I gazed back into her cold eyes. Given where I worked, I knew what that was.

"Is that the list?" I demanded, unable to keep the horror out of my voice. Now that I looked at it more closely, I recognized it as the same sheets that were issued to Reapers when we crossed the Veil to collect new souls.

The printer whined in the background as it inked another line. Atty stared at me, her fingers still flying. I wondered how much longer it would be until she ran out last names that started with *D*.

"He doesn't make the list?"

"Death is not Fate," the old woman replied with a haughty scoff. "He makes deliveries, not decisions." I was silent for a moment, trying to process. My eyes flicked back to the names she was typing. I wondered where they really came from. Did Fate have its own set of offices in the Nothing, where its staff compiled the list and faxed it to Atty? Once on a case with Orion, I met someone who had been an Oracle, so it seemed plausible to me.

"Now tell me what you want or get out of here. Some of us have *real* work to do."

"I need to see him," I replied, nodding toward the big glass wall that led to Kane's office.

"He's busy."

"Not making the list or checking it twice, apparently."

Atty gave me a dour glare. "He's busy all the same."

"I'm his heir. Surely that means I can snag a few minutes from his schedule from time to time?" I let a little of his cold Authority creep into my tone, reminding her that I spoke with the voice of Death, whether or not she found that impressive.

"He's got some time next century." She dismissed me with a nod of her head. "Now shoo."

I stared at her for a moment, feeling anger beginning to boil up my neck like magma in a volcano. She might know when people are supposed to die, but she didn't know everything. She had been wrong about me, after all.

Well, kinda.

With a flash of insight, I wondered if that was why she didn't like me. If her job was organizing Fate's list of mortal deaths for the Reapers, then I could see how someone showing up at the wrong time might be a problem. Maybe everyone else thought she had made a mistake and missed me on the roster. Was my showing up early a demerit on her personal record? I doubted Death's HR department would tell me.

"Did you ever figure out how I ended up here early?" I asked, watching her closely. For the first time Atty's fingers paused, and she turned to stare at me with open hostility. I had been going for something a bit more conversational, but I think I missed the mark. Small talk is not one of my strengths. Oops.

"I just feel bad if you got blamed," I rushed to explain, holding up my hands in a placating gesture. "I didn't even know that you collected Fate's list. I hope I didn't cause you any problems."

Atty's expression softened ever so slightly, and her fingers resumed their lightning-fast typing. The printer whined as it spun back to life, spitting out the names she fed it. "It's not unheard of," she told me gently. "Usually, it revolves around someone's Fate being changed by an unexpected circumstance."

"Like maybe some sort of forged demonic contract?" I asked, arching an eyebrow. I wondered if I could get her to give me this testimony in writing, just in case.

"Could be," she said with a shrug. "Once someone's thread has been cut, Fate cannot see it anymore. Whatever happened to bring you here early is hidden now." I remembered how Beatrice and her technomancers had shown me runes designed to obscure my journey from Fate. They must have worked.

"Well, I'm still sorry," I said honestly. "I promise I didn't *want* to die early. Not a lot of fun waiting for me on this side."

To my absolute surprise, Atty chuckled slightly, her features softening like a melting iceberg. Had she really just been mad at me for dying too soon this whole time? I guess if that made it look like she had made a mistake, it wasn't completely insane. But still.

"You can have five minutes," she warned, eyebrows narrowing into angles.

"Thank you," I replied genuinely, giving her a small bow. "I promise to not overstay my welcome. If anything, I'd argue that me arriving here early proves that. Didn't even use up all my time in the Living World." Atty gave another chuckle and shook her head.

Delighted by my good fortune, I hustled past her desk, heading toward Death's door. I was absolutely going to add "charmer of Fate" to my résumé, right next to the bit about making Fae princesses laugh.

I raised my hand and knocked on the door as I turned the handle, letting it be more of a warning than a chance for Kane to ignore me. I had already made it past his sentinel; no way would I risk being stopped now. Too much was riding on this conversation.

The door swung open to reveal Death sitting behind his desk with a black book in his hands. His eyes lifted from the page, and a grim expression settled on his features when he saw me. "Come in," he said, sighing, letting the book fall to his desk carelessly.

"Something tells me you've been expecting me." I made my way to one of the leather chairs in front of his desk and flopped down, trying to act more relaxed than I felt. I don't care how brave you are, facing Death himself is intimidating, even if he is an oddly pleasant person.

"You're the last of my grounded Reapers to come to complain."

"I heard," I grunted noncommittally. "I guess they're eager to get back out there."

"Apparently," Kane muttered, glancing down at the book on his desk. I paused for a moment, trying to decide how I should handle this.

Yuki and Rex were both working with Jack, who was obviously running some sort of Reaper mafia, stealing souls. Although how exactly that business worked, I couldn't tell. It's not like we could be bribed with money. Where would we spend it? We were dead, and the rules were pretty clear that you can't take anything with you. The Veil itself guaranteed it, acting like a big pool strainer between the living world and the Underworlds. There must be some sort of leverage, but I hadn't cracked whatever it was yet.

Jack certainly had leverage on me so I couldn't tell Kane what was going on directly, but maybe I could bury a few clues that would make the whole house of cards come tumbling down after I was safe and sound on the other side. That would make my conscience feel a lot better.

"Being chained to a desk isn't exactly helping me uncover the traitors inside the Reapers," I lied.

Death let out a grunt of acknowledgment but didn't seem inclined to comment.

"I'm trying to get closer to Jack, there's something going on there." I resisted the urge to bite my lip as I watched Death's face. I felt like Icarus, flying far too close to the sun.

Kane let out an annoyed hiss.

"Not a big fan of Jack?"

"His tenure here is almost concluded. Originally, I thought he would excel at the role, but he has proven to be one of my least favorite recruits of all time."

"Why is that?"

"He was a killer. Killers make excellent Reapers." A cold hand of terror stroked my spine as I realized that the same could be said of me. For a brief second, I felt a pang of loss for my innocence, which had been taken from me along with my soul.

"But he's never learned to let go," Kane continued with an irritated mutter.

"Let go of what?"

"Life. Some Reapers struggle to accept that they are truly dead and see their time in my service as a sort of second life, second chance. It is not."

I did my best to keep my face very still.

"Souls are vanishing at an alarming rate." Death's face grew darker as a shadow of anger passed over it. "I had already begun to suspect that something deeper was going on before you told me about the Dragon Dons and their ten thousand stolen souls."

"Why did that add to it?"

"Because the dragons do not have an Underworld of their own."

I paused for a moment to process that. Obviously, the Dons had implied that the souls were stolen, but that was before I had been to the other side of the Veil and seen how everything worked.

Even to get the souls, the Dons must have worked with someone else and then put them somewhere.

"Are you sure it's not the demons?" I asked. "That was the implication I got."

"You've met Zagan." Death chuckled darkly. "You tell me if you think it's likely that he's unaware of souls being stolen from his coffers."

That was a very good point. I rubbed a hand over my face as I tried to think through all the implications. The CFO of Hell had proven more than capable in all my encounters with him. If Doyle had ten thousand souls that were missing from the Pit, that implied there were more on the market.

I looked up at Kane in horror. "You're talking about a con-spiracy."

"Ten thousand of my souls don't just go *missing*."

I suddenly felt very small. The Nothing that spread out behind Death's windows was oppressive. I've never been to space, but I imagine the first men who went to the moon might have experienced something similar.

"Hey," I asked, a different line of questions occurring to me. "Who is Mother Ruin?" Pluto had used her name as a weapon against Kane, but I had no idea who he had been talking about. Instinctively, I flinched at the snarl that crossed Death's face at the name. It occurred to me that I had seen him serious before, but I had never seen him angry.

"She is a chief servant of the Nothing—a goddess of entropy who embraced being Lost, seeking to devour worlds that cannot pay their soul mortgage. She killed Yama, one of the board members I trusted most, and ever since then the Lost have been plaguing us as if an anthill has been kicked over."

Uh-oh. I had assumed the mark that the Lost were always gibbering about was something that lots of people could see. Many supernatural creatures could tell that I had an infernal deal just by looking at me. Why should this be any different? Unless of course it was.

"I don't suppose," I managed through a suddenly dry throat, "that Mother Ruin is an Olympic goddess about six feet tall, with black hair and purple eyes?" My voice trailed off as Death's eyes pinned me in place like a pair of spikes.

"You've seen her?" His voice was colder than the North Pole.

"Yup."

"Where?"

"It was before I died, on the other side of the Veil," I replied, thinking as fast as I could. While I was super sympathetic to the whole soul stealing thing, and I definitely didn't want Death Delivery Corp to lose their contract, I didn't think it was the best idea for me to tell Kane about the Key of Portunus and Janus in my pocket.

"I didn't have a clue about what she was until I saw Pluto.

I'd never met an Olympian before." I paused, connecting another dot that I hadn't before. "But how does she serve the Nothing if she is part of the same pantheon as Pluto? That seems like a conflict of interest?"

"Previously, she was called Aite, and she was the goddess of ruin. Long ago, in the time of Homer, she betrayed Zeus, before he changed his name to Jupiter, and he banished her from the halls of Olympus. Over the centuries she began to serve a new master and earned her new name, Mother Ruin."

"Is she part of the Lost?"

"Yes. She is the prophetess of the Nothing. She seeks the end of all things."

My eyes tracked away from him to the endless void lurking outside the window. Oh yeah, that seemed way worse. "Is the Nothing alive?" I asked in horror.

"Not the way that things in Reality are," Death replied darkly, glancing over his shoulder at the encroaching dark. "But it has a hunger that drives it like a mind and creatures that serve it." I resisted the urge to gulp in fear.

My mind flashed back to the black-togaed woman who had accosted me in the Between. She had come out the door of a consumed world that had its seal broken. My best guess was that Aite—Mother Ruin—had managed to get into the Between because the dragoon that had been stranded in there, had broken the chains sealing one of the devoured worlds. If she was able to move through the Nothing, it would make sense that she could access those fallen doors.

"Yama's death is what led you to make me your heir. You needed another ally after losing someone you trusted?"

Death grunted but did not comment.

"Which means you don't trust all the other members of the board," I continued, heart racing. I still wasn't sure that I should tell Kane about my access to the Between, but if it would prevent the Underworlds from firing Death Delivery Corp, then it might be worth the sacrifice.

"I don't know who I can," he admitted after a moment. It occurred to me how much he had changed since I first met him. When I had come to the Veil, he had been surprisingly cheerful for the personification of Death. But now he was really putting the "Grim" in Reaper. Things must be getting worse at an alarming rate. I guess the Dreadknight and Elder waking were enough to have even him worried. "There's a layer to this that I cannot fathom. The Lost have always sought to feed on souls, and the Nothing has always tried to devour Reality. These are not new, and yet there is something about this time that troubles me. This is different from how it has always been."

I tried not to let that terrify me. If Death, who had been here since the beginning, had never seen anything like this, what was I supposed to do to help? I was twenty-five years old. I did not have a real college degree. This was so far above my pay grade that it wasn't even the same company.

But I was wearing the cold ring of Death on my right hand. I had accepted this burden as a price of power. The one thing that I did feel confident saying I knew anything about was making deals. Make no mistake, this was a deal, and I had to see it through.

"You wanted my help," I half whispered into the silence, reminded of the time that I convinced Dawn to bring Mav to the Constellation Convention. "In order for me to help, you have to use me. I'm no good to you pushing paper. Put me back out on the streets and I'll crack this case for you, Chief."

Death gave me another blank stare, his immortal, tired eyes cloudy with confusion. "Is this another one of your modern references?" he asked.

"Yes," I snapped, leaping to my feet. "You gave me a badge; you trusted me to get to the bottom of this. But you gotta get out of my way and let me do my job. Otherwise, the perps are going to get away with it." Kane mouthed the word *perps* to himself, which almost made me choke on a manic laugh. "Put me back on active duty, and let me hunt these rats."

"I don't know what you're talking about," Death told me, "but if going back out there is what you want, you're in luck. You and your fellow Reapers are going back on delivery duty."

"We are?" I paused mid-rant, giving him a surprised look. "I thought I was going to have to sell this harder."

"It's not your salesmanship that matters…"

"There's been another attack?"

"There's been another attack."

Feeling a little embarrassed at my unnecessary outburst, I lowered myself back into the plush leather seat. I don't know why he'd let me get my little speech started if he was going to give me what I wanted anyway.

"What happened?"

"A smaller convoy carrying a delivery to Hel was destroyed."

"Why is it always Hell?" I groaned.

"No, Hel," Death corrected me.

"That's what I said? Hell?"

"One *L*, the Norse Underworld."

"Ohhh," I breathed. "I always forget about that one."

"Five hundred souls were Lost, and two of my Reapers."

"So now the Death Board agrees that we're innocent?" I asked.

"I pointed out that the only convoy to completely fight off a raid recently was defended by the three Reapers that I was being prevented from using, and the tone changed." A grim smile flashed across Kane's face, reminiscent of his old self.

"Now we're talking." I rubbed my hands together, feeling a spark of hope and relief kindle in my chest. This would be enough to get Jack of my back. I had a chance to pull everything off, and I was going to take it. "I'm back in the game, Coach. Where do we start?"

"We've drastically reduced the number of souls carried in an individual convoy to make them less tempting targets. But this means that we need to make more deliveries in order to keep up with demand."

"That sounds like we're stretching pretty thin keeping them all covered."

"On top of that, some of the trucks are decoys, completely empty."

"Have any of those been hit?"

"No." We shared a dark, knowing look. That meant that someone with insider knowledge was guiding the strikes. I couldn't help but feel bad for the guy, surrounded on all sides.

We mortals tend to think of Death as a vicious and cruel moment in someone's story—especially when it is a story that ends too soon. But having seen behind the curtain, or Veil, I knew that this wasn't the case. Kane took no delight in the purpose he served. He reminded me of an ER doctor, used to seeing his patients' lights go out but still showing up to work every day.

Plus, all the other options seemed *way* worse.

"Has anyone gone to check on the destroyed convoy?" I asked, a shadow of a plan beginning to form in my mind.

"There's been no time. If a delivery doesn't come back, we move on. We don't have the people to cover it all."

I nodded. That was the answer I was expecting. The Veil was a lot like the Panama Canal: a choke point for shipping. If something slowed down or got stuck, their ability to process the souls coming in ground to a halt. But that didn't affect the rate at which their backlog was filling up. People kept dying at the same rate. The Veil had to keep moving or get buried under the avalanche.

"Is there a route that would take me past it?"

Death was silent for a moment as he considered my request. "It would be easy enough to do," he mused. "You could be assigned to one of the circuits."

"What's a circuit?"

"Some of our clients deal in volumes that aren't worth a single trip. So instead, we send one truck to make several stops. It would be simple to make sure you retrace the steps of the missing convoy." His eyes narrowed. "What are you looking for?"

"I don't know," I admitted, "but it seems like the logical place to start."

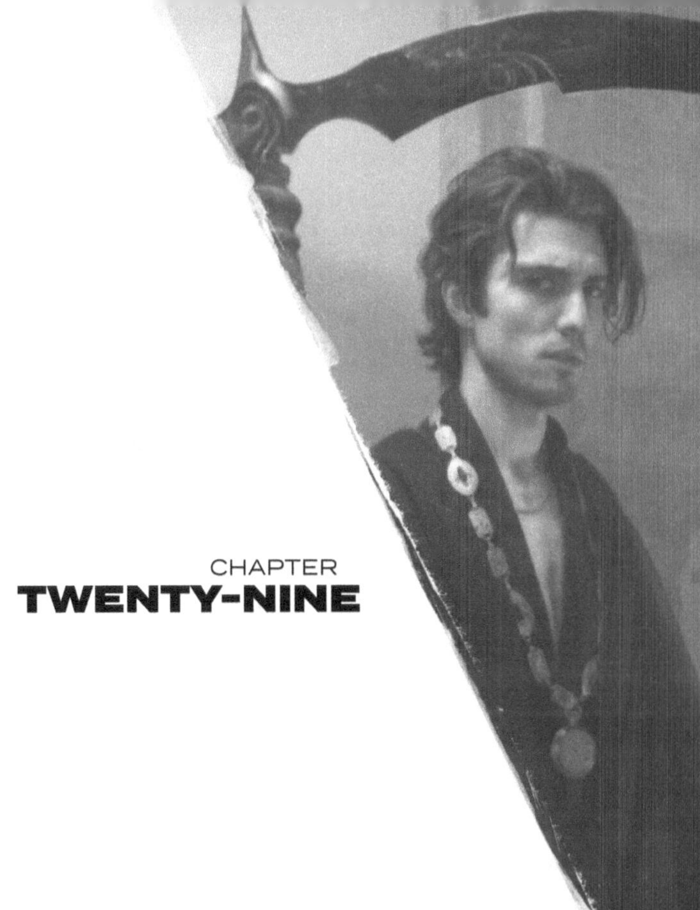

TWENTY-NINE

TRUE TO HIS word, Kane restored the three of us to duty and sent me out into the field with the next shipment. I spent the undefinable period of time between our meeting and actually returning to the Nothing staring at my silver pocket watch, watching my time trickle away. Somehow, I knew, the moment was not quite right. It was maddening and stupid, but Orion had taught me to trust my gut, and I was doing my best to listen to my teacher.

I still had to get to Midas and end his suffering. The deed itself shouldn't take much time, but it was a matter of finding the window of opportunity before the game was over. Then I had to get my grubby hands on the crown, and I had no idea how I was going to get back into Death's vault.

But here I was, trying to figure out who was stealing souls from the Grim Reaper.

It was enough to be very overwhelming.

I let out a long sigh as I kept watch from the top of the small truck rolling along the Rainbow Bridge. My Reality Anchor bounced around my neck, glowing orange as it kept the gnawing hunger of the Nothing at bay.

"Something on your mind, boss?" Yuki asked from where she stood next to me, watching the other side of the inky dark. As we'd planned, Kane had assigned me to one of the convoys that carried a smaller shipment to several of the smaller resorts in the Underworld. But the idea wasn't just to make deliveries—I was searching for information too.

In total, our manifest had fewer than three hundred souls, so we had been given a much smaller vehicle and an even smaller support team. One of the orange-jumpsuited factory workers had been pressed into driving, and I had been allowed to take one other Reaper with me as a guard. Given what I now knew about Jack's influence on my peers, I didn't like most of my options, but they were better than going alone. I chose Yuki for two reasons: She was nicer to me than Rex, and I was pretty sure that she had access to less Authority to use on me.

"One or two things," I replied dryly, my eyes still scanning the Nothing for anything moving in the murk. While I understood that a couple hundred souls was not nearly as tempting a target for the Lost as the thirty thousand we'd escorted on our last trip, I couldn't help but feel the heavy weight of Megan's orb in my pocket.

I was breaking the cardinal rule of transporting souls

through the Nothing by carrying hers outside a dampening crate. I was hoping that hers being only half full would make it less likely to attract predators.

The problem was, I couldn't find anywhere that seemed safe enough to hide it. It felt wrong to just leave her lying around somewhere, unattended. After losing her a year and a half ago, I wasn't letting this ball out of my sight—not even for a second.

Yuki was quiet for a long moment, but I knew that it wouldn't last forever. There had been a need to her question that told me something was lurking just below the surface. She was far chattier than stoic Rex, which made her a better target for getting information out of.

"Do you want to talk about it?" I asked, my instincts telling me now was the moment.

"About what?" A defensive tone crept into her voice.

"About Jack, perhaps?" I offered, trying to keep my voice free of judgment. But that was harder than I'd thought. We both knew what I was talking about. We both knew that he and his little group knew where the missing souls had gone.

"You must think I'm a monster."

"I just want to understand," I told her gently.

The Reaper was silent for so long that I began to think I had misjudged her earlier attitude. Curious, I glanced over my shoulder to check on her. I figured that even the Lost couldn't sneak up on us in an instant. To my surprise, she wasn't looking out into the dark. Her head was bowed, and she stared at the black handle of her scythe in her hands.

"You're going to Hell when this is all over, right?" she asked, not looking up. A chill that had nothing to do with the abyss we stood in ran down my spine. "I felt your nervousness when we took the shipment through the gates." I remembered her asking me a single question: *You too?*

"That seems to be the current trajectory," I confirmed, not trusting my own voice to speak above a whisper. "I assume that makes two of us?"

Yuki didn't answer for another long moment. Only the soft hum of the truck rolling across the Rainbow Bridge broke the echoing silence of the void. I tilted my head in thought, trying to guess where she would take this. I began to mentally list the Reapers I knew and wonder where they might be going.

Jack seemed like an easy name to place in the "Hell" column. I know you're not supposed to judge and all that, but he didn't strike me as a particularly good guy. Now that I thought about it, Death himself had told me that the cold-eyed Brit was a killer. While it's technically possible to be a good guy and a killer, I'm not sure that's the kind Kane was talking about. If I had to guess, Rex was probably on the Naughty list too. Same for anyone who was in the little gang.

The more I thought about it, the more I struggled to find a Reaper whom I wouldn't judge as bad. I hadn't seen any heroes running around wearing the black uniform of Death.

Which actually made total sense.

"It's all of us, isn't it?" I asked.

"All of us what?" Yuki stirred from her reverie, glancing up from her weapon to look at me. Her dark eyes were somber, shimmering with some sort of pain.

"All of the Reapers are going to Hell."

"No." She shook her head. "I don't think we're *all* going there." I frowned slightly, my theory ruined a little. I had begun to suspect that only certain type of people were recruited to work at Death Delivery Corp. Seeing my expression, she continued, "But none of us are going to Paradise, that's for sure."

"It's harder to recruit someone who's going where they want to go," I allowed, arching a single eyebrow. My hiring process had gone differently due to my Death Tax. That was a unique situation. Most people don't have bills racked up on their behalf by Hell. The rest of the employees were volunteers. I could imagine that if your number was called, and you got to the window and were told you were going upstairs to an eternal pizza party, you had little motivation to delay gratification and risk your immortal soul. But someone who had unending pain and suffering to look forward to would be only too happy to postpone it by a few centuries.

No wonder the Reapers were so jealous of my status as heir. Kane told me that his second could not be compelled to go to his Underworld when his time was up. It was literally a get-out-of-Hell-free card.

"Exactly."

"Okay, so we're all the bad guys," I continued, trying to keep her talking. "But how does that matter? Why steal or risk ourselves against Death himself?"

Yuki's eyes were full of despair as she held my gaze. "What would you do to alleviate some of the suffering you know is waiting for you when you cross through the Gates?"

Ah. Of course.

That was the key to the corruption, I realized. Kane had suggested it was impossible to bribe a Reaper. They had no bank accounts, needed no food. What could they possibly be given that would make them risk a True Death?

"Hell will let you go?" I gasped in horror. A dark and terrible feeling began to form in the pit of my stomach. Not fear—something worse, the icy hand of temptation. If souls were already being traded anyway, could I trade for my own?

That would be horrendous. A crime beyond words or comprehension.

But would it work?

I shoved those dark thoughts down, trying to silence their whispers. I was *not* going to do that. Even if it would work. I may not have traded my soul to the Devil the first time, but making a deal like that would truly make me worthy of the fiery pit.

"Let us go?" Yuki let out a scornful chuckle that dashed my dark hopes to pieces. "Any Underworld would rather implode than see a single soul slip their clutches. No, they won't let us go. But most of them are willing to *negotiate*." Disgust filled her words, but after a moment of reflection, I realized it was aimed at herself.

"An upgrade?" I breathed, understanding.

"When I'm finally boxed up and sent off to Perdition, they are supposed to put me in the Seventh Circle," Yuki told me, her eyes gaining a faraway look. "But thanks to Jack and his deals, the devils will put me in the First Circle instead."

I'd seen those circles with my own eyes, and I got the appeal immediately. The First Circle was miserable and boring, but the Seventh was pain and suffering for eternity. I held back a low whistle of surprise. That was quite an upgrade.

It would be so easy for a master tempter—like, say, Zagan, or Samael, or their CEO himself—to pull those levers and make a bunch of desperate humans dance to their tune. It was a fatal flaw in the security of the Death Treaty.

"So you're stealing souls for Hell?" Of course Zagan was behind this.

To my surprise, Yuki shook her head, still not meeting my eyes. "No, not directly. It's more complicated than that. There are brokers and fences."

"Dark Abyss," I swore, finally feeling like I understood the nightmare that Orion had invoked with that oath. Of course there were. Kane had said every organization had its own corruption. There must be demons inside Hell itself who made souls appear and disappear while cooking the books. The mafia had made it to the Underworlds.

"What circle are you going to?" Yuki asked me in a small voice. For a moment, I thought about telling her the truth. Even though she had just confessed to a horrible conspiracy, I couldn't help but feel a bit of camaraderie. We were both terminal patients, counting down our days. I wouldn't make the decision she made—*I wouldn't*—but that didn't mean I couldn't understand how someone ended up down the dark alley.

I had to swallow once or twice as I thought about the new Tenth Circle of Hell that I had seen under construction. It was still terrifying knowing that the Devil was personally building a place to torture little old me.

But that felt like something I should keep to myself.

"Probably the Seventh too," I croaked, not having to fake my throat being a little dry. That was the place where people guilty of murder and violence went. That seemed close enough for the purpose of this conversation.

"What would you do to not go there?" Yuki's voice was a tortured whisper.

"A lot," I admitted, looking back out into the void we were traveling through. "A lot."

"But you wouldn't do what we've done."

"What do you mean?"

"You're different from the rest of us. Don't get me wrong, you're scary as hell when you fight, but you're not a schemer like Jack. You say you'd do a lot to get out of the Seventh Circle, but you wouldn't stoop to our level."

I was quiet for a moment, trying to digest her words. No one had ever called me scary before. But then I'd usually been overshadowed by Orion. He was the star, and I was his backup dancer. But maybe some of his teaching had rubbed off on me.

"I wouldn't," I told her after a moment of reflection. "But I was fortunate enough to have someone who stood up for me when I was defenseless, and he paid for it. Who would I be if I didn't do the same?"

We rode in silence for a while, both of us lost in thought as we stared out into the deep. Despite my fear, no hunting horns sounded, and no raiding parties appeared in the distance. Maybe being marked wasn't as powerful a call as thirty thousand souls had been.

"One thing I don't understand," I said eventually, "is how you manage to hide losing so many."

"What are you talking about?" Yuki glanced back at me, brow furrowed.

"You and your crew have facilitated the theft of tens of thousands of souls. How is that possible without getting caught?"

Yuki gaped at me for a moment, mouth opening and closing like a fish. "What are you *talking about*?" she repeated in horror.

My eyes narrowed as the threads I had gathered and sewn up began to pull free. "How many souls would you say that you have helped Jack steal?"

"A few...hundred?" Something akin to real panic filled her

voice now. Startled, I turned away from the Nothing to face her. She had banished her scythe and stood with her shoulders bowed and arms crossed.

"Are you sure?" I hissed, taking a step toward her, my mind racing. The woman fell back a step, her pupils growing wider. It occurred to me that she'd seen me give the True Death to Sunburn; I might be more intimidating than I had been before.

"Yes—yes! I swear it!" Her throat visibly moved as she swallowed and backed up another step, right to the edge of the top of the truck that we stood on. Fear is a weapon, as sharp and deadly as any blade, and I wasn't going to waste it.

"Don't lie to me," I commanded, pulling on the Authority of Death through my ring, summoning my scythe to rest in my hand.

"I'm not—I wouldn't. We move some around on deliveries when the right people are working reception. It's a handful at a time. It would take generations of Reapers to steal that many. We're watched too closely."

I searched her eyes for any hint of a lie, but all I could see was her terror of being sent into the final dark. After a moment, I nodded once, letting the scythe slip back out of existence to wherever it lurked when it wasn't needed.

"I believe you," I murmured. Kane was right. There was more going on.

The truck let out a little groan as the driver began to apply the brakes. Yuki's expression changed from fearful to suspicious as we slid to a halt in the middle of the Rainbow Bridge.

"Why are we stopping?"

"Come find out," I told her, walking to the front and leaping off without looking behind me.

I landed in a light crouch in front of the vehicle, glancing back at the driver's cab to nod at the nervous warehouse worker who had been shoved out into the Nothing with us. He paled even further under my gaze, and I let out a little sigh. I had been trying to reassure him with my look, but I only intimidated him more. Probably another thing I learned from Orion.

Our path had taken us right to the lost transport, just like Kane and I had planned. I felt the bridge shake like pudding struck by a spoon as Yuki landed next to me.

I could already tell that something was wrong.

I'd never seen the Lost tear into one of our trucks and consume the souls before, but the vibe that the Dreadknight had given off had been something like an alligator about to rip into a tin can full of meat. I expected to find our vehicle torn to shreds. I was prepared to sort through the wreckage like a homeowner after a tornado.

I did not expect to find the truck in one piece, with its back doors hanging open.

"What is this?" Yuki breathed, staring at the abandoned truck with bug eyes.

"A mystery our master has sent us to solve," I replied grimly, striding toward the scene.

There was no sign of the two Reapers assigned to this delivery. I approached the truck cautiously, some instinct warning me of a trap. Slowly, I circled it, looking for anything that seemed out of place. But the more I studied it, the more concerned I grew by how *normal* everything seemed.

After completing a full revolution, I clenched my teeth and took a step forward. With a shadow of dread hovering over me, I made my way to the cab and peered inside. No bodies, no blood, no signs of a struggle. It was as if the Reapers had brought the truck to a stop and gotten out. Maybe they had seen the raiders coming and decided to meet them on foot instead of trying to run.

I walked down the side of the vehicle, running a gloved hand along the intact cargo bay. I could feel the tremors of the bridge as Yuki trailed behind me, silent.

Steeling myself a second time, I walked around the open rear door to see what was left. The doors themselves looked like they had been unlocked with the key. There was no damage to the locks or handles. As I feared, the souls were gone; not a single glowing orb remained. The interior was completely bare. There were no shards of broken containers, no torn-up crates. The entire back of the truck had been stripped down with precision.

If I didn't know better, I'd say that professional dockworkers had unloaded every single item worth having, put it in their own vehicle, and left. They hadn't even bothered to cover their tracks, I realized, blown away at the audacity. Whoever had done this hadn't expected Kane to send anyone looking. Which meant they knew how thin the Reapers were stretched right now. The dread hovering over me grew as I followed that line of thought.

What if there was another player in this game? The Lost raided the convoys, tore them up, and consumed their contents. But what if someone else was using their attacks as cover to steal from Death himself? Someone different from Jack and his team of small-time thieves.

This wasn't just the work of some light-fingered Reapers; I was sure of that now. It was too big. Maybe Jack told someone where to wait for the shipment, but there was a difference between being an informant and being a mastermind. I wondered if he even knew this was happening. This wasn't an operation that could be pulled off by Reapers alone.

This was something else. Something worse.

CHAPTER
THIRTY

WE DIDN'T STAY at the abandoned truck long. There wasn't much to see, but it had told me plenty, and everything it had to say was bad news. Yuki and I returned to the top of our own truck to keep watch while we resumed our steady pace down the Rainbow Bridge.

The other Reaper was even quieter now, and I was content to let her stew on what she had just seen. I thought of her as a monster, at least in some ways, and she knew it. Stealing souls was the work of a monster no matter how you sliced it.

But.

I too have stood on the precipice of dark and terrible temptations and heard their song. I'd like to think I've resisted the worst of them, but that doesn't mean I don't have a bit of sympathy for anyone corrupted. They call it falling, but sometimes it's more like being hooked. Before you know it, you've been pulled to vicious, crushing depths and have no idea how to get out.

It didn't excuse her. Not even a little bit. But it did make me feel bad for her.

I left her to simmer while I tried to untangle the webs of conspiracy surrounding me. I knew that souls are important. Before she died, Gloriana had described them as the fuel that powered Reality. When the Fae had failed to collect new souls, they had lost much of their lands to the Nothing. Kane said that without them, the universe itself would fall apart. Dan had been so worried about being behind on his quota of souls that he had forged my signature. That's sort of how I got here to begin with.

A better way to think about it was that souls were how the Underworlds paid their mortgages. If they couldn't pay their bills, they got foreclosed on and kicked out into the dark. It's always about rent at the end of the day.

But knowing that souls were being stolen didn't tell me what they were being used *for* exactly. I know when Doyle offered Ash ten thousand souls, the implication had been that they could be used to reclaim the parts of the Faerie Lands that had fallen into the Nothing.

Was that the only use for them, though? Were the worlds of fading and forgotten Immortals all suffering the same fate? I thought about the empty halls of Hades and decided it was likely. In fact, if it turned out that Pluto was trying to buy stolen souls I wouldn't be surprised. He sure seemed desperate enough.

So, races falling into their twilight would be likely candidates to buy the stolen souls. But with what? Doyle had tried to use them to smooth over a dispute between the Dragon Dons and the Dandelion Court, so I guess it was the same thing money was always used for.

It all made sense, but I couldn't help feeling like I was missing something. The gears moving the world on this side of the Veil were cosmically huge. We were talking about places like Hades and Hell, for Pete's sake. It was reasonable for me to assume that I didn't know everything about the entire universe.

Huh, look at that, a smidge of humility.

Resolving to keep my eyes open, I settled back into my watch of the Nothing as we rolled onward. Even though I didn't see anything crawling in the inky dark, I couldn't shake the feeling that I was being watched.

—— ✕ ——

My skin was still crawling with the pressure of unseen eyes when we arrived at our first Underworld. As I suspected, it was significantly less intimidating than the Gates of Hell. The Rainbow Bridge dead-ended into an expanse of desert that appeared out of nowhere. Long limestone walls carved with hieroglyphics crumbled along the edges, and the rusty gate hung open, its hinges sagging dangerously.

Our driver stopped the truck right at the border, and I eyed the sand with distrust. Whatever inventor had brought the combustion engine to Kane when he died hadn't designed him a vehicle that made me confident in its off-road capabilities.

I dropped from the top, landing next to the driver's side, and motioned for him to open the door. He did, then passed me the clipboard carrying our manifest. I glanced down at the first page, trying to figure out where the heck we were.

"Duat," I read slowly. Its name didn't ring any bells, although I got a very ancient Egypt vibe as I studied the crumbling ruins. "Seven souls total," I continued, turning to the next column. Glancing at the dangerous road conditions ahead of us, I made a snap decision.

"Yuki, you stay with the truck. I'm gonna walk these in myself."

"You sure?" she called, appearing at the top of the truck to stare down at me. There was a surprising amount of hesitation in her voice. "Splitting up seems like a bad idea."

"Better than getting a whole bunch of extra souls stuck in an Underworld we don't know much about," I pointed out.

"Just leave them at the front and let's get out of here. Some of these old forgotten places aren't exactly safe, and their keepers aren't sane, either."

I hesitated, considering her suggestion. It was tempting to just deliver our package and get out, but even these smaller shipments were supposed to be signature-only. I checked the manifest: Sure enough, the spot for the recipient's mark had been highlighted by the administration team before we left.

"Gotta get it signed," I called, giving her a frown.

"Fair enough," she grunted. "Just hurry, okay?"

I nodded and made my way to the back of the truck. The heavy iron key I had been assigned as the excursion leader sank into the lock, and the bolt retracted with a heavy *thunk*. Moving quickly, I swung the door open, letting the orange light of the orbs bathe me as I leapt inside.

It took me only a moment to find the crate labeled DUAT. I cracked it open, scooping them into the pockets of my jacket.

That might not be the most dignified way to carry people's souls, but I only had so many hands.

I tucked the clipboard under my left arm and put the last orb in my hand. Locking the truck behind me, I stepped off the glowing road, and summoned my scythe, using it like a wizard's staff to help me keep my footing as I stepped back into Reality.

Oh, here comes gravity.

I let out a gasp of surprise as my body immediately sank into the sand with its new weight. I leaned harder on my weapon as I got used to feeling real again. After a moment, I got my feet under me and began my trek into what seemed to be an actual desert.

Hot winds buffeted me with sand particles, and I felt my skin begin to warm under an oppressive sun that beat down on me from a cloudless blue sky. I hoped this wouldn't take too long. I hadn't brought sunscreen, and it would be embarrassing to have sent that tomatoey Reaper to the True Death and then come back all red myself. Once again I was grateful for the cold of Grim's power. It was like having my own air-conditioning with me.

Now completely in the Underworld, I paused, looking across the horizon for a clue on where I was supposed to take these souls. But all I could see was the swelling of sand dunes. Grumbling under my breath, I resumed my hike, heading in a straight line from the gate.

After ten minutes I ran out of patience. "Hello?" I called, letting the power within me carry my voice unnaturally far.

"Hello—Hello—Hello" my own voice echoed back to me, despite the terrain lacking mountains. A chill settled down my spine as my words continued, growing louder and closer together as if the wind itself were mocking me.

I froze, slowly crouching to set the seventh soul that I carried on the sand at my feet. I had a bad feeling I was going to need to be able to use both hands in a moment. After thirty seconds my echo faded as the wind that had been playfully dancing around me abruptly changed course and shot away from me, carrying my greeting with it.

It left only an oppressive stillness.

I swallowed nervously as I eyed the empty horizon before me. I didn't know what, but I knew that *something* was about to happen. How did I keep getting myself in these situations? I should have listened to Yuki.

I had just enough time to see the sand in front of me begin dancing to brace myself for the wind's return. The air slammed into me like a linebacker, carrying with it someone's reply in the form of a long wolf howl. The bestial cry echoed like mine had as the wind swirled around me, mocking me once more. The sound began to build as the gale picked up speed, turning into a miniature sandstorm.

I raised my arm, using the sleeve to shield my face from the grains of sand that tore at me. I wondered how long I had before whatever creature had made that cry would come to find me. All I had to do was turn around and march right out, signatures be damned—

Like a candle being blown out, the wind vanished.

One moment I was in the heart of a raging sandstorm.

The next it was a perfectly clear desert day, just like before.

But I wasn't alone anymore.

The howling creature stood in front of me. Well, I assumed that it was the howler on account of the fact that it wasn't a man. Or maybe it would be better to say that it had the body of the man but the head of a dog. His skin was dark, the same color as the fur that covered his canine head. Two black eyes stared at me as he panted with ragged breaths.

I'd never seen Anubis before, but I couldn't think of any other dogmen of death off the top of my head. The god's mouth hung open and a long red tongue lolled out of its maw. I didn't know if IMMORTALS could catch rabies, but the longer I looked at this one, the more I worried about his health.

"What are you doing in my realm, manling?" he hissed after a long pause. His voice was dry and cracked as if it hadn't been used in millennia. Which, given the crumbling infrastructure around us, might be possible.

"I'm here with a delivery," I told him, letting the clipboard beneath my left arm drop into my hand. "Death Delivery Corp is pleased to bring you seven souls."

"*Seven?*" Anubis hissed in fury, taking a long step toward me.

I don't know why I hadn't noticed before, but his feet were more like paws, complete with wicked-looking claws that I had no interest in seeing any closer.

"Once, thousands flocked to my realm, but now you bring me *seven*?" A mad gleam shone in his lupine eyes—and was it my imagination, or was his mouth beginning to look particularly frothy?

"That sounds like a marketing issue," I told the god, doing my best to keep my voice even. Even though I carried the ring of Death and held his scythe in my right hand, I somehow doubted I had the Authority to claim one of the old-school gods.

"Maybe you brought me seven, mortal, but I smell eight," he growled, taking another step. My heart skipped a beat as I realized that he meant Megan's.

To the best of my knowledge, one of Anubis's tasks had been to bring souls to the Underworld. I wondered if we Reapers had taken his job in the Death Treaty. If he decided to keep me here, I wasn't sure there was much I could do about it.

"No, no, just seven," I emphasized, giving the glowing orange orb at my feet a light kick. Anubis's head snapped down, locking on the round soul as it rolled across the sand toward him. His entire body froze, and I watched in bemused horror as his gaze flicked between the…ball and me.

There was no way.

I twitched my body, feinting a step forward, and Anubis leapt into action, diving onto the sphere like a…well, like a dog protecting a ball. As he stood over the soul, his head came up to fix on me, and I felt a thrill of fear as his lips peeled back in a sinister snarl. A rumbling growl filled the sky like thunder.

As doglike as he was, he was still a god, and I was still in his domain.

I risked a glance over my shoulder. With the wind gone, I could just make out the wall in the distance, hovering on the horizon. All I had to do was make it there and I would be fine.

Good thing I had six more balls.

Anubis let out another vicious growl and walked toward me with slow, deliberate paces like a hunting dog. My left hand shot into my jacket pocket and clamped down on one of the souls that I had stuffed in there. I held it up so that he would see it. Instantly he froze.

"That's a good death god," I called in a high-pitched tone, a frantic chuckle escaping from my lips. What was wrong with me? Was I really taunting *Anubis*? Fortunately for me, his dog brain seemed to be in control, and he ignored my words, eyes locked on the ball.

Here went nothing, I guess.

Calling upon Death's aura to give me strength, I cocked my arm back and threw the orb with all of our combined power. The orange sphere glinted in the desert light as it shot out of my hand at a speed any quarterback would be jealous of.

With a vicious growl, Anubis leapt after it, vanishing in a spray of sand as his paws tore up the ground beneath him. The second the god moved, I spun, banishing my scythe and sprinting as fast as my legs would carry me over the sand.

Far too quickly, a howl sounded behind me, and I glanced over my shoulder in terror. The dark-furred god was blurring across the ground back toward me, the orange soul container glowing in his mouth like a radioactive tennis ball.

"Ack!" I shouted, skidding to a stop and turning to face the approaching death god. My right hand flashed into my pocket like a gunslinger's, and I snatched one of the orbs out to hold up like a shield.

This had better work a second time.

As before, Anubis slid to a halt in front of me, his dark eyes fixated on the new soul before him. His canine snout opened, and the old orb dropped to the sand, covered in saliva and forgotten. It seemed to me that eternity had not been kind to this IMMORTAL's mental health.

"This is fun, right?" I panted. Once again, he did not reply, just stared at the glowing orange ball in my hand and waited for me to throw. Of all the dumb situations I had ever found myself in, playing fetch with Anubis had not been on my bucket list.

What happened when I ran out of souls to distract him

with? No matter what, I wasn't going to give him Megan's. This place might be a step up from Hell, but I was going to bring her home. A glance over my shoulder told me that while I had made progress toward the exit, I still had a long way to go. That was Future Matt's problem—Near Future Matt to be sure, but I was Present Matt, and he didn't have to deal with that. All I had to do was throw the ball in my hand into the next postal code.

Once again, I called on Death's power and did my best imitation of a baseball pitcher. The orange orb shot into the sky, and Anubis gave chase with a thrilled howl that sent fear down my spine.

I used that fear as fuel and raced across the treacherous desert, my legs pumping like pistons. Distantly, I began to be aware of the sound of panting under the thudding of my footsteps, growing louder every second. Casting a terrified glance over my shoulder, I felt a jolt of surprise as I saw how close he had gotten.

Stupid, stupid Matt. I had to pay more attention, or I was going to die.

Once again, I slid to a stop and produced another soul for the dog god to play with. He dropped the old one and stared at my shinier, less slobbery new one. I sent it flying and resumed my terrified sprint.

I still had four souls.

We repeated the cycle, and I felt a shiver of dread as I checked my progress toward the edge of the Underworld. I didn't think I had enough balls to get me to the end before I ran out. Anubis let out a growl so low I felt it rattle in my chest.

Three more left.

Then two.

One.

Panting, I rested one hand on my knee as I stared at the dangerous death dog staring at me from across the small gap between us. Was it my imagination or had his fangs gotten bigger? Were there more bubbles in his frothing saliva? I'm no vet; did this mean he was just excited, or that he had rabies?

I eyed the last soul orb in my hand with a sense of dread. I was too far from the exit to make it on a single run. No matter what happened, after this throw I would be out of distractions. I licked my dry lips, scanning the horizon for some way out, but apart from the crowd of sand dunes we were alone. On the plus side, if Anubis really locked me in Duat for the remainder of Time, then the Devil would be so pissed. I found more comfort in that pettiness than I probably should have.

As I glanced down at my last orange ball, a vision of playing fetch with my childhood puppy flashed through my mind. Sometimes you didn't actually have to throw the ball in order to get a dog to chase it.

Feeling a smirk tug at my mouth, I drew my hand back like a professional baseball pitcher, letting my knuckles curl around the sphere. I narrowed my eyes, focusing on a spot far in the distance, cocked back my arm, and snapped it forward like I was throwing a fastball not even Babe Ruth could hit.

But I didn't let go.

Just as I had hoped, Anubis took the bait, spinning on a dime and tearing off through the sand like a hunting dog. As he raced, my eyes fell to the slobbery orb he had left behind. I wrinkled my nose in disgust, but before I could even think too much about it, I reached for the slimy ball. Two souls might just be enough to get me out of here.

The sphere was wet and warm, which made me want to throw up, but I had no time to waste. I raced toward the gate, stumbling through the sand, gasping for air. The next time Anubis cornered me, there was even more menace in his growl than before. I couldn't believe that I had pulled a fast one over on two mythological dogs in the Underworlds.

"Yeah, yeah," I panted, staring at him. Was he hairier than he had been a few moments ago? It looked like the fur covering his snout had begun to spread over the rest of his body, as if his more of his dog aspect was taking over. To think, mortal mail carriers went through this every day.

Curious, I raised my right hand with the still-unthrown ball and cocked my arm back. Anubis tensed, like a foxhound waiting to be released. I jerked my arm forward, faking another throw. The canine god twitched but did not give chase to my phantom toss. A low growl emerged from his throat as he glared at the glowing orb in my hand. No more tricks.

"I figured," I sighed, taking a moment to pump some more fake oxygen into my fake lungs before my next sprint. Anubis began to fidget, and I knew the game was losing his attention. So I hurled the poor soul and ran.

That was how, with one slobbery orb left, I found myself seventy yards from the barrier between Duat and the Nothing. I was pretty confident I hadn't been gaining that much distance per throw; maybe fifty if I was lucky. Which left me with twenty yards that I was going to have to cover without any soul to distract the death god other than Megan's and mine.

Sick.

Determination began to glow in my chest, like a warm fire. It made me miss the Faerie fire spirit. I could really use their rocket boost right now. We could have crossed the distance with ease. But my faithful fiery companion was not here. None of my friends were. I was going to have to save myself for once.

Here goes everything.

I pulled back my arm and threw with all the power that my body could summon, drawing deeply on Death's aid through the ring. The dark chill filled me to the brim, keeping the desert's heat at bay.

Then I was running.

Dunes flashed by me as I raced. There were no thoughts in my head, only a singular focus: the open gate before me. As far as my body was concerned, there were only three functions that it cared about:

Breathe in. Step-step-step. Breathe out.

I was no longer a man. I was an arrow, and I shot toward my target, the wind whistling past me. My legs may have ached, my lungs might have burned, but I didn't feel them. A bolt does not have those, so neither did I.

Thirty yards to go.

Then twenty.

Ten.

Something heavy and dark hit me from the side, sending me flying like I had just been tackled by one of the LA Metro's runaway trains. I sailed through the air, landing on my back on the hard sand, bouncing as I rolled.

I screamed in rage, letting the force of my tumble bring me to my feet. I continued sliding backward as I crouched, traveling another couple yards. My feet dug two long furrows in the sand as I came to a stop.

I had just enough time to make out the dark blur of Anubis

before he was on me like a junkyard dog. The god dove toward me on all fours, mouth open wide. I leapt in the direction of the exit, desperately trying to dodge his lunge.

A shock ran through me as his jaws closed around my right boot, stopping me short. I face-planted into the desert sand, getting a mouthful of crunchy little particles.

No! This could not be it. I was so close. I kicked viciously, trying to free myself from his mouth. But his bite might as well have been from an alligator. The canine god let out a snarl as he doubled down on his grip, and after a moment of struggle, we both lay there in the sand. Steeling myself, I glanced down at my right ankle in his mouth, worried I would find a mangled mess where my limb used to be.

But as I studied it, I realized that Anubis hadn't caught me high on enough on my ankle to get over my boot. His teeth were digging into the thick leather instead of my flesh. It hurt terribly—but in more of a crushing and less of a piercing kind of way. I aimed a kick at the canine's head with my left boot, but the god ignored it.

In my pocket, I felt the round shape of my sister's soul pressing into my thigh, reminding me that I had an easy way out. Screaming in rage, I stomped at the god's skull, but I might as well have been trying to beat up a statue for all the impression it made.

Anubis seemed more interested in holding me in place than opening his mouth to get a better bite, which meant that there might be a way out of this for both me and Megan. Gingerly, I lowered my hand to the laces of my right boot, just above where his mouth was clamped down. Grateful that I had never learned how to double-knot my shoes, I undid them with shaky hands. This was a dumb idea, but I had to do something. My boot loosened, and I lay back for a second, wincing under the pressure that Anubis's jaw was exerting.

"Come on Matt, you can do this," I gasped to myself, and with a wrench, I jerked my foot free of the leather, turning to lunge to my feet at the same time. There was a vicious *crunch* as Anubis's jaw snapped shut, crushing the now empty boot I left behind, but the moment of confusion it provided was all I needed.

I shot across the final ten yards of Duat and out into the Nothing like a bullet, not slowing my charge until the gravity around me lessened and I felt the spongy surface of the Rainbow Bridge under my feet. As my socked right foot landed on the bridge, it convulsed, and a black wave appeared where I stepped. It rippled down the road and continued off into the distant dark. I watched it go with a sense of apprehension. I don't like it when things I don't understand happen on the edge of Reality. It makes me nervous.

You are marked, Legion had said.

Yuki stood at the front of the truck, arms crossed. Behind me, Anubis drew to a halt at the edge of the Underworld, a chilling howl escaping from him as he gave up the chase.

The Reaper's brown eyes flicked from the enraged canine to me and from my sandy face down to my missing boot. A single eyebrow quirked in amused disappointment.

"I told you to leave them at the front door."

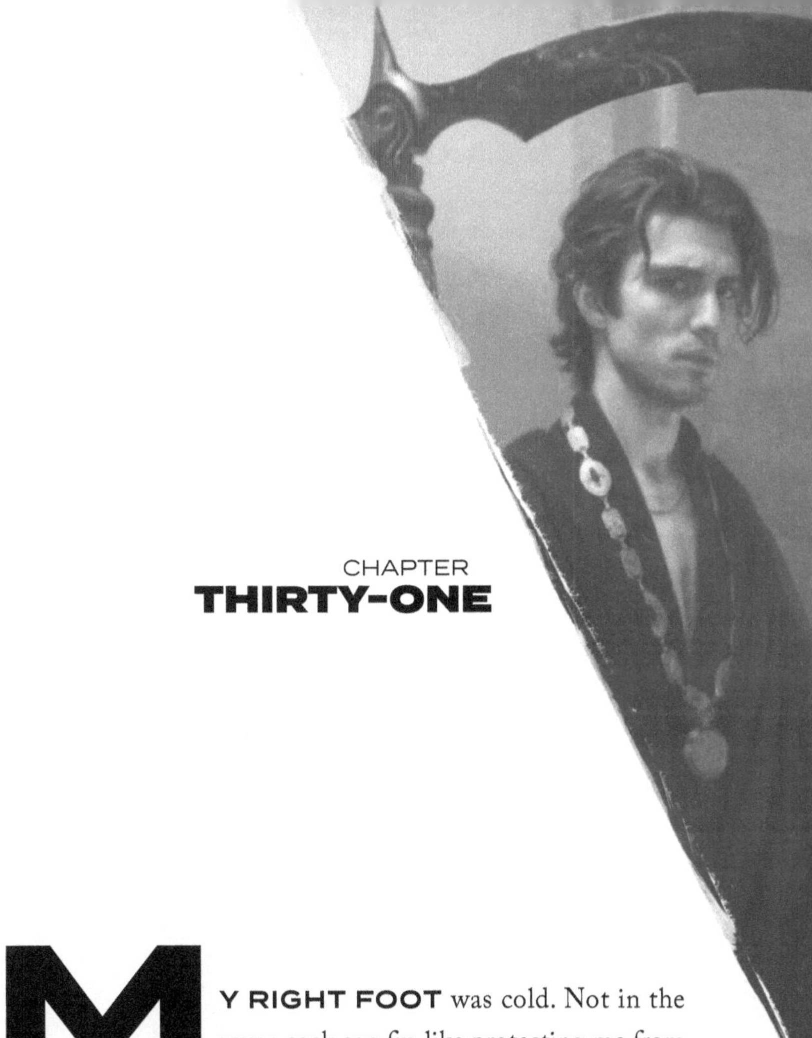

THIRTY-ONE

MY RIGHT FOOT was cold. Not in the way a sock can fix, like protecting me from a winter morning or a marble floor. This was a different kind of cold, the rot of the Nothing, eating at me like a ravenous frostbite. The longer I was out in the dark, the more the feeling began to grow.

Without my boot, the Reality Anchor didn't seem to be up to the task of keeping the chill of the abyss away. Fortunately, we only had a few deliveries left before I could get back to the Veil and prop it up in front of a fire or something.

"I still can't believe you let him just rip your boot off," Yuki chuckled, her mood not at all soured by my situation. "Death's heir chased out of a third-rate Underworld by a forgotten death god."

I shot her a glare, which she ignored. It seemed that seeing me humbled by Anubis had made her a lot less afraid of me. Sure, I had executed a Reaper in front of her, but now I only had one shoe. I guess that does something to one's image.

"I didn't let him rip my boot off," I explained for the half-dozenth time. "I pulled my foot out of the boot before he crushed it into a pulp."

"Right, right."

I sighed as we pulled away from the most recent delivery we had made, to a place called Irkalla, which given that it was another sandy ruin, I had refused to set foot in. No more desert Underworlds for me—no thank you.

"How many more stops do we have?" Yuki asked me from her side of the top of the truck. "We've got like maybe eight souls left, so that's one, maybe two places max."

I shrugged and pulled out the clipboard. So far, our driver had known where to go, so I hadn't paid much attention to our itinerary. You don't really need to give directions when there's one straight road.

Running a finger down the sheet, I realized we had finished that page and flipped to the next one, which was also completed. Yuki must be right: We had to be almost done. Feeling a little bit of hope for my freezing foot, I turned to the final page, which had only one entry. My heart plummeted as I read the details for our final stop:

UNDERWORLD DELIVERY ADDRESS: HADES

AUTHORIZED SIGNATORY: PLUTO

"Oh great." I groaned, letting my hand drop.

"Are there a lot more?" Yuki sounded surprised.

"No, it's just one more stop, but it's Hades."

"So? That's an easy one. He's on the Death Board, so he hasn't gone completely insane like some of these other ruins."

"He hates me," I confided in her, choosing to ignore her comment about whether or not Pluto was entirely sane.

"Well, I'm sure you deserve it," the Reaper commented loftily.

Now that I was dreading our final stop, the rest of our journey seemed to take no time at all, despite my freezing foot. No matter what Yuki claimed, Pluto was crazy. Maybe he wasn't rabies-infected-dogman crazy, but the little guy was clearly a few gods short of a pantheon.

Plus, he really, really wanted to get his hands on the Key of Portunus—or was it technically Janus's when I was on this side of the Veil? It didn't matter, he wanted both. The last time he had tried to make an issue out of it, Santa Muerte had made him back down. But out here in the dark, away from prying eyes, I didn't think I would get the same kind of protection.

"Listen," I told Yuki as we began our final approach to what had to be Hades in the distance. "Just stick with me, okay? I have something he wants, and he might decide to throw a fit about it."

"Obviously." She rolled her eyes at me from across the truck. "Everyone wants the ring, Matt. Or did you think even old Anubis failed to notice the power you were channeling?"

Idiot. I am an idiot. The canine god had referenced my extra soul, and I had assumed that since he was poor in souls and likely far behind on his rent, he would be looking to get his hands on some any way he could. But that wasn't the only prize I had carried into his domain. Death had told me that even the gods would want his ring.

"Yup, glad you're tracking," I told her, as if I had known that the whole time. "Let's keep it with the Reapers, okay? It'll be easier for you to get your hands on it when I kick the final bucket." Yuki didn't say anything, but then again, she didn't have to.

I had only seen Hades from the inside, but even I was impressed as we drew close to the ancient Underworld. A dark mountain reared its head out of the Nothing. It rose in harsh, jagged lines that not even the most intrepid climbers could hope to scale. Thick black clouds clung around it like lovers, and as I watched, some of them flashed with contained lightning. I had no doubt each of them could birth a vicious storm. At the very tip, a sinister red light glowed as lava boiled near the surface of the volcano, ready to blow.

The Rainbow Bridge dead-ended into a giant tunnel dug right at the base of the mountain. Its wrought-iron gates hung open but seemed to still be working.

Although given the condition of its inner mausoleum, I knew very well that appearances could be deceiving. You can slap some paint on the outside of a fixer-upper, but that doesn't mean it's not full of mold or that its toilets work.

My expression soured as my gaze fell on a figure standing in the open mouth of the tunnel, hands clasped behind his back like Napoleon Bonaparte. Pluto, the Romanic god of death, waited for us with a small smile on his face, dressed in a black suit.

Our driver parked the truck on the edge of the Rainbow Bridge, just short of the massive mountain's entrance. Heart in my chest, I leapt down from my perch, thankful that I could feel

Yuki following me. I was hoping I could count on her presence to keep the short deity from stealing all my stuff. As I landed in a crouch, another one of those black waves surged out like a ripple from my almost bare foot. I tried not to think about it.

"Hail, Lord Pluto," I called as we approached the waiting Immortal. I don't know what possessed me to say that, but it felt suitably Roman to me. "We come bearing souls for your vaults, as bidden by our master, in the name of the Death Treaty."

Pluto didn't respond right away, his purple eyes took in my disheveled, slightly sandy uniform. I could feel the pressure of his pupil-less gaze drop to my feet, where they settled on my sock with a physical force.

For once in my life, I chose not to comment.

"Yes, of course," Pluto replied after a moment of pointed staring. "Death honors me by sending his most distinguished servant to deliver my souls personally." Something about his tone and the wry twist of his mouth told me he didn't mean this as nicely as it sounded.

"Death Delivery Corp takes each and every shipment incredibly seriously," I informed him in my best customer service voice. "All of our staff members are expected to make their rounds with excellence."

"I'm sure." He gave another pointed glance to my bootless right foot.

Irritated, but not wanting to get further into the weeds, I took a step toward him and held out the clipboard. "We have a delivery of eight souls for Hades today, and I just need to get your signature while my associate gets them out from the back."

Pluto nodded affably, scanning the sheet, and I tossed Yuki the key to the truck. Maybe this wouldn't turn into a scene. My co-worker strode to get the delivery, leaving me alone with the tiny god. I scuffed my sock against the edge of the Rainbow Bridge while I waited for him to sign everything. Something about this whole thing felt fishy, but I couldn't quite put my finger on it…

"Give me the key," he mused softly, not looking up.

"Huh?" I started out of my idle thoughts and looked at him in surprise.

"My cousins' key. Give. It. To. Me." Each word was said with the force of a hammer striking an anvil, and I flinched at the raw power in his tone.

"No," I told him, lifting my chin in defiance and taking another step back from the edge of his realm and into the Nothing. I wasn't completely sure why Anubis hadn't been willing to leave his Underworld and enter the Nothing, but I suspected it had to do with limits on his power. In his domain, he was a god, but in the abyss that stretched between Underworlds? That was a place where hunger and Death were kings. Which meant Pluto was stuck on the other side too. "I don't think I will."

The short god eyed me with irritation, but he signed the sheet and tossed the clipboard at my feet. I heard Yuki's footsteps behind me as she returned with the crate of orbs destined for Hades.

Rolling my eyes, I bent over to pick up the fallen clipboard. My co-worker passed me as I tucked the manifest into the inside of my jacket. I looked up just in time to see her cross the line between realms with her delivery.

A violent smile crossed the death god's face, and he blurred into motion, grabbing my fellow Reaper by her pigtails and hurling her against the side of the cave's wall with enough force to shake the whole mountain. The crate of souls fell from Yuki's surprised grip, some of the golden orbs spilling out of on either side of the border as it crashed to the ground.

"PERHAPS YOU DID NOT HEAR ME," Pluto raged, his voice full of his divine fury. **"GIVE ME THE KEY, OR I WILL PULL HER BONES FROM HER FLESH."**

Yuki let out a whimper from where she had collapsed against the ground, completely caught off guard by the Roman's aggression. I stood flat-footed on the edge of the barrier, trying to decide what to do.

On the one hand, Yuki was my co-worker, and she had saved my life before. On the other, she wasn't a great person before or after dying. I don't know what she had done to get herself on a path to the seventh level of the Bad Place, but her corruption as a Reaper wasn't exactly a sign that she had turned over a new leaf.

As long as I stood on this side of the line, Pluto couldn't do anything to me. He wanted my key and my ring, and I had very important plans for them. Not just for me—the Impossible Task would set Megan free too. Those were very, very good reasons to let Yuki lie in the bed she had made.

Pluto snarled in fury at my hesitation and turned to the fallen form of Yuki, drawing back one of his fists as he reached down to grab a fistful of her hair. I closed my eyes as a long sigh built in my chest.

I hate bullies.

I have always hated them. I was bullied as a child. I didn't need a therapist to tell me that this was a reaction tied directly to my own experiences. Once, when I was smaller, weaker, and more insecure, I didn't know how to stand up for myself, and plenty of cruel people took advantage of that.

But I'm not helpless anymore.

I had power, training, and a really bad attitude.

The sigh that came out of me was full of the excess steam from my Wisdom generator working overtime, trying to convince me to be smart. It knew I should stay in my lane and not pick a fight with a god. But it also knew—before I even took a step—that there was no way I was going to do that.

I crossed over the border before I opened my eyes, calling on Death's Authority through the ring. As I did, Pluto turned from Yuki's prostrate form, the slice of a cruel smile splitting his face.

I tried to carve him a new one with my black scythe, summoning it out of thin air as I whipped my hands across my body. Pluto raised his arms in an X to shield himself from the blow. As the edge of my weapon bit into his arm, I felt a pressure pushing back on me, like a wickedly strong magnet rejecting its opposite pole.

Gritting my teeth, I poured my will into the scythe, commanding it to cut, to claim. Slowly, like a dull knife carving through a steak, my attack pushed through his defense. A thin gold line began to appear on his arms as my blade sliced through his own power.

Pluto let out a grunt of anger and took a step forward, shoving out with his arms. The burst of his rage and will sent me staggering backward. For a moment, he glared daggers at me.

Drip. Drip.

A low sound echoed in the cavern entrance, and his face wrinkled in confusion. Slowly, he raised his right arm to inspect the sliced sleeve of his black jacket. Golden blood, bright and pure, fell from his cut like divine rain. His purple eyes flicked from his wound to me, true hate flashing in their depths now. I met his fury with a smile so wide, it made my cheeks hurt.

It seemed even gods could bleed.

Pluto blurred forward, hands extended to grab me like he had Yuki. Even though I knew I could cut him, I didn't let that knowledge make me an idiot. Orion had taught me how to dance with a bull, and I hadn't forgotten his lessons.

I sidestepped the god's charge, letting him career toward the wall as I twirled around him. My scythe was like a cobra in my hands, rearing back and then licking forward to strike at his back as he shot past. My blow bounced off his magnetic shielding, which I was pretty sure was just the sheer force of his will. Whatever it was, it sure made him madder.

He spun faster than he had any business doing, ditching his momentum in an instant. Sir Newton would weep to see his laws so thoroughly broken. The rules aren't the same when you are fighting a god in his own realm.

Again he dashed toward me, and this time I took a risk and met him head-on. I set the butt of my scythe against the floor like a pike and angled the curving blade to point the tip right at the charging Roman.

Pluto's eyes widened, and he narrowly avoided impaling himself on my weapon, which would have just made things so much easier. He ducked out of the way, heading deeper into the tunnel that I assumed led to the forests and the River Styx that I had seen before.

It occurred to me that Pluto, being the second god I had ever disagreed with, wasn't really putting up as impressive of a showing as his cousin Aite had. Mother Ruin had held me still with her mind and made it clear that I was barely more of an inconvenience than a rat.

Pluto, on the other hand, was bleeding.

The difference between the two was shocking. Granted, I hadn't been a Reaper when I ran into Aite in the Between. Still, either Pluto was trying to play me, or he wasn't nearly as powerful as his relative.

"Been skipping the gym?" I taunted him as he eyed me warily from the darker part of his tunnel. "Maybe a few centuries in front of the couch reading scrolls and drinking wine wasn't the best for your health."

Pluto sneered at me, but the short god didn't strike. Instead, he began to pace toward the side of the tunnel where Yuki sat, still unscrambling her brains. A classic move used by bullies since the beginning of Time—I had been afraid of that.

I lifted my scythe off the ground and interposed myself between him and my co-worker, drawing the bladed end of the weapon back to strike. Pluto eyed me warily but let me intercept him.

"You will never leave this place," Pluto hissed, his purple eyes flashing. "I will consume you and make you into nothing."

Honestly, I probably should have been more bothered by his threats. He was a god of death. But it had just been so much more intimidating when Zagan had said it. Pluto just didn't have the same chutzpah as the fallen angel, and that wasn't even figuring in the CFO's boss.

"Is that the best you got?" I asked, arching an eyebrow. "An eternal stay in your crumbling motel until I fade into nothing? Do you know who is on the list of people that I have pissed off? They are so much scarier than you. Get some new material, dude."

Not breaking eye contact with the Roman, I began to inch backward, shoving Yuki with the back of my ankles. The Reaper let out a groan but responded to my nudging with a slow crawl in the direction I was urging. As cool as it was that I could cut Pluto, I didn't think I'd be able to *kill* him. Which meant that the only win condition for Team Matt was getting across the border and back into the Nothing, where he had no jurisdiction.

"Look on the bright side," I told him as we shuffled toward freedom. "At least you finally have some friends who can play with Midas." I cocked my head toward the fallen crate and saw that one glowing orb had rolled free of the packaging. "Also, the damage to the packaging was done after delivery, so don't call customer support crying about it," I warned him.

But Pluto wasn't listening anymore. His heavy gaze had fallen on the soul delivery, and I could practically see the hamster wheel inside his head turning as he tried to make a decision. There was something he didn't want to do but was tempted to try. A bad feeling began to grow in my chest, and I tried to urge the crawling Yuki to go faster with my feet.

All we had to do was get across the line. His Authority and Power had no standing in the hungry expanse of the Nothing, and we both knew it. Even with his new souls, he barely had the power to keep his own Underworld afloat. His attention flicked back to us for a moment as we neared the border. Seeing our progress pushed him over the edge of whatever his hesitation was, and he leapt into action.

He thrust his right hand at the crate, and my skin crawled as the rest of the orbs that were on his side of the boundary responded to his power. Seven of them rose into the air and hovered at chest height, and for a moment I thought he was going to throw them at me like baseballs.

Then in a streak of orange light, they shot down the tunnel like a meteor shower, vanishing into the dark depths of Hades. Only one soul remained, just out of his reach. For a moment there was silence as I stared at the god in confusion. Then a warmth pulsed through the tunnel and before my eyes, torches burst into light all the way down to the distant gate.

It was as if someone had just turned the power back on after centuries of it being off. Which, now that I thought about it, made only too much sense. Gloriana had told me the Faerie Lands had been put into low-power mode to prevent complete destruction.

As far as I knew, Hades had only had one soul in it before the seven that Pluto had just plugged in like batteries. A terrible thought occurred to me: What if the lack of extra soul power had been exactly why he wasn't as scary as Mother Ruin?

"Yuki, time to go," I shouted, shoving at her with all my might. I glanced over my shoulder in time to see her make it across the line. Now all I had to do was get out myself. I spun, crouching to spring into a dive that would carry me to safety.

I jumped, but as I soared, I felt familiar iron bands of will wrap around me like they were a hot dog bun, and I was the sausage. My dive halted, and I hung in the air like one of those soul orbs, halfway over the border between the Underworld and the Nothing. Yuki, still lying on the ground, stared up at me in horror. I had just enough time to let out a strangled, "Oh crap!" before I was yanked back into Pluto's domain.

My back slammed against the wall of the cave, and my fake lungs gasped, trying to find the air they still thought I needed. Pluto stood in front of me, and somehow he no longer seemed small. His Presence filled the narrow passage, practically thrumming with power.

I struggled against his mental bonds with no luck—even Death's Authority failed to cut through the will he held me with. Panic began to settle in as I wiggled. This one wasn't looking so good for the home team. I probably shouldn't have made fun of him for being weak.

"Ah, that's much better," he purred, eyeing me with sadistic delight.

"Urk," I replied.

"Oh right, I always forget about how you need to be able to breathe to speak," he acknowledged, and the pressure on my chest and neck loosened slightly. I gasped for breath, which, even if there was no air around us, still tasted delicious. There's nothing like being lightly strangled to make breathing suddenly sweeter than candy.

"I believe you were just about to give me my family's key," Pluto growled when I finally finished sucking in enough air to function. He held out his hand, and I felt the bonds around my right arm vanish. I was still pinned against the wall, but I had enough motion to fish something out of my pocket.

Yeah, he definitely leveled up once he had plugged in the batteries.

I glared at him spitefully, my mind trying to find a way out of this, but it kept running into the same walls and bouncing right off them. A god was holding me down with his entire attention. *A god* in the seat of his power. I had no idea what Pluto actually was in the cosmic sense of truth and realism, but it didn't really matter. He was the lion and I, the newborn gazelle. I didn't have a lot of cards to play, and we both knew it.

Now that he had me, Pluto had found his patience. He stood in front of me and smirked as I tried to figure out how to get out of his clutches. He knew there was no way out for Matthew Carver, and he was enjoying watching me figure that out too.

"Give me the key," he insisted. The pressure around my skull began to tighten, like a vise being slowly twisted.

"Bite me," I managed, the entire weight of Reality closing around my mind. I was just being stubborn. I knew there was no way for me to get out of this, but I *needed* the key.

Out of the darkness came a surprise—my own *deus ex nihilo*. In the deeps a horrifying moan began, like the call of a humpback in the ocean but twisted and warped. All of the Nothing shook with power as it echoed through the emptiness. I don't speak whale, but even I could tell that this was a sound of hunger. It could only be one thing.

An Elder stirred in the dark.

Despite my crushing circumstances, I felt a flash of delight at seeing the blood drain out of Pluto's face. He looked away from me to the gates of his kingdom as if noticing them for the first time. Like a moth drawn to the flame, the Lost were coming to devour his world, because he had left the doors open and a soul on his front doorstep.

With a panicked hiss, he turned his attention back to me, right hand squeezing into a ball, and the tremendous pressure he was exerting on my skull followed his instructions. My vision began to grow dark and watery as my cranium hung together by a thread.

"The key! Give it to me!" the tiny god raged. Despite his power-up, he seemed so small next to the haunting sound of a true monster that hunted him.

"I hope that nightmare cracks you open like a cold one," I managed through gritted teeth.

Pluto let out another roar of frustration, and for a second, I thought that was the end, that my skull was about to pop like a champagne cork. The pressure built for a few heartbeats, then vanished as Pluto threw me across the border with his mind. I crashed into the ground next to the crouching Yuki and felt a shudder of fear as the black ripple echoed down the Rainbow Bridge. In the distance, the Elder let out another hungry cry.

You are marked. Aite's mocking voice echoed in the back of my mind.

Slowly, I rose to my feet, staring at the insane little god who was glaring at me from his side of the border. His chest rose and fell as he hyperventilated, but his greedy purple eyes were fixed on me. For a second, I wondered why he had bothered throwing me away instead of killing me. My only theory was that this key was one of those things you had to give someone of your own free will, and not something he could take from my corpse after he finished juicing me.

"Deliver my last soul," he snapped, holding his hand out toward the one that had fallen on the Nothing side when he ambushed Yuki. For a second, I considered keeping it, just to spite him. But I was a delivery driver, and when I made my report to Death, I wanted to be able to tell him that we had done everything right.

I struggled to my feet and gave the orb a kick with my booted left foot, sending it rolling the last few inches over the line. Pluto opened his mouth to complain, but the deep roar of the hunting Elder cut him off.

"Better flee, Reaper," he snapped in the silence of the aftershocks. "The Lost are coming, and we have unfinished business." Ah, so he was counting on me to live, so he could take the key from me another day. Well, I hated to do anything he told me, but I had every intention of living—so that I could kill him later.

"Be seeing you," I promised, grabbing the dazed Yuki by the arm and dragging her toward the truck. There would be time to sass Pluto later.

Right now, we needed to run.

THIRTY-TWO

THE LOST WERE coming. I pulled my friend to her feet, wrapping an arm around her waist to support her as I hustled her toward our vehicle. "Come on," I panted to her, giving her an encouraging squeeze. "We can't stay here."

"Just need a second," Yuki groaned, raising a hand to her forehead.

Out of the corner of my eye, I caught a blur of movement as something stepped onto the Rainbow Bridge in front of us. I turned, feeling my heart sink as I spotted one of the Legion barring our path.

"I taste you, marked one," the twisted creature hissed. Its face flickered through the souls it had stolen. Suspicious, I glanced around looking for the rest of its raiding crew, but there were no other ones to be seen. This one had come on its own. I felt the corner of my mouth twitch in something like grim amusement. It exuded confidence, seeing a Reaper on his own, trying to protect his wounded friend. But I was not afraid. I'd slain a Dreadknight. What did I have to fear from a simple Legionnaire? I wasn't running from this thing, but its older, older brother.

"Come and claim me then, Lost One," I taunted, summoning my scythe to my free right hand, not letting go of Yuki with my left.

Legion was only too happy to oblige. With a roar it leapt forward, its twisted body thundering down the glowing road as it raced toward me. So confident. With a contemptuous flick, I drew my scythe back and swung as it stepped into my range. The black blade sliced through the Lost with ease. It had just enough time to register horror on its stolen face before it faded, unmade.

A cluster of orange lights shot out of the creature and into me, but I barely felt them. Next to the torrent that had poured out of the Dreadknight, this was nothing. Still, my skin glowed a little when I glanced at my hand. Suddenly I was protecting more than just my two co-workers.

The horrible call of the Elder echoed in the deep once more.

No time to wait. I shoved Yuki into the cabin of the truck and jumped in next to her, squeezing in with the terrified factory worker like a sardines in a can. "Drive, drive, drive!" I shouted before I even pulled the door shut behind us.

He needed no more encouragement, and with a tight turn he sent us speeding away from the dark Mount Olympus that housed Hades and its puny master. We seemed to be going faster now. Granted, there was no speedometer in this world's version of a vehicle, and when the only thing shooting past you is darkness, it's a little hard to judge.

"Yuki, are you okay?" I turned my attention to my co-worker who was squished between us like the meat of a sandwich. "How many fingers am I holding up?" I waved three of my glowing digits in front of her face.

Groggily, she reached out with a hand and grabbed my wrist, pulling it down. "Mm fine," she mumbled unconvincingly. "Just a little seasick is all."

"I don't know how to tell you this, but we are *nowhere* near the ocean," I informed her. The Elder let out another of its echoing whale cries in the deep, and I was forced to reevaluate that opinion. Maybe we were closer to one than I thought.

"I'll be okay, just hit my…everything," she breathed, eyes closed.

I let her rest, turning in my seat to scan the abyss around us for any signs of the Elder or its children. I hadn't gotten a very good look at the last one, for which I was pretty sure I was grateful.

"Thanks for coming for me," Yuki whispered after a few moments of tense silence. A different sort of chill ran down my spine as her arm snaked through my left one and she leaned more on me, her eyes still closed.

"Yeah, uh, no—no problem," I stammered, doing my best not to move. A thousand conflicted emotions ran through me at once. The biggest and most confused of them was the fact that I was *betrothed*. Which was a weird business transaction that also was something more. It also didn't have the clearest rules.

But given Ash's reaction to a few other moments along the way, I suspected that she would not be a fan of this one. Guilt bloomed in my gut, a sickly warm thing like a fever of my soul. But also, I was dead. Which was sort of like being on a break. They say "till Death do you part" for a reason. I shook my head slightly to clear it.

This was not the time. We were on the run from one of the ancient dark beings that lurked on the edge of Reality while jammed three-deep into a cabin designed for two. I wasn't doing anything wrong and had much bigger problems than this.

"How far are we from home base?" I shouted at the driver as I turned my attention back out the window and scanned the darkness.

"How the hell would I know?" he shot back, voice tight with stress. Fair question. Time and Space weren't really consistent this far from the Veil. Plus, we had meandered through the dark making our delivery run, which meant I didn't even have a sense of where we were—not that it would make much of a difference if I did.

The echoing cry sounded again, somehow even louder this time.

"Not long now," Yuki observed from where her head rested on my shoulder. I wasn't sure if she was talking about getting to the Veil or the Elder finding us, but I had a feeling it wasn't going to be the option I wanted.

Out of the corner of my eye, I caught the motion of darkness on top of darkness. My head snapped to the right, and my jaw fell open as I tried to comprehend what I was seeing. A thing the size of the Los Angeles metro area was wriggling through the dark.

Although it had sounded like a whale, to my observation the Elder was more like one of those emperor squids that live in the crushing depths—if it had been exposed to extreme amounts of nuclear radiation for a century.

It had too many heads, bodies, and tentacles. My brain rebelled at my attempts to categorize and quantify it. There were and are no words to explain some of its characteristics. The Elder was made of the true forms of Fear, Despair, and Loathing. But it was more than the sum of those parts. Dark whispers began to speak in my head, in languages I had never heard, but I understood their commands perfectly.

Devour them.

Devour yourself.

Come to me.

Feed me.

With an extreme force of will, I managed to rip my eyes away from the great horror. I placed my right hand on the dashboard and bowed my head, trying to find my center. I was sweating as if I had just done a dozen rounds in the ring with a heavyweight boxer.

"There it is!" Our driver let out a shout of glee as the Veil swam into view out of the dark. The massive barrier to the Nothing shone like a beacon, calling us home.

"We're not going to make it," I told him grimly. Somehow in my heart, I knew that it was too late. The Elder was here, woe to all who fell under its gaze.

"What?" he said in a strangled squeak.

"We're not going to make it," I repeated softly.

Then we were spinning. One moment we were shooting along in a straight line, and the next we were corkscrewing in a death spiral. Our driver began to scream, and I was tempted to do the same, but instead I called on the power of Death. It was like plunging into an ice bath, and I used it to keep myself clinical and cold. Now was no time to panic. The view through our windshield was a riot of colors; the empty black of the Nothing, the vibrant rainbow lights of the bridge, and the bone-white of the Veil flashed past us in a kaleidoscope as our velocity increased. Without the Rainbow Bridge to anchor us, there was no friction to slow us down.

As we shot forward, more and more of the melting pot became white, until only the Veil filled my vision. We raced at it like a runaway train, and I realized with a flash of grim realization that we were going to slam into the wall at speeds no crash dummies had ever survived.

I reached for the passenger-side door and wrenched it open with my glowing hand. I grabbed a fistful of Yuki's and the driver's clothes with my left.

"Time to bail," I growled, voice full of Death.

No one resisted as I leaned out the door, trying to time our spins. It was a miracle that I wasn't dizzy. I didn't know if that was a side effect of having no gravity or if some aspect of Kane's power was keeping it at bay. Either way, it was the only thing that gave me a chance to save our lives.

When I thought I had the timing of the revolutions down, I crouched, counting the seconds till our window returned. We were running out of time. Either I made a move, or we became a collective pancake.

Three, two, one!

With explosive force, I leapt out the door, pulling my comrades behind me in a line. Together we shot out of the spinning vehicle like a stone from a sling. As we soared, I glanced down in time to watch it slam into the Veil at top speed. The truck disintegrated, exploding into a thousand tiny pieces. Its impact didn't even scratch the dam between Life and Death.

The driver let out a wail, but I ignored him, focusing on keeping my grip on my friends tight.

We had survived the first danger, but there were plenty more to go around. We shot what felt like upward, parallel to the eternally tall Veil. I had cut it close; there were only a few yards to go, but those yards might as well have been miles. Like astronauts who had been separated from their anchor lines in a spacewalk, we had no way to stop our momentum. There's no friction in a vacuum.

In the deeps behind us, a shadow moved once more against the darkness. My mouth went dry at the eldritch being moving toward us. The remnants of the Rainbow Bridge we had been driving on still flailed wildly, like a lizard's tail after it had been cut off.

My best guess was that the Elder had smashed the road behind us, snapping it in two, and the aftershock had launched us free of gravity and sent us hurtling at the Veil. I don't know what the bridge is made of outside of, like, magic and dreams, but the fact that the Lost had *broken* it spoke to power on an order of magnitude I couldn't even fathom.

Shaking my head, I tried to snap out of my spiral. I could theorize about how strong existential beings were later. Right now I had to get us out of this mess before we were devoured.

We needed a way to stop our movement. The only thing close to us was the Veil, but it was still out of reach. A dark inspiration built in the back of my mind, and I seized on it, unsure if it came from my own brain or was a subtle suggestion from the power that I was calling on.

When I executed Sunburn, my scythe had grown, shifting in shape and size. Could I do that again, then use the weapon like an ice pick to dig into the Veil itself? I could—I was almost certain.

The Veil hadn't even noticed the truck slamming into it, but my scythe was something else entirely. The edge on it was sharper than Reality. We Reapers used it to cut our way through to the Living World when we went to collect souls, although that was more of a metaphysical cut than an actual one.

What would happen if I cut the Veil itself?

Hopefully nothing.

With my free right hand, I summoned the scythe and forced my will into it, commanding the weapon to grow and extend. At first it resisted; it was a scythe. That was what it had been made to be. But I was more than a Reaper, I was the heir of Death and could not be denied. Reluctantly, it grew like a supple willow tree in my hand, reaching toward the white barrier like the sun.

"What are you doing?" Yuki had just enough time to howl before the curved edge of my weapon bit into the surface of the Veil like an anchor into the sandy bottom of the sea. I let out a grunt of pain as we jerked to a stop, the sockets of both my arms protesting.

Yuki was screaming, but I ignored her, focusing all my willpower into keeping both my hands tight. It had worked. Slowly, using every ounce of my Authority, I commanded my scythe to shrink to its normal proportions.

The blade was still stuck in the white barrier of the Veil, so the path of least resistance caused the three of us to be pulled toward the wall like we were in a tractor beam. Our driver let out a whimper as we moved through the dark, but I ignored his complaints too. We were almost home.

When my weapon was back to its normal size, I pulled on the haft, using it to bring us in for a landing on the wall. Then I banished the weapon, not even trying to pull it out of the hole it had gouged, because that could only make it bigger.

The smooth white surface of the Veil was marred by a single dark scratch where my scythe had bit in deeply. Yuki let out a low moan of fear as she saw the mark, but I couldn't help but feel relieved.

The Veil was incredibly thick. This was no more than a paper cut. I saw no exposed wires or bolts, nothing that looked important. It was a tiny blemish on a superstructure that wouldn't be noticed for an eternity or more. I gave my companions a small smile.

"Well, that could have been way worse," I said.

The Elder's deep call sounded once more in the murk.

"Whoops, forgot about him," I grumbled, eyeing the swirling darkness, trying to see how close the abomination was.

Too close.

"Come on," I shouted, pushing my feet off the surface beneath me and shooting along the wall. "We gotta find the entrance." The other Reaper and the driver followed in my wake, the three of us bounding off the Veil, using it to correct our direction as we tried to get back on track. It felt warmer than I would have expected, its heat poured through my sock to put some feeling back into my right foot.

I frantically scanned the surface for clues as we moved. There were no street signs to follow. I used my best guess based off the direction that I remembered seeing the flailing Rainbow Bridge, praying that we would find the massive orange shielded entrance eventually. The eldritch cry sounded again, definitely closer.

"This way!" Yuki shouted, cutting to the right, clearly having recovered some of her mental faculties. Happy to hear someone sound like they knew where we were going, I threw myself in her wake, glancing behind me to make sure our driver was keeping up.

Some sixth sense made me turn to look out into the expanse beyond the Veil, and my stomach dropped as I saw how close the Elder had gotten. A malicious red eye the size of a skyscraper burned in hatred as the thing came toward us, radiating madness. But the cold pillar of Death's power thrumming through my veins anchored me, letting me tear my gaze free from its eldritch stare.

Then a dozen of its dark arms shot toward us, and dread filled me.

"Yuki! Find us that entrance!" I screamed, forcing myself to look away even as this thing held me down with absolute power.

"I see it!" she promised, giving me a tiny spark of hope. The white Veil blurred beneath us as we picked up speed. There was no more time to be safe. A horrific crunching sounded behind us. I snapped my head back to look over my shoulder and immediately wished I hadn't.

One of the Elder's monstrous tentacles had smashed into the Veil only a few feet behind us. A dozen heartbeats later another struck to my right, no longer behind us, just a little too far up. I checked again and saw a dozen more missiles cruising toward us, like a nuclear apocalypse. I didn't like our odds of dodging them all.

"We're out of time!" I screamed, but the other Reaper ignored me. I opened my mouth to berate her; didn't she know that we were about to squashed by a cosmic horror?

Then the ground rushing beneath us turned from white to an orange barrier, and my heart leapt in my chest. Freedom! But we were going too fast, and our momentum was moving us across the doorway, how could we—

The orange force field bubbled out like someone had blown on it, enveloping us as it bulged. I let out a yelp as the world shifted. Suddenly gravity and friction existed again. The three of us thudded to the ground of the warehouse bay, and I slid a dozen feet on my back, coming to rest at the feet of the Grim Reaper himself.

The Veil shuddered as the cruising tentacles that had been looking for us slammed all around the entrance. For a second I thought the lights in the room flickered. The workers and Reapers in the room all flinched, but Death didn't even blink.

Kane stared down at me for a long moment, his brown eyed unreadable.

"Hey, boss," I managed, when I could finally breathe again. "We delivered all those souls for you."

THIRTY-THREE

DEATH DIDN'T SPEAK for what felt like an eternity. Silent, he stood at the edge of the orange barrier between the Veil and the Nothing watching the Elder rage. Despite its horrifying power, Kane didn't seem worried it might actually get through. No, his attention reminded me of a dog stuck inside its fence staring at a deer just out of reach. Orion was the same way when something kept him from hunting his prey. No wonder Grim was a fan.

After we made it back inside, he banished everyone with a gesture before taking up his vigil alone. Before I could leave, he stopped me with a word. "Matthew, deposit those souls you liberated," he called without turning to look at me.

"Oh right." I eyed my lightly glowing hands with a sigh. "Don't I need you to get in the vault?"

"You are my heir; it will open for you."

"Oh right." Feeling more than a little dumb, I beat a retreat out of the cargo bay where Death brooded. Why hadn't I thought about that before? Kane had literally handed me a key to his kingdom, and I hadn't thought to try it to unlock the vault.

How I had survived this far is a mystery.

"I told you that delivering to Hades was going to suck," I muttered to Yuki under my breath as we walked down the path to the weird skull soul vacuum that I had used before.

"I don't know," she shot back, sounding more like herself now. "I've done it hundreds of times without any issue. Maybe you're the problem."

"Did we date or something?" I grumbled to no one, only half listening. "It's not my fault that he—" My banter died on my tongue as my brain finally processed what she had just told me. My head whipped around, and I stared at her with wide eyes. "You've delivered souls to Hades before?" I demanded.

"All the time," Yuki said with a shrug, confused by my sudden attention. "He is one of Jack's biggest fences for the souls we skim. Plus, the Romans might not be around, but there's still a steady trickle compared with some of the truly forgotten places—why does your face look like that?"

And suddenly all of Death's problems made sense. Kane was right. It was so much worse than a few rogue Reapers.

"I gotta go," I managed to stammer out before turning on my heel and sprinting back toward the warehouse we had left, my task of depositing souls forgotten. If I was right, and I was willing to bet just about everything that I was, then I had to warn Kane immediately. All my enemies would know that it was only a matter of time before I connected the dots.

My feet alternated with the heavy clomp of my left boot and the soft pad of my right sock as I raced toward Death. I could feel the tension in my chest rise as I drew to where I had left the boss. Somehow, I knew that I wasn't going to be able to get back to Kane without trouble. That would be too easy, and Matthew Carver *never* gets to do things the easy way.

Like a prophet of my own doom, I turned the final corner only to find my way barred by someone who had slipped my mind. I had been expecting to run into Jack and his Reapers, or an angry Pluto, but I felt the fake blood in my veins turn to ice as I met my blocker's black-eyed gaze.

Zagan was here.

The CFO looked much worse for wear than the last time I had seen him. His hair was still styled, and he wore a fashionable suit. But the fallen angel's face was covered by an angry purple bruise and a trio of red lines that on a mortal would become wicked scars slashed over his right eye.

His black gaze flashed with inhuman anger as he stared at me. If I had thought he didn't like me before I rescued Megan's soul, I was certain that he hated me now. That's okay, the feeling was mutual.

"Give it to me," the fallen angel of Hell hissed, blurring across the room in an instant. Something hit me with the force of a freight train and slammed me against the wall. I let out a choked gasp as all the air in my lungs exploded out. I was seeing stars, and not the celebrity kind. Zagan wasn't in the mood to play with his food anymore.

"Ack," I managed weakly through the iron band of his hand

clamped down on my neck. "I can't breathe."

"Where is it?" he demanded, leaning in so close I could smell a hint of brimstone on his breath, which I found *shocking*. It was like seeing a mortal executive sweat through his suit. Vainly, I struggled with his hand, trying to gain even an inch to let air in.

My vision began to fade in a familiar way as my body burned up whatever my lungs had used. This all felt normal. Clearly, I had far too much experience with getting choked out.

"Enough," a voice commanded, its power was so strong that the room shook like a gong. To my surprise, Zagan dropped me instantly. I slid down to the floor, gasping as the CFO spun to face the interloper.

I leaned to the side, trying to catch a glimpse of my savior. It must be Kane; who else would dare to command Zagan in this place? But instead of the Grim Reaper, I saw a different figure standing behind the demon.

The white eyes of Azrael blazed as he looked from his opposite to me. He was dressed in his plain black outfit, but his right fist was clenched as he faced down Zagan. For a moment, angel and fallen angel just glared, like two predators surprised to find each other in the same bush.

"This Reaper stole a soul from Hell!" Zagan practically shouted after it became clear that Azrael was not going to speak first. "He has shattered the Death Treaty, and Lucifer demands that he answer for his crime." The Angel of Death's eyes flicked to me, and I winced as I felt the judgment in them.

How had this all gone so wrong? All I wanted to do was save my sister. I wasn't trying to end the world. It was so incredibly unfair that my mess-ups even had the chance to do that. No one else I knew could start an apocalypse on accident.

"Is this true?" he asked softly.

Still panting, I levered myself back to my feet, leaning against the office wall for support. Steeling myself, I met his heavy stare and summoned every ounce of cleverness I possessed. I had to be very careful here. I did not think it was a good idea to lie to an angel.

"No," I replied finally. Azrael arched an eyebrow in surprise, and I lifted my chin defiantly. Technically I had only stolen half a soul. That was an entirely different thing—probably.

"You stole your miserable sister's shade from us," Zagan hissed, whirling back on me. His black eyes were burning with rage-filled flames. The last time I had seen the CFO this bent out of shape, he had tried to crush me like a bug.

But this was no time to let him cow me. Everything depended on it.

"Prove it," I sneered, leaning in.

Zagan blinked in shock, and I thought I saw something like an amused smile cross the angel's face over his shoulder. I wondered how often the demon got a taste of his own medicine. I made a mental note to thank Robin for all the tutoring. It was worth a million dollars and then some.

A white pulse of power burst out of Azrael, and I stiffened as it passed over me like a smoke ring. As it did, I felt a sudden burning in my right pocket. My heart plummeted, and I tossed the Angel of Death a betrayed look before glancing down. A brilliant white light was shining so brightly that it was visible through my pants.

"What is that, I wonder?" Azrael murmured, his eyes half lidded.

Slowly, I reached into my pocket and pulled out Megan's

soul. The half-filled orb was blazing like a sun as I held it out for inspection. I guess angels and demons are cut from the same cloth after all.

"You see? He's guilty," Zagan crowed.

"What have you done to this soul?" Azrael demanded, his voice full of horror.

"It is none of your concern," the CFO snapped, turning back to face his rival. "It was the work of that hag Lilith. But it belongs to us, and the treaty says that we may do with it as we see fit." The demon looked at me and held out his hand for the orb. I retreated a step, clutching Megan's soul to my chest.

This couldn't be how it ended. I had been so close to saving her! Megan wasn't going back. I couldn't bear it. I'd sooner die for real.

"That's…not true," I mumbled, working my way through a half-formed thought. Something was there, a thread that I began to pull on as I spoke. "It doesn't belong to you."

"Of course it does, that's why it was in *Hell*," Zagan sneered.

"He has a point," Azrael agreed in a completely neutral tone. I shot him a dirty look, unsure why he didn't want to help me. I had thought the angel liked me a little.

"No, he doesn't," I insisted, continuing down the path I had begun to see. "Because even *if* my sister's soul was in Hell—which I am neither confirming nor denying, by the way—" I held up my hand to stop either of them from interrupting. "It should not have been. My infernal deal made her alive again, which means her whole soul should be on the other side of the Veil. If Hell had it in their possession, then that would be a violation of the agreement."

I had just enough time to see a disappointed expression

cross Azrael's face before my gaze leapt to Zagan. The CFO no longer looked upset at all. Instead, he looked…smug? The fallen angel withdrew a step from me and gave me a short, mocking bow. My heart began to sink.

"You raise an excellent point, Master Carver," he said cheerfully. "There must have been some sort of administrative mix-up. As you know, I took over your account after poor Lilith's untimely demise. Forgive me, as it has taken me a little time to catch up on all the specifics. But I am so glad that we could resolve this and have you take your sister's soul into custody, per our contract, in front of this *witness*."

A low moan of despair escaped my lips as I realized what had just happened. The whole thing—the entire soul fraud freaking ordeal—had to do with one simple question: Did I sign the contract or not?

My defense was predicated on being able to prove that I did not. There was a signature, it matched my name, how was I to prove otherwise? By not taking advantage of the contract. Imagine if someone forged my signature on a lease for a car, but then I drove the car around for six months. Whether or not I actually was the one to sign the agreement hardly mattered when I obviously had been using the thing.

By claiming Megan's soul through the contract and in front of a senior member of the opposite team, I had done some serious damage to the credibility of my claim.

My eyes closed as I saw my mistake. I could see the trap so clearly now. It might even have been the plan from the beginning. Zagan hadn't wanted to imprison me in Hell; that whole event had been orchestrated for this very outcome. As far as they knew, I was already dead. What were a few more chronons before they got me in their clutches? This had all been about strengthening their case that they deserved to claim my soul when my service to Death was done. I had been even more hubristic than I thought to believe that I was being sneakier than the Devil and his lieutenants.

"Well, now that that's settled," Zagan offered brightly, turning from me and nodding to the angel in the corridor, "I have some meetings to get to. So glad we could get this little hiccup sorted out. Be seeing you, Matthew, I'm sure we'll chat soon." That last part sounded like a threat. The CFO of Hell gave me a cheery wave and strode down the hall, dress shoes clicking on the floor.

Now I was alone with the Angel of Death.

With a sigh, I opened my eyes and glanced at Azrael. He gave me a sad shake of his head, like a parent who is watching a toddler struggle with something unbelievably easy, like Velcro shoe straps.

"If you're going to survive, you will need to learn how to play the game," he told me at last. "That was poorly done."

"Yeah, I got that now, thank you," I snapped, momentarily forgetting who I was talking to. I had gotten too comfortable mouthing off to Orion for my own good.

"Don't be angry with me because you fell for a trap that any Immortal with eyes would have seen coming from a thousand miles away."

"I'm not an Immortal!"

Only silence greeted my assertion. I remembered the solution that Dawn had offered me and felt a new chill run down my spine. Did everyone know that I could just choose to become a Fae? Is that how they thought this would all play out?

"Whose side are you on anyway?" I grumbled.

"Not yours, but you are the student of one of my students. It pains me to see you leap into the spider's web and thrash around."

"You taught Orion?"

"Where do you think he learned to use the sword I gave him?" Azrael shot me an amused grin. For the first time since meeting those other angels, I wondered why he didn't carry one.

"Do you not have one too?" I tried to ask politely.

"Let's just say I loaned it to someone who could put it to better use." A thrill ran through me as I realized that Orion's blade was Azrael's personal weapon. That I had used the *Angel of Death's* own sword to kill Lilith. I glanced down at my right palm, where I saw a burn scar in the shape of that blade's grip.

Oh.

It was a testament to how overwhelmed I was that I didn't even really know what to do with this information. It was too much. My brain was full and no longer accepting any new details. I made a mental note to freak out about it later and tried to move on.

"Well, if you are feeling at all sympathetic to the cause, tell me how to get this back into my sister," I demanded, holding out the half-filled soul orb that was in my left hand.

The angel cocked his head to the side and studied it for a moment, pursing his lips in thought. "Did your sister really return from the dead when your deal began?" I noticed that he didn't assert that I *signed* it, only that it started. I appreciated his neutrality.

"Yes." A troubled frown passed over his face. Kane told me there had not been a resurrection in my lifetime. I wondered if the Angel of Death knew that too.

"It's not really my area of expertise," he admitted after a moment. "But like calls to like. The rest of her soul is currently in her body?"

"As far as I know."

"If you can get it back to the other side of the Veil and destroy it, it should seek to return to its home."

"Are you sure?"

"No." Azrael shrugged, looking back at me. "I take lives. I don't give them."

CHAPTER
THIRTY-FOUR

AFTER PARTING WAYS with the Angel of Death, I took a moment to compose myself. To an outside observer it might have looked like I was banging my head against the wall over and over, but in truth I was practicing a centering technique. The coldness of the wall would calm me, while the impact on my skull would slowly shake all the self-hatred out. It is traditional to chant a relevant truth over and over while you do this. In my case, I went with "You are the stupidest man ever to live."

It felt particularly true in this moment.

Once the ancient technique had been observed, I lifted my forehead from the wall and spun on my heel, starting the long journey back to where the docks of the Veil pointed into the Nothing. I needed to tell Kane what I had figured out: that some of the very members of the Death Board were in on the thefts.

The Grim Reaper had promised absolute, apocalyptic judgment on anyone involved in the soul stealing syndicate. It hadn't occurred to me when he had made that threat that a god might be on that list. That was why Pluto had gotten so itchy about me sneaking into Hades in the first place.

He wasn't embarrassed that he was almost out of souls. He was terrified that I would realize he was missing all the rest that he was supposed to have. That was why when I teased him about the place being empty, he had backed off. I was probably the only Reaper who knew that the souls he was smuggling weren't staying in Hades after they got delivered there.

The real question was: Why? It went against everything I knew about how the rules worked. If souls were essentially batteries or money—depending on how you looked at them—what sense did it make to give them away?

My foot froze mid-stride when it hit me: Death's vengeance might mean Pluto and Hades would abruptly cease to exist. On the one hand, I was fine with that. Pluto was a jerk and responsible for who knows how many souls ending up in places they didn't belong.

But on the other…the order of operations had some repercussions for me. If I told Kane the truth now, and he went all final-judgment on the little death god, that might wipe out Hades before I had a chance to complete my deal with Midas and get my Impossible Task.

Which, given how massively I had just screwed up on the whole fake-contract side of things, seemed more important than ever. So, if I was going to save the entire world's Death Treaty, hopefully it wouldn't be that big a deal if I waited a few minutes.

In fact, there was no reason for me to even keep walking to the other side of the Veil. I paused, eyeing an unattended door right next to me. Why waste the time? I could simply use the key to— Time. How much did I have left?

In all the excitement, I had completely lost track of what time it was. I reached into my shirt and pulled out my pocket watch. My stomach immediately curdled. It was almost 11:52 p.m. Idiot! In all the excitement of Elders, angels, and demons I had stopped paying attention to the game clock when I stepped back into the space where Time swims.

A cold hand of fear clutched at my heart for a second. If I hadn't checked…I shook my head, forcing the bad thoughts out. This was no time to panic. Well, no time to *only* panic. I could do that while I moved.

Any hesitation I had about going for the Impossible Task first had vanished under the realization that I couldn't afford to wait any longer. If I went looking for Kane now, I might very well run out of my last few moments. But the Between and Hades were farther from the Veil's dam of Time, which meant that the clock would be paused while I made those plays.

Go get my Impossible Task, kill Midas, then tell Death so he could handle the rest.

What about the souls I carried and the crown? I didn't know. I'd have to figure it out. Every fake heartbeat that I stood still for in the hallway of the Veil was a wasted one. Glancing over my shoulder to make sure the coast was clear, I shoved my hand into my pocket and fished out the key to the Between.

I turned to the door and slid it home, letting the magic

settle it into the knob with a familiar *click*. Taking a deep breath, I unlocked the door and reached for the—

"Matthew?" a voice called from down the hall.

With a startled curse, I jumped, turning toward the person calling for me. My brain froze for a second when my eyes met the deep brown gaze of Death. Kane stared at me with a blank expression, the weight of his question evident in the cold aura radiating off him.

"Oh, for crying out loud," I groaned. I knew how this must look, me about to step out of Veil, still carrying undocumented souls. But it was too late to stop now. "I'm working on it, I promise," I shouted, turning the knob and shoving the door open. Even Death couldn't follow me into the Between. I just needed to finish my errand and then I would explain what was—

Wham! A force slammed into me like I was a baseball, and it a bat, sending me flying backward from the doorway in a home run. I let out a grunt of pain as my back crashed into the wall behind me.

I kept my wits well enough to turn to stare desperately at Kane. I wasn't betraying him! He just needed to understand that I had to rescue my sister. Then we were going to save the Death Treaty together. But the Grim Reaper's eyes were not fixed on me anymore.

Gone was the quiet man who ruled the Veil. In his place stood a cold avatar of judgment. His scythe was so black that it seemed to devour the light around the room. A cloak of shadows had grown over him, shrouding him in a hood darker than night.

More shadows began to grow along the walls like mold as darkness rushed toward him like the inverse of a moth to a flame. My ring flared with a frigid burn that made any other chill I had experienced from it feel like a mild spring day.

This was the true face of Death, I realized, not the man who bore its power like a yoke. This was the hungry thing that waited for every mortal soul at the end of the rope. This was an absolute force, Entropy given form. I feared it, but mostly I feared its inevitability. There was no true escape from it, only a short delay.

But Death's final gaze was not fixed on me. His dark hood stared at the door I had opened with a hungry intensity, like a Doberman. Slowly, I followed the line of his stare back to the doorway, and I gasped in shock. Something had gone horribly wrong.

Through the open door I could make out the mustard-yellow walls and faded carpet of the Place Between Worlds that I was used to traversing when I went to visit the Faerie Lands. The one on the *living* side of the Veil. Wide-eyed, I glanced down at the key that was still in my hand, which now bore the smiling mask of Portunus at the top, instead of the frowning one of Janus. What the hell had just happened?

But the biggest problem about opening the wrong door wasn't the place that it had opened to, but who was waiting on the other side. That was the true horror of my mistake.

"At last," a harsh voice breathed in delight. Aite, goddess of destruction, Mother of Ruin, stood in the doorway, her purple eyes blazing with madness. The shadowy tattoos on her arm wriggled wildly like a Gorgon's snakes in a blood frenzy.

"Fool, did you think that the secrets of my cousins' halls would hold me forever?" she demanded, stepping out of the Between into the Veil with an easy grace. "You are an interloper. This place is my birthright."

She tossed me a contemptuous sneer before turning to face Death himself. A cruel smile curved her lips as she saw him in his true form. "Well, someone missed me," she purred. "Where were we before you cast me out into the darkness?"

Kane didn't reply. Instead, the Grim Reaper simply blinked forward, his scythe moving faster than my eye could track. But the goddess was made of power, and she too winked out of existence, reappearing a dozen feet farther down the hall, just out of reach of Death's weapon. In her hand a black gladius appeared, short and straight like a Roman legionnaire's blade, but made of the void.

"Oh yes," she murmured, her eyes half lidded. "I remember." Red lights began flashing, and a klaxon began to sound. The Veil had been breached, and it was my fault.

The two Immortals flashed up and down the hall, their weapons moving faster than a thought. To a poor mortal like me, it was like watching a martial arts battle with a strobe light. The two fighters would appear for a heartbeat, moving so fast they seemed frozen. Then the light would go out and they would be a dozen feet away, locked in a different struggle.

Not even Orion could have kept up with their frantic pace. The Veil itself shook as they threw their weight around. Which, in the case of the goddess and Death, had nothing to do with any physical attribute and everything to do with something deeper.

Aite lunged forward, vanishing and appearing in front of Kane a dozen yards away, her black sword extended like a lance. Death warped away, and her weapon speared into the wall like a hot knife into butter.

Black ichor spread across the white wall, and the room seemed to shudder as the dark power of Mother Ruin tore at it. Snarling, the goddess spun, ripping her blade free from the Veil and chasing after Kane.

Their battle raged down the hall, and I slowly pulled myself to my feet. I might be his heir, with access to most of his power, but I could never hope to compete with that. But how had she even gotten in here? Feeling betrayed, I stared down at the changed key in my hand. The smiling face of Portunus grinned back at me, mocking me for a fool.

Usually, when I wanted to go somewhere with the key, I gave it some mental guidelines on what I was looking for, like when I found the Trust and Safety offices in Hell. But that had only been when I entered a different world from the Between. The hallways were always just there. I hadn't done anything different this time, so why the change?

The Veil continued to shake as Aite and Kane's battle moved deeper. No longer sure what I should do, I glanced in the direction the two powers had gone. Aite being unleashed into the Veil was bad—really bad. But it didn't really change my priority list. The game clock was still ticking.

I needed to get to Hades before it was too late.

Out of ideas, I drifted down the hallway, following the sounds of fighting. The power that Kane exuded as they fought was like gravity, it pulled on me like a leash. Unable to resist its siren call, I raced down the hall, back toward the docks.

If Mother Ruin managed to escape back into the Nothing…well, I didn't exactly know what would happen, but I was confident that it would be bad. As I ran, I still grasped Portunus's traitorous key in my left hand. So this time when it shifted, I felt it.

Stunned, I skidded to a halt and held up the key in my

hand. The frowning mask that signified access to Janus's side of the Between glowered at me from the top position and I could only stare back at it blankly.

What was going on here? Why would it just randomly change while I was—

On instinct, I took three large steps backward, heading the way I had come. After the second one, the key shifted, blurring for a moment as the masks turned liquid and swapped places. The leering smile of Portunus was now the top one.

I took a step forward and turned that smile right back into a frown. Back and forth I stepped, watching in shock as the key flawlessly transitioned from one version to the other. My mind raced, trying to process this behavior. Clearly it was based on location, but why? Mentally, I tried to graph where I was in the Veil. No small task when it didn't really have a beginning or end.

But it did have two sides. Suddenly I felt so dumb that I wanted to smack myself in the forehead with the key. It seemed obvious once I knew what to look for. The Veil was a dam between the Living World and the dead one. The key changed based on which half of the wall I was in. The docks were on the edge that bordered the Underworlds, so as I followed Death's battle with Aite I had moved back to the correct side to open the path to Hades.

It had only been chance that had resulted in my quarters being on the Underworld side of the Veil and had led me to finding my way into Janus's halls. A little quiver of fear shook me as I realized how lucky I had been to make it this far. If I had opened the wrong hallway the first time, I would have unleashed the Mother of Ruin right into my bedroom.

Buoyed by my new understanding of the keys, I resumed

my sprint down the hall, racing toward the sound of battle. As I did, a voice in the back of my mind raged that I was being an idiot. *Why don't you just escape now?* it demanded.

A great question. I had no good answer.

People streamed by me, office staff fleeing from the rampage, and Reapers following the heavy summons of their master. I flew like a fool, and as I rounded one of the corners, I burst into a large cafeteria-like room that was nothing but carnage.

Death and Ruin danced in the center, a blur of hungry darkness that chased itself like a tornado. Reapers circled like hungry sharks, some brave or foolish enough to leap into the maelstrom, only to come flying back out.

My eyes narrowed as I spotted two figures who were paying more attention to me than the cataclysmic battle happening in front of us. Jack and Rex lurked to the side, their greedy gazes fixed on me, their heads close together as they discussed something. I felt a sudden spike of worry. Jack and his crew were the definition of jackals. I've survived enough high school lunchrooms with cheerleaders to know when I'm being talked about. I doubted it was anything complimentary about my haircut.

Jack said something and Rex nodded. As one, the two Reapers began making their way toward me. They split up to go around the battle on either side, catching me in a pincer movement. Suddenly, I really regretted not listening to my inner voice and leaving when I could.

"Seriously?" I demanded from the cold-eyed Brit who approached from my left. "We don't have anything more important to do right now?"

"I dunno, seemed like the right moment to me, old chap," Jack replied airily. A black scythe appeared in his hands as he drew close. "Daddy's rather busy at the moment."

I rolled my eyes and shoved the key back in my pocket as I squared my shoulders. He should have learned his lesson from Sunburn's tragic end. No matter; he had threatened Megan's safety, I was happy to give this monster a permanent end. With a snarl, I pulled on the dark power through my ring, calling on Death's Authority to let me strike down this arrogant soul stealer.

My own scythe appeared, but something was different. Instead of a raging torrent of frigid strength, what answered my summons felt like a trickle. The shadows that made up my weapon were no deeper than the ones that Jack carried as he strolled toward me.

"What's the matter? Not as much power as you were expecting?" Jack let out a dark chuckle. "Did you think that Death was omnipotent?" He tossed his head at the fight raging behind us. "I reckon there's barely anything left over for the heir to borrow right now."

A cold drop of sweat sprouted at the back of my neck and rolled down my spine. He was right. It felt like my roommate had turned on his shower, taking all the water pressure and leaving me with a fraction. Death had called on all his power reserves, and until he was done, there wasn't any more to go around.

Facing Jack and Rex as the heir was one thing, but as a regular Reaper, they both had more experience and Authority than I did. I might put up a good fight, but I had no illusions about my ability to beat them. I felt a moment of guilt for the souls that I was still carrying under my skin. I hoped that if I fell, they would still get to return to the Vault of Souls.

I felt the watch around my neck tug as I shifted and wanted to scream. Frustrated, cornered, and out of time, I did what any wild animal would do—I attacked. Rex was still a few yards away, his path around the battling powers longer, so I leapt at Jack, my scythe slashing for his throat.

The cold-eyed Reaper danced back, using the haft of his weapon to knock my strike to the side. Unlike Sunburn's, his weapon didn't crack under the pressure of my Authority. His cruel smile grew as we both took that in. My advantage was definitely gone.

I kept up the attack, driving toward him in a relentless, reckless series of blows. In only a few seconds, Rex would be here, and then I would be fighting two instead of one. I had to finish off Jack before it was too late.

The Brit was of course aware of this, and he casually retreated under my barrage, taking no risks as he waited for his compatriot to flank me. Growling, I shifted tactics, letting him disengage and checking Rex's approach. Maybe he had less Authority than his boss. If I could break his weapon, that would give me a chance.

I leapt backward, making space between Jack and me before turning on the balls of my feet and slashing at the second Reaper. The bald man blocked my swing easily, and his weapon also showed no sign of cracking. He shot me a vague look of contempt. I shifted my angle and slashed again, hoping to bisect him with brute force.

But the dark-skinned warrior caught my attack with his own blade, hooking it around mine and twisting it with savage strength, locking our weapons together. Panic bloomed in me as I realized that I wouldn't be able to disengage my scythe in time to block Jack's attack from the side. All Rex had to do was hold me still and let his partner carve me into the abyss.

Jack drew his weapon back for the killing blow, blue eyes glittering evilly. I grimaced, bracing for the cold welcome of the end. Instead, a long, dark blur hammered into him from the side, tackling the boss to the ground. Wilbur rose above the British Reaper, naked rage on his face as his own weapon appeared in his hands.

"Yes!" I screamed, turning my attention back to Rex, who was staring at my friend with a look of stunned surprise. I guess the tall boy had been listening after all. No longer outnumbered, I set my feet firmly, wrestling with the bald Reaper for control of our locked weapons.

Over his shoulder, a fifth fighter made her way toward our scuffle. I watched as Yuki bounded toward us, pigtails and scythe trailing behind her. Fear returned as she drew close. She had been here longer than Wilbur, and her time was almost up. We had saved each other's lives, but I didn't know if I could trust her. My opponent glanced over his shoulder to see what I was looking at and let out a grim chuckle.

"You're both dead now," Rex grunted out as she drew near. It was his turn to brace, keeping my weapon locked in place. "Yuki! Cut him down." The woman drew back her scythe as she came into range. I was forced to let go of my weapon to leap backward as she swung her blade horizontally through the air so fast that it whistled as it came.

Her attack cut cleanly through the bald Reaper, slicing him in half so quickly his face didn't even shift as the two parts of him separated. His shade vanished before the top fell to the floor, consumed by whatever void waits beyond the Underworld.

Yuki slid to a stop on the other side of him, leaning on her weapon like a cane. Her breath came in ragged gasps as she stared at where Rex had been just a few moments ago.

"Now we're even," she panted.

"I don't know, I feel like saving you from a god and an Elder Lost is way better than one measly Reaper."

"Technically it was two." She pointed at Jack, who was still wrestling with the scrawny form of Wilbur.

"Oh crap, right." I turned from her and dashed toward my friend. The tall man's tackle had brought him inside Jack's guard, which made fighting with scythes very tricky. They're closer to a halberd or spear than a sword or knife. This close, the two of them held their weapons in upside-down grips, trying to gut each other with the curved blades.

Awkward as using the scythes might be in close quarters, the blades of Death were very sharp. A slight amount of pressure was all it would take for one to slice his way into the other.

But numbers went a long way. With a savage grin, I closed in on the Brit from behind, blade angled to rip through his spine. The gangster clearly sensed my approach, however, and reacted with lightning speed.

In the blink of an eye, he stepped inside Wilbur's guard, driving a knee up into the taller man's crotch. We might not be real, but even the memory of that *hurts*. Wilbur let out a deep *whoof* of pain and curled slightly.

That was just enough for the shorter Reaper to knock his scythe aside and stab as he pushed his weapon into my savior. The curved black blade bit greedily into Wilbur's abdomen, cutting like a shark's dorsal fin through the ocean.

"No!" I cried, leaping toward them, drawing back my blade.

Wilbur screamed as Jack shoved him aside, clutching his stomach as he fell. The cold-eyed Reaper spun, triumph on his face. It was still there as my scythe cut his head from his shoulders like a guillotine. Jack's body slumped, then faded to nothing before it finished, leaving me standing over my fallen friend.

"No, no, no," I muttered incoherently, dropping to my knees next to him. He looked up at me weakly. His hands were pressed to his torso, holding the bloodless hole.

"You were right," he mumbled, his words coming out thickly. "It matters."

"You matter too. You did it. I'm so proud." I was babbling incoherently, trying to tell him everything and keep him focused on me. Could I even help him? Did our bodies on this side possess the ability to heal? That really seemed like something that wouldn't make it through the Veil.

As I knelt, my pocket watch necklace fell forward out of my shirt. I ignored it as it dangled in front of me. But Wilbur's foggy eyes focused on it as it swung in front of him like a pendulum.

"Oh, look it's almost midnight," he hummed, his voice a singsong tone. "Almost bedtime," he giggled. Shock must have taken over, which given the extent of his injuries was certainly a blessing. Yuki came to crouch next to me.

Startled by what he'd said, I glanced down at the timepiece and swore bitterly. He might be loopy, but he wasn't wrong. There were less than three minutes left on the clock. But how long would that be in realized time? Minutes? Seconds?

Stupid Time and its stupid swimming.

It didn't matter. I had to go now. But, I realized, that didn't mean I had to leave my friend. A plan began to form in my mind. There was a way to get Aite out of the Veil, save Wilbur, and accomplish everything else on my to-do list. It wasn't a good plan by any means; it was born of desperation more than anything else. But it just might work.

"Yuki, I need your help."

"What do you want me to do?"

"Carry him and follow me." I rose to my feet, eyeing the blinking whirlwind that was Kane and Aite. The battle between the two of them still raged. From the brief glimpses I got of them, neither seemed winded or wounded. I suspected that if left unattended, the two of them could keep this up forever, which would be a problem for me.

"Oh, and get ready to run," I tossed over my shoulder as I strode toward the nearest door.

"What?" Yuki's disbelief was so strong that I almost laughed. It was time to really roll the dice. How I wished Alex and Orion were here to watch my back.

I fished the key out of my pocket, and after confirming that it showed the frowny face of Janus, meaning that we were on the Underworld half of the Veil, I jammed it into the doorknob and opened the path to the Between. I breathed a small sigh of relief as I saw the marble walls greet me. I had been right.

"What the hell is that?" Yuki breathed in awe as she looked into the space I had unlocked. "That's not where that door goes."

"When I tell you, run into that hallway and go to the right—wait, no! You go left, I'll go right." Yuki gave me an odd look, but I shook my head. It was too complicated to explain my bad experiences with sending friends to the right. "Keep Wilbur in there until I come to get you, and whatever you do...don't come back."

"Where will you be?"

"I'm going right," I told her grimly. I knew that wasn't an answer, but it was all we had time for. I drew on what little of

Death's power I could claim, sucking it all up like the last bit of soda in a can. With my will I forged that power into my scythe and set myself, waiting for the moment.

Mother Ruin blinked across the room, stopping in front of me with her back turned as she faced my boss. The second she settled, I threw my weapon overhand at her like a giant ax. The scythe had never been designed for throwing, but I was charged with enough power that it crossed the distance between us in a heartbeat, spinning end-over-end.

Before the blade could strike her, she flickered out of existence, appearing in the same spot as the weapon went past her, but now she faced me with a snarl.

"Hi." I gave her a small wave. "I'm going this way, in case you ever want to see your cousins' key again. Thought you should know." Without another word, I spun and raced toward the door.

"Oh fu—" Yuki began, cutting off as I shoved her and Wilbur through the door ahead of me.

"Run!" I commanded, following my own instructions and breaking right. I was relatively sure that the Between was outside Time and Space, which meant Wilbur couldn't die while he waited here—probably. I'm not a doctor or a scientist, but it seemed like a pretty good guess to me. As far as I knew, that dragoon was still suffering in the other half.

Once Aite was dealt with, maybe Kane could give him a hall pass or something. I didn't have the whole plan worked out. That was another one of Future Matt's problems. Present Matt was entirely focused on surviving a footrace with a goddess. As my feet pounded the carpet, I scanned the signs looking for my least favorite Underworld.

Mother Ruin let out a primal hunting screech as she burst

into the Between. I risked a glance over my shoulder and watched as she slammed the door shut in Kane's face. This had been part of my—admittedly questionable—plan, but I still felt a tremor of nervousness as my reinforcements were cut off.

No one would be coming to save me from Aite now.

It was just me versus an angry, hungry goddess.

Joy.

This was the moment that things could go very, very wrong. If Mother Ruin caught me while we were in this hall, my story would end. She would take the key from my undying corpse and leave, free to use the Between for her own machinations. I'd spent the rest of infinity wishing I were in Hell.

Now that I thought about it, giving the avatar of the Nothing access to travel between worlds did seem like quite the risk to take on the behalf of humanity. Sorry, everyone. But just as I was beginning to panic that the house was going to win, I saw the sign I had been praying for: HADES.

I slammed into the gate, unlocking it with a savage twist of the key, spinning as I shoved it open to make sure that Aite was coming. The goddess of ruin was walking toward me at a sedate, leisurely pace. A wide smile split her face, and with one hand she twirled her midnight tresses. She seemed more like someone who was out for a stroll than a deity on a mission.

I tried not to let that make me doubt my plan more than I already did.

Without another look, I turned from her and dashed into the mists of Hades, leaving the gates open behind me.

THE RIVER STYX roared as I exited the mists. My heart was pounding from the exertion and fear as I raced toward the winding path that led to Pluto's strip mall of souls. This was where things would get dicey. Well, that wasn't completely true—they had been dicey the whole time.

I sprinted up the switchbacks, past the remains of Sisyphus, through the corpses of trees, not pausing to take it all in. I had seen everything these ruins had to offer. The only thing that this place could give me was freedom, and I was here to take it.

There was a tremendous clash of thunder, like a dozen lightning strikes had all been hurled at once, and the whole Underworld shook. In the distance I heard a chorus of howls from a wolfpack that I hoped was just all of Cerberus's heads and not some of his children. I took the cacophony as a sign that the goddess had taken the bait and followed me through the gate.

Because it was bait.

I breathed a sigh of relief as I crested the final part of the hill and saw the stone façade of Pluto's mall of pain. I was almost there. Mentally, I thanked Orion for the absurd physical training regimen he had put me through. Cardio saves lives.

Now all I had to do was—get past the death god waiting for me.

Crap.

Pluto stood in front of the open gate, his arms crossed as if that could overcome the fact that he was five foot four on a good day. He glowered at me, his purple eyes glowing with anger. I slid to a stop, kicking up a cloud of dust from the fallow ground. My heart sank as I saw him. I might have survived a scuffle with him at the border of his realm, but I knew that I stood no chance next to him here, at the seat of his power.

Fortunately, I had a trump card ready. I just had to hope it worked.

"I told you not to come back here," he snarled, dropping his arms to clench his fists at his sides. "What have you done?"

"Pluto, you have to help me," I managed to gasp out between panting breaths. "I'm being chased by a monster—"

"Spare me your nonsense," he spat.

"You don't understand! She's come to take your throne from you!"

"I told you—what—who has? What are you talking about?"

"Aite," I wheezed. "She broke into the Veil, and she's come

for you." I felt a smug sense of satisfaction as I watched the color drain from the god's face. Although if the Roman god of death is so scared of the goddess of entropy from his own pantheon that he literally pales, maybe that should be a warning to stupid mortals like me.

Nah.

"What?" he snapped. "Mother Ruin is here?"

"Didn't you hear the thunder and wolves?" I jerked a thumb over my shoulder in the direction of the howls. "Death told me to warn you before it was too late."

Pluto eyed me for a moment, distrust warring with naked fear on his face. There was a rumble behind me, and I turned in time to see several of the dead trees of the forest topple as if felled by a woodsman's ax. Something was making its way toward us.

"**PLUTO**," a voice thundered from the copse. "What have you done to my father's house?" I spun back to the god before me, taking no small amount of delight in the fact that his eyes were as round as saucers. I guess he hadn't had any of the family over in a while to see the ruin that Olympus had fallen into.

"Told you," I sneered.

But Pluto wasn't listening to me anymore. Instead, he raised his hand toward the forest. There was a tremendous cracking. I turned in time to see all the trees began to rise from the ground, walking on their roots like legs, swinging their branches like arms. An entire tree army—granted, one made of emaciated, dying trees—began marching down the hill in the direction of Aite's voice. I could only hope his soldiers' bite was worse than their bark.

Glancing back at the master of Hades, I saw his eyes were

unfocused as he commanded his forces. Slowly, I risked a step around him. Pluto didn't react. I took another, and still he did not seem to notice.

With a shrug, I trotted around the death god generaling his troops and made my way into the mall. It was time to go find Midas and get an Impossible Task. The inside of the mall was exactly as I remembered: a three-story structure with open stairways.

Without hesitating I made my way to the third floor where the dead Sorcerer King waited for me behind the roped-off section, exactly where I'd left him. His gilded exhibit was jumbo-sized compared with most of the other storefronts of suffering, but when you're the last soul standing, I guess it's to be expected that you get the penthouse. All I could see of him was his feet dangling over the edge of his throne's armrest.

"Hey, golden boy," I shouted as I drew near. "Guess who's here to kill you?" Midas sat up in a jingle of rattling metal clothes. His eyes widened as he focused on me, and with sprightly movements he leapt out of his chair and trotted toward the rope barrier. Despite his regal air, there was a glint of desperate hope in his eyes.

"Back so soon?" he murmured. "I wondered what all the commotion was about."

"Oh, that's not me. Mother Ruin is performing an inspection of the facilities."

"Who?"

"You'd probably have known her as Aite."

"You brought Aite here?" Something like horror crossed across his face. "She cannot gain control of this place."

"I'm working on it," I promised, holding up a hand to calm

him—although the attempt was probably wasted by the entire Underworld shaking as the two gods had their discussion out in the forest. I just hoped that Pluto was as distracting for her as Kane had been. "Before we get to your sweet release, I need your help."

"We already made a deal, young Reaper."

"Not with our bargain, but just a little housekeeping information. Recently Pluto brought several souls into Hades. Are they still here?"

"No," Midas growled, something like jealousy in his voice. "No one remains here for long—apart from me." I nodded in sympathy, unsurprised but a little relieved. I had been counting on Pluto's greed for my plan.

"Great, that's all I needed to know. So now let's get to the good part. One Impossible Task, please." I held out an expectant hand.

Midas's eyes narrowed. "First you must prove that your power has grown since you were here last. How is it that you have gained enough mastery of Death to be able to unmake me in such a short amount of time?"

"I got a promotion," I said, shrugging.

"Show me," the dead king insisted again. I bit my lip and closed my eyes, trying to hide my nervousness. I only had one shot at this. That was why I had taunted Mother Ruin into following me. I knew I would never have access to enough power to kill Midas while Kane was battling with her, so I had to break up their fight before I ran out of time.

Using the signet ring, I called on my scythe, pumping it with as much power as I could draw. I almost sagged in relief as Death's Authority poured into me at full force. The water pressure was back to normal. My plan had worked. Once Aite had fled, Old Grim must have released his grip on the source, which meant there was plenty for me.

Cold hunger radiated from the weapon in my hands, and I felt my lips twitch in a sardonic smile as Midas instinctively fell a step back in the face of True Death. Even a king who wanted to die was afraid of the power of the Reaper. I stared at the golden man for a moment before banishing the weapon and arching an eyebrow. "Satisfied?"

"Second, you must swear to uphold your end of the bargain. Once you have the task, you must destroy me."

"Done."

"Swear on your soul, Reaper."

"Sure, I swear on my soul that I shall end your suffering once you have given me an Impossible Task," I told him, rolling my eyes. At this rate, who wouldn't have some sort of claim on my soul?

Midas stared at me for a long moment before nodding, some of the tension in his fading. "Very well. Let us see what Fate and the others have in store for you."

"Fate? What do they have to do with it?" I hadn't realized that we were going to be consulting with outside parties for this assignment.

"Who do you think governs the Impossible Tasks?"

I didn't have a response for that one.

The king strode back into his prison and began rooting around through the pile of junk, looking for something. I was trying to be patient, but the Underworld shook again as Pluto and Aite battled outside the gate, and I felt my blood pressure rising.

"How long will this take?"

"There is no Time here."

"Yeah, but there are several angry gods, so chop chop if you want to die."

Midas ignored my jibe, but he did return to the rope barrier between us, arms full of golden objects. Carefully he placed three candlesticks in front of him in a row. Then he laid an oversized golden scroll next to them. Finally, he produced a large knife, like a gilded butcher's blade, and held out his hand expectantly.

"This requires blood," he demanded.

I eyed the dead king suspiciously before sighing and holding out my left arm. From what little I knew about magic, giving someone access to your blood was a *very bad idea*. But in the Underworld, was it even real blood? Besides, Midas was going to be dead soon. What was the worst that could happen?

The king twisted my wrist and made a slight slice across my palm, then gestured for me to drip my blood on the scroll. Gritting my teeth against the sting, I clenched my fist a few times, pumping a little stream of red out of my body. Midas held out his own hand and repeated the slice, letting some of his royal blood dribble onto the scroll to pair with my own.

Apparently satisfied, he tossed the knife over his shoulder, where it fell among his scattering of objects with a clatter. I guess he really wasn't too worried about organization what with kicking the bucket in a few moments.

Closing his eyes, he raised both hands and in a deep, formal voice intoned, "Attend to me, keepers of prophecy. I am Midas, King of Phrygia, who commands the knowledge of the Muses, Oracles, and Fates." I shifted uncomfortably at the list of people who would be joining the call. They were all too familiar for my liking. I'd met a retired Oracle before, and from what I'd been told, her organization was as dirty as they come. I was also in the middle of defrauding the Fates. At least I helped Orion save the granddaughter of a Muse once.[1] That should be good for at least one favor.

"One stands before you who wishes to prove his worth to the gods in the tradition of Odysseus and Jason before him. Taste his blood and my royal essence to judge them acceptable. Come and set before this one, who has traveled to the depths of Hades itself, tasks to prove himself worthy of the night sky."

The hairs on my arms began to stand on end as he spoke, and by the time he finished his invocation, I felt like I was about to be struck by lightning. With each word, I'd sensed the building of the pressure that comes from the attention of powerful Immortal beings—as if many giant pairs of eyes had opened in the sky above and were staring down directly at us. Midas lowered his hands and gazed down at the three candles standing watch over the bloody scroll.

"Now what?"

"Now we see what they say," he said, shrugging. "I'm merely a conduit."

My emotions swung between hope and fear as I waited for a response. The heavy focus of many ancient things continued to grow in me, like a pot approaching a boiling point. Midas looked unconcerned, so I tried to follow his lead. This was totally normal; the Oracles and Fates scrutinized me all the time.

Suddenly the pressure spiked, and I dropped to my knee with a gasp. Midas remained standing, but I doubted he was bearing the weight of the attention that I was. One of the

---

1. Featured in the novella PIPER'S PRICE. (Coming in 2025).

candles burst into flame as I knelt before it, then after a few more heartbeats the next one did too.

My breath came out in ragged gasps. There was so much strain on me that I felt like I was being crushed. I could not fill my lungs all the way. I was hyperventilating as something studied me from the inside out, scrutinizing the very splicing of my DNA.

"Come on," I grunted, glaring at the candle to my left, which was the only one still unlit. "You know you want to see what happens."

Begrudgingly, the final candle burst into flame, although its fire seemed smaller and not nearly as bright as the other two, as if the entity was reluctant. For a second, all three shone in a row, then abruptly, they winked out. Immediately the pressure holding me down vanished, and the eyes above me closed. Not that I could see them, but I could *tell*.

Inhaling my first full breath in moments, I rose to my feet. I had done it. I had been given an Impossible Task. Lightning of a different kind flashed through me as I resisted the urge to jump for joy. I had my task. I could force-majeure my way out of going to Hell and save Megan.

Finally, something had gone my way.

"Well, that was more dramatic than usual," Midas muttered, eyeing the candles for a moment before bending down to pick up the scroll.

"Which candle was the holdout?" I asked, reaching for the bloody scroll with eagerness.

"The Fates seemed reluctant to accept you, but the Muses and Oracles must have been enough to convince them." His eyes narrowed in thought. "You haven't upset any of the Fates, have you, boy?"

It must have something to do with the reason Death's assistant Atty had been upset with me. I wondered if it was my dying early or Beatrice's Fate-hiding runes had caused the delay. Midas studied me for a moment, then shrugged, his expression clearly that of one who knew he wasn't going to be around to deal with this crap much longer. "I hope it was worth it."

Hades rattled once more under the fury of the gods raging within its borders.

With shaking hands, I accepted the scroll and unrolled it, the golden sheet rattling. My heart sank as I gazed down at it. It had been composed by a master of calligraphy. The letters flowed in beautiful order.

But they weren't in English. I couldn't read a damn word on the page. I went to college; I can recognize Greek letters well enough thanks to the fraternity system, not the education one. It seemed that whatever magic translated our voices didn't extend to the written word.

"Um, is there a way to get this done in a different language?" I asked.

"You think you're ready to complete an Impossible Task, and you aren't able to read Greek?" Midas's eyebrows shot up. "Surely you speak at least the other languages?"

"What other languages?"

"All of them."

"Oh yeah." I coughed, ignoring the blossoming dread in my stomach. "Most of them, definitely."

"I warned him," Midas sighed to no one in particular.

"Since you're here and you speak ancient Greek—"

"It's just Greek to me."

"Sure, that's what I meant. Since you speak Greek, I don't suppose you'd mind just giving it a quick read for me?"

"The word *impossible* must mean something different in your tongue," Midas sniffed, but he held out his hand for the scroll. "Very well, let's get this over with." His eyes narrowed as he began to read.

"The Oracles, Muses, and Fates have accepted Matthew Steven Carver, Lord of Fire, as an eligible noble of the Dandelion Court to prove his merit before the stars of the night sky. In order to judge his worthiness, they have set before him an Impossible Task composed of three parts:

"The first is that he must eat a golden apple of Iðunn. The second—he must slay the beast known as Leviathan. For his third, he must destroy the Four Seals of the Apocalypse."

"I'm sorry, the *what*?" My voice rose into a shriek. Whatever joy I had felt at getting an Impossible Task had just been crushed under the reality of the actual tasks. Each one seemed more…well, more impossible than the last.

"Void where prohibited," Midas continued, giving me an unamused stare. "Some conditions apply. The Oracles, Muses, Fates, and their agents are not liable for any temporary or permanent injuries that result from attempting to complete these tasks. See back for a complete list of exceptions."

With a grunt, he slammed the golden scroll shut, its metal page shrieking in protest, then held it out to me.

"There you go, now unmake me." Hades shook again.

"What was that bit about the Apocalypse?" I demanded, not taking the scroll from him. "What the hell are the Seals of the Apocalypse?"

"It's called an Impossible Task for a reason, Reaper. *Now*

do as you promised." A look of frustrated desperation crossed the golden king's face.

With a sigh, I accepted the scroll, tucking it away in my pocket, next to the soul of my sister. "So be it," I intoned, summoning the dark power of Death once more. The frigid scythe filled my right fist, and I lowered it, grasping the weapon firmly with both my hands as I prepared to swing. "Do you have any final words?"

"You know that this place will cease to exist once I die, don't you? It is hanging on by but a thread." A shrewd look crossed Midas's face.

"I'm counting on it," I told him, and I swung. Like I had learned with Sunburn's soul, I banished his spark into the darkness, unmaking him once and for all.

The golden king's body faded before it collapsed to the ground, and he was gone. Even though we weren't exactly friends, I hoped he found what he was looking for. Around me Hades began to rattle like an old roller coaster, and I turned to head back to the exit.

If I didn't hurry, I'd join him.

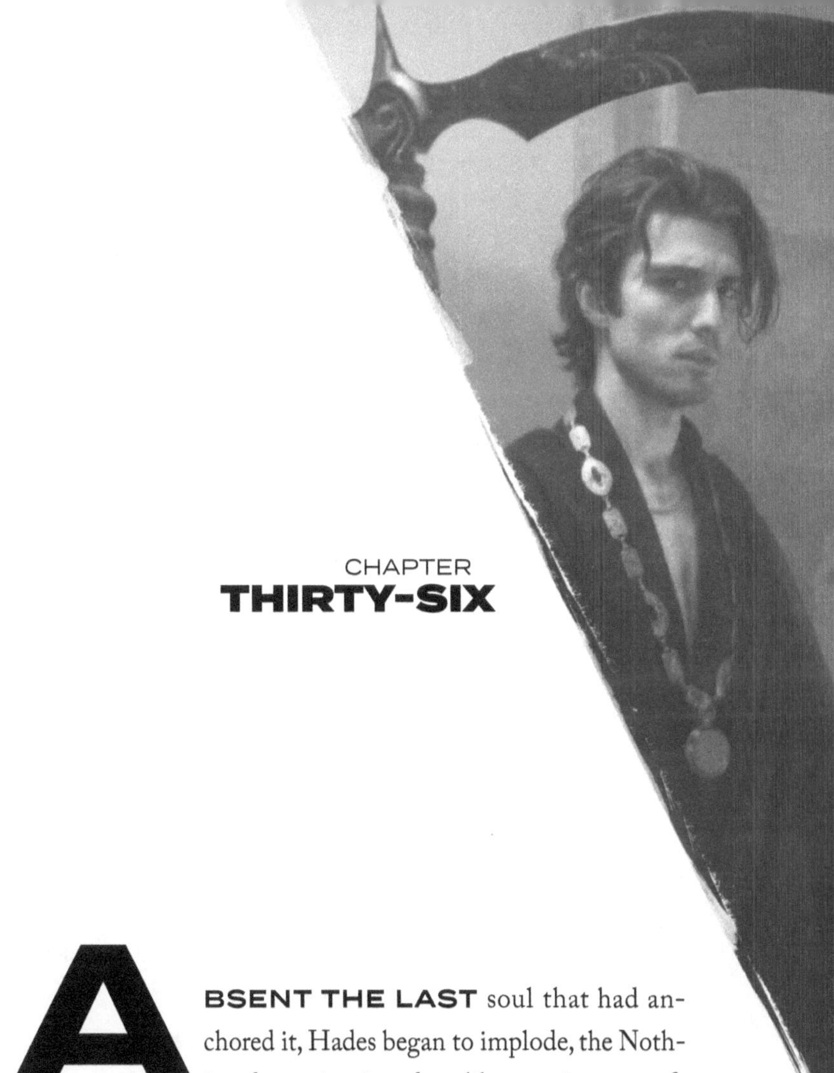

ABSENT THE LAST soul that had anchored it, Hades began to implode, the Nothing devouring its edges like termites on caffeine. While Pluto and Aite were battling, the place had been shaking, but now it was coming apart at the seams.

Sprinting at full tilt, I held as much of Death's Authority as I could, letting its cold power add springs to my legs. I bounded down the stairs of the mall, out the open gate, and into the forest.

Despite my panic, the destruction from the battle between the two gods drew me up short. The forest had been torn to shreds. The trees that had marched as soldiers were now only splinters, as if they had been hit by a Category 5 hurricane, an

EF5 tornado, and an 8.0 earthquake—at the same time.

In the center of the ruined woods, Aite stood tall, a wriggling Pluto in her hands as she choked the life out of him. Pluto's eyes were wide. Things were clearly not going the tiny death god's way.

My heart broke for him, truly.

Pluto clawed at his relative's grip with his hands, but they didn't have the strength to pry even a single finger off his neck. I couldn't help but grin as I realized that his power was gone. A death god with no Underworld was like a battery with no charge—he might as well have been a paperweight. The landscape shook again as if we were in a snow globe, and even Aite staggered under the assault of the Nothing devouring this corner of the world.

Right, no time for watching monsters get their just desserts. I had to get out of here. Cutting to the left, I raced past the fighting gods, letting my momentum carry me down the mountain.

"Aite, stop him! If he leaves, there is no escape!" Pluto wheezed behind me, spotting me as I fled.

"Fool," she hissed at the wriggling god in her grip. "What do I have to fear from the Dark?" The prophet of the Nothing shoved her hand into Pluto's chest like it was made of paper mâché and pulled. Golden blood and gore exploded as she ripped his heart from his chest. Despite the color, it looked distressingly similar to the organ that beat behind my own ribs.

"Then take with you my *mors maledicto*," hissed Pluto. His purple eyes flashed, and for a moment everything was still. A power not unlike Death's absolute silence descended upon the war-torn glade.

Pluto threw back his head and screamed his impotent rage

into that stillness. A dark orb of power coalesced into being in front of the gaping hole of his ruined chest. Before Aite could react, it detonated, shattering the silence like a thunderstroke.

Its shock wave expanded like a mushroom cloud, sweeping over me in a tempest. Everything turned to black. Deep whispers spoke ruinous tidings in my ears in languages I could not understand, then were silent. For a moment I thought I died, caught in the sweeping aftershocks of Pluto's final counterstroke.

But the darkness did not last. As quickly as it came, it was gone.

Mother Ruin stood at the epicenter of the blast, Pluto's lifeless form in her hands. Her black toga was a ruin, and streaks of ash marred her porcelain skin. Aite dropped the carcass of the Roman god of death at her feet, and my heart leapt with hope as I saw her stagger a step to her left.

"Your death curse missed, dear uncle," she murmured almost drunkenly into the fading Underworld.

Slowly, her gaze tracked from Pluto's body to me. One of her eyebrows was missing. She held eye contact with me and took a bite out of her cousin's heart like an apple. Whatever the god had done wounded her, but clearly it had not been enough.

I ran.

Without the trees, I was able to make a straight shot to the River Styx. As I drew near to the bank, I felt a thrill of fear. The other side had already vanished into the void. The empty dark of the Nothing lurked just across the rapids.

Pluto was right: The only way out of here was the gate to the Between, and I was the key. I raced along the close bank, cruising into the fog that shrouded the exit. My heart soared as I saw the warm light of the marble hallway.

Not only had I gotten my Impossible Task, I had bested not one, but two gods. Maybe I was a worthy student of Orion. "Thanks for the invite, but I gotta jet!" I cried over my shoulder as I leapt for the doorway.

Raw will wrapped around me like an anaconda, halting my progress in midair. I grunted in shock as the iron bands of power slammed into me. Slowly, they began to constrict, squeezing me like a tube of toothpaste.

"Urk," I protested, staring at the glowing exit only a few feet in front of me. I should know better than to gloat. "Yuki, help. Yuki!" My voice came out weak and wheezy as my torso began to constrict like an empty soda can. I knew that it was wasted breath. I had told my friends to run in the opposite direction. Yuki wouldn't be close enough to hear me, let alone get to me in time. The pressure built, and my vision began to blur.

So close. I had been so close.

A shadowy figure appeared in the entryway ahead of me, blocking the light. For a second, I thought that I had died and gone to the empty abyss beyond Death. Then I realized I was still being crushed, and the person was coming toward me.

Despite my circumstances, I still felt a twinge of fear as I saw the figure draw back their scythe and swing at me with all the force of a professional baseball player. But I was not their target. Slowly, the weapon carved through the hard air of Mother Ruin's will.

The pressure on my chest lightened as the band of power snapped like a hair tie. I gasped, sucking in a full breath as the lights went back to normal. Somewhere behind us, Aite let out a scream of rage and pain. Even a goddess did not appreciate Death's kiss.

We had to get out of here before she came to make us pay for our insult. Hades rattled again as the Nothing continued to devour it like a flock of piranhas. I glanced over my shoulder, but all I could see was the empty dark. A note of hope flared in my chest as I realized that the decay had cut off the goddess's approach. We had a little more time.

Grim-faced, Yuki drew back her weapon again and aimed at my legs. Her strike cleaved through open air, and she staggered when she met no resistance. I guess it's hard to cut through invisible power without something to aim at.

"Lower," I gasped, wiggling my legs to show how my ankles were stuck together. The Reaper nodded, sending her pigtails dancing, but she drew and slashed again, this time hitting the mark and cutting me free of my bonds.

With a plop, I dropped the final six inches to the ground, landing in a light crouch. Aite let out another primal scream in the distance. Pluto had really done me a solid with his death curse. I wondered if I would have stood any chance of escaping Mother Ruin without him weakening her.

"Take my oath with you, Matthew Carver," she cried, voice echoing from the abyss that was swallowing her ancestral Underworld. "You are marked by the Lost and shall always be lost. When your soul ventures forth from the Veil, know that my masters shall devour you in the dark!"

"Yeah, yeah," I grumbled. "Get in line."

Hades began to tear itself apart as if some key foundation had been dissolved, shaking me out of my stunned silence. Lacking anything close to a witty response, I pointed out the door to Yuki and dashed through with my fellow Reaper.

I shot through the gate, letting the brightly lit hallway

banish the cold that had settled over my soul. Taking a deep breath, I turned to Yuki and gave her a small nod of thanks. As far as I was concerned, we were even now.

"Surprise," called a soft, mocking voice.

Heart leaping in my chest, I spun to see Aite emerge from the darkness of the void that had consumed most of Hades. I should have guessed that the prophet of the Nothing would be able to make her way through the abyss.

Without even pausing to think, I summoned my scythe and hurled it at her, letting the weapon spin end-over-end as it shot toward her. Mother Ruin's face twitched in surprise, and she ducked to the side. But I didn't even bother to wait and see if my throw found its mark.

I grabbed the gate to Hades with my left hand and slammed it shut, cutting off her scream of rage as the exit sealed. Panting, I staggered back a few steps, and as I watched, the iron of the gate began to rust before my eyes, the stones of the entrance crumbled, and the Underworld beyond fell into ruin. I glanced at the carved sign and watched in awe as an invisible hand carved an addendum to the title: HADES—DEVOURED.

The Greco-Roman Underworld was no more.

Matthew Carver: 2

Gods: 0

Holy crap. My plan had actually worked! Now all I had to do was steal a crown and go home. My heart leapt in my chest as my gaze settled on the still form of Wilbur, lying against the wall where Yuki had set him when she had come looking for me. My friend's eyes were half lidded, and his chest still rose and fell in labored breaths.

I rushed to his side and dropped to my knees, placing a hand on his shoulder. "Come on, dude, you got this," I whispered.

"I don't reckon I do." He coughed wetly, and my heart broke at the horrific sound. "But you were right. It was worth it." A giant smile spread across my face, even though my eyes were still threatening to rain.

"I'm proud of you," I told him. "Proud of you both," I added, glancing up at Yuki. The woman gave me a small nod, her own eyes misty as she looked down at us.

"Thanks," he mumbled. "This hurts. I wonder how soon I'm gonna die?"

"I'm…not sure you can," I admitted. "Not here. We're sort of between places right now."

"Great." Wilbur let out a weak chuckle. "So, I'm just suffering for no reason."

A flash of guilt ran through me, but I shook my head, giving his shoulder a squeeze. "No, you're buying us time to figure out how to stop you from bleeding out."

"We don't actually *bleed*."

"Metaphorically bleeding out then," I snapped. "There has to be a way. Yuki, do we have a first-aid kit or doctors or… anything?"

Silently, the woman shook her head, giving me a sad smile. "We're Death."

"We don't even get dental," Wilbur reminded me.

"There has to be a way!" I shouted, my frustration rising. My friend had overcome so much and proved that he was the good guy I had always known he was. This couldn't be the end. He didn't deserve to simply end.

My right hand curled into a fist, and I felt Death's icy signet ring rub against my fingers. Struck by a thought, I glanced down at the band. There was no denying that being the heir let me draw on more power, which made me stronger...

What would happen if I gave it to Wilbur? Would he be able to give himself enough Authority to reject the Death that Jack had given him? It made a weird sort of sense. Kane had told me that the heir could not be compelled to leave the Veil against their wishes. Heart racing, I reached for the ring and pulled, twisting it to get it around my knuckle. As it popped free, I felt something leave me, as if I had just taken off my jacket. The little knot of cold power still lurked in the back of my mind, but it was weaker—warmer than before. No more drinking straight from the firehose for me. I was back to being a regular Reaper instead of the heir.

"Here," I panted, not wanting to explain. "Put this on." I grabbed his hand and jammed the signet ring over his middle finger.

"Ow, what are you—" Wilbur's voice cut out as the power took hold.

"Use it," I commanded, rising to my feet. Yuki came to hover next to me, a shocked expression on her face.

Eyes wide, Wilbur nodded, his neck convulsing as he swallowed in fear. Then his gaze unfocused, and as we watched the dark tear in his side began to close. With a gasp, he sat up and looked at me, mouth hanging open. Slowly, he climbed to his feet and stared at us, a wide smile beginning to grow on his face.

It had worked.

Laughing, I tackled the gangly Reaper, hugging him and pounding on his back. "You're okay, you're okay!" I shouted. Even Yuki joined in. After a few moments, we separated, and I had to surreptitiously wipe a tear out of the corner of my eye.

My relief that Wilbur and Yuki were okay was overwhelming. I had set out to do something that Orion would have done, and I felt like I'd succeeded. I hoped he would be proud of me. Maybe Alex could tell him about it in five hundred years.

The silence began to build as each of us began to realize the repercussions of what I had done. When I gave Wilbur the ring, I had thought of it as a loan, a way for him to draw more power when he needed it most. But he now possessed a weapon that would save him from being sent to Hell when his time was up, and I had no way to force him to give it back. There was a reason Jack and every other Reaper had been willing to kill for it.

Slowly, the mood turned from joyful to tense.

"Here," Wilbur said after a few moments. With deft hands he reached up to pull the ring off his finger. I relaxed, relieved that my trust in my friend hadn't been misplaced. As it came free, he staggered, and I watched in horror as the wound in his side reopened in slow motion.

"Put it back, put it back on!" I shouted, waving my hands at him. Grimacing, Wilbur slid it back on, and after a moment, his wound sealed once more. I guess that's how being one foot in the grave works.

The three of us were silent as we processed this development. If Wilbur couldn't give me the ring back, he would have to remain the heir to avoid dying. That was fine with me, I was about to blow this Popsicle stand, but Kane might have something to say about it.

Wilbur had proven himself to me. Why shouldn't he be the new heir? Clearly Death needed some help. I had found the major pipeline of corruption in the Underworlds, but who was to say there weren't more? If not right now, then in the future.

That is the way of things. Corruption grows like mold, getting into everything. It was only right of me to leave this place in capable hands.

"Keep it for now," I told him firmly, looking into his eyes. "I trust you to hold on to it for me for a bit." Wilbur's eyes flicked down in shame, but then they came back up, and he nodded tightly.

I led the two Reapers back up to the hall to the door for the Veil. Digging into my pockets, I pulled out Janus's key and hesitated. With my other hand, I fished out the pocket watch.

My stomach curdled as I stared at the hands: 11:58 p.m. I wasn't sure I had enough time to pull off Lazarus's heist. But I was going to have to try.

"Say, are you ever gonna tell us what's going on?" Wilbur asked from behind me.

"What do you mean?" I shoved the watch back down my shirt. I took a deep breath and squared my shoulders.

"We have eyes, Matthew," Yuki pointed out. "You have taken us somewhere we are not supposed to be with a key I doubt any of us are supposed to have."

I let my hand drop from the knob and sighed. I didn't really have a good way to explain my access to the Between. "I don't suppose you'd just let me just walk away?" I asked, turning to look at them.

Wilbur shook his head slowly. Yuki only stared, arms crossed.

"Okay, so you know how my soul is going to Hell?"

"Just like the rest of us."

"Well…not quite." I told them the basics, about how Dan had forged the deal and stolen my soul, and how I was here to get an Impossible Task to undo it.

"Did you do it?" Wilbur asked eagerly, stepping toward me. "Did you get your task from the Sorcerer King?"

"I did." I fished the scroll out of my pocket and held it up for him to see. Yuki didn't look nearly as interested.

"All this time you were judging us for trying to get our souls out of Hell, and you were doing the same thing? What's the difference?" Enraged disbelief had entered her voice.

"I told you that I understood," I said flatly. "But the difference is that I wasn't willing to step on other people to save myself."

The tough Reaper glanced away, cheeks turning slightly pink in shame.

"One thing I don't understand," Wilbur continued, picking up the awkward pieces of our conversation. "Don't you have to be alive to do tasks like that?"

"Oh, there are ways around that," I replied airily, giving him a cheeky wink. I did my best to look unconcerned, but on the inside I was terrified. They couldn't know that I was still alive. I trusted them, but there's trust and then there's *trust*.

"Any more questions?" I arched an eyebrow at the two of them, and they both shrugged. "I'll fill you guys in more later," I lied, feeling a little sick to my stomach. There was but one way through this, and I was going to take it.

"Now." I turned back down the hall. "I need you to help me drop off these souls before I get in *more* trouble."

THIRTY-SEVEN

THE DOOR FROM the Between into the Veil followed my unspoken instructions and opened in an empty hallway just around the corner from Death's vault. I hesitated at the threshold, taking a deep breath like a diver at the top of a cliff. Time was short. I had to do this perfectly. Lazarus's threats hung over my head as I stepped back into the flow of time.

"Are you sure shouldn't we go find Death first?" Wilbur asked as he and Yuki followed me out the door, looking around in confusion. I was too desensitized to the Key of Portunus slash Janus to remember how disorienting the journey could be.

"I told you," I said as reassuringly as I could, "he told me to off-load these souls I rescued before doing anything else." That wasn't a lie, exactly. He had ordered me to do that, before Aite had been unleashed on the Veil. It wasn't unreasonable to assume his priorities would have changed, but he hadn't updated me on that yet.

"If you're sure…" Even though he was the heir now, Wilbur seemed more nervous than before.

"Let's do it fast, just in case." I broke into a jog, turning the corner and entering the dark hallway where the Vault of Souls waited. The round door was sealed, its golden skull leering at us from the darkness.

"Wilbur, tell it to open!" I shouted, not slowing.

"How?"

"Use the ring and command it!" I guessed. I hadn't performed this particular task while I had been the heir, but that sounded right. Sure enough, the vault door began to grind open as we raced toward it. I let out a whoop, dodging through its narrow opening without slowing. I could hear the footsteps of my friends behind me as we entered.

I stopped myself from checking my pocket watch as I raced through the room of treasures, heading toward the door shrouded in shadows at the back. I had to get these souls out of me. I didn't know what would happen if I came back to life carrying a bunch of other people with me, but I didn't want to find out. I thundered into the deepest part of the dark.

"I'll be just a second," I promised, hoping that was true. The crystal skull sat on its altar as it had before. The whole bone motif was starting to get a little played out, but when you're Death what else can you do? I raced toward it, slapping my right hand over its face without a moment of hesitation.

I shivered as the dark power reached into me, pulling out the orbs of light that lurked under my skin like a swarm of fireflies. Each felt like a bursting pimple as it popped out of my skin and into the skull.

With my left hand, I checked the time. 11:59.

Less than a minute left.

Fear tore at me like a wild, feral thing. I jerked my right hand, trying to free it from the skull, but it was frozen in place, waiting for the last couple of souls to get sucked out.

"Come on!" I shouted in frustration.

"Everything alright in there?" Yuki's voice came from the hall.

"Oh, uh, yeah. Just got something stuck."

"I don't think that's how it works."

I ignored her as I felt the last pop, and the crystal released my hand. My mind went numb as I turned to race out the door. The only thing I could hear was the ticking of a clock that drowned out everything else.

This was the final race.

I burst out of the altar room past the waiting Yuki and Wilbur. They followed in my wake, confused. Back in the main room of the vault, I frantically cast around the shelves of Kane's treasures trying to remember where the Crown of Immortality had been. Believe it or not, that was harder than I'd expected. There were crowns everywhere, each marked with a meticulously inscribed placard.

I saw the Crown of Stars, the Crown of Thorns, the Crown of the Seas, and the Crown of the Oceans, which seemed repetitive to me, but maybe they're different things. Each of them was beautiful and powerful in its own way, but none of them would protect me from Lazarus's wrath.

Then I saw it. The place where it should be. CROWN OF IM-MORTALITY read the little sign next to the purple pillow. But there was no crown resting on it, just an indent where it had once sat.

"I always knew there was something wrong with you," a furious voice hissed from the doorway behind me, freezing me in my tracks. I turned to face Atty. Death's assistant held a crown in her left hand and a dark, wicked pair of scissors in her right. Her eyes danced with smug rage as she stared at me.

"Looking for this?" She gestured with the crown. Its seven black diamonds glittered in the light, and I twitched toward it. But the old woman danced back, extending the scissors toward me like a knife. "I thought so."

"Matt, what's going on?" Yuki's voice was tense.

Panicked, I took another step toward Atty. I didn't have time for this. There had been a minute on the clock. One single time surge and the game would be over. I just needed to get my hands on it…

"You're a fool," Atty hissed. "I should have seen it from the beginning. Your name wasn't on the list. I never make mistakes."

"I don't know what you're talking about," I lied, stalling for time. I knew she wouldn't believe me, but if I could keep her talking, maybe I could catch her off guard.

"When Midas invoked the Fates' approval for the Impossible Task, did you think those were empty names?" Haughty scorn filled her voice as she mocked me. "Did you think that I was not *listening*?"

Oh crap. That was why she made the list. She wasn't the assistant. She was one of the Fates. If I recalled correctly there were three of them: the maiden, the maid, and the crone. Each was responsible for a different aspect of life, but the eldest decided when the thread of someone's existence was cut.

"Atty isn't your real name, is it?" I asked softly.

The crone gave me a smile that was all teeth. "Men have called me many things over the eons, but I have always been partial to Atropos." I suppressed a shudder at the dread her real name sent crawling down my spine.

When Midas had performed the invocation of the Impossible Task, the Fates' candle had taken the longest to light. That was because Atty had been learning the truth of what I was. I'd assumed that the Fates were pissed at me because I had died without being on their list, not that Death's right hand was one of them.

The eldest Fate didn't answer, but she took a step toward me, her scissors glinting in the bright lights of Death's vault.

"I can explain," I told her, holding up my hands in a placating gesture. "It's not what you think—"

"I know exactly what you are, faithless one. You will never leave this place." She raised the sharp black scissors once more. "I will trim you myself."

"Matt, what do we do?" Wilbur's voice was full of panic. I could only imagine how confusing this was for the new heir. I felt bad, but I'd saved his life. He could endure a little bit of awkwardness. I glanced over my shoulder and waved him back.

Time was almost up. I leapt toward the crone, calling on what Authority of Death I still had. Compared with the fire-hose of power I was used to, this was only a trickle. But it was better than nothing.

Atty was an ancient and powerful being, but she wasn't a warrior. Her stab was slow and predictable. It was child's play for me to block her attack and divert it. She let out a shriek and twisted, holding the crown farther from me, flailing.

I reached for it, but my fingers only barely brushed its sharp edges before she forced me to twist to avoid her cruel scissors. My bumbled grab knocked the Crown of Immortality from her grasp, and we both watched in horror as it crashed to the ground, shattering into a thousand pieces.

"No!" I screamed as I watched the shards scatter around the room like shrapnel. Despair gripped me. I had failed. Lazarus would go after my sister.

"Die forever!" Atty cried, lunging toward me with wild eyes. Caught off guard, I dodged back, retreating from the Fate's cruel weapon. I knew that if she stabbed me with her scissors, I would be unmade. Frantic with rage, she followed and cornered me in the back of the vault. I had nowhere to run. Atty cackled as she raised her blade to clip my thread.

I had failed.

A loud thump interrupted her. It echoed across the entire Veil like it had been on the PA system. The world seemed to slow, and my vision turned black-and-white for a moment before the color slowly leached back.

Thump.

Thump. Thump.

Thump. Thump. Thump.

Slowly, I raised my hand to my breastbone. With each thud, I felt something pulse in my chest. Then as the pace picked up, I realized that it was a heartbeat. My real one. I pulled out the watch to check the time. Midnight.

Time's up.

"What?" snarled Atty, her eyes going wide. "This isn't possible, you can't—"

Whatever I could or couldn't do, I would never find out. Something that felt like a hook settled around my sternum and *pulled*. I had just enough time to start screaming in horror as I shot backward through the wall that the Fate had cornered me against. Over her shoulder I saw the shocked expressions of Yuki and Wilbur. Then I was gone.

I passed through solid objects as if I were a ghost, traveling faster and faster as I went. Sterile white walls flashed past, along with colorful blurs of people whom I couldn't make out. With my heart restarting, the Veil seemed intent on spitting me out like a whale. I was terrified. Completely out of control, I could only hope that this was going according to plan. There hadn't been a safety briefing about how I would reenter the living world.

I was still screaming when I abruptly jerked to a halt.

As the world swam into focus, I realized that I wasn't back in Lazarus's lab; this was still the white of the Veil. The pressure tugging on me hadn't abated—if anything, it was growing. It felt like an entire professional tug-of-war team was pulling on a robe attached to my spine, and every second they added another player.

A cold, vise-like grip was wrapped around my ankle—the one without a boot—pulling me in the other direction like a wishbone. Dangling between these two forces, I glanced down my body to see what had caught me and found myself staring into the dark eyes of Death.

Oh double crap.

The Grim Reaper was still in his battle form, wreathed in shadows. He held me in one hand and his infamous scythe in the other. My newly beating heart skipped some of its real beats at the sight of old Death holding me in place.

"What have you done?" he demanded in tones of ice.

Terror jerked in my heart as the hook in my chest from the living side of the Veil pulled on me, stretching me like a Matt-sized accordion. "I can explain!" I gasped. The shadowy figure was silent, waiting for my excuse.

"It was Pluto! He was the one selling souls. He had drained all of Hades except for one that he was using to keep the lights on."

"*What?*" Kane's rage flared like a match at my words.

"He was working with Jack and some of your Reapers, funneling lost souls into Hades, then helping them make deals with their future Underworlds for lighter sentences."

Death was as silent as himself for a long moment. While he brooded, I stretched, torn between the two forces pulling on my soul.

"I took care of it," I wheezed. "That's my job, right, as your heir?"

"How?"

"Hades is no more. I claimed its final soul, and it fell to the Nothing. Pluto and Mother Ruin were inside it when it was consumed. There were no survivors. Jack and Rex have been dealt with too."

"What of the buyers? Where were the souls going?"

"I don't know," I admitted after a moment of thought. "Some are clearly going to the places that were willing to give the Reapers bribes. But there were a lot more missing."

"We know the Dragon Dons have access to the missing souls as well, and they do not have an Underworld of their own," Death pointed out, his hand still tight on my socked ankle.

"What does that mean?"

"It means that there is more going on."

"Whoever hit the shipment you sent me to investigate was not the Lost," I acknowledged, doing my best to think through complicated plots while being pulled in two. "They didn't tear the convoy apart but unloaded it like professionals. Another player is still taking souls that is not Pluto or a Reaper."

"And now we will never get the chance to interrogate any of them. I wanted you to solve this problem, but it seems that you have only made it harder to unravel."

"I brought justice to those who abused their power in your name," I snarled, surprised by the heat entering my voice. "Each of them was responsible for souls being stolen and lost in the dark. They got what they deserved. Maybe there are more people involved, but that is *your* responsibility, *Death*."

Kane stared at me for a moment before letting out a mildly satisfied grunt. "I guess that's what I get for naming a student of the Hunter as my heir," he grumbled. Neither of us mentioned that Mother Ruin, as a prophet of the Nothing, was more than likely fine. At least she was on this side of the Veil now. She wouldn't be able to follow me to the other side, which was much warmer and nicer.

"In my defense, Aite killed Pluto, not me."

"Did you think that I didn't know what you are?" he mused softly, changing topics. I tensed, trying to stare into his shadowy hood. He didn't seem as angry as I had expected. Certainly less than Atty had been.

"I...don't know," I admitted.

"This is my realm. I am Death. There is no counterfeit to me."

"Then why let me in? Why make me a Reaper?"

"Because you are the Harbinger."

"I'm sorry, the what? Can you, like…define that for me?"

"In time you will discover what you are," Death said with a laugh. "Our work together is not done yet, Matthew Carver." The tension from the living world increased; I gasped as I was stretched even thinner.

"Okay, well, do you think we could do this other part later? I'm sort of being pulled in multiple directions right now."

"You're not wearing the ring." His tone took on a rigid anger that hadn't been present before.

"I figured since I was going to be out of the office for a while, I should give you a new heir," I said, doing my best to explain. "Congratulations, it's a Wilbur!"

"Wilbur? One of Jack's associates?"

"He's seen the error of his ways. He and Yuki helped me take down Jack and Rex. I trust them both to carry on your directives in my absence."

"You had no right to give away my signet ring!" For the first time, he seemed truly angry. Kane's rage seemed to shake the Veil itself, but that might also have been my vision as Life and Death fought over me like spoiled children.

"It was to save his life—"

"Is that a *soul* in your pocket?" His voice rose to a shriek as he noticed Megan's presence.

"I could be just happy to see you?"

Death glared at me, unmoving.

"Yeah, about that. Someone definitely resurrected my sister a year ago. Which I get the sense was not cleared by you or the Death Board? Hell stole her soul after that, so I'm just taking it back. You should ask Zagan about it. I'm sure he'd love to explain it all."

Kane was silent for a moment. When he finally spoke, his voice was cold and hard. "You came into my house, lied, stole, and forsook my gifts. You may be returning to the Living World, but you are a mortal. Your road will always end with me. I pronounce a new lien upon your soul." It was about then I realized that he didn't know I had broken his crown yet. I decided not to bring that up. The bill was already large enough.

"This is your Death Tax: Half a soul you are taking from me, so half a soul I demand. Balance the scales between us before your days come to an end or face the consequences." I did my best not to gulp. Turned out Old Grim was pretty good at threats too.

"Half a soul?" I croaked after a few moments.

"To match your sister's."

"But she's not supposed to be here!"

"This part of her is dead, and now she will not be. There are prices that must be paid for that transit." I winced at that. Freaking Zagan.

The tension pulling on me increased, and I arched my back in pain, but Kane didn't move an inch. All of the give came from my joints, which freaking *hurt*.

"What about a whole soul? You could keep the extra as, like, a…tip."

"The scales must be balanced. That would leave them imbalanced."

"But then you could maybe give *me* half a soul, and we could, like…" I trailed off as I stared into the darkness of Death's hood, sensing that my prattle was only going to get me in more trouble. Kane might have a sense of humor, but the Grim Reaper was more primal than that.

"I don't suppose there are a lot of half souls floating out in the living world?" I asked, already knowing the answer. It was always going to end this way, I realized, broken crown or no. Death and his greatest enemy had me in their clutches. Suddenly the tugging felt like an apt metaphor.

"There are three. Any of them would be acceptable. For you, one would be much easier than the others."

"Lazarus."

"Lazarus."

"I understand." I sighed, closing my eyes in defeat.

"Also, where is your boot?" For a moment, an amused tone crept into Kane's voice.

"Anubis took it."

Death let out a tiny, almost disappointed sigh. "See that you remember my price," he told me, his tone once again icy. "We will meet again, you and I." Before I could reply, he released his grip on my ankle, and I shot out of the Veil like an arrow. The world flashed by me, in a burst of colors, lights, and sounds.

Then everything went black.

When I opened my eyes, I was back in Lazarus's lab, exactly where I had left me, and everything was on fire.

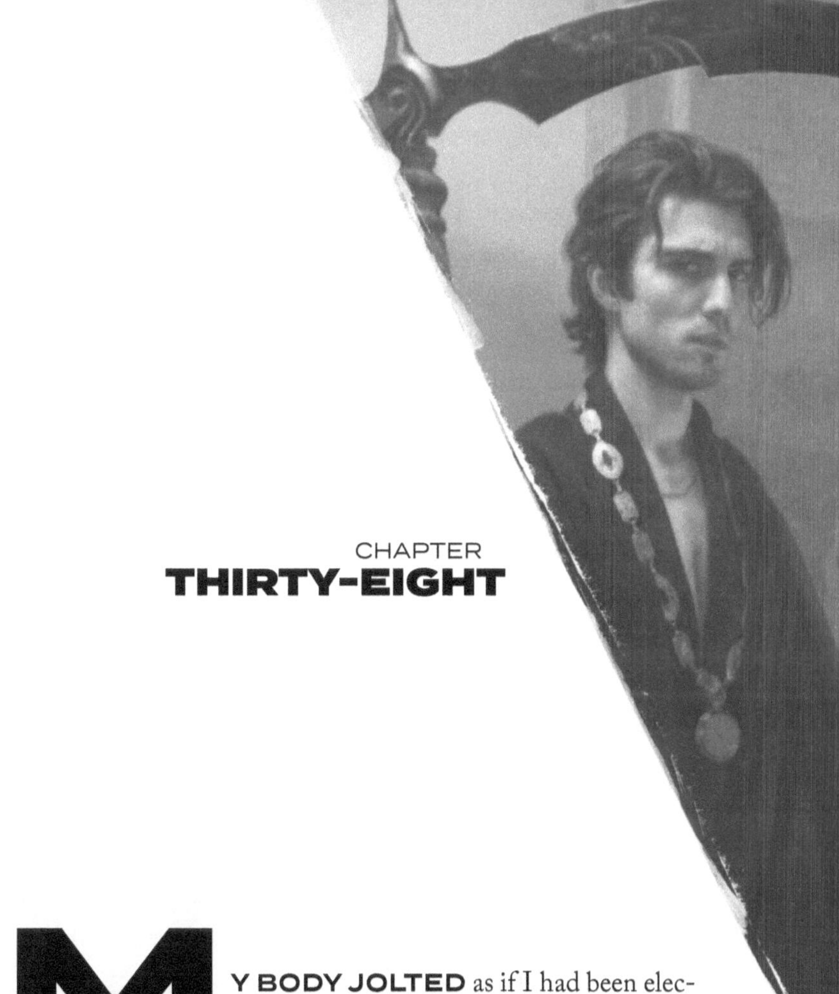

THIRTY-EIGHT

MY BODY JOLTED as if I had been electrocuted. I staggered, taking several steps to the right and then collapsing. I would have to get used to having real legs again. They felt the same as I recalled, and yet different. They had a weight to them that was real—not imagined or remembered.

I was *so cold*. My lungs ached as if they had long since given up on oxygen. I tried to inhale, but nothing happened. My diaphragm contracted, but no air came rushing into my body.

My hearing was muted as I gazed out at the pandemonium erupting around me. I was back in Lazarus' lab. My body was still in the center of the circle where his team had killed me.

The ring glowed with power, but the machines around the edges were shooting sparks and several burned with a full-on flame.

In the corner, Alex was gesturing wildly with a rifle he must have taken from a security guard. In his other hand, he held the demonic mask that turned him into a berserker. Scientists were running around while armed guards faced off with my friend.

If only I could get a breath, I would probably be able to do something. Ahead of me, the giant hourglass that held the Sands of Time was empty, just like my lungs. Gasping on nothing, I threw one of my hands forward, desperate to crawl out of the ring.

When they had killed me, they had used magic or something to make the space around me some sort of super-freezer. The idea was that if they could stop my body from decaying, it would be easier for my soul to get back into its meat suit.

But in all the excitement, someone had forgotten to turn Reality back on now that I was alive. Or maybe they hadn't noticed I was back. If I could just get out of the circle, things should go back to normal—I hoped.

My head pulled backward as I ran out of slack in the tube that was connected to my mask, stopping me like a dog on his leash. With frozen hands I flailed at the latches on my cheek, trying to tear myself free. My numb fingers felt like bricks; I had no dexterity to manipulate any of the clasps.

A familiar darkness crept through my body as my soul began to be choked out by real Death. All that work to break out of the Veil, just to be sent back to the Underworlds sixty seconds later. I could only hope that Kane would be willing to accept something else as my Death Tax. Maybe, if I asked nicely, Alex would put some hundred-dollar bills over my eyes instead of coins.

My friend must have seen my flailing out of the corner of his eye, because he spun, gesturing at the circle and shouting furiously. Dim and dull as my world was, I couldn't hear any of it, but he got his point across.

The muzzle on his assault rifle flared, and I saw a light built into the circle ahead of me shatter. He kept firing, and chunks of the floor exploded. One of the bullets must have hit something vital, because atmosphere shoved its way through.

The warmth of Reality poured into me, and my hand clutching at my mask burst into flame, filling me with joy. Willow's power had returned to me, taking up residence in the same corner of my brain it had always been. If I wasn't afraid that I was about to die for real, I could have sobbed with relief. I hadn't lost my friend, and suddenly I could *feel* again. Still gasping, I ripped the mask free and took the sweetest inhale that I've ever had.

Sound slammed back into me, and I staggered under the weight of the sonar assault. Alarms blared, machines beeped, and people shouted. It was overwhelming and chaotic. After an age spent in the sterile realm of Death, it was beautiful.

"Matt! Matt, are you okay?" Alex demanded, still brandishing his rifle and mask. The people in the room had grown still after he fired his weapon, and now they all were staring at me, shock apparent on their faces. Beatrice's mouth hung open in blatant disbelief.

Standing across from Alex was Lazarus. The tweed-wearing mobster's eyes burned with a greedy light as he saw me. A thrill of fear ran through me as I met his watery gaze. He was about to face several disappointments.

"I'm alive," I croaked, giving my friend a grin. "Why does

everyone look so surprised? The Sands of Time ran out and I came back."

"Matthew," Beatrice said slowly, stepping toward me with wide eyes. "The hourglass ran out twelve hours ago. We had begun to worry." I felt my eyes widen. I guess my final conversation with Death had run a little longer than I'd thought.

"You had given up," Alex snapped at the technomancer, shedding some light on why he might have felt the need to get himself a gun.

"It seems that once again, you prove to be a surprising young man," Lazarus offered, clasping his hands behind his back as if all were going according to plan. "Welcome back to the land of the living, Matthew. What have you brought us from the other side?"

For a moment, I was struck by the staggering hubris of this old man. He may think that he stood a chance against Death, but he had not seen what I had seen. He had no idea of the yawning, hungry dark that waited for us all. He thought that Death was a thing to be conquered—but you cannot conquer THE END. It is inevitable.

Steeling myself as I stared at the man with half a soul, I met his eyes and tried not to feel fear. "Let's talk," I told him. As I did, I banished Willow's flames. I wasn't trying to look threatening—not yet anyway. A dark shadow flashed over his face but was quickly hidden by his normal placid expression. After a moment, he nodded and gestured for me to follow.

I gave Alex a reassuring pat on the shoulder as I passed him. It was good to see him again. My friend eyed me warily but lowered his hands. I was glad he was armed—I didn't know how this was going to go. My number one priority was protecting Megan, but depending on how Lazarus reacted, we might have to do so aggressively.

Speaking of Megan, where was her soul? Had it made it through the Veil? Something tugged against my wet suit's thigh as I walked, and I reached down to pat the round lump under my outfit. Relief flooded through me as I realized the soul container had stayed about level with where my pocket had been despite the wardrobe change. Suddenly curious, I patted the other side, only to feel the bulge of my scroll and the smaller lump of the key. Looked like everything had made it home okay.

A smile broke out on my face as I followed the mobster. At least that part of the plan had worked.

I was grateful for my brief chance to collect myself. It was disorienting having a physical body again, and I needed to be oriented. I might not be in the Veil anymore, but the danger was far from over.

Then despair settled around my shoulders like a heavy yoke. I could feel Death's hand on me, there was no escaping it. As I now knew better than most, Death always finds his man in the end. With each step drawing us closer to Lazarus's office, I could feel my heart—the flesh-and-blood one now—beating faster in preparation for a fight.

But my conscience didn't love what was coming. Lazarus was not a good man; I had no illusions about that. It's not possible to build an organization with the kind of reach he had without breaking a few eggs. That's not how this world works.

But he wasn't a monster.

Well, that wasn't true either. He wasn't a monster that I couldn't understand. What lengths would I go to try to save the world? Is killing a million people to save a billion lives ever the right choice? I don't know, but I'm certainly glad that those decisions aren't on my plate. Granted, if Lazarus ever managed to stop mortals from dying, the universe would fall apart—at least according to Kane—but I doubted the old man knew that.

I owed him for taking care of Megan and helping me get her soul back. I couldn't have done it without him. Killing him felt like a betrayal. He had dealt with me in good faith, or as close to it as anyone in the supernatural world seems to come—and yet Death had named his price.

Weighed down by my burdens, I followed him into his same mahogany library where he had threatened me what felt like weeks ago but had really been only a couple of days. The old man slid around his desk and dropped into his leather chair. He pulled his horn-rimmed glasses off his face and fixed me with a stern look as he pulled a cloth from his jacket pocket and began to clean them.

I didn't have to tell him that I didn't have the crown. He knew.

"You failed," he said without preamble.

"In a manner of speaking," I agreed, my voice just as flat. "I found the Crown of Immortality in the Vault of Souls, but I was prevented from stealing it."

"Prevented by whom?"

"Atropos, the crone of Fate. She destroyed it." Lazarus's thick white eyebrows twitched upward in surprise, but he didn't interrupt. "My entire time in the Veil was a trap," I told him. "Death knew that I was not really dead, and they were watching me. He knows what you are trying to do."

Lazarus was still. He cocked his head to the side as he studied me, inscrutable thoughts running behind his eyes. The tension inside me rose as I stared back at those cold, calculating blues. They reminded me of Jack's for some reason. He looked like a man, but there was frighteningly little humanity behind them.

"Death claims that if everyone stops dying, the universe will fall apart," I pressed as the silence grew. "That Reality is constantly expanding, and as such it needs a constantly expanding number of souls to keep it alive."

"An interesting thought," Lazarus grunted after a moment. "Apparently Einstein was more right than he knew." I blinked in surprise in his willingness to accept Kane's word. Maybe if I told Death that Lazarus had abandoned his project, it would be enough to pay off my tax. Then Death wouldn't need to threaten Megan. A small smile tugged at the corner of my mouth. There was a way out of this.

"So you'll stop?" I asked, a note of hope filling my voice.

"Stop what?"

"The whole curing-death thing?"

"Good heavens, of course not, boy." He looked at me like I was an idiot.

"What about the whole destroying-the-universe thing?"

"Well, perhaps some sacrifices will still need to be made." A chill settled on me as I realized that he was a monster after all. Maybe he'd always known that some humans would have to keep dying even after he and his friends became immortal. Even if he didn't, he would never have let that stop him.

Death's cold, heavy hand settled around my heart. I knew how the rest of this conversation was going to go.

"Well, what do you propose?" he asked eventually, placing his glasses back on his face and leaning back in his chair. "I warned you what your failure would force me to do."

"I can tell you how the Underworlds are organized. How souls are stored, how it all works," I offered. Despite his grim designs, part of me still wanted to give him an out. He had helped Megan when no one else could. If he hadn't turned on me, I would owe him as much as I did Orion.

"I'm afraid, Matthew, that we had a deal, and you have not lived up to your end of it." Lazarus shook his head sadly like a disappointed teacher. "For the sake of humanity, I will have no choice but to begin *studying* your sister in earnest." *Studying* is such a normal word. Everyone studies. But somehow when he said it, he managed to fill my head with images of saws and drills.

That was it, then.

Anger ran through me, and unbidden Willow leapt to my call. My hands burst into flames, and I felt a rush of appreciation for my fiery companion. It was good to have them back in my head. *I missed you too*, I thought in their direction. The spirit rarely spoke in the mortal realm. Being here was kind of like free-diving for them—they had to hold their breath. But I felt a warm nudge against my brain that was like a cat bumping into my legs. I took that as their cheerful reply.

Lazarus's gaze flicked down to my burning hands, and he smiled thinly. "We've discussed this before," he commented. "Your fire is no threat to me, I'm afraid."

A cold weight of judgment settled around my shoulders like a headsman's hood. Mentally, I reached inward, to the part of my brain that was collecting powers like party favors. I brushed past the bright spot that was Willow and seized the dark Authority of Death.

My right hand grew cold, though not as frigid as I expected; I guess the Faerie fire's warmth kept some of the chill at bay as the weight of my Reaper's scythe filled my palm. "What about this?" I asked softly, still holding his gaze. "Do you feel as confident that your science will protect you from Death himself?"

Lazarus's blue eyes widened in surprise as the chill of the grave emanated from my weapon. For a second, he went very still, in a dim parody of a surprised immortal. "It seems, that you have a new bargaining chip, young man" he said after a long moment. "That power can certainly claim me."

I leered at him with a smile full of teeth.

"What do you want?" he demanded eventually, his eyes still fixed on the scythe in my hands.

"You promised to get the FBI off our backs. Make them go away."

"Already done."

I arched a skeptical eyebrow.

"It's much more convenient to shelter people who think they are being hunted than to actually have to hide them from the authorities," the old man explained with a shrug. I held back a snarl of annoyance. Smug bastard really had been playing as if he held all the cards, hadn't he. Fool. He had played his whole hand, and the game was over.

"Then what do you say we call it square and move on?" I asked. Even now, part of me wanted him to take it, to give me a reason not to do what I had to do.

"Square?" Lazarus laughed, a cruel note entering his voice. "We are not even, Matthew. We are not equals. Do not suppose that just because you have found a new weapon, you are my better. I own you."

"Well then." I shrugged, letting the motion lift the butt of the scythe off the ground slightly. "It seems we have a problem, *sir*, because that's all I need from you."

"You forget your sister so easily?" Lazarus scoffed, a smug look in his eyes. "I still have her in my care, and no one else is equipped to handle her current situation. There is nothing you can do for her."

A cruel smile grew on my face as I stared at this monster that had manipulated me and my family. He was right. With Megan's soul split and her stuck in Limbo, there was no one better equipped to care for her. As far as he was concerned, that gave him a trump card in our negotiations. Little did he know, I brought a couple of surprises back with me from the Underworld.

"I think we can take it from here," I told him, lifting my scythe. "Kane asked me to say hello." Lazarus's eyes went wide as I drew back the weapon and summoned all the Authority that I still had at my beck and call. I wasn't Death's heir any longer, but I had more than enough for this. I swung the weapon with all my might.

The old man twitched as the blade cut at him. Instead of being sliced in half, he began to wither. His blue eyes stared into mine as his body turned to dust and wasted away. In a few heartbeats, there was only a pair of horn-rimmed glasses sitting on his chair to show that he had ever been here. I stared at them for a moment before I banished the scythe. I couldn't help but feel like that had been too easy. For all his schemes, the mobster had gone quietly when his time was up. The cold power retreated to its corner of my mind, lurking like a cat. I guess I wasn't done with it yet.

A deeper cold filled the room. The shadows all grew and stretched as if pulled by a gravity that affected only them. I knew this chill well. It was the bigger, badder version of the one that lurked within me. The Grim Reaper had come to claim his old foe personally.

"He's all yours," I told the empty room.

I'd paid my Death Tax. Now it was time to make my sister whole.

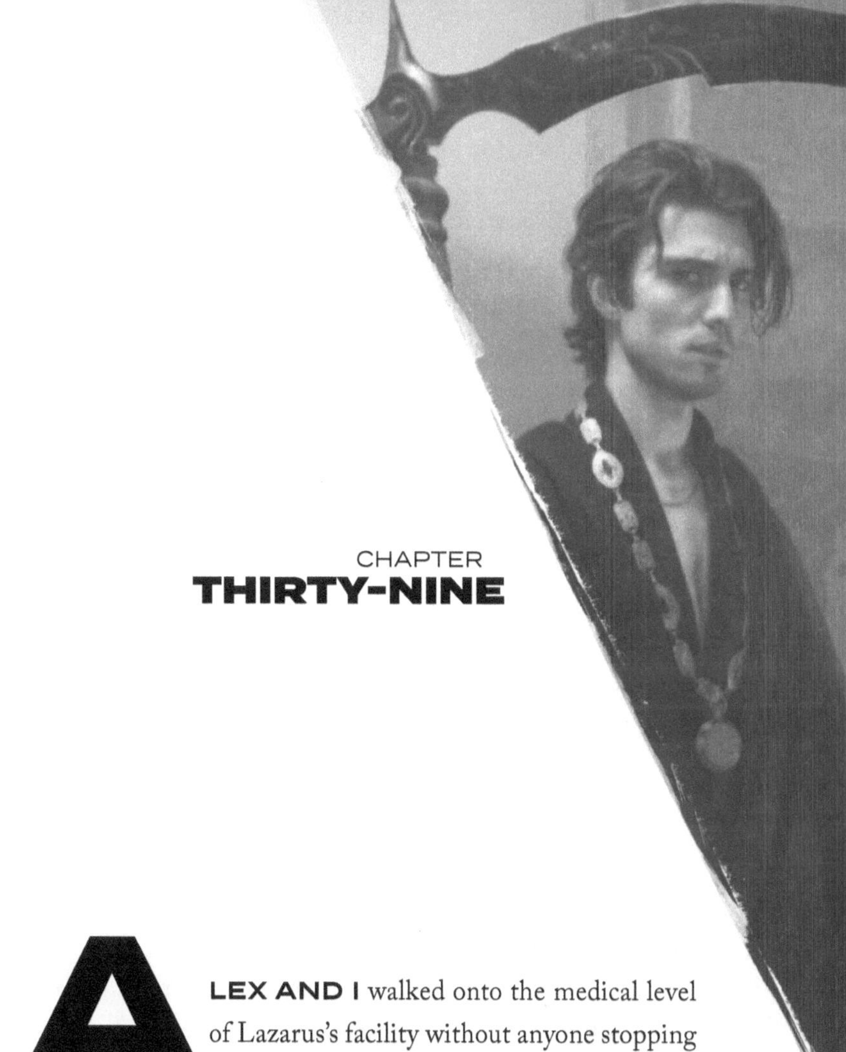

THIRTY-NINE

ALEX AND I walked onto the medical level of Lazarus's facility without anyone stopping us. There were probably two reasons. No one knew that the boss was dead yet. There was no body for anyone to find, just a pile of dust. Lazarus's horn-rimmed glasses were stuffed down my wet suit, which felt weird but was still better than leaving them lying around.

The other reason was that we were armed to the teeth. Flames wreathed my fists, the Angel of Death's sword was strapped over my shoulder, and Alex carried the assault rifle he had taken from some guard. It was obvious that stopping us would take *effort*, and that kind of strenuous activity usually ended up with someone getting hurt.

Even crack security guards like the ones Lazarus employed weren't getting paid enough to pick fights that no one had told them to start. Together we made our way through the halls, past rooms that I knew held patients who also needed saving. I could only hope that striking the head off the serpent would lead to that, but I doubted that Beatrice and the rest would stop their quest to beat Death just because Lazarus was gone.

Finally, I spotted the placard that read CARVER, MEGAN. I hesitated at the door, suddenly terrified.

"You got this," Alex murmured encouragingly from my side. My friend hadn't even questioned me when I came back to our barracks alone from my meeting with Lazarus and told him it was time to break out. That's real ride-or-die friendship. I had died, and he was still ready to ride.

I nodded in appreciation and twisted the handle of the door with more force than was necessary. We burst into Megan's room, and the sight drew me up short.

She looked much the same as she had before I died. Her skin was thin and pallid, as if she was wasting away. The arcane circle etched in the floor around her hospital bed gleamed in the bright light. A dozen whirring machines were still hooked up to her, as if she were a terminally ill patient in a coma.

I swallowed hard at the signs of all the trauma she had suffered because of me. But that all ended today—I hoped. It was time to make her whole and bring her back into the world of the living. I could only hope we weren't too late. Her shade hadn't seemed particularly unbalanced when I saw it in the Tenth Circle, but when my father had woken her on this side, she had been hysterical. Even now, her face twitched as she slept, as if she was plagued by nightmares.

There was no way to go but forward. I channeled some of my fire into the floor, scoring a line in the linoleum over the circle, breaking it. The terrible smell of burning plastic filled the air. I ignored it, my attention focused on the still form of my sister. Several of the machines began to frantically beep as whatever stasis she had been held in was shattered.

Stepping over the line, I extinguished Willow's flames and dug into my wet suit, fishing out the half-filled orange orb that contained the missing part of her soul. The sphere seemed brighter now, and it flashed in time to the beeping of her heart monitor.

"Is that…?" Alex's voice trailed off in hushed awe as he looked at what I was holding in my hands. I nodded, not trusting myself to speak. Here went everything. Megan's eyelids fluttered, and I knew it was time to act.

Once more, I called upon the power of Death, letting the scythe materialize in my right hand like a pillar of ice. Alex let out a surprised hiss behind me, but I didn't look at him. There would be time to explain my new powers later. Gently, I lowered the curved blade to the orb. Inch by cautious inch, I pressed it into the sphere. The weapon's black edge bit in easily, as if I were peeling an orange.

As the blade sliced through the skin, I twisted it, cutting all the way around. Megan let out a low groan, and I went faster—being careful not to cut my fingers on my weapon. No amount of stitches would fix the damage this thing could do.

My hands were shaking when I finished cutting the soul container in half. I released my hold on Death's cold power and gripped part of the sphere in each hand. With a grunt, I wrenched the top and bottom apart with all my strength.

There was a brilliant burst like the flash of a camera, and a stream of orange light shot out of my hands and made a beeline for Megan. It crashed into her chest, and I watched with bated breath as a warmth began to spread through her body, coming up her neck and sweeping across her face.

"No way," Alex breathed from next to me.

Megan's eyes flicked open, and she froze with the panic of someone who wasn't sure where she was waking up. That terror broke my heart more completely than ever before. How awful had her nightmares been that she feared waking?

"Megan," I croaked, my voice hushed and raw. "It's okay, you're safe now."

Slowly, her head turned to stare at me, and if anything, the fear deepened. "Is this real?" she asked, a desperate plea in her voice.

"It's real. I swear it." I took a step toward her, but she flinched, and I drew up short. I wondered if Zagan and the Devil had twisted Hell around her to the point that she couldn't trust her senses anymore. "Megs, I got you out," I continued softly. "I found your other half in our old neighborhood and brought you back."

Tension flowed out of her shoulders at my words. "That was real?" She let out a sob that was both relieved and devastated. "There are two sets of memories in my head, and they don't make sense. It's like I was in two places, but neither."

"Not anymore," I promised. "You're back."

"I'm good. I'm good," she repeated to herself like a mantra.

Shaking with a thousand emotions, I stepped toward her, and she sat up, which was a struggle after a year and some change in a coma-like state. I reached out to clasp her hands in mine. She was finally back—I had done it.

Our hands touched, and a spark leapt from me to her. Not a shocking burst of static electricity, but a warm one, like the striking of a match. Both of our hands burst into flame, casting warm light throughout the sterile hospital room. My heart skipped a beat in my chest as I watched Willow's spirit kindle in another body.

"*The returning Flame!*" the spirit's voice echoed in both of our minds with a joyous shout. A wild smile spread across my face as I stared into Megan's confused eyes.

"Here we go again," Alex muttered behind me.

"Okay, someone is going to have to tell me what the hell—" Megan winced slightly. "—what in the world is going on?"

"Congratulations, you're a Faerie Noble now," I told her, a bubbling laugh escaping my chest at her thunderstruck expression. "Blame Dad. But all in due time." I held up my hand, cutting off her questions. "First, we gotta get out of here."

My stomach rumbled, reminding me that technically I hadn't eaten in a few days. "You hungry?" I asked my sister. "I'm *dying* for a good burger."

——— ✕ ———

No one tried to stop us when we left. Maybe it was because they thought Lazarus had let us go. Maybe it was the coldness of Death lurking behind my eyes and the assault rifle in Alex's hands. Whatever the cause, I was grateful.

We went to the Island, a favorite family restaurant during our childhood. Megan was silent as we rode in Alex's minivan, eyes glued to the world outside the window as we navigated

LA's unrelenting traffic. She drank it all in with the hunger of someone returning home after being gone for far too long.

It occurred to me that by being beyond the bounds of Time, she might very well have seen eons go by since she'd traveled the streets we grew up on. I let her absorb it all in peace. It felt like part of the healing process. Besides, it was my first time outdoors since the FBI had tried to arrest us. It felt good for me to see the sun too.

In a way, I took her melancholy as a good sign. When she first came back, there had been something…wrong with her. She didn't know that she had been dead. Now she did. I could only hope that meant she was more alive now. Maybe since Death himself let me take the other half of her soul through the Veil, there were different rules?

While we drove, I demonstrated that I can in fact learn from my mistakes and texted Ash. She had never completely let it go that I'd forgotten to call her after escaping the dragoons with Alex at the Constellation Convention a few months ago.

I'm alive! I sent. Granted, cell phones were an unreliable way to get ahold of my Faerie betrothed. It doesn't matter what carrier you have; you're not getting service in Goldhall.

Are you okay?

I smiled at her instant response. *Want to grab a burger and meet my sister?*

Some of the chill that still clung to me began to fade. I turned to see my sister watching me. She looked so thin and pale; I should have saved her sooner. "Feel familiar?" I asked.

"I still can't believe it's real," she murmured. "How did you…"

"Uh-uh." I held up a finger to stop her. "My brilliant chef-sister once told me there are conversations that can't be had without food."

"That sounds wise. It must be something I said."

—— ✕ ——

You're telling me that *Damien*, our father, is a fairy?" Megan demanded incredulously from across the table, her burger forgotten in her hands.

"Faerie technically," Alex offered, since my mouth was full of cheeseburger. The Island wasn't one of those fad burger joints obsessed with smash burgers—those skinny little patties with no substance. Theirs are hefty and thick and take a bit of chewing.

I probably should have been more focused on explaining everything to Megan, but I was having a borderline religious experience with each bite. I hadn't needed to eat while in the Underworld, but damn had I missed it. Being alive rocks.

"What's the difference?"

"Less Tinkerbell, more Shakespeare," Alex offered after a moment of thought.

"I don't know what that means."

"Well—glug—well you're about to find out," I laughed as I managed to swallow. Over Megan's shoulder, a golden SUV careened into the parking lot, turning far too sharply to slide perfectly into an empty spot.

It had to be Robin at the wheel.

The doors popped open, and three Fae emerged. Two took their sweet time getting out, but the third shot from the passenger door and beelined for us. Fiery red hair trailed behind her as she raced toward me.

"How about that?" Alex mused to no one in particular.

"How about that," I agreed, putting my burger down and

standing up. My heart raced as I tracked the beautiful Faerie princess heading straight for me.

"Who's this?" Megan asked, her older-sister senses clearly tingling.

"This…" I trailed off, not even sure where to begin.

"Is his fiancée."

"His what?"

"*Betrothed*, technically." I glared at my best friend. But suddenly I was enveloped in a warm, soft hug, and I forgot that I was upset. Ash's body molded to mine, and all I could smell was her floral scent. For a moment, I closed my eyes and rested my head on her neck.

She shifted, pulling away, and reluctantly I let her go. She paused as she leaned back, her hands coming up to frame my face. Her green eyes stared into me, sparkling with deep joy. "You are never allowed to do that again," she commanded.

Then she kissed me, and my ability to form words fled. She tasted of cinnamon, sweet yet almost spicy. For a brief instant, I felt like I was back on the other side of the Veil. Time had no meaning.

Then the moment faded, and I came crashing to earth. Ash pulled back and looked at me, a note of uncertainty lurking beneath her expression. I stared blankly for a moment while my stupid brain rebooted.

"What were we talking about?" I asked breathlessly when I could finally form sentences. "Honestly it doesn't matter, whatever you want."

"Somehow I doubt that," Ash murmured, wrapping her arm around my waist. After a second's thought, I copied her. She leaned against me, setting my already speeding heart racing at a dangerous pace. It sounds silly, but this was new behavior. Maybe I should have died a while ago.

"You must be Megan," my betrothed said to my sister warmly.

"I am." It took everything in my power to keep from laughing at the flabbergasted look on my sibling's face. In her defense, she had every right to be shocked. Ash was way out of my league.

"Who are the other two?" Megan demanded, turning back to me. "Any other secrets I should know?"

"That is my sister Dawn." Ash pointed at the approaching blond woman.

"She's our Queen," I offered helpfully.

"Naturally." Megan seemed to realize she was still holding her burger and set it down on her plate, rising as the rest of the Dandelion Court approached.

Never one to be shy, the blond ruler stepped up to the table and fixed me with a heavy stare. "You lived, I see."

"You did tell me not to die."

She snorted, turning her attention to my sister. "I'm Dawn. I'm your Queen."

"So I hear," my sister replied dryly.

"Ugh, that tone," the Queen complained. "It's all I ever hear anymore. You two are your father's children." I felt my brow wrinkle in irritation. I am nothing like Damien. I turned to Robin, deciding not to dwell on my family tree.

"Hey, lawyer guy," I called, reaching down to grab the Impossible Task scroll from the chair next to mine. "I got something you need to review."

With deft fingers, he unfurled the document, his eyes growing to the size of saucers as he read it at top speed. When he got to the three tasks, he froze. A chill ran down my spine, extinguishing my good mood like a rainstorm kills a fire.

"Oh, Matthew," he breathed, his voice full of sympathy. The other two Fae didn't bother hiding their curiosity as they peered over his shoulder. I guess both of them could read ancient Greek.

"That bad, huh?" I croaked.

"There are no more apples of Iðunn—"

I waved his objection away with a huff. "And all the Sorcerer Kings are dead. I've heard that one before. It's going to be solvable."

"Levithan…"

"I was trained by the Hunter. Killing is what we do best." I forced bravado into my voice. I'd helped kill a dragon and a Dreadknight. Leviathan could get in line.

"Even if you accomplish the first two, though…the third is another matter entirely."

"Something about destroying the Four Seals of the Apocalypse? I wasn't sure what that was about."

Ash gasped in horror.

"Traditionally, they are called the Four Horsemen," my lawyer replied quietly. "Their names are War, Pestilence, Famine, and—"

"And Death," I finished for him softly.

Harbinger.

"Sorry, I'm still catching up. Why do you have to do these things again?"

"Now that we've rescued your soul, I have to complete three Impossible Tasks to save mine."

Megan was quiet for a moment, processing. "Can you have help?"

"Definitely," Alex shot in, tossing me a grin. "That's what he keeps me around for."

"And me," Ash murmured softly.

"Well then, I'm coming too." My sister stepped around the table to place her hand on my free shoulder. As we touched, her own Willow burst into flame, causing all three of the Fae to twitch in surprise. I turned to grin at Ash, who was beaming at my sister. The fire grew.

"Straight into the frying pan, eh?" Alex observed dryly.

"Isn't that how the expression goes?"

"I believe it's usually *out* of the frying pan and *into* the fire."

"Oh. Well, here's to doing it backward." I regretted the words the moment they were out of my mouth. Alex and I both tensed and turned to look at Megan. I wasn't sure if we were at the stage where we were joking about her stay in Hell yet.

To my relief, she laughed. "Out of the fire and into the frying pan. I like it."

Thanks for reading DEATH TAX!

If you enjoyed it, don't forget to leave a rating on Amazon and Goodreads. It makes a huge difference for independent authors like me.

If you want to keep up with me, go to: andrewgivler.com/links or scan this (different) QR code on your phone!

ACKNOWLEDGEMENTS

Here we are again, time to thank everyone who makes making a book like this possible. I may be an "independent" author in the sense that I do not have a publisher who handles this for me, but that does not mean that I do this on my own. I have a team that makes this possible, and they rock.

Thanks as always to Laura and Taya whose keen editing skills make you all think I know what a comma does, or where a semicolon goes. (I don't.)

A huge shoutout goes to the early readers who spend their time poking holes in everything to help make the final version perfect. The Alpha reading team: Aki, Caleb, Taylor, and Molly, thanks for always being the first place I can drop off a disjointed book, knowing you will help me bring it in for a landing. To the Beta readers: Alex, Casey, Cris, Erica, Erin, Galen, Nathan, Rachel, and Seb, you all helped me fill in gaps that I never would have noticed on my own. As always, a huge shoutout to Austin and Rich from 2ToRamble who AGAIN made a single piece of feedback that changed this book for the better. (Be sure to check out their BookTube channel, they're some of my favorite reviewers.)

(I pray that I have not forgotten anyone, if I have, I owe you a drink and a formal apology. Know that it was because I'm an idiot, not because I do not appreciate you.)

Chris McGrath is an artist without equal and this cover is my favorite yet.

Likewise, Shawn King is a wizard, and the reason this book looks so good on a shelf.

To all the readers who have sent me emails asking when *Death Tax* would be out, your enthusiasm is electric and keeps me going. Buckle up because it's going to get wild from here.

www.ingramcontent.com/pod-product-compliance
Lightning Source LLC
Chambersburg PA
CBHW061535190726
48289CB00004B/1052